Andries.

Andries.

MELANIE MARTINS

Melanie Martins

VAN DEN BOSCH SERIES

BOOK TWO

Melanie Martins, LLC
www.melaniemartins.com

Copyright © Melanie Martins 2022

First published in the United States by Melanie Martins, LLC in 2022.

ISBSN ebook 979-8-9861626-0-7

ISBN Paperback 979-8-9861626-2-1

Printed and bound in Great Britain by Clays Ltd, Elcograf S.p.A

This is a 1st Edition.

DISCLAIMER

To all my dear readers, thank you.

READING ORDER

While you don't need to have read the *Blossom in Winter* series to start this book, we recommend the following order to get the very best reading experience:

Blossom in Winter series (Petra & Alex's story)

1. Blossom in Winter
2. Lured into Love
3. Lured into Lies
4. Defying Eternity
5. Happily Ever After: Part 1, 2, 3, and 4

Van Den Bosch series

1. Roxanne.
2. Andries. (You are here)
3. Elise.
4. Dan.

CHAPTER 1

I'm burning up. Burning alive with everything that I'm feeling, it's almost like I'm being pulled backward by some imaginary tether around my waist as I leave Roxanne's office. I'm so keenly aware of her presence standing behind the door that I just closed.

I keep walking as fast as I can, crossing the open layout with her staff around, feeling that tether pull tighter and tighter as I do so. *Fuck it.* I know it'll eventually have to snap one way or another.

As I finally step outside of her building, the air is cold on my cheeks and running through my hair like frozen fingers, but even that isn't enough to stop me, not even long enough to pull my hood up. If I stop, I'm afraid I'll turn around and run back to that office where I was just humiliated so deeply. There's still enough rage inside me, being the catalyst that propels me forward, and I can't give up that advantage while I still have it.

I remember how far from her office I'd asked my driver to drop me off, not wanting to let him know the exact address I was heading to. I had to walk a few blocks to get to her building, which had been torturous when I had been dreading the encounter, but now that I'm fleeing, I appreciate that I have those few moments to gather myself before I reach the car.

I truly have no idea what will happen now. I feel like I've experienced so much in the last few days that my body and mind can't hold it all. This heartbreak is a gut-punch of feeling, and while it's just as intense as the love I still hold for that woman, it's infinitely more miserable.

How could she do this to me? Why wasn't she just honest?

Questions I had contemplated over and over again the past few days. What exactly would have been different if Roxanne had told me the truth? The fact that I still don't know how exactly things would have gone down tells me that I'm not as sure of myself as I'd like to think. I find her job of choice to be disgusting, but her insistence that she herself doesn't escort anymore does change things, at least minutely. Not enough for me to be able to forgive her lies, but enough that I don't want to go home and scrub my entire body down to the bone to remove the memories of her. I can live with the fact I've been her lover, but living with having been in love with her? That's a different story.

Do I want to die? No, that's foolish. But right now, I'd be perfectly content not existing on this Earth, at least for a brief period of time.

I don't look behind me as I spot my driver pulling my door open and I slide inside without a second glance. Both possibilities would've been too painful; if Roxanne had followed me, I'd have had to turn her away again in anger, but if I had turned back to see an empty sidewalk... that would have been just as terrible. Part of me had hoped she'd chase after me, but there were no words from her wicked mouth that could change my mind. Not now. Not ever.

I might be a poet and student, but I'm also a man who often feels too young for the soul which occupies his body. Today is one of those days, because missing and hating Roxanne at the same time feels like some grudge that should have been built over decades of longing. If it hurts this badly now, I can't even imagine what it would feel like when it's old and concentrated. Less at the forefront of my mind, but sharper and deeper than ever before.

I love her, still, and I hate her more than I thought possible for a man to hate a woman he knew through and through.

Except you're not the only one that knows her that way, my traitorous mind hisses.

I resist the urge to sink my fist into the back of the headrest, and I can see my driver's nervous glance in the rearview mirror as I work my jaw to try and dispel my more violent desires.

For a few valiant minutes, I try to concentrate on other things. Class, the upcoming events I will be required to spend with my family, all the projects I'm still working on... but nothing occupies me long enough to keep me entirely distracted. I blow out a breath slowly, playing the last hour over again in my thoughts. Roxanne's shock when she saw it was me, the hollow look she wore as she figured out what it all meant, and the rising anger that I could easily read in her frame as I tore her down.... I used words I never imagined I would attribute to the woman I love, but suddenly they all fit her so perfectly.

She had been glorious in her rage, though, raising herself onto her toes, spine as straight as an arrow and storms brewing in the depths of her eyes. Under any other circumstances, it'd have drawn me to her. Roxanne's passion in any form did that, at least before. Now it's all dirty and tainted.

If everything goes the way I planned it, I'd never have to see her in person again. It'll take some time to remove her things completely out of my apartment, since we had been all but living together, but with each piece I remove I'll be a step closer to having her be a thing of my past and my past only.

I feel my phone buzz in my pocket, and I hesitate to even check to see who is calling, wanting to take this time of painful reflection alone, but curiosity gets the better of me. It's Elise, which is both a relief and a disappointment. The toxic part of me wanted it to be Roxanne, but it's certainly good that it wasn't. I can only hope this hysteria dies down quickly.

I accept the call and put the phone against my cheek. "Hello, Elise."

"How did it go?" she asks curtly. No time for pleasantries when it comes to my sister.

"As miserable as could be expected."

"I bet she was shocked. It serves her right." There's a note of satisfaction in Elise's voice that rubs me the wrong way, but I let it go.

"Yes, it was every bit as awful as you wanted it to be, I'm sure. Did you want anything else, or were you only calling to soak up that negative energy you love so much?"

Elise scoffs. "I was calling to check up on you too, you know. How are you doing?"

I grit my teeth. "I'm doing awful, Elise. What do you think? This is the biggest shock of my life, but I'm assuming you think I should be taking it in stride?"

"I'm going to meet you at the apartment, and we'll get that witch's things out today so you can fully move on." She ignores my miniature rant, and I can hear her gathering her things as she speaks, ready to head to my place.

It's a good idea, purging Roxanne completely from my life immediately, but I hate the idea of it being over so rapidly. Part of me still needed to hold on to at least part of her. One day Roxie was completely ingrained in my life, and the next she'd be completely gone, as if she had never been there in the first place.

"We don't have to rush," I offer.

"Yes, we do. The less time you have to think about her, the better," my sister insists.

"Nothing short of a mind wipe or a lobotomy would get her out of my brain completely, but whatever you say."

I can hear her sliding inside the backseat of a car, right before she shuts the door behind her. "You guys weren't even together that long, Andries. You'll be okay."

"Again. Whatever you say."

I hear her exhale in frustration. "This conversation is going nowhere. I'll see you soon."

I hang up without saying anything else. She's right, of course, but I fear that for some time, no conversation with me will bear much fruit. I need time to reflect, rage, mourn, and heal. Whether I'm strong enough to get to that last step is yet to be seen.

I close my eyes and lean my head back against the headrest, trying to zone out until we reach my apartment again, but right behind my eyelids is everything I'm trying to forget. With nothing else to do, I give in, and let it all wash over me.

* * *

No lights are on in my home, and the gray light from outside casts everything in somber colors, a fitting setting for how I'm feeling. I quickly try to calculate how much time I have before Elise arrives, and if I have time for a drink before she gets here. I've just reached the liquor cabinet and pulled it open when I hear the hydraulic hiss of the elevator reaching my floor. Cursing, I let the cabinet door close and turn to face my sister as she opens the door. I should've known Mom gave her a spare key.

Only it isn't just Elise.

Behind her is Dan, looking sheepish as he follows my sister inside. I can tell immediately from his posture that it wasn't his idea to tag along, but that Elise had forced him to. If I was in a better state of mind, I'd almost be impressed by my sister's tenacity. She is going to be a tour de force as she changes from young woman to adult, and I'm not sure if the world is quite ready for her.

"You can leave, Dan. This is a family matter," I say, but Elise is already shaking her head.

"No. I told him everything, and you need another man here. Being babied by a bunch of women is just going to make you sink further into your 'woe-is-me' mindset, and that's the last thing we need."

I narrow my eyes. "You had no right to tell anyone my business like that."

"He's your best friend! Who, frankly, you have been neglecting just like the rest of us while you were off being obsessed with that harlot, so why don't you wipe that pouty look off your face and greet him properly."

I slide my gaze to Dan, who has gone from looking slightly embarrassed to slightly offended, shooting a glance at Elise. "Come on, lady. I'm not a puppy, I'm not feeling *neglected*," he sputters.

I know the moment should be funny, but my world is still too gray for all of that. "Stay or go, Dan. I don't care either way."

He turns to me now, an understanding look in his eyes as he walks over and claps his hand on my shoulder. "I'm going to stay, man. And I'm here if you need me, whether you want to talk or just drink ourselves stupid. Although honestly, I prefer drinking."

Fake it till you make it, my dad's voice whispers through my consciousness, giving me enough energy to return Dan's half-embrace. "Yeah, I figured that's what you'd prefer."

Elise watches us with her arms crossed, and when she has judged our greeting is complete, she starts to wave us into action. She digs underneath my sink until she finds a box of trash bags, throwing them onto the counter.

"All of Roxanne's things are to be put in the garbage bags where they belong, and then right out into the hallway. I'll put them on the curb and call her when we're done. Then we can wash our hands of this whole mess. Now, chop-chop, get to bagging."

Elise is a pain in my ass, but I feel like a puppet on strings right now and having someone plan my actions out for me helps more than she can know. I need someone to give me commands because my thoughts are somewhere outside my body.

I go to reach for a trash bag, but as I do, my phone goes off. Dan and Elise both freeze and look at me, but before I can pull it out of my pocket, my sister holds her hand out. I hand her the phone without a second thought, eyes toward the ceiling so I can't even see the contact photo on the screen. I know it's Roxanne, and if my sister has the phone, then at least I won't have the temptation to answer it. I'd like to think I'd just tell her to fuck off, but there is that little traitorous part of me that might beg her to forgive me, and it isn't worth the risk.

She's a liar and part of an industry I don't want to associate myself with. I have to keep that at the forefront of my mind. Not the smell of her hair or the feeling of her skin under my fingertips.

Fuck, I hate this.

Elise silences the phone and tucks it into the pocket of her pants, wiping her hands on them afterward, as if just the idea of the woman calling is distasteful. I can't really blame her.

The conversation is stilted as we work, with Dan trying to keep things light and humorous while Elise wants to be all business, planning my days going forward out loud as if I'm completely incapable of living my own life. Well, I guess she isn't wrong for the time being, but she reminds me so much of Mom when she's like this that I find myself becoming exasperated to the point that I tune her out completely.

"How are you really doing, Andries?" Dan asks when we have a second alone. "Like, *really*. Not putting up a tough face in front of your sister, but the honest truth."

"Like shit."

"Yeah, obviously." Dan shoots a glance around us, but Elise is still in the bathroom, so he continues, talking quickly. "Listen, I'm not going to harangue you, but is there any way you might have acted too rashly here? Did you get Roxie's whole side of the story before you made your decision or—"

Elise returns, and my friend jumps like a little kid caught with his hand in the cookie jar. She squints as she looks between the two of us, hands on her hips, but she grabs her half-full bag without saying anything.

"Make sure to ask before getting rid of any lace underwear, Elise, they might be your brother's!" Dan jokes, and my sister makes a gagging motion in response. I feel the corner of my mouth twitch, but I can't manage the smile Dan is looking for, and he seems defeated by it.

I want to tell him it's just too soon, and that I do appreciate him coming to help and be with me, even if I am humiliated that he knows the entire story now. But if there was ever a person to never pass judgment on my actions, it would be Dan. Short of murder or assault, I'm not sure there is much I could do to offend the guy. He's the loyal sort.

What's more is that I know Dan liked Roxanne, but there's no disappointment coming from him about the breakup. Just concern for me.

My efforts in bagging Roxie's things up is haphazard at best. Every time I pick up something of hers—from a small set of pearl earrings she had set down next to a candle as an afterthought or a coffee cup with a ring of red lipstick on it —I'm thrown through a loop of remembering our moments here together. How am I supposed to live in this miasma of her memory? It seems impossible. I spend most of that sad afternoon rearranging things, avoiding the little clues of Roxanne's existence whenever possible, and letting Elise or Dan bag them up instead. Unfortunately, they aren't sure what is hers and what isn't, so I have to involve myself somewhat, and each time they ask me about something of hers, my palms itch more and more for the liquor bottles in my cabinet. So while my sister isn't around, I go and serve myself a glass of bourbon, which I drink in two gulps.

The most miserable moments are those in my bedroom, opening drawers and smelling her scent as it washes over me with each piece of clothing I hold. Jaw working to hold off the tears that threaten to fill my eyes, I jerk open the drawer in my dresser that has all my old t-shirts; threadbare things from concerts, schools, and festivals that I'd wear around the house. It was the drawer Roxanne would always gravitate toward after we made love, pulling one of them over her head so it fell nearly to her knees as she puttered around the apartment. Seeing her in my things had made me feel so deliciously possessive, but now... now they just made me sick to my stomach.

I tug the entire drawer off its track and out of the dresser, dumping the whole thing into the bag and throwing the empty drawer aside. The metal on the bottom scuffs the floorboards as it skitters away. I can see Dan's silhouette in the doorway, watching me sadly, and I shove the bag of shirts into his hands as I push past him and into the bathroom.

I breathe in through my nose and out through my mouth, over and over again, until the breaths stop shuddering out of me and come smoothly. It's a battle. I run cold water, splashing it over my face again and again until my teeth are chattering, and my mind is sharp again. I'm in control. I can do this. If I tell myself those lies enough, they might become true.

Suddenly, I can hear Dan and Elise talking quietly in the living room.

"We should take a break. Come back tomorrow. I can give him a Xanax so he can sleep. He looks like he's been up for days."

"No," Elise hisses. "It has to be like pulling a Band-Aid off. We are purging that bitch from my brother's life today. I'm not going to have him spending his days in this apartment with traces of her all over the place. You know he'll just forlornly look out the window and never leave."

"You're pushing him too hard, Elise. You're going to burn him out and then it'll take even longer for him to recover."

"Excuse me for saying so, but I think I know my brother better than you."

Dan laughs. "Sure you do, sweetie."

I hear Elise gasp in indignation, so I exit the bathroom before they can continue. They are both so quiet when they see me, and I know they're wondering if I overheard everything or not.

"I think we're about finished," I tell them, and they look relieved.

"Do you want to come stay with me?" Elise offers, and Dan does the same, but I turn them both down.

"I just need to be alone."

Elise approaches me, and before I can balk, she lays her hands on my cheeks. The authoritarian look she had worn since she arrived earlier had faded and in her eyes was the sweetness and empathy of my little sister, a look I rarely saw anymore as Elise grew into her own. She'd be an unstoppable powerhouse of a woman, but it was endearing to know there were still traces of the little girl she had been not so long ago.

"Heartbroken poets write their best work, don't you know that?" she tells me, patting my face before tapping the tip of my nose with her finger. I brush her off, but not before I hear Dan snickering in the background.

We pile the bags by the door. Seeing me and Roxie's life together packaged up into three black plastic bags makes my heart lurch in my chest. Was it really so little? So insignificant to be quantified like that?

"There. Trash packed up like trash, as is proper," Elise declares, dusting her hands off. I want to retort, and tell her that her harsh language isn't helping, but as I open my mouth, the buzzer for the front door downstairs sounds.

We all look at each other as the buzzer sounds three times and goes silent, but as soon as the buzzer ceases, I see Elise pull my phone out from her pocket and frown at it. Then the buzzer begins again.

I walk over to the window and look down, my stomach dropping to my feet. Of course, it's Roxanne. From this angle, I can only see the top of her head, but I can tell she's stiff as a board, her phone in her hand as she tries to call me again and again.

"She's not going to leave," Dan points out.

"Thank you for stating the obvious!" Elise gripes. "Okay, here is the plan. I'll handle her. The two of you just go to the office and lock the door. Stay quiet. I'll let her come get her things and go, and she'll never have to know you're home."

"This is just kicking the can down the street, Elise. She'll be back. We might as well bite the bullet now," I say.

"No way. It's still too new. It's only been a few hours since the breakup! Please trust me on this."

The entire time we speak, the buzzer continues to sound. I hate it, but I know my sister is right. The confrontation between Roxanne and me will be nothing but ugly, and it'll just make things even worse. With a tight nod, I motion to Dan, and the both of us head to the back of the apartment. I let him walk in before me and shut the door behind us, locking it before sinking down onto the leather loveseat and holding my head in my hands.

"This is a nightmare," I say, more to myself than anyone else.

"It's only temporary," Dan responds. I feel his weight as he sits down next to me.

"It doesn't feel that way. It feels like something that is going to haunt me for the rest of my life. I've felt the highest highs and the lowest lows in my entire life over the past few days. How is a man supposed to come back from something like that? I don't think I'll ever be able to trust a woman again."

"You're so dramatic," Dan groans. I look at him sharply and he holds up his hands. "Fine! Sorry! It's just... I think Elise forced you into a corner that you didn't want to be in and now you're stuck."

"Elise is in no way responsible for Roxanne's fuck ups." My voice is incredulous.

"I never said she was. But there's no way of knowing that Roxanne wouldn't have come clean with you sooner rather than later. Her career isn't exactly one that is safe for a woman. I can almost see where she was coming from making up an alibi at first. She had no idea what kind of person you'd be, and by the time she started falling for you, it was probably too late."

"Doesn't matter. I'd have never been with someone in her line of work. It's better that I know now instead of finding out when I was even more attached to her down the line." I examine my friend closely. "It sounds like you don't think her job is a problem, though."

"Come on," Dan says with a shrug. "It's Amsterdam. It's just part of life here. I mean, it's fine if it's a hard line for you, but none of that shit surprises me anymore."

"She's exploiting other girls after years of selling her body. I'll never be convinced that's okay. Sex isn't something to just be... be given out like it's nothing! It's between you and someone you love."

Dan chuckles. "Whatever you say, Andries. I'm here for you no matter what, anyway. Any breakup sucks, but you really fell hard, didn't you?"

Trying to drown out any potential sounds of my ex talking to my sister, I blow out a breath. "That's the understatement of the century."

"No way to help it, then. Want to get wasted?"

I give him a hollow smile. "I thought you'd never ask."

CHAPTER 2

Amsterdam, December 29, 2021
Roxanne

I made and discarded a lot of plans in the last few hours; from getting stupendously drunk, booking a flight out of the blue so I couldn't be found, finding my sister and crying in her arms, and even tearing my office apart and leaving the mess to fester like an open wound. I'm pissed beyond belief, humiliated, but most of all, heartbroken.

What did you think would happen dating someone so young!? This is your own fault. You should have known better. You should have been smarter than this.

I hate so many people at this moment. Elise, Andries, but mostly myself. I had built my business from the ground up, literally on my own shoulders, and it's something I take pride in. To be torn down by someone I love, in my own office, is unfathomable. Andries had sneered at me like I was no better than the dirt under his shoe, and for a second, I had believed him. Yeah, that was exactly how I had felt.

It isn't fair, and I've been too taken aback to do anything but respond in anger. Now that it's drained away, I want to have a real conversation. Adult to adult, so he can at least know that nothing I did was meant to hurt him. I wasn't trying to be shady or underhanded. I just had run out of time to tell him the truth and have it not implode our relationship, and I wasn't ready to give it up yet.

After all this time, I guess I'm still a selfish girl.

Now I'm standing in front of Andries' building, hoping that he'll be willing to see me. Andries is a lot of things; prideful, unshakeable in his convictions, and he comes from old money, but he's also in love with me, as I am with him, and it's going to take more than a fight in my office to do away with everything that had been between us. He has to give me a chance to explain. Explain, and, more than likely, say goodbye. I desperately need closure.

And yes, a part of me is still hoping we can work through this. He has some serious apologizing to do, as do I, but is our love strong enough to pull us through?

It's time to give up this fairytale bullshit and face the facts, Roxie. He doesn't want a used-up old hooker. It's time to move along. It was a nice interlude, but it's over.

My heart wants something different, but the logical part of my mind speaks the truth.

I stare up at the windows, hoping to catch a glimpse of him, but any fantasies I had about Andries watching for me seem to have been misguided. I need to get this over with before I lose my nerve.

I hesitate at the door. I have the code, but as his now-ex, it seems a bit inappropriate to just go up unannounced. Yet… There's a good chance he won't let me in if I just keep pressing the buzzer. Decided, I square my shoulders and type in the passcode. To my shock, the light flashes red, and I'm not admitted. I try the code again, but it isn't a mistype. The light goes red for a second time.

"Oh, this asshole," I mutter to myself.

I hit the buzzer once more, given no choice, and wait. Predictably, he doesn't let me in. I hit it twice more, my annoyance growing by the second. I'd been calling him all day, and of course he had been ignoring me, but I try it again anyway. Maybe the calls plus the buzzing will be enough to get me a moment of his oh-so-precious time.

At this point, my finger is jamming into the buzzer with no small amount of rage, when to my surprise, the door clicks and the light around the keypad goes green. Not wanting to waste any time on a possible mistake, I jerk it open.

When the elevator spits me out in front of Andries' apartment, I don't even have time to reach for the doorknob before it's opened for me. My heart is ready to pound out of my chest, but instead of Andries standing in front of me, tall and irresistible, it's his smaller female counterpart.

"Oh," I utter in shock at the sight of Elise.

She raises a perfectly arched, brown eyebrow. "What are you doing here?"

"I just wanted to talk to your brother," I reply.

"He isn't here," she says, crossing her arms. "But your clothes and belongings are." She kicks her leg slightly to the side, hitting a stack of black garbage bags that I assume contain all my things. "So feel free to take them out, since this is exactly what I was doing."

"I…" I look past her at the bags, temporarily lost for words, and then back up at Elise.

Am I really going to let this little girl talk to me like this? I fight back a sneer and begin grabbing the bags, tossing them in the elevator behind me while Elise watches. The way she holds a pretentious air in front of me feels like she's watching her maid or something, and it pisses me off immediately, but I have to keep my cool. To get to Andries, I clearly have to go through his sister first.

After I throw the last bag behind me, I stand back up straight and say, "I left some of my jewelry in the case where he keeps his watches. I've never mentioned it, so I'm sure he wouldn't have gotten them out. Can I get them?"

Elise sighs. "Very well. Andries isn't home anyway. He went to the family estate to recharge and reset. I think he invited Dan and–" she pauses for dramatic effects, a small smirk forming at the corner of her mouth, "Tatiana."

"Whatever," I reply, hiding my disappointment in the fact that Andries isn't here. All of my plans to talk to him are useless, and now I'll have to wait for him to return. I clock the subtle way Elise slips in Tatiana's name, but I ignore it, not wanting to give her the satisfaction.

I follow Elise inside, forcing myself not to get distracted by everything around me. Every space, every surface, is a memory. I feel tears pricking at the corner of my eyes and blink them away.

"Listen, Elise…." She raises an eyebrow as I pause for a moment. "Can I leave a note with you or something? Since Andries isn't here. Or I could just leave it on his nightstand. We sort of ended things on a bad note and—"

"Absolutely not," she snaps instantly.

Her snotty tone raises my hackles, but I keep my face blank. "Me leaving him a note doesn't affect you at all, and it isn't like I'm forcing my way into his face to talk, either."

Elise lets out a single laugh. Stopping on a dime and turning to face me, she gives a step forward in my direction. "Let's make it clear here. Do you see how kind, romantic, innocent, and naive my brother is? I'm the opposite. And I've got zero patience for your bullshit. So if I were you, I'd just move on and find someone else."

I don't back down. "My relationship with your brother is none of your business," I tell her.

"Well, it kinda is." She looks me up and down, and her expression says that she finds me lacking. I feel like she thinks that way about a lot of people, though. "His reputation and good name matter to me. And you have done enough to ruin it."

"I understand you are mad at me for what I did but—"

"Oh, I'm not," she interrupts. "I had a feeling something wasn't right about you, and I'm glad we figured it out sooner rather than later." She lowers her voice, sounding serious and threatening. "Andries was blindsided by his love for you, but I'm glad he finally managed to see who you truly are."

"Elise—"

She makes a cutting motion in the air with her hand, and I stop mid-sentence. "Are you done?"

"I love your brother! I really do—but I knew once he found out, he'd break up with me."

"So you were selfish enough to keep your true identity to yourself, huh?" she sneers.

I shake my head in denial. "I'm no longer an escort. I stopped doing that a long time ago."

"Yet, you are still selling pussy, aren't you?" Her voice is acidic, and her top lip curls in disgust at the words she's saying. Hearing her prim and proper voice speaking that way even makes me freeze.

"It's all consensual," I insist. "I'm helping these girls. I am giving them real, lucrative work."

"Yeah, right. Since when is laying on your back lucrative work? I'm pretty sure those women all have something in common." Elise leans forward, bringing her face closer to mine, and it takes all my willpower not to slap the holier-than-thou look off her face. "Lack of money. Easy girls, easy money."

"You have no idea what you're talking about. It's a good way for them to earn money while still having time to live their lives. It's a hard world out there for people who aren't born with a silver spoon in their mouths." My voice gets shriller the angrier I get, but Elise just rolls her eyes. "Most of them make more money than graduate students do," I continue. "Some of them have even graduated in law and economics, but they still do it part time, because no one wants to hire you right out of university. But you wouldn't know anything about having to pay the bills, would you?"

"Reducing sex to a financial transaction is beyond disgusting," Elise retorts, tossing her hair over her shoulder as she straightens. "And the fact you don't see how wrong it is, is the very reason why I'm glad you guys broke up."

"Your mindset is a flagrant display of how ignorant and privileged you are, Elise," I grit between my teeth. "But I guess you don't care about those who are out of your little bubble, do you?"

I don't give her time to respond, pushing past her close enough that her shoulder meets mine, and she gasps at the contact. I ignore her, yanking my things out of Andries's watch box and shoving them into the purse slung over my shoulder. Elise comes into the doorway to watch me, as if I'm some common thief, and I can't hold my tongue anymore.

She acts as if she's going to block my way until the last second, but when she moves, instead of walking by her, I stop so we are both in the doorframe, closer than is comfortable for either of us.

"Despite not being as wealthy as you are, I've taken way more women out of poverty than you or your mom will ever do," I hiss, looking her up and down the way she did me before I finally leave. I, too, find her lacking.

"Goodbye, Roxanne," Elise says to my back as I storm out of the apartment.

I'm so emotionally exhausted that all of my anger disappears into thin air the moment Elise can't see my face anymore. My expression crumbles and the tears fall in earnest. In the privacy of the elevator, I cover my face with my hands and sob.

The Uber driver watches me from his seat with a bored expression as I lug all the bags out and throw them into the trunk. I'm annoyed, thinking how Andries' driver would have never let me do all of this by myself. Why on earth did I decide to leave my car at the office? Now that Andries knows the truth, him seeing me driving a Porsche wouldn't have mattered.

At first, face red from exertion and crying, I thought home would be the best place to go, but once we reach the block of my building, I realize I'm not ready to be left alone in my apartment, so I ask the driver to wait for me at the curb while I carry the bags up to the concierge and ask him to leave them in my living room. Then I return to my Uber and I change the address to my sister's bookstore, which he accepts with a sigh.

My sister's store is somehow more comforting than even my own home, and the knot of emotions in me starts to unravel as soon as I see the entryway. Outside, the world is dreary, but inside there is an innate warmth. It's in the smell of paper and ink, the kitschy string lights and antique lamps that light the place, and the soft indie music that seems to creep and crawl through the stacks of new and used books.

Most of all, it feels like home because of Lili, who stands behind the counter with her hair caught up in a clip on the top of her head as she flips through a pile of donated books with an overly serious look on her face. I don't even need to say anything when she sees me. As soon as the bell above the door tinkles softly, she turns in my direction, snapping the book shut and rushing around the counter to wrap me in her arms.

The hug carries on for a few long minutes, Lili rubbing my back as I hold back my sobs that still manage to escape in choked little hiccups. It's humiliating, but it's been a humiliating day, and at least Lili accepts my embarrassing outburst with love and light.

It's silly. I've always been the grownup who never faced heartbreaks... until now. But I know I don't have to be strong or prideful with her. I can come apart, and she knows it'll be the same if things were reversed.

Lili leads me over to a worn corduroy chair, where I sit, exhausted. She moves through the bookshop, locking the door of the store and turning the "Open" sign around to read "Closed."

"Tea or coffee?" she asks.

"Brandy."

Lili brings me tea anyway, something bitter and black that she insists will revitalize my soul. All it does is give me goosebumps from the sharp taste, but at least it's hot. Inside, I'm so cold, and it helps. A little, at least.

She drags another chair over, ignoring the way it scrapes across the floor. "It's the boy, isn't it?"

I groan. "It doesn't help when you call him a boy. How about man?" Lili doesn't answer, looking at me over the rim of her teacup, and I relent. "Fine. Yes. I fucked up with *the boy*."

"Well, go on. Do tell."

I hesitate, biting my bottom lip. I don't want to relive it all, but if Lili is going to give me advice, then I need to be completely honest. Closing my eyes, I launch into the entire story, from arriving at my office to find Andries all the way to my confrontation with Elise. Lili makes noises of agreement as she listens, grabbing me a handful of tissues when I get choked up again, and even refilling my awful tea. This time there are two sugar cubes dissolving in the black void of it, and I'm thankful.

"If you had been truthful at first, this would have never happened, but it seems like you would have never had Andries, either."

"I know," I say. "He pursued me so intently. I never thought he'd be so anti-sex work that it'd make him so horrified by what I do for a living, but it became all too clear as we got serious. I had already dug my grave and there was no way out."

"This was inevitable," Lili says sagely. "It was headed for disaster from the start."

"I know," I repeat, sighing miserably.

"So, you need to let this go. It was beautiful while it lasted, but it's over now."

"You don't understand, though. I've never felt for anyone the way I feel about Andries. What if I never find that kind of love again?"

Lili lays a hand on my knee. "Maybe he was just a part of your life to open up your heart for that kind of love. Now you know that it's possible, you'll be ready for it with the right person. Someone who will love you just as you are, not as some idealized version of you."

"I just can't imagine ever feeling the same for another person…"

"Then just be with yourself, Roxie. Love yourself, and before you know it, you'll feel better again."

I tap my nails against the ceramic cup, trying to imagine how my days will move forward from here, and it all just feels like static. "You know the stupid thing? I actually felt for a moment that he was right. That my business, the one I've built so carefully, really is despicable. I felt *ashamed*. Why would I feel shame for not only building a business to keep my bills paid and stomach full but doing the same for other girls that would have been left destitute if not? I can't help it though. Every time I think of his face in my office, twisted in disgust, I feel that little twinge of shame again."

"I won't pretend to like your business, Roxie, but up until now, it's something you've been proud of. Don't tie yourself up in knots just to please someone that isn't going to be with you now either way."

"Hmm," I sigh, lost for words. At least, I feel slightly better, now that I had emptied out all of my troubles in front of my sister, but there's a hollow emptiness left behind that I know I won't be able to fill anytime soon.

"We don't have to talk about this anymore," Lili offers. "Do you have any plans for New Year's Eve? Why don't you come to stay with Mama and me? It will be like old times!" She scoots closer to the edge of her chair so we're closer, reaching out to take my hands in hers. "You don't need to be alone."

The idea sounds nice, but I know the comforting thought of it is just that; a thought, and nothing more, because my real life won't leave me behind. In the real world, Mama doesn't talk to me and then there's my heartbreak, making any little escape impossible. I give Lili's hands an affectionate squeeze but shake my head.

"I appreciate the offer, but all of my responsibilities don't just disappear because I'm feeling bad," I explain, pulling my hands away gently and standing. "Thank you for hearing me out, but I think I have to go home and figure out how to deal with everything and not just fall apart."

"Okay. But if you change your mind, just call me, okay?"

"Of course."

Seeing Lili was supposed to give me some perspective, and I guess it did, but now that I was alone and heading home a lot of the same awful feelings felt like they were still just waiting there in the wings for me to let my guard down. It's getting late, and the temptation of just going home and drinking myself to sleep is all too obvious. It seems like just as good of an idea as anything else.

Elise had said that Andries had gone to his family estate, which means that he was probably going to spend the rest of the holiday there. It also means I won't be able to see him until he comes back for class, and while it's technically only in a few days, it feels like an eternity. I want this whole thing resolved. I want closure, and I want it right now.

On a whim, I try to call Andries again, but as I expected there is no answer. It's another little jab to my heart, and my mind is nearly made up to just go home and call it a night when I get a call.

Adrenaline courses through me at the brief thought it could be Andries, but my heart dies a little more when I see it's just Poppy. My first instinct is to ignore the call and let the cab continue to take me home, but once the first call ends, Poppy immediately calls again, and I give in and answer.

"Sorry to bother you," she opens with, most likely knowing that I'm not exactly having the best day. "But I was wondering if we could go over a few things that I don't think can wait…?"

Internally I'm cringing, but I tell her, "Yes, go ahead."

"Okay! Great. Well, we've got Charlie's NYE party coming up after tomorrow and he phoned earlier to say he wants a redhead, a brunette, *and* a blonde—"

As Poppy goes on and on, I let the manager side of me take over, even if it feels exhausting. I hold my phone over my hand so Poppy doesn't hear me, and quietly tell the driver to take me to my office instead. There's nothing else to do about it. Work doesn't wait for grief, it seems. Even when you are the boss.

CHAPTER 3

V.D.B estate, December 31, 2021
Andries

There isn't really anywhere else for me to go but home for the New Year. Of course, there are dozens of parties and soirees back in Amsterdam, but none of them hold any interest for me. So, like the pathetic mess I am, I migrate back to the family estate, spending my hours alone in my darkened room like the depressed poet my fifteen-year-old self always thought I would become.

Spending the holiday at the Van Den Bosch estate holds a few benefits—I'm not technically alone, even though I feel like I am. I don't have to subsist off takeout, because God knows I'm in no shape to be cooking three meals a day for myself. And most of all, there's no way that Roxanne is going to travel here to harass me in front of my family. She'd be arrested before she could even draw her first breath after stepping onto the property.

The last point is by far the most important: I still don't trust myself not to give in and talk to her if I had remained in Amsterdam. Here, I'm safe not only from her persistent affections but from my own untrustworthy habits too. It'd be ludicrous to say that she isn't still invading every crack and crevice of my mind. I'm obsessing, and not in a way that can be thought of as hopelessly in love.

I'm obsessed with Roxanne in that dark and dirty way that polite society would sneer at. When I sleep, I dream of her, all pale limbs and soft skin, and when I'm awake I'm overcome by horror at the things I had discovered about her. The dichotomy of it is slowly driving me insane, and I don't know how long I can live with it before my mind well and truly shatters.

Everyone says the same thing: time heals all wounds. Well, time is passing, but these mental wounds are just festering day by day. There is no healing in sight, at least for the near future, it seems.

So, the positives are my isolation. The negatives are that my family, no matter how good-intentioned, refuse to accept said isolation. Every hour there is someone knocking on my door; a sister, the housekeeper with a small snack, my mother wanting to talk about school or life or, God-forbid, business school. Worst of all is my father, with his hands stuffed in his pockets as he shuffles his feet, making stilted conversation with me about whatever safe, masculine topic he could pluck out of thin air. It seems he just remembered that I fenced, so that was the current safe conversation he has been falling back on recently, and I am curious to know what he will replace it with once that wheel has run dry.

Everyone knows I'm suffering, and everyone but the children know why. My situation is so unique and strange that no one knows quite how to deal with my grief, though, and they have all become painfully frustrating distractions while I try to work through the tangles of my mind.

Elise borders on tolerable... maybe because we are so close in age, or maybe because she has been more involved than anyone with the split between Roxanne and me. Though even she has begun to wear my nerves thin. I'm tempted to pack a small bag and leave for a hotel, but the moment my family thinks I'm having some sort of mental break, they will follow me to the ends of the Earth to get to the bottom of what is going on with me. If I thought they were obsessed with me now, I know it would be tenfold if I disappeared on them.

Tonight is New Year's Eve, and my grandmother has just arrived for the celebration. The normal huge bash that would be thrown at the estate is to be more subdued than usual tonight, for which I'm relieved, but now there's a chance I'll have to go through my entire story another time for Grandma... I sigh. I love the woman, but I'm well and truly exhausted.

The sights and sounds of the New Year's Eve party being set up are all around me. Even if I close myself in my room completely, I know I'll have to face it, eventually. The clinking of glasses, the never-ending cacophony of footsteps going to and from, and the increasingly frazzled butler coming to my door with outfit suggestions for the party tonight... It makes it impossible for me to prepare myself mentally for wearing the mask of the "well-adjusted Van Den Bosch son." So much of my life in recent years has been spent wearing that mask for my parents and all their peers, that I don't even know what it would be like to go in front of them being my honest self. My parents would be in shock if they knew about their poet son; the one who had been living under their roof all this time masquerading as a business major.

I honestly can't believe they still haven't figured out my secret, but I'm not about to shout it from the rooftops for them.

My biggest worry tonight is Grandma.

If my mother is shrewd and calculating, then Lady Margaret is all that tenfold. She can extricate secrets from people without them even knowing what happened, and all of us grandchildren had confessed things to her that we never planned to share. I have no plan to tell her about being an English major, but it wouldn't surprise me if it spilled out of my mouth. I'll have to limit my alone time with her tonight, even if her company is much more tolerable than the rest of my family's.

There's another secret I'm harboring that I need to keep close to my chest tonight... and it's about how much I've been relying on alcohol to get me through this breakup. Looking at the perfectly tailored, casual gray suit in my closet, I can't help but pull the flask I had been hiding under my pillow. The whiskey isn't the aged vintage I'm used to, and the rough burn of it in my throat is hard to ignore, but I need all the numbness the drink can provide if I'm actually going to make an appearance at dinner.

So I drink, cap the flask, and go to the closet to change. My stomach is burning, and I can already feel the slight haziness settle over my brain. From here on I swear that I will drink no more tonight. I have to ride the edge of comfortably tipsy and drunk, so I don't go sharing my sins with the entire dinner table, or with Grandma, if she manages to corner me and ask the tough questions.

I stay hidden until the absolute last moment when Elise comes knocking on my door to command me down to the dinner table. I oblige, letting the mask slip into place and following her down into the main dining area. The immediate smell of roasted meat washes over me, and my stomach rumbles with interest. It makes me realize that I've done nothing but graze on whatever has been brought to my room for the past two days, and the idea of a real meal is almost enough to shake me out of my current fugue.

It's a smaller than usual affair, as I had expected, and there are minimal people for me to greet, for which I'm thankful. The brief interlude of the food being a distraction is quickly done away with as the pressure of even this minuscule gathering begins to get to me. There is so much laughing, so much chatter, and everything is just so bright and garish. It's enough to make my head pound, and I'm about to use said ailment as an excuse to leave back to my room, but it turns out the last person I need to greet is nothing less than my grandmother, Margaret van Dieren. My seat just so happens to be next to hers, which means leaving is now off the table.

"Andries." She smiles affectionately. "You become more handsome every time I see you."

"Thank you, *Oma*," I reply, unable to match the excitement in her tone.

Her delicate perfume fills my nostrils as she embraces me briefly. I kiss her cheek, once again surprised by how much taller I am than her these days. If I was in a better state of mind, it might make me a little melancholic, but with how I feel currently it's just another footnote.

I take my seat beside her, letting her pat my hand a few times when I'm seated. The whole overly sweet grandma routine is just that, a routine, but I let her indulge the audience around us. Appearing this way makes her less threatening, but no one, including myself, should ever forget that she's really a viper in cashmere.

Grandma isn't the only one who seems to be fixated on me. Mom and Dad exchange hopeful glances, likely having to do with my put-together visage and willing appearance that the party and the subsequent smiles sent my way make me want to roll my eyes. Everyone thinks this is a positive thing, me being at dinner, but it's just me going through the motions to avoid any uncomfortable questioning.

Once dinner begins in earnest, the champagne flows like a river. No one's glass is staying empty for long. It's the only thing that gets me through all the courses, even if the sparkling wine doesn't sit well with the whiskey I had already consumed.

It's just family and close friends, and it's only later than I notice who is sitting next to Elise further down the table: Tatiana. She catches my eye, her sweet, shy smile making me groan internally. Of course, she had to know about Roxanne and me being separated since she was Elise's friend, and my family would stop at nothing to get me to commit to Tatiana.

I can't lie. The night I left Roxanne, I considered it, if only briefly. Tatiana is objectively beautiful, so bright and sunny in nature that there isn't anyone in the world that could deny it. She's the innocent, youthful type of beauty that never held much interest for me, but I'd have to be blind to not see that she'd have been a great girlfriend, had I been the man my family so wanted me to be. Being with her would be so easy, and she clearly wants that chance, even after we had discussed remaining friends. But if I gave in and got into a relationship with her, it'd have to be once I had completely given up on ever experiencing true love, because if we dated and slept together, I could never leave her. I couldn't bear to put that kind of shame on such a gentle soul, even if I knew I could never love her in the romantic sense. On the other hand, it would just be… so, *so easy*. I could even marry her straight away and be done with it. My family would be pleased, Tatiana's family would be pleased, and Tatiana herself would be over the moon. She would be the perfect wife…the perfect wife for the man everyone thinks I am, not the one that I truly am.

Lying in bed at night I toyed with the idea of marrying Tatiana and letting my heart die for good. She would still be a good friend and lifelong companion, but the fact that it meant I'd keep her from finding someone that would love her as much as she loved them stopped me. I'm ready to give into the idea of feeling dead inside all the time, but I'm not about to do that to her.

Down the table, Tatiana waves with a quick wiggle of her fingers, cheeks flushed from the champagne and her natural nervousness. Beside me, my grandmother chuckles, before leaning toward me.

"Why don't you put the poor girl out of her misery and just date her already?" she asks, her voice low and discreet. "Even I know she has stars in her eyes for you. And she's gorgeous. What's not to like?"

I think about the kind of women I'm attracted to. They had to be older than me, confident in themselves, established, and intelligent. A fully realized woman. Tatiana is still a girl.

"There is just no spark," I explain, my tone nonchalant, between bites.

"That's the last thing you should be worried about," Grandma says. "Real, long-lasting relationships are built on the foundation of two people that are better as a whole than they ever were single. Trust and respect come first, love and lust second."

I sit my fork down on my plate with a click. "I don't need to hear your stories about lust, Oma. But thanks."

"Oh, don't be silly, Andries. You know what I mean."

"It sounds like an arranged marriage," I comment.

"No. It's a smart match, based on logic, and not the whims of the heart and groin, child."

I lean my head back against the chair and close my eyes. "I wish you didn't have to keep inserting lust and... genitals into this conversation."

Grandma puffs at me, head shaking. "All I'm saying is that you should heavily consider Ms. Jansen for a more serious commitment. It isn't often that life drops the perfect solution to our problems in our laps. You shouldn't ignore this sign."

"Are you sure you're ready to see your favorite grandson tied down already?" I ask, taking the rare chance to tease her.

She scowls in response, and I feel the distinct urge to laugh. "You might think it's a joke, but I still stick by the point. You should date her. This would give you more than enough time to get to know each other."

"I know her already pretty well," I counter. "Which is one reason why I'm positive that I don't want to date her."

Grandma cranes her head around the other guests to get a better look at Tatiana, who is deep in conversation with Elise. Again, I am struck by how lovely she truly is, with her brownish hair pulled behind her ears and her glossy lips curved in a smile. My grandmother looks back at me, both of her thin eyebrows raised.

"I can't for the life of me figure out what it is that you find lacking in that girl, Andries."

I sigh, pushing my food around on my plate. "If Mom had closed her eyes and conjured up the perfect bride for me out of her own mind, it'd be Tatiana. Now this may shock you, but Mom and I don't exactly have the same taste in women."

Grandma makes a delicate amused sound that could almost be considered a snort. "Oh, Andries—"

"She's the human equivalent of a glass of milk. Good for you, nutritious, even, but utterly boring."

My grandmother coughs into her napkin to smother her laugh, and I can't help the twitch of my own mouth in response. It was a funny quip, I had to give myself some credit. Once Grandma gets herself under control, she takes a drink of water and gives me a scathing look that doesn't quite hide the reluctant amusement dancing in her eyes.

"You're a very rude boy. That poor girl."

"Oh, cut the crap. As if you'd ever be forced into doing something that you didn't want to do."

"Fair enough. But I've earned that right. I'm old enough to be a great grandmother, after all." She's quiet for a time, but I can tell she has more she wants to say to me. I'm not under any illusions that she doesn't know about my breakup already, but I still hope she doesn't bring it up. It's been nice to get a break from talking or thinking about it.

Finally, Grandma leans closer to me to whisper, "Is it that you like…well, you know… men?"

This time it's me who coughs, but not to cover up a laugh. It's shocked surprise. "No! Good lord, no, Oma."

I let the childish affectionate name slip out, earning me a pat on the hand from her. "Alright. I guess your sister was telling the truth then, about this all having to do with your split from some older woman." She waves her hand when I tense. "Don't fret, I'm not going to ask you to talk about it."

"As if this whole conversation hasn't been about my love life," I mutter.

"Fine, I'm finished. Just relax and try to enjoy yourself. It's a night of new beginnings, after all."

I look around the table, feeling the familiar tension that comes with all the fake song and dance I have to do for these people. "I'm trying. Really, I am."

* * *

This wasn't an event that I would enjoy at the best of times, but now it is almost unbearable. There is no way I'm joining anyone on the dance floor, or joining in any polite conversation, since I've to spend all my energy focused on keeping my sneer at bay as I lean on the wall and watch, an Old Fashioned clutched in my fist like a lifeline.

The decor is modest enough by NYE standards, most of it consisting of nets filled with shimmering metallic balloons. Here at the Van Den Bosch estate, there are no party poppers or cardboard top hats. Mom simply would not abide by such immature antics.

I guess my presence is enough to keep my parents at bay, but I can't help feeling Tatiana's eyes on me the entire time. There are a few moments when I think she's going to approach me, but she aborts the effort prematurely and disappears into the crowd again. I check my watch again and again, the minutes dragging by like hours as the New Year approaches.

I fish an ice-cube out of my now-empty glass and crunch the cube between my teeth, relishing the shards and the faint hint of alcohol left on them, but my momentary distraction allows me to miss the person who had finally gathered the nerve to approach me.

Tatiana looks at me from beneath her long lashes as the music slows to a low sonorous purr. I vaguely recognize the song, but not well enough to name it.

"I love this song," she comments. "Don't you?"

"I'm not familiar with it," I say dryly.

Her lips quirk up. "I bet you spend your spare time listening to Beethoven or Mozart. Only the best symphonies for Andries."

"I'm shocked, was that a joke from you, Tatiana?"

"An attempt at one, at least," she replies with a self-conscious chuckle. "Was it funny?"

"Very."

She shuffles her feet as the music plays on before she takes an enormous breath and takes her chances. "Will you dance with me? It's a slow dance, at least, so it shouldn't be too embarrassing for you."

I'm going to say no. In my brain, I send her away, but to my surprise, the words that come out of my mouth are, "Fine, but only this one song."

Damn that Old Fashioned.

Her face lights up as she grabs my hand, and I lead her out to the dance floor. To my relief, she doesn't try to press herself against me, but respects the distance I leave between us, and the way I rest my hand above the swell of her hips instead of on them. She seems to just be thrilled to have this dance.

Tatiana smells like lemons and sugary sweetness, and she's an easy dance partner, moving with me as if she weighs less than a feather. If I didn't see and feel her right in front of me, I wouldn't even know she was there.

The last time I held a woman, there was no denying her presence. Roxanne is more like a night blooming jasmine, dark and sultry, powerfully feminine. I felt her every pulse, movement, and breath when she was with me.

It makes me think about all the other men who paid for the same experience she had given me for free.

It infuriates me, and Tatiana jumps when my grip on her tightens suddenly. I relax immediately, muttering a quick apology and forcing all thoughts of my ex as far away as I possibly can. How long can this song possibly be, anyway? It has to be nearly over.

"You've seemed distracted all night," Tatiana comments quietly. "Is it–?"

"I'm sure Elise has already enlightened you, and I'd rather not discuss it further."

"Okay…sorry."

The song does eventually end, but to my displeasure, the next sound over the speaker is the damned countdown to midnight. I'm glued in place as everyone around me, including my dance partner, chants the countdown, and I'm stuck holding a girl I have no interest in as it happens.

"3, 2, 1—HAPPY NEW YEAR!" Everyone around me echoes in unison, like some sort of incantation.

Being a party put on by my mother, the celebration of the moment isn't too garish, all things considered. As if on cue, the nets above holding the golden, silver, and black balloons release and the balloons float down in a cloud of shining confetti. Other than that, the only symbol of the change of the year is the fact that all the coupled-off adults are currently kissing like their lives depend on it.

Tatiana looks wistful, her gaze lingering on my mouth longer than I'm comfortable with. Not wanting to shatter her heart completely, I take one of her hands and place a chaste kiss on the back of it, earning me a half-hearted smile from her. Obviously, she'd still been hoping for something more.

"Happy New Year," I tell her, and she replies kindly.

At least feeling uncomfortable with Tatiana kept me busy when I'd have been wishing for another woman's kiss to ring in the new year. I'm granted another boon when I feel my phone start to vibrate in my pocket with a call.

I step back from Tatiana. "I have to take this call. I'll talk to you later."

"Sure…" she mutters, disappointed, but I'm long gone before she can even finish the word.

I make a beeline for the terrace, where the cold is keeping the rest of the party away. It's too loud in here for any conversation, and on the off chance this is a call I want to take, I don't want to waste any time.

Cold air wallops me, but I ignore it, pulling my phone out and frowning at the unknown number. I should know better, but there's still a significant amount of alcohol in my system, and it makes me impulsive.

"Hello?" I ask.

"Happy New Year," Roxanne replies, and my heart skips a beat at the sound of her voice.

I grit my teeth. I had known on some level that it would have to be her but having to actually hear her voice is on a whole other level. What is someone even supposed to say to a person they hate, but simultaneously long for like nothing else in the world?

"Never call me again, Roxanne. Stop wasting both our time."

"Andries, wait—"

"This is over," I reply, cutting her off. "Do you hear me? Over!"

And I end the call before I can second guess myself, and at the same moment, a riot of fireworks begins to explode amid the dark night right in front of my eyes. Of course fireworks had to be expected for New Year's Eve, but the suddenness of it all still takes me off guard.

There's a commotion from people inside moving forward to observe the celebration from the safety of the warm house, as well as some spillover on the ground floor of the braver guests coming out onto the balustrade, the buzz of their appreciative conversation drifting up to me. Still, I'm completely alone out here, which is exactly what I want.

Well, at least I thought I was alone.

Leaning over the railing on the terrace, watching the fireworks apathetically, I'm numbed to the chill in the air by the copious amount I've drank throughout the night. It's probably the alcohol too that lets my grandmother sneak up behind me. I don't notice her until she appears beside me, leaning on the railing in a mirror image of my posture, only wrapped in a fur coat that is nearly as big as she is. Her sudden appearance makes me jump, and she chuckles.

"That was a short phone conversation," she comments blandly, speaking loudly between the explosions.

"Indeed."

"Was it a wrong number?"

I look at her out of the corner of my eye. "How long were you out here exactly?"

Her lips spread slightly up. "Long enough."

"Then I'm sure you know it was my ex. Which, as I've told multiple people tonight, I don't want to talk about."

"Are you sure? Although I've been told what has happened, it's always best to hear all the possible gossip from the source."

I scrub my hands over my face as the firework display ends. I want to flee back to my room, but I also don't want the truth about my situation to get diluted being passed from person to person.

So I launch into the story for her, from the opera to the day I confronted her in her office, leaving out all of the sordid details and only painting the picture of my brief love affair in broad strokes. My grandmother listens intently, never interrupting me, and I have to admit it's nice to lay it all bare without the person I'm talking to trying to immediately comfort me or belittle my feelings. I had been wanting this more logical approach that she was offering me.

Even with a lot of the emotion removed from the retelling, I have to swallow past the lump in my throat multiple times, lest it choke me.

Once I've finished, she looks thoughtful for a minute before nodding. My grandmother is the image of high-class sophistication, with her perfectly coiffed white hair, gracefully aged face and discreet jewelry worth hundreds of thousands of euros, so talking to her about falling in love with a former prostitute isn't exactly a comfortable situation, and I'm glad it's over.

"You did well, it seems. For as attached as you were, you extricated yourself completely without any additional drama, so a job well done in my book, son."

"Yeah, well, it doesn't feel that way. But thanks."

She pats my shoulder with a thin hand, wearing a sympathetic expression. "We've all had great and small loves in our lives, my darling, but that first love will always be something different. It's normal to feel like the world is ending, but it won't feel like that forever. It only hurts in the beginning, but even if it sounds cliche, time does heal all wounds."

Unbidden, more thoughts of Roxanne flit through my mind. I wonder where she was when she just called me... at home, or at some party where she and her employees moved through the crowds wordlessly selling sex and seduction. It's a shock she even had time to call me tonight if that was the case. Who was she going home with? Did she wish it were me?

I feel the cold skin of my grandmother's fingers on my hands, which are clutching the terrace railing in a white knuckled grip. Her touch snaps me out of my thoughts, which were quickly spiraling out of my control. Everything is spiraling out of my control.

"My husband Hendrik was deceitful, as well. I hated for a long time that I let myself fall for him the way I did, and once he was gone, I swore I'd never let myself be that vulnerable again. He lied, betrayed me, even knocked up some harlot while I waited at home for him like the doting wife I was. So trust me when I say I understand what you're feeling, dear, and that there's a light at the end of this dark, dark tunnel."

I relax my grip on the railing, replacing my hands with my elbows so I can hold my head, rubbing my temples to try and ward off the headache I knew was on the horizon. "I'll try to believe you," I tell her finally. "I swear."

"Then that's all I can ask."

The silence is companionable but sad, and I think we are both probably lost in thought. Me, thinking about Roxie in the embrace of another, and my grandmother reliving her painful past with a man she had put her trust in so long ago.

"How's business school?" she asks, closing the book on the previous subject for the time being.

"Fine," I say simply.

"Just fine?"

"It's business school. It isn't exactly something I'll ever consider 'fun' or 'enjoyable,'" I say, already wishing I could busy myself with a new drink.

"Fair enough. So, I'm assuming your plan is to take over the family business, not to open your own venture, correct?"

"So far that's the plan… I'm not sure if things will change in the future though." It's all a lie, and I try to avoid more detailed questions, because keeping things vague allows me to keep track of all the little lies that I have to continue to make about business school. The more answers I give, the more chances there are for things to go wrong.

I have the odd urge to just blurt out the truth to her and be done with the whole thing, letting my secret of being an English major trickle down to my parents, but I keep my mouth shut.

"You know, your father's company has an internship you could take. I know it'd take up a lot of your time since you also have school, but I think it could be a good distraction for you. And practice for once you graduate, of course."

I shrug. There really isn't anything I'd rather do less than intern with my dad, but I don't tell her that. "I don't think so, Oma. Not now."

She looks like she wants to argue, but resists the urge, just humming to herself in annoyance instead. "You don't trust my judgment? It's the perfect chance to get your mind off women and back where it should be. School, work, and then somewhere much farther down the line you can worry about dating and marriage."

"Oma…"

"Just think about it, okay? Obviously no one can force you, but it'd be a stupid move to pass it up."

I chuckle sardonically. "Fine, I'll think it over."

She sighs, leaning into me and giving me a small side embrace while we watch the smoke from the fireworks twist and twirl into the sky. "Good," she says, her tone victorious. "Oma knows what's best, of course."

Despite how absolutely miserable I feel, I give her a quick squeeze back. "Of course."

CHAPTER 4

Amsterdam, January 1, 2022
Roxanne

For years, I've trained myself to keep my emotions off my face in any work-related situation, because there's nothing good that can come of clients being able to see what is really going on inside my head. Escorts are one part living, breathing person, and a second part walking fantasy. Emotional control has always been imperative.

But when I pull my phone away from my ear and stare at the home screen after Andries hangs up, I can't stop the scowl that pulls at my lips. There had been a brief second when I thought he'd speak to me, but that hope quickly died when he ended the call before I could begin to say my piece.

Hearing his voice had been almost a physical pain, and the loss of that combined with his refusal not only hurt like hell, but it also pissed me off. He's being so damn difficult, it's ridiculous.

Charlie's New Year's party is being held in the Waldorf-Astoria Hotel, sprawling through the ornate ballroom and bar, and the energy is electrifying. It's a damned good event, and I should be enjoying it as much as I can enjoy any work event, but heartbreak has soured everything for me. I should never have let myself be vulnerable. This wouldn't be happening to me if I hadn't!

The lights are low, and there's a small group of string players providing ambient music that can be heard between the snatches of conversation. There's an impressive turnout, and it's a miracle I'd even had time to sneak away and try to call Andries. I'd been helpless, though, when the countdown was over, and everyone had locked lips in celebration of a new year and all the beautiful things that came along with it.

Charlie had been next to me, dapper and clean cut in his suit, top three shirt buttons undone, while everyone rang in the new year. I allowed him to lean close enough to kiss my cheek briefly and was grateful when he didn't press the issue further, just murmuring, "Happy New Year, beautiful Roxanne," before returning to mingle amongst his crowd.

Unlike Karl, Charlie had taken my early retirement in stride, being disappointed but otherwise understanding my need to stop escorting to focus on the escort business itself. It was why I had agreed to join some of my girls that had been hired for the night, spread across the gathering like shimmering little jewels meant to charm guests and provide entertainment in the sultriest of ways. I, on the other hand, kept my involvement strictly to the charming conversation portion, both available and untouchable all at the same time.

Charlie had been thrilled to see me arrive with the other girls and was more than happy to let me join them in partaking in the open bar. Coming to the party had been a spur-of-the-moment decision, so I'd have something to do that would get Andries off my mind. Wearing a silky silver dress that hugged every curve of my body and hung off my shoulders, I stayed perfectly on the line between sexy and classy, and I'm enough of a professional to interact with everyone.

Everyone's inhibitions are slowly but surely falling to the wayside as the night goes on, everyone except for my girls, that is. They drink little and spend their time winding other guests around their fingers with nothing but a smile and brush of fingers. The newer girls still draw attention, but the more experienced girls are impossible to resist. Men and women alike stop in their tracks to speak with them, dance with them, or anything else that will keep them around a little longer. My little sirens... It's a good night for business, no doubt.

Throwing myself into work has been my saving grace, but as the night wears on, the more my thoughts begin to wander back to my ex. I shouldn't have called him... it was a moment of weakness, but it's too late now. I should have stayed in my office all night pouring over paperwork, applications, and client lists, streamlining everything to an inch of its life while also staying busy. This party, the romance and joy of it, is only making me feel worse by the minute.

Making up my mind, I quickly finish the glass of wine I had been nursing, setting it down on the bar-top with a clink, and scoping out the quickest way to escape the situation. I've made an appearance, proven I'm not a recluse to myself, my employees, and the public, and now I can go home and feel bad for myself in peace.

Sleep had been scant for me lately, every restless few minutes I managed to grasp filled with memories and images of Andries. As foolish as missing him makes me feel, it's nothing compared to the emptiness that is left behind.

I push through the crowd, smiling and stopping for a quick word with a few people, wearing my capable businesswoman facade like a suit of armor. I'm almost to the main lobby when I run into someone, and unlike the rest of the guests, this one doesn't move out of my way. Instead, I run into him almost head on, and he catches me by the elbows as if to steady me. Except, I hadn't lost my balance. Not even close.

Looking up, I feel a hot flash of anger cut through my melancholy. It's not just a random person, too distracted to have any social awareness. It's Karl, and his mere reappearance in my life makes my skin crawl.

"Roxanne," he says, his voice unusually polite and even pleased to see me. "I'd seen a few of your girls flitting about, so I hoped I'd see you here."

I jerk myself out of his grasp and step back. "You've seen me. Now move, please."

He looks astonished at my reaction. "Why so hasty? Don't you want to catch up with me? I know we've got some unfinished business, but I hope it won't affect our friendship."

I can't help it. I snort in a rather unladylike fashion. "Certainly you aren't insinuating that we are friends, Karl?"

For some reason, he finds my comment rather funny and his lips twice into a smirk. "Well, you are aware I'd rather that we be lovers, but you've taken that off the table, so…"

I tilt my chin up stubbornly. "I don't know how this has escaped you, but we were never friends. We were never lovers. You were just a client, Karl, and nothing more. Now your nasty behavior has made it so we can't even be business associates, but you burnt that bridge yourself, so please get out of my way."

His face, which I once considered handsome in that way that older gentlemen can be, turns ugly as he sneers. "I heard about your little breakup, by the way. Didn't I tell you karma would come for you, eventually?"

Infuriated, I try to push past him, and this time I make it, slipping past his larger frame and making a beeline for the exit. Before I can get there fully, I feel Karl grab my shoulder, and I whip around to give him a piece of my mind. Before I can, though, he holds up his hands in a gesture of surrender.

"I apologize. That was out of line." He clears his throat and has the decency to look slightly embarrassed. "I've got a private booth in the VIP area of the bar. Let me buy you a drink."

I pause, biting back my scathing retort in my confusion. "Karl, the drinks are free. Have you been paying for them?"

He laughs. "What I've bought is certainly not on the open bar's menu tonight, Roxanne. Come on, let me get you something special to apologize for my behavior."

I should say no. I really want to. But on the other hand, verbally tearing Karl to shreds seems to be a smidgen more entertaining than going home and crying into my pillowcase for the millionth time.

I don't trust Karl, not even for a second, but I have to admit being able to drop the put together facade would be nice, and Karl apparently already knows all my shame and heartbreak, so what did it even matter?

"Fine. But it better be something impressive."

Behind the main area of the bar there is a thick red curtain that separates the VIP area. I follow Karl, smelling thick cigar smoke rolling out from the cordoned off area, swatting Karl's hand away when he tries to lay it on the small of my back as he holds the curtain aside.

The VIP lounge reminds me of some secret club that only blue-blooded first-born sons would be allowed into, all dark reds, greens, and dark wood made shiny with years and years of use. There are about a dozen patrons back here, including Charlie, who gives Karl and I a quick nod before returning to his in-depth conversation with another man who has one of my girls perched in his lap like a sparkling accessory. I catch her eye, and she gives me a quick wink, rubbing two fingers together below the man's eye-line in the universal sign for "money," and I offer her a knowing grin in response.

I slide into a wine-red leather booth with Karl. It's in the shape of a horseshoe, but for the time being Karl respects my space enough to sit across from me instead of scooting until he is next to me. He signals the bartender before turning all his rapt attention back to me.

"So why did you bring me back here? To gloat in peace?" I ask.

"I was actually going to start out with an apology, if you'll let me, but I'm not so sure you will."

I wave my hand in a signal for him to continue.

"I want to apologize for our last few meetings; the unfortunate incident with your sister's bookshop and our meeting at the mall." His tone is more serious and humble than usual which catches me off guard. He sounds rather honest, but who knows for sure. It's Karl, after all. "I was still feeling quite stung and jilted by losing you from my life so suddenly, and I was lashing out. A behavior that I'm much too old for, no doubt."

"No shit."

He looks offended before sighing. "You continue to be a difficult part of my life that I seem to be addicted to."

I make a show of checking my nails, ignoring him for longer than is socially acceptable, before finally shrugging nonchalantly. "I can consider forgiving you if you promise me to never, and I mean *never* mess with my family in any way, shape, or form again. This is between you and me. You had no right to go and try to take that bookshop from us."

"Agreed."

"Like I said, I'll consider it." I can see he wants to talk about it more, so I move the conversation along before we can get any more in depth about his lingering feelings for me. Overly clingy clients are always a kind of risk for the work I do and dealing with them never fails to be distasteful. "Now what special libation did I come over here for?"

As if on cue, the bartender appears with a dark brown, nearly black bottle that he's cradling with both hands, wrapped in a pristine white towel, while another server places two round-bellied snifter glasses in front of each of us. Karl declines the offer to pour the drink for us and dismisses the bartender, so he and I are alone again.

I turn the dark bottle so I can better see its aged, tan label. It reads, in blood-red script "Vintage Port," "Special Label," and below that, "Dows." It's just slightly colder than room temperature, and while I don't know much about the port, I can tell it's special.

"Why do I feel like this is a ridiculously expensive bottle and you're going to lord it over me once we drink it?" I ask suspiciously.

"I told you I had something special. Something tells me that you could use a little indulgence after that week you've apparently had."

He sounds sincere, but I'm still skeptical, and I chew my lip as I consider it. Finally, I nod, and with a wolfish grin, Karl opens the bottle. He pours the ruby liquid into our snifters with careful precision, the port thick, dark, and aromatic.

My first sip of it is jammy and strong enough that I can feel it in my sinuses, but once it has time to mellow on my tongue, it's undoubtedly something incredible. The port is rich, earthy, and I actually sigh before I take another drink.

"Good?" Karl asks, and his tone is strained.

Realizing I'm probably looking almost indecent in my enjoyment, I straighten my posture and sit the snifter down. "Fantastic. Almost worth my time, even."

Karl chuckles as he relaxes, draping his arms over the back of the booth. "Since we've got some time with you finishing your drink, why don't you tell me what exactly happened with you and your boyfriend?"

Scowling at him over the rim of my snifter, I consider the idea. There's no way Karl is trying to comfort me. This has to be a tactic to get either under my skin or fish for information that can be used to manipulate me in the future. Still… I can give him a little information without it biting me in the ass, I think. I don't know if it's the port or seeing everyone else with their tongues down each other's throat, but I really want someone to talk to.

"I'm not going to get into specifics with you... it's just safe to say that we had conflicting ideas of the future and my business plans. That's all."

He leans forward in interest. "So does that mean it was an amicable split?"

"Ah, no, not really..." I let my words trail off, before giving another sip of my port.

"Hmm, interesting... Did he not like you being an escort, then?"

I bite the inside of my lip, trying to decide how to skate the subject safely without him figuring out how vague I'm being. "It just didn't work out, okay? Andries and I are two very different people. I thought we could work through our differences, and he didn't. It's that simple."

"It doesn't sound like it's simple at all for you, Roxie." Karl tips back the rest of his drink before reaching across the table to drag a finger down my cheek. I freeze, pushing him away, and to my surprise he backs off without any fight, just sad affection written on his face. "He's a fool. I'm sure he'll figure it out sooner rather than later."

"Speaking of splits... how's your divorce proceeding?"

"Actually, it's finished, finally. I thought we'd never agree to everything, but I just signed the papers recently." He holds up his left hand, empty of any ring. "I'm officially a free man."

"Congratulations," I say, and I mean it. "I know it was a difficult process for you."

"It's just nice to be able to move forward finally, instead of being mired in the past."

I nod. "Yes, I can understand that."

"In a way, you're kind of the reason I was finally able to put it all to rest," he says thoughtfully.

My brows raise in surprise. "What? How?"

"Had you not gotten me that promotion I wouldn't have been able to throw enough money at the whole ordeal to get it finished. Once my ex-wife and her attorney realized how outclassed they were going up against the Global Head of Sales for Van Den Bosch Industries, they folded pretty fast." Karl refills his glass and mine before holding his up. "So thank you, my dear, for going out of your way to get me that promotion. You're quite the useful ally to have in my corner, I'm beginning to realize. Even if we can't be together the way I'd prefer…."

I raise my glass and toast him, clinking our glasses together. "To allies, then."

Karl sighs after he drinks, sounding almost sad. "Ah, Roxanne, I wish I could believe that you felt that way, but I see the wariness on your face when we speak. How did we become enemies after all this time? We had so many good years."

"We can still have more, if you can accept that our relationship has changed and moved from personal to professional. And, well…" I think about the bookshop, and the shit he put me through. "Maybe a sizable donation to my sister's bookshop would help take some of the sting out of the nonsense you tried to pull. She's been wanting the extra funds to turn the attic into a children's reading area."

"Always scheming, aren't you?" I bristle, but he laughs warmly. "Oh, calm down. I mean it in a good way. It's what makes you such a clever woman. One step ahead at all times."

"Uh-huh. You're laying it on a little thick, you know?" I look around at the couples who are sinking further into each other, arms around necks and lips whispering in ears. The atmosphere, combined with the way Karl is looking at me, the lid of his eyes lowered, makes me sure that it's time to take my leave. As long as he and I end this conversation now, then I can count the night as a net positive.

"This was lovely," I tell him honestly. "But it's time for me to take my leave."

I curse under my breath when he closes the space between us, moving from sitting across from me to being hip to hip in one slick maneuver. This close, I can feel his body heat and smell the pomade he uses in his hair, and my stomach flips unpleasantly. I just need to get out before he tries something—

But it's too late, as he lays a hand over my bare knee and squeezes gently. "The night could be even more lovely from here. For old times' sake, spend the night with me. I'll double that bookstore donation if you do... out of friendship, of course, not as payment."

I hate that I consider it. After such a hard breakup, I'd almost sleep with Karl again in the hopes I can purge my ex out of my system, but in my heart I know that I still want to try and mend things between Andries and I. Plus, the idea of going home with Karl makes me feel ill.

I try to move my leg out from under his hand, but he just slides it further up my thigh. "What did I say about keeping this professional?" I plead, knowing I'm on the precipice of erasing all the good will we just built.

"It can be our swan song. A goodbye to the beautiful times we have shared." He moves closer into my space, face so close to mine that his nose brushes my cheek as he tells me softly. "Haven't I always treated you right, Roxie? Haven't I always made you feel good?"

I shudder, this time completely extricating myself from his grip before this can go any further. "I'm leaving, Karl."

There is a quick flash of anger that washes over his features before he gets them under control, going back to that slick, seductive look that is never going to work on me. In a last-ditch effort, Karl offers me something else, and I have to admit it's unexpected.

"Okay, I respect that you don't want to have a one-night stand. Instead, let's start fresh."

"That's what I'm trying to do," I point out, my frown becoming more evident.

"No, not like that." He grabs my shoulder to hold me in place, and his voice is low and serious. "We can be together, Roxanne. As a couple, a real one. No mistress or escort nonsense, no transactions, just us. Imagine how we could help each other grow… how my funds and business expertise could help transform your business."

"Please, Karl." I hate that I'm about to beg, but this is getting bad, and fast. "I want that too, but without the dating or the sex. I don't want to be with you like that. Why can't you understand that?"

It's like he doesn't even hear me, invading my space a second time, the push of his fingertips into the flesh of my thigh making frightened rage shoot through me. I am not going to be pushed around, but he could certainly make this difficult for me if he wants to.

"I've never stopped wanting you," he tells me, voice low and throaty. Karl slides his hand from my shoulder to my hand, and before I can register what he's doing, he grabs it and places it over his groin, where I can feel—

"You're being a pig!" I gasp, jerking my hand away and scrambling out of the booth without any grace. "Go fuck yourself, Karl. Don't contact me again until you can understand that no means no."

I flee then, past the bar and to the red curtain, pushing it aside as I hear Karl yelling my name behind me, but I'm done with him. Sickened, even. Every time I put any kind of trust or hope in a man behaving decently, they revert to being disgusting perverts, and I figure I see even more than usual because of my occupation. It's almost like since I slept with Karl in the past, he can never see me as a whole person. Just a woman he could coerce into bed if he tried hard enough.

I want a hot shower, complete with full body sugar-scrub, but I'm still destined to be stuck in this hotel, because when I pause to clip my clutch purse shut, I run right into another man.

"Fuck, sorry," I mutter. "I'm in a hurry."

"Hey!" he exclaims, but it's a happy sound, as if I was someone he had been searching for.

The man steps back, and in the dark bar area I just get the impression of a younger man in a crisp white oxford shirt and a pair of thick-rimmed glasses balancing on his face.

"You're Andries Van Den Bosch's girlfriend, right? Roxanne?"

I shiver, feeling cold all of a sudden. My relationship with Andries had not been public knowledge except for our friends and family, and now that we had broken up in a shameful fashion, it was even more imperative that it didn't slip out into the public sphere. If it got out that Andries had been dating the head of an escort service...

"I think you've got the wrong person," I say quickly.

"Don't worry, Ms. Feng, I don't wish you any ill will."

The use of my last name sets me on edge even more. "Who are you exactly?"

"Oh, me? I'm Kenneth, a journalist with RTL. I specialize in investigative journalism regarding prominent Dutch families. Maybe you've read some of my pieces featuring the Van Dierens?"

I quickly flip through the names that I know, finally making the connection. The Van Dierens were related to the Van Den Bosches, and Andries had briefly mentioned his uncle Alex Van Dieren being in the news lately.

Oh, shit, I think to myself. *This is really bad.*

"Never heard of them. Goodbye!" I try to slide past Kenneth, but he's dropped the casual patron act and doesn't move a centimeter, standing firmly in my way.

"I think you have. Your boyfriend's mother, Julia? Well, before she was Julia Van Den Bosch, she was Julia Van Dieren."

"I don't have a boyfriend," I insist, but every time I try to sidestep him he gets in my way.

Kenneth has a look in his eyes that reminds me of nothing so much as a shark, his white teeth almost glowing in the dim room. "I have to admit, I'm surprised to see you here! I'd heard Elise and Andries Van Den Bosch were spending the holiday back on the family estate, and I just assumed you'd be there with them. Why aren't you spending the holiday with your boyfriend, Roxanne?"

I'm well and truly sick of men tonight, and my anger drives me to shove Kenneth out of the way with both hands. He's shocked by the physicality of it, and actually moves, but as I weave through the crowd, he's right behind me, peppering me with questions loudly enough that I have to stop and shut him up. He's nearly yelling these questions about Andries and me, and I see more than a few other guests turning to see what the commotion is.

"Shut the fuck up," I hiss, but he's relentless.

"Who are you here with, Roxanne, if not Andries? Could it be a business venture? Or if you don't feel like answering that question, maybe you could tell me why that older man was yelling your name when you came out of the VIP lounge. He seemed pretty distressed, almost as if—"

"Is there a problem here?" A shadow appears beside Kenneth, and I could almost fall to the floor with relief when I see it's Charlie, maybe my only ally in this place that doesn't have some sort of agenda.

"No problem, sir," Kenneth replies, falling right back into that young, unsure persona he had worn to catch me off guard, but Charlie isn't falling for it. He must have seen more of the interaction between Kenneth and I than I thought.

Charlie looks him up and down, raising a steel-gray eyebrow. "This party is invite only. I don't recognize you, which means you aren't on my guest list. Who are you, exactly?"

"Just a plus one," Kenneth says with a self-conscious laugh. "But you just caught me on my way out." He turns his attention back to me, holding out a thick, cream-colored business card that he seems to pull from nowhere, and hands it to me. "It was lovely to meet you, Roxanne. If you have fun stories you want to tell, you can always shoot me an email." His eyes narrow, predatory. "My paper pays quite well."

I'd like to shove the business card down his throat, but like a thief in the night, he disappears into the crowd before I can get a word in edgewise. Charlie is still standing with me while I slip the card into my clutch, knowing that I might need it for information later. At least to see who this Kenneth person is.

Charlie looks concerned as he grabs my shoulders to look me over, turning me this way and that like a marionette. "Are you okay? I feel horrible that some slimy journalist was able to bother you here."

I wave him off me, but his genuine worry is the only warm spot of the past few hours. "I'm fine. Just shook up. You don't expect strangers to know your whole name, you know? Or your personal business. It scared me a little."

Charlie's eyes dart to my clutch. "Do you want me to dispose of that card for you?"

I shake my head, the pieces of my hair that have fallen loose throughout the night brushing against my cheeks. "No, thank you. I'm going to do a little digging of my own."

He doesn't look convinced that I'm making the right decision, but thankfully he doesn't try to prod me into giving him the card. Instead, Charlie just sighs. "Just be careful. Journalists like him publish these sensational articles as a way to get their own fame, and they don't care if they ruin lives in the process. It seems like he already knows enough to be dangerous, so just watch yourself."

"I will, I swear." In an impulsive move, I hug him quickly, feeling like I'm eighteen again with the world against me. "Thank you."

Unlike Karl, Charlie is happy to let me go, and escorts me personally to the exit.

Finally free of the New Year's Eve party of many problems, I suck in lungfuls of chilly night air not tainted with smoke, sweat, or the stench of alcohol, before hailing a cab. Alone in the backseat, I pull my phone out and toy with the idea of calling Andries again. Wanting to avoid the inevitable sadness that comes every time he sends me to voicemail, I decide against it, but I can't help sending a quick heart emoji along with the simple message, *I miss you.*

* * *

The shower I had been dreaming of is calling me as soon as I walk in the door, so I kick off my heels, pulling the dress over my head as I walk straight to the bathroom, my panties following not far behind. Under the scalding water, I wash away the sweat and scents of the night, along with the product from my hair, before scrubbing myself head to toe with my favorite sugar scrub.

I feel better afterwards, my limbs loose and heavy, but my mind is still buzzing from the last interaction of the night: Kenneth.

As much as I want to crawl between my sheets and try to get some rest, I think I need to do a little investigating first.

I grab my laptop from my work satchel along with the business card, settling cross-legged on the mattress and opening the computer up. The search doesn't take long. The first result, on the first search page, is the man that had confronted me at the party, looking sharp and intelligent in his headshot on the RTL website. I read the small bio for him, but it doesn't give me enough information. I need more.

This time, I search for some of his articles, and reading them makes my stomach drop. Every piece is like something out of the gossip magazines, except much more in depth and clearly well researched. There are articles about Andries' mom and dad, his uncle Alex van Dieren, and even his grandmother Margaret, spilling every personal detail that Kenneth could get a hold of out for everyone to read.

It makes me feel ill. There were very few people at the party who knew about Andries and me, but if Kenneth had asked the right people the right questions, he may have found out much more than I was comfortable with. If it got out that Andries had been dating me, it could hurt his reputation, and turn him even more against me. It would be horrible.

Tonight, though, it's almost three a.m. and there is nothing else I can do at the moment. I shut the computer and set it on my bedside table, tucking myself under the blanket and laying my head on my pillow. My body almost seems to sigh in relief at finally being able to lay down after so long in heels, but my brain is harder to convince. I comfort myself by plotting out my next move, and after some time, I fall into a restless sleep, the faces of all the men that have been manipulating my life in one way or the other infecting my dreams.

CHAPTER 5

Amsterdam, January 1, 2022
Roxanne

The next morning is still technically a holiday, so I grab my laptop bag and head down the street to a little cafe—the only one open today actually—to have breakfast while I work through all the problems that cropped up last night. I'm too exhausted to cook for myself, and being in a different location might help me organize my thoughts.

Once I have a scone and a coffee, I settle in at the most secluded table I can find and pull up the list of all the girls who were at the party last night. There were six of them in total, and it isn't until the fourth call that I hit pay-dirt.

The fourth girl I speak to is Natasha, and where the other girls had no idea what I was talking about, Natasha seems ready to burst as soon as I mention Kenneth's name.

"Yes!" she exclaims. "Once he realized I worked for you, he started asking a million questions, some that didn't even make sense."

She describes what he looks like, and there is no doubt that we're talking about the same person. I open the note app and have her tell me everything she can remember, especially the questions he asked her, but Natasha doesn't recall everything as clearly as I would like.

It doesn't help that she's also nervous once she connects the dots and realizes that Kenneth is a journalist.

"You don't think he'll publish anything with my name in it, do you? My parents would lose their minds if they found out that I'm an escort! They'd have heart attacks and drop dead on the spot."

I pinch the bridge of my nose and sigh. "I don't think he's interested in my employees, Natasha, just me. Try not to worry."

She makes an unsure noise on the other end of the phone. "I really don't like this, Roxanne. He was very pushy, and if it wasn't for the other guy I was talking to interjecting, I think he'd have bothered me the entire night. It feels like his intentions are like, really bad."

"...Natasha, you didn't tell him anything about me, did you? Especially about me and the man I was dating until recently?"

It takes her too long to answer, and I know I'm potentially fucked. Finally, she responds, "I don't think I did, but I was honestly pretty drunk at that point."

Cursing under my breath, I get off the phone with Natasha as quickly as I can, knowing that I'm backed into a corner. I had hoped to have more information before confronting Kenneth directly, but if he had gotten any information from any of my girls, I needed to get ahead of it before it ended up in an article or something.

I hesitate, but nothing else is coming to my mind, so I have to call him. After dialing the number on the business card, I'm connected directly to Kenneth's mobile number, and he answers on the third ring.

"This is Kenneth."

"Hi. So, we met at the party last night. Roxanne. I'm sure you remember me."

Kenneth laughs darkly. "Yes, of course. I'm surprised to hear from you so soon, Ms. Feng."

"I wish you didn't have to hear from me at all, but there is nothing else to be done, it sounds like, since an employee of mine said that you were harassing her last night?"

"Hmm. Harass is a pretty strong word. In my line of work, it's just called investigation."

I close my eyes and try to keep my temper in check. I want a cigarette so badly, but I need to get through this first. "Look. I know you have to have some professional integrity. Please stop whatever project you're working on if it includes anything about me or Andries. I'm not one of these wealthy upper-class individuals that can weather the sort of storm that destroys a person's career. You'd be fucking up my life."

Kenneth laughs again and takes his sweet time mulling over what I've said before answering. "You're right in that I don't often go after normal civilians, but you have just such an interesting career and connections I think I can make an exception."

"You little—"

"There is *something* I can do for you, though," he interposes before I can finish my sentence. "For a small price I can at least change your name in the article I'm writing. How does that sound?"

"My name and Andries name," I counter.

"Just yours, Roxanne. Take it or leave it."

I clench my fists, trying to dispel some of the anger, but it doesn't help. "Fine, say I accept. What's the price?"

"It's very affordable, actually. I just need you to collaborate on this article with me. Answer some questions, give me some insider information, that kind of thing."

I think about agreeing. It's better than nothing, but still insulting, so I tell him a few more colorful curses before hanging up, dropping my phone on the cafe table and groaning. This was bad news. Really bad news.

Nothing makes sense at first, about how Kenneth found out about my relationship and connections to the Van Den Bosch family. I feel exposed, laid bare, and like there is nothing I can do about it. Someone is leaking information to the press, and I just don't know if I'm up to solving the mystery.

"*A girl on campus that went to the party told my sister she works for you*," I remember Andries commenting when he entered my office. Would it be that girl on campus that works for me and knows Elise that tipped the info to Kenneth?

It's a long shot, but I call my personal assistant Poppy with a single possibility in mind.

"Poppy," I say when she picks up. "We've got some girls working for us that also attend the University of Amsterdam, right?"

"Yes, we do. Quite a few of them, actually."

"I'll be back to the office after tomorrow. Can you compile a list of which girls go there for me?"

"Absolutely!"

I can easily picture one of my girls telling Elise about me as soon as they saw me in the arms of her brother at his birthday party and then thinking to tip a journalist in exchange for some extra money. Now I just need to figure out who.

I finish my scone, but don't taste it much at all.

* * *

Back in the office on Monday, everything seems so normal and peaceful. The holiday weekend gave a lot of the girls time to rest and recharge, and everyone seems bright and chipper when I arrive.

I'd usually spend the first day back in the office working out schedules and events for the week, matching the right girls with the right clients, but I have one extra task today that has to be completed first.

On my desk is a neat list of all the girls that work for me and attend the University of Amsterdam, along with their phone numbers. Poppy works quickly, I have to give her that.

I like to consider myself a lenient boss, but the type of gossiping that could affect personal lives, mine included, is not acceptable. I hate making the calls I have to make, and it's a huge relief each time one of them tells me that they didn't even know Elise. I was getting close to the bottom of the list when I call an escort named Cassey, who, by the sound of her voice, already knows what I'm calling about.

I ask about Elise, and without hesitation, Cassey confirms she knows her.

"And did you tell Elise about me?"

She heaves a long sigh, a few beats of silence ensuing, before she finally tells me the truth. "Yeah, I told her. We're friends, and I didn't know your job was some shameful secret." Cassey sounds offended and combative. "We aren't doing anything illegal."

"You know that this line of work can become dangerous and ruin lives if we are too loose lipped with clients, family, and friends. This time it was me that you got into hot water, but next time, what if you say something to the wrong person and one of your coworkers gets hurt by a jealous ex?"

Cassey remains silent, and my eyes flutter shut. Fine, if she wanted it this way, then so be it.

"You're fired, Cassey. You can come pick up your check any time after Thursday."

"Cool," she bites out, bitter, and I can hear the tears in her voice. "Thanks for nothing, Roxanne."

I don't have anything else to say to her, so I let her hang up before pillowing my head on my arms that are folded on my desk in front of me. Cassey could have jeopardized my business, and has already ruined my relationship, and for what? The approval of Elise Van Den Bosch?

This whole issue was really causing me a lot of grief. Eventually, I was going to have to do something about it.

CHAPTER 6

"If I had known I'd be the newest circus attraction, I'd have stayed back at the estate and done online classes," I tell my sister as we get into one of the cafeterias for our lunch break.

It was clear as soon as I stepped foot into the lecture hall this morning that everyone knew that I had dated a former escort and current brothel keeper. Whether or not it was Cassey and Patricia that spread the news is a theory yet to be proven. Needless to say, I'm glad today I only have one last class at five p.m. It'll give me time to prepare myself mentally before facing one more wave of whispers, giggles, and stares.

Elise bumps me with her elbow, looking bright and lively in a pair of dark jeans and white blouse paired with her beige overcoat and boots. She doesn't look like she's been in class for hours working on a high-stress business degree, but instead like she'd just walked out of a shampoo commercial. Young, beautiful, carefree, but still my painfully annoying sister.

"It's just because you're so brooding and mysterious. Everyone is thinking about how much they want to soothe your darkened heart."

"Hilarious," I mutter as we start scanning the free tables around the open layout. "Darkened heart, huh? You want to take over as the family poet?"

Elise keeps looking around, pretending not to notice the weight of everyone's stares. "Um. No thanks. I think you've got it under control actually."

The cafeteria isn't usually part of my daily schedule at the university, but for Elise, it's the perfect opportunity to make a bunch of her social appearances at once. Since it's our first day of college after the winter holiday, she'd stuck to me like glue, no doubt commanded to do so by our mom. At least it isn't like a high school cafeteria, with everyone separated into firm groupings that no one could ever infiltrate.

The cafeterias on campus have the life and harmony I had craved back then, but not in the way I had anticipated. It's a conglomeration of exhausted juniors and seniors, some sleeping on their folded arms with a cold coffee cooling beside them, alongside freshmen taking full advantage of the meal pass they will soon grow tired of, and couples stealing private moments before they have to make their return to the hustle and bustle of class. Most students are looking to eat, drink, and get out.

Elise is the outlier, as she is in so many other portions of her life. It's like she holds court over the place as soon as she walks in, at least she does most of the time. Today, though, all eyes are on me. Unfortunately.

I'd tried to leave this morning in a hoodie and sweatpants, but Elise had acted as if I'd personally wounded her when she saw me, so I was at least dressed in a manner considered presentable to my sister. If she had her choice, I'd be in a suit jacket at all times, but she'd have to settle for a cardigan today.

"I think I'm going to go," I murmur to her, as the stares become more and more pointed. Some smaller groups are giggling behind their hands, and others are making more obscene gestures where they think I can't see them. I can, and it's making me more uncomfortable by the minute.

"Nonsense," Elise replies. Interlocking her arm with mine, she then drags me to one of the empty tables. "Let's at least get you a bagel and an orange juice. You look like you're about to expire on the spot. What are those dark circles all about, anyway?"

"I thought it was considered attractive to look like you're on death's doorstep."

She scowls up at me. "Yeah, when you're not *actually* on death's doorstep. Which I'm convinced you are. Sit down and I'll get your snack."

"Yes, mother," I huff.

As soon as she leaves my side, I feel... off. Like all the strange looks are something physical I can't shake off, and now that I'm alone, the target on my back seems to be even bigger than before. I can almost hear the tittering and muffled laughter at my expense, even if I have no idea why.

I focus my eyes on the clock above the entryway arch, counting the seconds to keep myself busy and unaware of what is going on around me. Sixty seconds, one hundred and twenty seconds, one hundred and eighty seconds...what in the hell is taking Elise so long?

I spot her still in the checkout line, the tray with our food balanced on her hip as she talks to another girl in hushed tones. The second girl is showing Elise something on her phone, and Elise's face goes from pale to bright red with anger. It looks like she is thanking the girl, and then she is coming back to our table, dropping the tray down with more force than is necessary.

"What was that all about?" I ask.

She is already on her phone, furiously typing. "Eat your bagel first and then we'll talk," she says, not even bothering to look up at me.

I eat in silence, my stomach complaining the entire time, washing down the dry hunks of bread with juice, faster than is probably healthy. I just want to see whatever has her in such a frenzy.

Once I'm done, I push the tray away from us, Elise's fruit bowl still sitting on it untouched. "Okay. Finished. Now tell me."

Lips pursed and expression tight, Elise lays her phone horizontally on the table in front of us, plucking her AirPods out of her backpack and handing me one. The video she pulls up on YouTube isn't very long, but within seconds, the rage I'm feeling is murderous.

The YouTuber is a guy about my age, talking to the audience like he has some big, ugly secret to spill. It turns out he does, only it isn't his secret. It's mine.

"My friend said his channel is all about exposing the rich and famous for their dalliances," Elise whispers. "She said he actually goes to school here, which was why he was able to get all the footage and information from your, and I quote, 'circle of friends.'"

"That can't be true," I say, all of my attention now on the video. The YouTuber is telling his audience about my birthday party, and the toast I had given in honor of Roxanne. Among all the negative feelings I have been having for her, that one was untainted until now.

Her beautiful face as she watched me toast her, the gentle warmth of the champagne I had drank earlier, and the thrill of complete happiness I was feeling for the first time in my life had made that night unforgettable.

Watching the event unfold on Elise's phone screen, through shaky footage that someone must have taken without me noticing, it didn't feel like that grand moment I remember. Instead, it seemed fake and over the top. I looked like a besotted teenager, and while in the moment I had eyes for nothing but Roxanne, watching the video made me see all the strained, uncomfortable looks on some of the guests' faces. They must have thought I was trashed and obsessed with the first woman to give me any attention. They couldn't see the love that had been burning between us. None of those people would ever understand.

Once the video of the toast ended, the YouTuber reappeared, a self-satisfied smirk on his lips as he revealed his big "gotcha" moment. Using pictures captured by the paparazzi of both Roxanne and I and Roxanne with other men, he narrated how Roxanne was an escort, and like a moron, I had fallen for her and was sparing no expense in pampering her. There was even a shot of Roxanne in my apartment window, her pale hair undone and floating around her face. It made my heart seize in my chest.

The video is already at 37,000 views and climbing. The stares pounding into me from all around changed from curious to damning, now that I knew what they were about. They saw me as a fool… a stupid rich kid who fell in love with a fucking escort. And I had been not only sleeping with her, but also dating her.

The YouTuber was still talking, but I couldn't take it anymore. I push the phone away, sick to my stomach. "Turn it off, Elise."

She doesn't ask any questions, just does as I say, tucking the phone away. There is a line of worry between her eyebrows as she watches me, but she doesn't prod at me just yet. I'm humiliated that she has to be the one to reveal this to me, especially in such a public venue, but at least I'm not alone. I don't know if I could handle it.

Noise in the cafeteria soon stops being just a faint buzz and becomes a dull roar in my ears. How can I go to class, walk through these halls, now that everyone knows what has happened to me?

"I need to get out of here," I tell Elise, who nods, taking my arm and leading me toward the entryway. I keep my eyes fixed firmly on the floor, not wanting to see any more of the student's faces or the judgment in their gazes.

We've almost made it back out into the main hall when a figure steps in front of us. With my head pointed stubbornly toward the floor, I see his feet first, and the disgusting old, tattered Vans covering them.

"Can you get out of the way?" I ask, raising my head, before I freeze at the sight of his all-too-familiar face.

The YouTuber grins at me, looking like every stereotype of a bully that there is, except he's in university now, and it looks pathetic on him. He might get away with dragging people like me through the dirt online, but in real life it was going to be a different story.

Elise reacts first, striking forward like a snake, pointing her manicured finger inches from his face. "Who do you think you are, huh? That video is totally fucked up! Our lawyer is going to tear you to pieces."

The infuriating smirk slips just a touch at the mention of our lawyer, but he doesn't let it fade completely, tipping back his head to laugh. "No number of civil suits is going to change the fact that everyone now knows that your big brother here has a bit of an obsession with hookers."

I can't let Elise fight this fight for me, not with the way the entire cafeteria has gone silent to watch us. It's not her bullshit to work through. I step forward in front of my sister, drawing my hunched shoulders up so I'm at my full height, tall enough to look down on the YouTuber with a sneer.

"It also doesn't change the fact that you're a leech that can only get attention by tearing down other people. Is it because you're jealous, I wonder?"

He doesn't even have the decency to look ashamed, which makes me think that I'm not the first target that has confronted him about this.

"You rich assholes are the ones who fuck up, and I just cover it for the general public. It's not like I'm out there causing you all to act the way you do. It just seems to come naturally."

I take another step forward, but he doesn't budge. "Why don't you get out of here, and if you're lucky, you won't hear from my attorney."

He shrugs. "Sure, buddy. Whatever you want. But can I ask you a quick favor first? The way you were so obsessed with that hooker… man. She must be an animal in the sack. Can I get her number now that you're done with her?"

It happens in a flash, so quickly that my mind doesn't even have time to catch up with my actions. The rage that had been simmering in me explodes, and I sink my fist into the YouTuber's face, all the strength I have built from fencing powering my arm forward with such force that he staggers back, holding his nose, which is now leaking blood.

"What the fuck!" he exclaims, voice muffled by his hands.

It's like a car crash from there, the sound of my own pulse lessening enough that I can finally hear the world around me again. Everyone's conversations have reached a fever pitch, and when I turn around, shaking my hand off, I see multiple of them filming the altercation. Elise grabs my sleeve, pulling me hard toward the exit, almost at a run. We leave the YouTuber hunched over, still holding his face, and the rest of the crowd following us with their eyes or their cameras.

It isn't until we pass through the main hallway and bust through the doors into the concourse, cold air slapping me hard, that Elise stops and whips round to face me.

"What is wrong with you?!" she hisses. "So many people recorded that, Andries! You could get thrown out of school!"

"I wasn't going to let him continue talking to me like that," I tell her, still shaking my hand to ease the sting from the punch. It had happened so fast that I didn't have time to do it properly, and my imperfect form was making me pay the price.

Elise looks frantic, and for a second I feel like she's going to slap me, but she clenches her small fists and breathes out slowly, trying to compose herself. "You're not a child,

Andries," she explains. "Nor do you have the luxury of being an unknown person. People know your face, and now people know that this thing with Roxanne is bothering you to the point that you'll lash out with violence. It's unacceptable."

"Let it go, sis, it doesn't have anything to do with you."

"If you think for one minute that your reputation doesn't affect mine, then you're crazy. I'll hear about this little punch of yours in class until I graduate, I'm sure. You really need to —"

"Sir. Ma'am." A security guard for the school sidles up to us, causing Elise to stop her diatribe. "I need you both to come with me."

"Wait," I tell him. "She didn't have anything to do with what just happened, she was just with me is all."

The guard shakes his head. "The rector wants to see you both, so come on."

My sister shoots daggers at me with her eyes as we follow the guard, clutching the straps of her bag like a lifeline. I do my best to ignore her, and the seed of guilt in my gut at having potentially gotten her in trouble. Elise might overstep her bounds sometimes, but she has still been here for me, in her own way.

As we approach the small brick office building where the school administration has their offices, I reach over to squeeze her arm. "I'll take all the blame, don't worry."

She still looks pissed, but she swallows hard, and nods. It isn't common for me to see my sister nervous, but the situation we are in makes it impossible for me to savor the moment for later sibling versus sibling insults.

The guard opens the ancient wooden door to the rector's office for us, and we enter, heads lowered in an almost identical gesture of humility. At her desk, the rector scoffs, waving us forward.

"Stop looking like kicked puppies and sit down."

We both take our seats. The rector folds her hands on her desk and looks us over, and I suddenly feel like I'm eight years old under her steely gaze. She has iron-gray hair pulled into a severe French twist, a thin face, and a dark hound's tooth suit jacket.

"This is my first time having any of the Van Den Bosch children in my office to be reprimanded. A family first!" When neither Elise nor I respond, she continues. "You know, the good thing about having all those ugly cameras installed around the campus is that the staff can see any nonsense happening in real time. Imagine my shock when the guard watching the cameras calls me in to show me one of my students punching another in the face, seemingly unprompted. Such a shock…"

"Ma'am, Elise wasn't involved at all. I think you should let her off the hook," I insist.

"Oh, I know, but I have a message for you both. But first, what exactly happened? I want to hear it in your own words."

Leaving out the part about me dating an escort, I explain the best I can how the YouTuber, who she tells me is called Wes, posted defamatory videos on his channel, meant to cause shame for my family and even around the university. The rector seems unamused at the mention of YouTube, but she takes quick, scratching notes as I speak, giving me her full attention.

"And you do realize, even with all that, violence is never acceptable on campus, right?"

"It was a single lapse in judgment," I assure her.

She leans forward minutely. "Is there anything else going on with you? Maybe mentally, or family issues that could cause you to act out like this?"

"Just a difficult breakup," I admit. "But nothing that excuses my behavior."

She sighs, tapping her nails on her desk as she thinks. "Okay. I will give you a warning *this time,* Andries, but if security checks this YouTube channel and finds nothing like what you're describing, then you'll be coming back to face harsher consequences."

"I understand."

Her face softens. "We have never had issues with anyone in your family or extended family before. If there's something we can help you with, we have counselors and programs for students suffering from mental health problems."

"I'm fine." I sigh.

She doesn't look convinced, but she makes another note before looking at Elise. "That brings me to you. I hope you aren't encouraging this type of behavior."

Elise shakes her head hard enough to send her hair flying around her. "Absolutely not."

"Good. Now, when possible, I'd like you to escort your brother to classes, and if anything goes awry with this new negative publicity he now has, I'm going to give you both a number to call that will have our campus security come to your location right away. I don't want either of you to feel unsafe, so for the time being, try to move in pairs. Understood?"

"Yes, ma'am," we both declare at the same time.

"Any more violence caused by you on this campus, Andries, and you will be suspended. This is your one and only warning."

Elise and I leave the office, her not relaxing until we are back outdoors. I can tell her first instinct is to tear into me about everything that just went down, but she holds back. After taking a few deep breaths for patience she hugs me quickly.

I pat her back as she does so, and when she pulls back, there is genuine worry in her eyes. "Andries," she starts. "I've never seen you do anything like that before. Do you think maybe… you might want to check out therapy? Or at least those school counselors like the rector suggested?"

"No," I bite out. "Reiterating the steps of my breakup isn't going to make me feel any better. The opposite actually. I'm perfectly capable of handling my emotions myself."

Elise frowns but doesn't argue. She checks her watch and grimaces. "I'm late for class. Go back to your apartment and I'll come pick you up for your next lecture."

I want to argue that I'm an adult man, and that I don't need a babysitter, but knowing I had just caused my sister a large amount of stress, I just nod instead, making my way home while she rushes to her class.

Biking through campus and back to my apartment is a quick affair, with me avoiding eye contact with anyone possible. When I am finally back in my apartment, the first order of business is to deactivate my social media for the time being, and the second is a cup of coffee from my Keurig with a healthy pour of Bailey's Irish Cream to settle my nerves. It's almost too much for me; the heartbreak of the breakup, Roxie's constant attempts to get in contact with me, having to keep it together at school, and now the entire student body knowing that I'd fallen in love with a former hooker. It's enough to make a man want to hide away for the rest of his days.

I want to skip class and drink more while working on a few of my manuscripts, but I know there is no point in even trying... not with Elise coming to the apartment to escort me to the lecture hall herself.

I try to nap after I finish my coffee but end up lying on top of my sheets and watching the sun travel across the sky. Waiting for my sister to come and take me to class makes me feel like some criminal that couldn't be trusted on their own. I should be studying, or writing, but there is no motivation within me.

I've lost myself completely in my melancholy daydreams when I hear the buzz from my front door. After a quick time check, I realize it's about time for Elise, so I crawl out of bed and straighten my clothes.

I pause halfway to the door. Why would my sister be buzzing in? She knows the code to get in on her own. Filled with dread that it's Roxanne outside again, I check the screen of the intercom before doing anything else. Instead of a blond head, I see a brown one, caught in two identical braids, both of them secured with a bright yellow tie. Tatiana.

If I could get away with ignoring her, I would, but I know she'd just call Elise at the first chance she got, so with a resigned huff, I let her in.

"Where's my sister?" I ask when I open the door for her.

"She had to stay late, so she asked me to come and get you." She smiles brightly. "Don't look so excited."

I fix my frown, but the best I can manage for her is a neutral expression. "I really can get to class myself, Tatiana."

"No no, go get your bag. I'm going to that part of campus anyway, so I don't mind!"

"Whatever," I grumble, grabbing my bag and following Tatiana out. The way she walks ahead of me, like there are clouds beneath her feet, is exhausting to me. The only thing missing from the scene is a flock of songbirds flying around her, and her princess appearance would be complete.

"You can't honestly like class this much," I comment.

"It's fine, but I have to say I was looking forward to this walk with you more than anything else." Tatiana blushes prettily. "Oops. That might have been too forward."

I smirk. "No, you're fine. Soon you won't be that shy girl I've always known. You'll be the demanding woman you've always dreamed of being."

"No way," she laughs. "I am who I am, no changes. Sorry."

There are more pointed looks as we move through the concourse, but they roll off Tatiana like water, for which I am thankful. Elise was born having to deal with her family's reputation, just like all of us were, but I'd have hated for Tatiana to feel awkward being seen with me. She didn't deserve anyone's negativity.

At the door of my lecture hall, she seems reluctant to leave me, twisting her fingers in the fabric of her white lace shirt.

"Hey," she asks, her nerves evident in her voice. "Do you want to go and eat something afterwards? Something low-key, just to unwind. Be out of the public's eye for a minute. I have the perfect place in mind."

With how terrible the day has been so far, I decide to throw caution to the wind, and accept the invite. Tatiana clasps her hands together happily, leaving for her own class and promising to meet me around six p.m. at the restaurant.

Class crawls by, and once it ends, I'm looking forward to dinner. Again, it's just something to keep my mind off my ex and also from the notoriety caused by that stupid YouTube video, but Tatiana isn't the worst company to have.

I return to my apartment long enough to throw a denim jacket on, wash my face, and slick my hair back. It's just enough of a departure from how I normally style myself that I might be able to go unnoticed, at least to a degree.

Tatiana is waiting for me, just like she said she would be, outside of a pho restaurant a few miles from the university. She's undone her braids, and her wavy hair hangs around her face and shoulders. She looks happily surprised that I showed up, and she takes my hand to lead me inside, babbling about the menu and her favorite options as she does so.

She isn't wrong about the restaurant being low key, either. It's clearly some place people of all income brackets come, not as a status symbol, but because of how stellar the food is. It's a small dining room, the spicy, savory scents of pho filling the air to a point that it's almost overwhelming. Tatiana takes me to a small table in the corner, and after I finally am able to fold my legs underneath it, I pull the menu over and browse.

"Your sister was in shock when I told her that you actually agreed to come," Tatiana tells me.

"It's because she's so unpleasant that everyone tries to avoid her dinner invites," I retort.

She laughs softly. "You two really are more alike than you think."

Tatiana is pointing out her favorite dishes when a shadow falls over the table, and when she and I look up, my heart nearly freezes in my chest.

For one brief moment, one that is both exhilarating and dreadful, I think it's Roxanne. The height, heart-shaped face, and posture fool me for a second, before my brain works out who it really is. Lili—Roxanne's sister.

Tatiana looks from Lili to me in quick succession, probably wondering who exactly this Roxanne look-alike is. It's the first time today that I've seen her look anything but cheery. Instead, she's reserved, leaning away from the new visitor at the table.

"Lili?"

"Andries," she responds. "Can I take a seat? Only for a moment, and then I will leave you two alone."

I nod tightly, even though it makes Tatiana's face shutter further, and Lili snags a nearby chair to sit down in. She's grasping a glass of white wine like a talisman, her body language uncomfortable but determined.

"Lili, this is my friend Tatiana. Tati, this is Roxanne's sister, Lili."

Tatiana smiles thinly but stays silent.

"I just wanted to say I'm sorry," Lili blurts out. "I know it doesn't mean anything coming from me, but Roxanne never should have lied to you about who she really was. You can't build a house on shaky ground, you know?"

"If she had been honest from the get-go, there would have never been any attempt on my end to court her, and all of this could've been avoided. Her lies have made everything explode outward like a bomb, and now I'm not just dealing with her betrayal, but the aftermath of it all, too."

Lili sucks in a breath, closing her eyes. "I know. I know. She's torn up about it too. I just wanted you to know I'd have told you, had I known how quickly this whole thing was coming off the rails."

"I don't blame you, Lili," I tell her. "There are no hard feelings between us."

She swallows hard before taking a drink of her wine. "Okay. Okay. Thank you for hearing me out." She grins weakly. "And… you're always welcome at the bookshop. It's not often we get genuine poets around."

"Maybe after some time has passed, and it doesn't hurt so much, okay?" I say, and Lili nods.

She hesitates, but after a moment, bids Tatiana and I goodbye, and returns to her table where she is sitting with a group of friends that look extremely relieved that she has survived her encounter with me. I watch my ex's sister settle into her seat and allow myself a second of wistfulness about how much she resembles her sister, before letting it go and turning my attention back to Tatiana.

I can tell she absolutely hated the meetup that just happened, and that she wants to crawl out of her skin, but she shakes it off and resumes showing me some of her favorite things to order.

I play along, knowing that she needs some time to process, and she eventually says, "So. A genuine poet, huh?"

"I was hoping you wouldn't catch that."

"That reminds me… how is the English program going?"

I freeze in the middle of pulling my chopsticks apart, gaping at her. "What did you just say?"

"Your English program, Andries?"

I look around us to make sure there is no one else we know before answering her. "It's fine, but how in the hell did you know about that? It's supposed to be a secret."

Tatiana pulls apart her own chopsticks, rubbing them together to get rid of any splinters, her lips pulled up at the corners. "I have my ways."

"Tatiana...."

"Oh, Andries. It's not hard to figure out. After an entire semester, I have never seen you attending one single business class."

"But who told you I was attending the English program?" I press on.

"I figured it out by myself."

I don't believe her. It was most likely my sister who told her, but I let it go. There's no point in creating a discussion with someone who has been so kind and helpful after such a chaotic day.

I sigh. "Fine. But please don't tell anyone, okay? A lot of people are going to be pissed and I want to be the one to break the news."

She makes a zipping motion over her mouth. "Your secret is safe with me."

A smidgen of my miserableness evaporates, prompting me to reach across the table and poke her in the arm with one of my chopsticks, "It better be, Flower Girl."

She mirrors my motion but pats me on the arms in a comforting gesture instead. "I promise. But only if you read me some of your poetry sometime."

I groan, and Tatiana laughs.

In the restaurant's corner, Lili looks over her shoulder at us, and frowns, but I just pretend I don't notice.

CHAPTER 7

Amsterdam, January 10, 2022
Roxanne

Sitting out on my balcony, wrapped in my warmest robe, I allow myself to feel in full everything that has been weighing me down so much. The wind combs through my hair like fingers, and while the things I'm thinking about are undoubtedly causing me pain, the softness of the breeze and beauty of the sunset make it a little easier to bear.

I've been fighting with my feelings about Andries for nearly two weeks now. At first, I was furious at him for talking to me and embarrassing me the way he did. But after that, as the anger cooled, I began to miss him, and in no time at all, I couldn't muster up any more fury to keep me warm at night. Missing Andries, wanting just to hear his voice speaking to me in any sort of tone besides disgust, was consuming me.

So now, as much as I know it's a fool's errand, I want him to give me a second chance. Give *us* another chance. I had stopped escorting for him, even though he had no idea. It'd been such a big part of my life, and such a large amount of extra income, and Andries just had no idea the significance of my sacrifice. If I could make him understand, then maybe he'd be okay with sacrificing a little for me too.

I flip through a lot of my memories with him in my mind, like a photo album, some of them making me smile, others bringing laughter, and the most bittersweet bringing tears to my eyes that I wipe away hastily. Hours pass this way, lost in thought, and by the time I click back into reality, it's fully dark out, stars twinkling overhead.

"Shit," I mutter, grabbing my phone from the small table beside my chair to check the time. It's just past 7 p.m., and I have a single missed text from Lili.

I open it, and smile at the picture of my sister and her friends and one of our favorite Pho restaurants. It's captioned *We just got here! Come grab a drink!*

If I had gotten the message when it was sent an hour ago, I might have taken her up on the offer, but at this point, they had to be nearly done with the meal. Still, I tap the picture to make it bigger, taking some solace in how at peace my sister is.

It's only after gazing at the photo for a moment that I see a familiar face in the background, framed by wavy, brown hair. Quickly, I zoom in, and just like I had expected, it's Tatiana. I zoom out a little to look closer at the other person at her table who is more in the shadows, and harder to identify.

But I can recognize him anywhere. It's Andries. He's out with Tatiana.

My mouth goes dry, and my fingers fly over the text keyboard.

Roxanne: Do you see who is in the background of that picture??

Lili: Ugh. Yes. I was hoping you wouldn't notice.

Roxanne: Oh, I noticed. Fuck him.

After spending hours of my time parsing through memories of my ex, trying to determine the right course of action, and finally determining that I still wanted to be with him, it just figures that the universe would give me a big fat sign that he had already moved on.

I don't want to accept it. I can't. He had sworn so many times that Tatiana wasn't appealing to him at all as a romantic partner; she was too innocent, too naive, and that they were just friends. I believed him completely, and even in Lili's picture, they aren't posed like two lovers would be. It was probably just a dinner between friends.

None of that matters, though. He was still there, at one of my favorite restaurants, flaunting his young new thing in front of my sister. Like a trophy. As if to say, *"I dare you to send this to your sister"* or *"This is what I really want. A young, pure girl. Not your whore of a sister."*

I throw my phone hard, like a softball, onto the couch, pacing the floor like someone who has gone mad. I was staying in tonight, taking some self-care time to gather my emotions back into something more manageable. I'm definitely not going to go to the pho restaurant and tell Andries everything he hasn't given me the chance to.

"Fuck!" I mutter to myself. "Fuck him!"

There are a million other things I could do. I can throw myself into work, working out the schedules for the next week, or I could drink myself into a stupor and forget that Andries had ever been out with Tatiana. I would love to be able to shower, and fall asleep watching some random movie, but I was so full of angry energy that there was no hope for it.

I find my box of cigarettes, pulling one out and stomping back out to the balcony, lighting it, and taking a long drag. Smoke fills my lungs, hot and soothing, and hangs heavy in the air as I exhale. My robe flutters around me as I finish the cigarette, trying and failing to come up with any other plan besides the ones that involve me going to that damned restaurant and giving out to Andries like I've been wanting to for days now.

I light another cigarette, pulling the robe closer around me as I repeat a mantra in my head.

I'm not going, I'm not going, I'm not going.

It doesn't help, though. I have no control over the intrusive thoughts that are bombarding me. Andries and Tatiana laughing together in the restaurant, her foot running up his leg under the table. Andries holding the car door open for Tatiana, and sliding in beside her, close enough for their hips to touch. Him inviting her up to his apartment, freshly scrubbed of any trace of me, ready for Tatiana to leave her mark. Andries' bedroom door—

"Dammit," I sigh, putting out the cigarette in the ashtray on the side table and pulling my phone back out. There's no help for it. I'm going to the restaurant.

Roxanne: Are they still there?

Lili: They just left. Roxie, don't make a scene.

I have two options. Try to cut them off before they get too far from the restaurant, which would be nearly impossible, considering they'd probably take a cab. My other option is to meet Andries back at his apartment. It didn't matter if he still had Tatiana in tow, because at least I'd get a chance to speak with him.

And show that perfect little girl that I am not done with Andries. Not by a long shot.

Mind made up, I order an Uber on my phone, and take fifteen minutes till arrival to dress myself for a fight. Dark denim jeans, leather boots that reach past my knees, and a matching leather jacket. Dark enough that I could stand in the shadows and Andries won't see me from the street, and sexy enough that he will get a good look at what he's missing out on.

It's a brief ride to Andries's place, and I let out a relieved breath that all the lights are still off inside. There is a small patch of space between his building and the neighboring one; not quite an alley, but a large enough recess that I can lean into it and wait, almost invisible from the road.

It isn't exactly a balmy night, but thankfully it doesn't take long for the sleek, blacked out coupe to roll up at the apartment building and drop Andries off. He's dressed casually, like I noticed in the picture, and his posture is more relaxed than I expected. The few times I've seen him in the flesh recently he's been stiffer than a board, but I guess dinner and conversation with *Tatiana* relaxes him. Asshole.

I hold my breath after he steps out of the car, expecting the perfect flower girl to follow him out into the night, but to my immense happiness he simply closes the car door behind him, and it departs, exhaust fumes visible as it goes. Andries came home alone. He wasn't bringing his date home to sleep with.

Could it mean that he hasn't really moved on? Could it really have been just a friendly dinner?

I wait until the car is out of sight and Andries is nearly to his door before I appear. He's always been so perceptive, and he turns to see me approaching immediately. At first, he freezes, mouth forming the first syllable of my name, before he snaps out of it and tries to beat me into the building, no doubt planning to lock me out as soon as he has the door closed.

I'm past the point of shame, running to cut him off, and grabbing him by his jacket sleeve to stop him.

"Andries!" I gasp. "One fucking minute! Please!"

"Damn you," he growls, jerking his arm out of my grasp. "Leave me alone."

I'm not done, though, and I shove my arm between him and the door. I can see his jaw clenching with frustration, but he breathes through it.

"Roxanne…" He rubs one hand down his face. "Fine, okay? Fine. In the lobby though, not out on the street. I've had enough publicity for one day."

I follow him inside, asking, "What do you mean by publicity?"

He waves the question off. "Just go on YouTube and type my name when you get home. You'll figure it out."

In the lobby, I move toward a bench, thinking we'd sit and talk, but he's having none of it, keeping his arms crossed and spine stiff as he stands. With a sigh, I forgo sitting down and stay standing as well.

"You have a minute, two if you're lucky, so get started," he snaps. "But first, how the fuck did you know when I'd be home? Do I need to get a new place now that you're stalking me?" I hesitate, and he laughs darkly, shaking his head. "Never mind. Lili, of course."

"In her defense, she sent a selfie of her and her friends. She didn't even realize you were in the picture until after she sent it."

"Hm…" He shrugs one shoulder. "Fine. Go on."

I take in a huge breath, letting it out slowly. "Where do I even start?"

"Get on with it, Roxanne."

"Okay, okay…" I close my eyes for a brief moment, trying to calm my thundering heart. When I reopen them, my gaze lands on his mesmerizing blue eyes, and I can't help but say, "I miss you. Terribly. Every morning, every night, every waking moment something else isn't taking up my energy, I'm thinking of you, missing you. I know this is my fault, and that I fucked up royally, but you have to understand… I've never been in love before. What I feel for you is something brand new for me, and I'm not willing to let it go without a fight."

"You don't have a choice. I broke up with you."

"But you loved me, right? It was as all-consuming on your end as it was on mine. I know it was!"

The laugh he gives me is full of self-loathing. "And it was all fake. Every second of it, because I had no idea who you really were."

"I wasn't lying when I told you that I stopped escorting the moment I even considered being with you, Andries. I was never sleeping with you and someone else."

His gaze sharpens. "And since?"

"Of course not," my voice sounds small and pathetic to my ears.

There's a moment of indecision in his expression, I'm sure of it, but he seems to shake himself out of it. "It doesn't even matter. You lied about who you were, and now that I know the real you, I'm not interested. I'd never date a prostitute."

I flinch from the harness of his words. "I'm not a prostitute."

"But you're still managing that fucking brothel, aren't you?"

"It's not a brothel; it's an escort agency."

He cocks his head to the side. "But you're still selling sex there, no?"

"Well, sometimes, but—" I stop mid-sentence, knowing this argument is going to escalate. "None of that matters right now. I'm here because I want you to give me a second chance. It was *me* you fell for. Just because you didn't know my occupation doesn't mean that it wasn't really me, love. It's always been me. And I love you." I take a step closer to him, and when he doesn't immediately move away, another. "Give me another chance."

Andries watches me, his face shuttered, but real, unmistakable yearning in his gaze. For one brilliant moment, I think he's going to accept, so I close the distance between us, taking his beloved face between my palms, attempting to slant our mouths together and end this wretched time apart. His breathing is shaky, and his eyes are hooded. He wants this. He wants this as much as I do.

It isn't to be, though. Nothing in my life has ever been easy, but the heartbreak I feel when he pushes me away is beyond anything I've ever felt before. I sob his name, and try to kiss him again, or at least just touch him, but he grasps my wrists firmly and holds me at a distance.

"We're done. I'm serious." He releases me but holds a hand up to stop me from trying to move closer again. "I'm going to move, Roxie, and then maybe when you can't find me anymore you'll finally accept that this is over. For good. I'm moving on from you."

He jams his finger into the elevator button as he speaks, and as the doors part almost immediately, he disappears between them. Right there in front of me, able to be touched, and then... gone.

"Andries," I whisper uselessly, clenching my fists until my fingernails make little indentations in my palms with the force of it.

I could throw a fit, jamming the buzzer until he finally had to face me again, but this confrontation had taken everything in me. I'm humiliated, and I leave the lobby in a haze of tears, the sidewalk blurring as I flee. I have no idea where to go, so I just walk for a few minutes, my head down, trying to swallow my sobs.

Suddenly, on my right side, I stumble on a jazz piano bar that I had heard about from some of my older past clients. Well, I desperately need a drink right now. Figuring a bar is a bar, I jerk the door open and enter, making a beeline for a bar stool. The interior is dark, smoke from cigarettes, cigars, and other smokeables curling in the air like a low fog that never dissipates. Someone is in the corner playing a rollicking song, faster than I'd have thought a man his age could play, and it makes for a rather bizarre soundtrack for my misery drinking.

As the bartender slides me a brandy, the next bizarre thing happens. As I take my first drink, someone lowers themselves into the stool next to me, and to my surprise, it's Dan.

"I have to say," he starts. "This is not the place I'd have guessed would be your haunt, Ms. Feng."

I chuckle. "Any port in a storm at this point."

He orders his own drink but continues talking to me. "So why are you here, then? Secret jazz fan? Love going home smelling like an ashtray and old man cologne?"

I raise an eyebrow. "I could ask you the same question."

"The former. And maybe a tiny bit of the latter. But don't tell anyone."

I smile in spite of myself. Dan is loose-limbed and calm next to me, without a care in the world. It's an attitude I wish I could copy. Still, I can't pull myself out of the misery I'm feeling, and it shows in my words.

"I'm surprised that you're giving me the time of day, considering how everything went down between Andries and I."

Dan swirls his glass, ice clinking against the sides and the pianist launches into yet another tune that is wholly inappropriate for what I'm feeling. Dan looks at me for a long moment, considering.

"You really love him, huh?"

"Yes," I answer miserably.

He blows out a breath. "Can I tell you something, Roxanne?"

He sounds strangely serious, so I nod, wondering what kind of new misery he's going to put on me. Maybe explaining like Elise had, but in kinder terms, how Tatiana is the right person for Andries, or letting me know that Andries is moving far from here and I'll lose any chance of reconciling. Or, even worse, Andries hates me completely and utterly, and I was wasting my energy trying to fix things between us.

It isn't any of those things, but it still manages to surprise me, nonetheless.

"I knew who you were from the very beginning," Dan confesses. "Well, from the first time I met you in Ghent, that is."

My eyes go wide. "You knew I was an escort? Since Ghent?"

"Uh-huh. I was floored, naturally, but I didn't want to ruin anything between the two of you by sticking my nose where it didn't belong. I didn't put the pieces together in my mind that he didn't know what your job was until after we left the dinner where he introduced you, and at that point I could see how smitten he was with you." He seems genuinely regretful as he continues, which surprises me. "I sort of knew that things were going to implode as the secret went on longer and longer, but you two were so in love. I really thought you'd pull through."

This news has me reeling, more confused than ever. "How could you possibly have known me?"

"You probably don't remember, but I hired some of your girls for my red-light party a while back at my home. It was packed and chaotic, but I noticed you in the crowd, with some of the girls I hired, and I could tell they looked at you with respect. I pulled one aside and asked who you were, since I didn't recall your photo on the page where I selected who to hire, and she replied, 'My boss.'"

I remember perfectly well the party he's talking about. It's the one Karl told me to attend, knowing that Andries would be there. It feels like ages ago.

"You're right, I'm sorry if I didn't recognize you at Ghent."

"Nah, don't worry about that. I just wanted you to know I didn't go digging around the Internet to find your identity or anything. And that I have zero issue with what you and your employees do for a living. Obviously, since I've... well... partaken of your services, I guess you could say."

I open and close my mouth, trying to think of what to say. Dan breaks the silence with an added, "I was a very satisfied customer! I mean, wow, what a glorious business you're running."

"Thanks, I think." I take a long drink, holding up my finger to signal the bartender for another. "I guess I'm just surprised to hear that you're so pro sex-work when your best friend views it as a mortal sin."

"Ah. Well. Andries is... the product of his family and the environment he grew up in, you know what I mean?" I shake my head, so he continues. "He grew up in a bubble and can't understand the concept of women willingly selling sex in a first world country. He hasn't been on his own long, and all those old money lessons of properness and honor are still with him. He's the most intense monogamist you'll ever meet."

"Christ, Dan. This is a lot to swallow." He raises an eyebrow, mouth quirking up, and I punch him in the arm. "Oh, fuck you, Dan. Don't be gross."

After laughing for a minute, Dan rubbing his arm in mock injury, the mood sobers up again.

"Hey," I ask. "Why didn't you tell Andries? Isn't he your best friend?"

"More than that. He's like a brother to me. But... I've never seen him as happy as he was with you. He has all these morality issues that have been hammered into him by his parents, but his heart just isn't like theirs. It's why he's a writer, and not the cunning businessman they imagined he would be. I think he just needs time, Roxie. Time to come around."

Fingers tracing the whorls on the wooden bar, I don't look up at him as I respond. "I don't think so, Dan. I just talked to him. He told me he's moving on from me. Getting a new apartment. He was even out having dinner with Tatiana before I confronted him tonight. I think he's done with me for good."

"He might say that, but I just don't think it's true. And don't worry too much about Tatiana. She's a cute girl, but not at all Andries' type. I've always gotten big brother little sister vibes from the two of them until last year when Tatiana had the sudden realization that Andries grew up handsome. He's not interested, though."

"I have to give it to her," I grumble. "She's persistent, if nothing else."

"I think you should be prepared for the inevitability that they might be friends for life. Where Andries is secretly wild at heart, too wild for his family, Tatiana is too sunny and innocent for hers. She'll never fall into the scheming, underhanded work those families are all so fond of. I think she and Andries bond over being outcasts, even if they don't know it yet. It's friendship, not romance."

I blink a few times, stunned at how much sense Dan, the goofy friend, is making. "I guess that tracks. Huh. I never would have thought about it like that."

Dan loops his arm around my shoulder, and where I'd throw any other man off me like the plague, it's comforting coming from him. Like he had just said about Tatiana and Andries… it was friendly, not romantic.

"I understand you, lady. My parents are self-made. We know what it's like to crawl our way to the top through the mud, and it taught me that the world is much more nuanced than what these old money families realize. Once Andries calms down, and the anger is gone, there will be nothing left but the love he has for you. Then he'll be ready to listen, and maybe even ready to give you a second chance."

There's a lump in my throat, so instead of answering him, I lay my head on his shoulder. The only sentence I can get past the tightness of the lump is, "I love him, Dan," to which he nods understandingly.

We stay like that for a while, Dan silently comforting me while we drink. I feel better having talked to him; lighter, in a way. I have made progress tonight, even if it came from unexpected places.

I'm getting ready to throw the rest of my drink back and call it a night, when Dan's phone, sitting on the bar beside him, begins to ring. The bar is loud, but he still picks it up and checks the screen, shooting me a quick, worried glance.

"It's Andries," he says.

"Go ahead. I won't say anything."

Dan answers, putting Andries on speaker phone. "Hello?"

"Hey, man. I know it's late, but I need a favor."

"Sure. What's up?"

On the other line, Andries sighs. I can almost see him pinching the bridge of his nose. "Roxie came by. I've got to get out of this apartment. Can you call your friend in real estate tomorrow and see what's on the market?"

Dan frowns, but tells him, "Yeah, no problem. But I have to warn you, nothing is going to be as nice as where you are. Aren't your fucking floors heated?"

Andries laughs dryly. "We'll see. Just tell me if you find something."

"Yeah, yeah." Dan pauses. "You doing okay, man?"

The line is quiet for some time before Andries offers an unconvincing, "I'm fine."

"Okay," Dan sounds skeptical. "I'll call you tomorrow, okay?"

"Okay. Talk to you later."

Dan sits the phone down, and we exchange looks. "He's miserable," he says.

I know Andries so well, like he's a part of me, and I, too, could tell how messed up he was feeling. It's nice to know I'm not suffering alone, but I also don't want the man I love to be hating his life. If he'd only give me another chance, neither of us would have to feel this way.

"I agree," I say quietly. "I don't know if that's a good thing or a bad thing."

"Can go either way, really."

"Yeah." I bite my lip, mind racing and body exhausted. "I guess it can."

CHAPTER 8

Amsterdam, January 11, 2022
Andries

Nothing makes me feel more inadequate than not being able to succeed at being a student. All I have to do is sit here and absorb everything that is thrown at me. Being an English major is my dream, and here it's becoming a reality, and yet, I'm too busy daydreaming about Roxanne. That, and being hungover... on a fucking Tuesday!

I'm falling apart and no one seems to see it but me. Once some of this work is due, I'm sure my prof will also notice, but I'm sure she has better things to do than check up on a failing student who can't keep his shit together. I'd even planned to give today my all, to make up for the lack of attention I've been paying to lectures, but I'm even more useless today than I was yesterday. So much had happened in such a short span of time that I'm still reeling from it.

Dinner with Tatiana had set me on a good path. A reconciliation with Lili, good food, and Tati's bubbly personality had been a balm on my savaged soul, and I had gone home thinking that I might have the first good night of sleep in a long time.

Then, walking out of the shadows like a wraith, was the one person who I had been trying to keep from my thoughts. Roxanne looked incredible in almost head to toe leather, but where her outward appearance might have served as armor, she was clearly heartbroken and miserable inside. In the harsh overhead lights of my building's lobby, I could see so clearly how much she missed me. It echoed how much I missed her too.

I wanted to throw it all away for her. Every hard-won second of standing my ground, all of the attempts to build up my walls and move on, I just wanted to burn it all down for her, just to hold her in my arms. Just once. But I just fucking couldn't.

Because as beautiful as she was, as much as I was pulled toward her, she was still running a fucking brothel, and it turned my stomach. Had she come to me last night, telling me she'd quit and give up sex work for good, I'd have folded and brought her upstairs. Mended fences, made up for lost time... I'd have done it all if she had done that one thing for me.

Of course, she has no intention of quitting. Roxanne might have wanted me back badly enough to nearly make a fool of herself, but she's too stubborn to give up on her... line of work. So I left her there in the lobby, went upstairs, and drank myself sick.

Which is why I'm sitting in class, where my head's pounding, vision's blurry, and I'm entirely unable to concentrate. If none of my classmates are kind enough to share notes with me, then this day will be a wash. I'll get nothing from it besides a mark for attending class. To make things worse, I can't even go home once I'm done here. Dan secured a realtor in the middle of the night somehow, to show me some properties as soon as class lets out. I'm long, long hours away from being able to sleep this hangover off, unfortunately.

Mercifully, the lecture dismisses early, and besides a few sideways glances from other people in the class, I make it out unscathed. I'm sure I look like death, but there are plenty of students that pull all-nighters to study or complete projects, so my appearance shouldn't attract too much attention.

Dan picks me up, his vintage car bright red and ostentatious as it pulls into the campus. My head pounds as I climb in, the engine rattling my teeth.

"You look like shit," Dan says.

"Thanks. You too."

He rattles off some information about the apartments we're going to go see, and he wasn't lying when he said they weren't going to live up to my current place. My parents must have paid an exorbitant amount to get me into my current penthouse, and they'd no doubt be disappointed to see me leaving it empty for something less luxurious.

Dan finishes up with, "Or, you know, you could suck it up and just stay at your place."

"Not an option," I chip back.

"Man, you and Roxanne weren't even together that long. People don't break their leases and move because of a breakup. Give it a few weeks before you make any major decisions. Trust me."

I know he's right on some level. Probably all levels, if I'm being honest with myself, but if it means I'm mentally weak, so be it. I can't live like this anymore, with her ghost around every corner and lying next to me at night.

Dan understands what my silence means, and he tilts his head back, groaning. "You're a stubborn asshole, you know that?"

Stubborn, just like Roxie. No wonder we made such a good pairing. "So I've been told."

Dan drums his fingers on the steering wheel as he fights through traffic, the thrumming of his car making me want to scream from the way it vibrates my skull. It's a perfect day, as perfect as January can be, with the sun bright and buttery above us, glinting off the river as we pass. Without asking, I open Dan's glove box and paw through it until I find an old, tattered paper packet of migraine medicine, the kind of packets you can buy out of machines in gas station bathrooms. I tear the paper and swallow the pills dry, their taste bitter on my tongue. Forcing them down is almost impossible, but I manage it. Now there is nothing to do but hope they work.

"Dude, those pills were absolutely expired."

"Death by hangover or expired pills, what does it matter? Either way I'm dead," I lament.

"I hope you used this natural sulkiness of yours to write some amazing poetry. Otherwise, it's just wasted."

That's another thing that is pissing me off. Everyone's little jokes about how sad poets write their best work had never been funny, but I had kind of expected there to be some truth in the statement, but no matter how many times I sat down to write, nothing would come out. Nothing except things about Roxanne... bleeding heart narratives about how intensely I love and hate her… and no one wants to read shit like that.

The last option is what I'm doing right now: starting over, completely fresh. Once I leave my apartment and move out, I'll be able to pretend that Roxanne never existed. Except when I dream of her face, which I'm afraid I might do for the rest of my life.

It isn't just her face, either. Besides the dreams where I just see her, hold her, and touch her skin, the most common is the memory of our first time together playing on repeat. Giving Roxanne my virginity was something I know I should regret, now that the truth has come out, but I can't bring myself to feel that way. My entire adult life, I had sworn to never sleep with anyone unless we were in love, and at that time, I loved Roxanne. I barely knew her, but the obsessive need to make her mine burned like a beacon inside me. I don't think I will ever love anyone like that ever again, which means, despite all that had happened, she was still the right choice.

The only thing that upset me about losing my virginity with her is that now it isn't something I can share with my eventual wife. I could never have expected to love someone so desperately, but then never marry her. It fucked with my plans for the future, but who cares? At this point in my life, I don't believe I'll ever find love again. In fact, I hope I don't. It's a terrible thing, to care for someone so much that they could tear you apart, and make you want to die.

I'm startles out of my reverie when Dan speaks. "We're here," he informs me, and it's then I notice the car has indeed stopped.

We're walking across the driveway, toward the white and tan condominiums, and the sunlight feels like daggers in my eyes. I cover them with my forearm, wincing.

"Are you good, dude?" Dan inquires. "Do you want to reschedule this for another time? One when you're fully alive?"

"I just want to get this over with," I grit out between my teeth. "The sooner, the better."

My friend isn't convinced, but he still leads me into the building, where we meet the realtor. He seems around Dan's age, maybe a bit older, and I can see that he's skeptical as he looks me over before turning back to Dan, as if to suggest he isn't sure I had any potential as a client.

"I swear he's fine, just hungover," Dan assures his realtor friend, who purses his mouth in doubt, before he shrugs and takes us upstairs to the penthouse unit.

These condos are further from campus than I would like, and where my current apartment was made with comfort in mind, this one was clearly created for visual appeal. It's a sprawling open concept, exposed brick and metalwork, giving it an industrial look that is popular with younger Amsterdam residents. The bedroom and bathroom are toward the back of the apartment, but everything else is completely open and visible.

The crowning jewel of the less than perfect apartment is the wall of floor to ceiling windows that overlook the city. They bathe the apartment in natural light, and the lack of walls to separate anything besides the bath and bedroom, allows everywhere else to benefit from the glow. It isn't exactly what I'm looking for, but if I can sweet talk my mother into sending one of her interior designers over, there is real potential.

"It's like, the biggest bachelor pad of all time," Dan says as he walks the perimeter. "I don't love the pale wood, but otherwise, it's pretty nice."

I turn my back to the windows, the dull roar of my headache having receded enough to function but not disappearing entirely. "It's fine."

The realtor, who is pointing out the state-of-the-art stainless steel kitchen appliances, pauses in his description. "...Fine? Only fine?"

Herding me toward the bedroom, Dan makes some excuse for me to the realtor before shutting the door behind us. The bedroom is more of the same; brick and steel, but it also has a stunning view. It's immediately clear that Dan hasn't brought me here just to see the room, though. He crosses his arms, looking at me with the most serious face he can muster.

"If you're going to be miserable, you can at least tell me what made you this way."

"Besides the obvious?" I grunt. Dan nods, so despite my better judgment, I launch into the story of the night before.

I tell him everything, from the cafeteria fight, to dinner with Tatiana, talking to Lili, and finally, finding Roxanne outside of my apartment. I have to pause mid-story for Dan to look up the video of me punching the YouTuber, and after we watch it twice, with Dan getting hyped each time, I'm able to continue. When I tell him about her trying to kiss me, and how I had almost given in, he shakes his head sadly.

"What?" I grouse. "What do you have to say about it?"

"You should have just kissed her, man. This whole thing —you know what? Never mind. You don't want to hear what I have to say."

His tone is pointed, and for whatever reason, it bothers me. "No, I do. Tell me."

Dan throws his hands into the air. "Fine. You're overreacting, Andries. You're still in love with this woman and she's all but begging for your forgiveness, and you're acting like you're making some righteous decision. In my opinion, Roxanne is a catch."

Shocked, I blink a few times before I can respond. "A *catch*? She's a prostitute, Dan!"

"Not anymore, right? Isn't that what she told you? So her only sin is running her own escort service, and you can't move past that?" He laughs sardonically. "Let me lay it out for you; she's a self-made woman, driven, smart enough to build her own business out of *nothing*, beautiful, compassionate, and obviously head over heels for you. She's a catch, and you're just throwing her back despite the feelings you have for her."

I hate that he's right. On paper, she's everything I've ever wanted, but when you drop the word "escort" back into the mix, everything is ruined. Not to mention the lies.

"She lied to me the entire time about who she really was," I point out. "Even if I was okay with the escort stuff, am I just supposed to let the lying go too? How could I ever trust her again?"

"She made a mistake. A colossal one, sure, but still just a mistake." Dan is clearly stressed by all of this, and it's a state I've never seen him in before. He rakes a hand through his hair, pacing through the empty bedroom. "I'm just worried about you, man, and I don't want this to be something you regret for the rest of your life. If you move, I truly believe you'll be able to erase her from your life like you want to, but forgetting her isn't going to be nearly that easy. Especially if you love her as much as you say you do."

We stare at each other, seconds ticking by, neither of us really knowing how to navigate this more serious portion of our friendship.

"You really think there is nothing wrong with her job, do you?" I ask finally, astounded.

"It's twenty-twenty-two, Andries. Sex work isn't the taboo you think it is. It doesn't make Roxanne someone else entirely, just because she manages a company of sex workers."

A tiny, hair thin crack shoots through the walls I've put up regarding Roxanne. As horrible as I've been feeling, the fact that I was making the right choice is the only thing keeping me from breaking down entirely. Dan had seemed bummed out that Roxie and I had split, but seeing his real, raw opinion on the whole thing, makes me question myself. If Dan, my best friend, is okay with what Roxanne does, can it really be all that terrible?

Head spinning, I pinch the bridge of my nose. "Dan, I–"

I can't finish my thought, interrupted by my phone ringing. It's almost painfully loud in the empty apartment. I fumble it out of my pocket, frowning when I see it's Elise. The infinitesimal chance that it could be something important makes the call impossible to ignore, even if I want to.

"Elise," I say shortly as I answer.

"Hello, lover boy. How was your hot date with Tatiana last night?"

"Oh, fuck off," I snap, hanging up. She calls right back immediately, and against my better judgment, I pick up.

"Okay, okay! Jeez, I didn't realize you'd be so sensitive."

"Say whatever you need to say, Elise. I'm not feeling up to your shenanigans."

I hear her huff in indignation, but she takes me seriously. "Fine. I was just calling because I talked to Tatiana this morning. Andries, you were *all she could talk about.* She had such an amazing time with you last night."

"Great."

"Don't be that way. Tatiana thinks you're this flawless human being, and you're so dismissive!"

I sigh. "I'm just... tired. I don't want to talk about this right now. I'm touring apartments."

"You're really going through with moving!?" she exclaims. "We put so much work into your apartment. You can't just leave!"

"We can talk later, okay?"

My sister makes a frustrated noise that tells me she has a lot more to say on the matter, but she reluctantly tells me goodbye, and I hang up for the second time.

Knowing Tatiana enjoyed herself is nice, of course, but I don't have the capacity at the moment to feel anything other than sick and tired. I have told Tati, time and time again, that we are just friends. Strangely enough, she seems to accept it better than Elise, content to spend time with me as friends while my sister tries to make everything into a date between Tatiana and me. It makes me realize that the two of them must be closer than I thought.

I've always known they were friends, but if the two of them are planning out my future with Tatiana when I'm around, then they must be together more than just occasionally. What worries me is that Tatiana is too sweet for Elise. She's easy to manipulate because she trusts so easily, and if I know my sister, she'll take advantage of anyone that she can to get ahead in life. Elise has already expressed unhappiness at how my increasingly sordid reputation is bleeding over to her. If I got with Tatiana, with her pristine reputation and ability to make anyone and everyone smile, it'd make things much easier for Elise. And if Tatiana and I hypothetically went the distance, she'd have a friend entering the family, instead of a random woman. It's a win-win for my family, even if it meant I'd be bored out of my mind in my marriage for the rest of time.

Tatiana feeding off Elise is a dangerous thing that I'll have to keep a better eye on. I care for them both, but there is potential for something bad there. Hopefully I'm wrong, but just in case…

"Uh… everything alright?" Dan asks.

"Yeah…" The conversation with Elise has taken all the wind out of my sails in regard to my argument with Dan, and I just don't feel like starting it anew. "Let's go talk to the agent."

Once we're back in the main part of the apartment, the agent jumps up from where he is leaning on the counter. "Well, what do you think?" he asks, sounding unsure.

"It's fine. I'll take it. When can I move in?"

Dan and the agent look at each other before they both turn back to me. "Are you sure?" Dan asks.

"We've got five other properties to look at," the agent adds.

I'm sure I'm going to regret the decision later, but the feeling of being completely drained and unable to do a single other thing, or make any more decisions, is drowning me. I just need this to be over. Plus, it's just a lease.

"Positive. Just e-mail me the leasing contract. Dan, can you drive me home?"

The ride is weirdly stilted, with my friend looking over at me like he wants to say something, before he gives up and looks back to the road. How can it be so early, but feel like I've been up for ages?

He eventually pulls up to the curb outside my apartment, and as he slows the car to a stop, he finally speaks up.

"You don't have to do any of this, you know. I think you should take some time off, fly somewhere far away and let all these things that are weighing on you fade. It'd be more manageable, and you'd have a clearer head to think."

"I know what I want to do, Dan, which is why I'm doing it. I can't figure out why everyone is so annoyed with me doing something as simple as switching apartments."

"Andries, we've all done stupid stuff because of a woman before. There's no reason to be embarrassed."

After giving him a withering look, I step out onto the curb, giving him a brief, "Goodbye, Dan."

I'm so close to being upstairs in my apartment, alone, that I can almost taste it. I adjust my backpack on my shoulder, already running through the excuses for missing my study group later tonight, when I reach the door to my building.

Sitting on the stoop next door to my building is a man I've never seen before, on his phone, and I only barely take note of him until I see him standing out of the corner of my eye. For some reason, his movements, which are obviously intentional, make me hesitate.

"Hey, you're Andries, right?"

Slowly, I turn to face him. I've never seen him before, with his average brown hair and thick glasses, but he's looking at me with clear familiarity. And he knows my name.

"Who's asking?"

He sticks his hand out for me to shake, but instead of taking it, I raise an eyebrow and wait for him to identify himself. His dopey grin falls at the same time as his hand goes back to his side, and I get the instant impression that he's wearing some sort of mask, trying to catch me off guard. Maybe it's the glasses, or the clothing that make him look like any other student, but it rings false.

"My name's Kenneth. I was just wondering if I could have a word—"

Alarm bells start ringing in my head, the name and the odd behavior coalescing into an identity of a man I never would have thought I would find on my door.

"Kenneth, who works for RTL? The journalist?"

I see surprise flutter across his face, but it's gone in an instant. "Yes. Wow, you're a pretty informed guy, huh?"

"Well, considering you did a hit piece on my mother that included an interview with her professional enemy, Tess Hagen, your name is sort of well-known in my home," I tell him, my voice icy and hard. "Get the fuck away from my apartment before I call the police."

Kenneth fully drops the act, tilting his chin up stubbornly, his smile cruel. "I see you're a fan of my work. Well, you're going to love what I'm working on right now. I'm blowing the lid off a local escort agency that has a number of high-profile clients, some of whom are married. The owner of this certain house of ill repute is Roxanne Feng. Does that name sound familiar to you?"

Two minutes ago, I'd have said there was not enough energy in my entire body to dredge up any anger, but this bastard, standing nearly on my doorstep and threatening me after already damaging my mother's reputation years ago, manages to find some untapped well of rage deep within my soul.

I don't touch him, but I shoot my hand out to grab the collar of his sweatshirt, pulling him forward until he stumbles. Kenneth nearly loses his balance, yelping in surprise, and I release him, so his own momentum carries him forward. It allows me to push past him, and yank open the door of my building, turning back to Kenneth long enough for a few last words.

"Next time I see you out here, you're going to prison."

Finally, fucking *finally* I'm able to unlock my door and enter my own apartment. I throw my bag on the floor, jerking my shirt over my head and throwing it somewhere to the side, and moving directly to the liquor cabinet.

I've depleted nearly all of my alcohol, and the harsh, cheap whiskey I find in the back burns my throat like acid, but I suck it down, anyway. I feel it in my nasal passages and lungs, it's so terribly potent, but I couldn't care less if I tried.

Head spinning, my hangover blossoms back into true drunkenness. I discard the nearly empty bottle on the counter and stumble to my room. With the curtains yanked shut, it's blessedly dark, and my sheets are perfectly cold against my burning face.

Still, no matter how comfortable the room is, and how tired my entire being is, I cannot find rest. I know it's still the middle of the day, and many of the people who I love are worried about me, but the thing keeping me up the most is the empty spot on the bed beside me.

I reach over and lay my hand down where Roxanne should be, but the hollow space is no comfort to me. So, I imagine that she is there, and close my eyes. In my imagination, she smells like night blooming jasmine, and in the darkness, we talk about going to Paris in the spring.

CHAPTER 9

Amsterdam, January 14, 2022
Andries

Days are passing, but they are like mirror images of one another. I wake up, head pounding, and fumble for the bottle of aspirin on the bedside table, swallowing the pills before my eyes are even open. If I'm lucky, I will have remembered to leave myself a glass of water the night before, but if not, I choke them down with nothing but my own saliva before I let my head fall back to the pillow, watching the ceiling spin around me as I wait for the pain to abate.

Next is a cup of scalding black coffee, burning even worse than it normally would on my ravaged throat and mouth, damaged from the amount of straight liquor I've been pouring down my gullet this past week. The pain from it all is sharp in contrast to the dull pounding in my skull, and it actually helps to clear some of the fog away from my thoughts.

Then it's a shower; again, scalding. Class comes after that. I'm infinitely grateful that I didn't end up pursuing some sort of science or medical degree where I would have to attend labs, because staying upright and paying attention during the lectures is almost too much for me to bear. Thankfully, I have a few sympathetic classmates that have seen through the facade I try to keep up, and I will often have a ping indicating a new message in my university inbox, only to find copies of notes that one of them has taken. Hopefully, I won't tank finals later this semester, and I'll be able to return the favor in the future. For right now, though, I'm upright in my seat in the lecture hall, and my eyes are open. I was even a few minutes early. All in all, it's a success, as far as I'm concerned.

This English linguistics class is a required credit, so I do try and give it my all, but the ghost of Roxanne is weighing so heavily on me that, despite my best efforts, I can't give it one hundred percent. The professor for this class, Professor Josianne, is younger than a lot of the other teachers at the university, and while it makes her lesson plans more approachable and easier to digest for me, it also means she isn't as jaded as some of the older professors, who don't even bother to learn their students' names. Her genuine interest in her class means that she notices me, slumped over in my seat, apparently looking like death warmed over.

I catch her glancing my direction a few times during class, a small frown flitting across her face when she does so. I know that she's going to confront me, probably today, and I just hope that it happens sooner rather than later so it can be done and over with. She walks between the rows of desks, up the stone stairs that give away the age of the lecture halls, her hands clasped behind her back as she speaks. As I suspected would happen, she pauses near me, and looks down until I reluctantly meet her eyes.

"Andries, I'd like to see you in my office after class."

It isn't a request, but a quiet command. I give her a single nod and she moves on, continuing her lesson without breaking her stride even a little bit. If I had any thoughts about going into academics, I'd want to be a professor like her; fully engaged and aware, still full of passion for the subject and her job. Not like some of the dusty dinosaurs that seem to teach while half asleep.

That doesn't mean I want to have a one on one with her, though, and the rest of the lecture drags on forever as I await my fate.

It's only been a short amount of time, but the burning interest the rest of the student body has had for my private affairs...and public cafeteria fights... has begun to wane. There are some of the more gossip-heavy groups that whisper as I walk by, but a lot of students, especially the older ones, seem empathetic to my plight, hence the freely shared notes. One morning, there was even a bottle of orange juice on the desk I normally use when I got to class, a Post-it note with my name scrawled on it stuck to the cap. At least I wouldn't be getting scurvy anytime soon.

The lecture wraps up, and while the rest of the class is closing laptops and packing paper up, I don't move, waiting for them all to depart before I gather my own things. Professor Josianne is still on the lecture floor, sitting on the corner of her desk, legs crossed and foot bouncing as she waits. I'm struck by how young she is, and in another life, I would have found her beautiful, with her makeup-free face and loose, dark hair. Now, though, I don't register anyone at all as attractive... at least not since Roxanne. She has ruined me for other women, maybe forever.

Once it's just the professor and I left, she hops down off the desk and motions for me to follow her. I descend to the lecture floor and through the door at the end of the room, down a short hallway, and into her office. Where the rector's office was everything a high-ranking university employee's should be, Josianne's office is lighter, her single window bare of any curtains besides a gauzy thing currently tied into a knot, a plethora of plants dotted around the space, and the quintessential English professor decoration; a bookshelf full of novels and encyclopedias. Some of them are pulled out and opened on her desk, and even the floor, neon tabs marking places all throughout the pages.

I sit in the soft rolling chair across from her desk, as she takes hers. She doesn't say anything at first, just looks me over in the natural light of her office, dust motes floating in the air between us. Finally, she plucks one of the framed photos off her desk and hands it to me.

Confused, I take it. It's a wide panoramic shot of the professor's graduating class, everyone dressed in identical black gowns and caps. Josianne leans forward and taps a figure in the middle of the crowd, and when I squint, I can see it's her.

"What—?" I start, but she moves her finger to tap another figure, this one in the front row. As soon as I move my gaze to the next person she's pointing out for me, I can't believe I didn't notice it before. Front and center of the group is Roxanne, her hair still black and longer than I've ever seen it, flowing out the bottom of her cap. She's smiling, a carefree expression of youth that I've never seen her wear, and my heart squeezes in my chest.

Professor Josianne leans back in her chair, still watching me closely. "I didn't seek out the video that's going around of you and Roxanne, but the rector recommended anyone that had you in class view it, just so we knew to act if any of the other students bothered you. Imagine my surprise to see the woman who has been causing all this upset is my old classmate Roxanne Feng."

I breathe a sad chuckle, still holding the picture, unable to look away from this younger, sweeter version of the woman I still love so desperately. "Small world, I guess."

"Not really. We were both English majors living in Amsterdam, but it's a strange enough coincidence that I wanted to talk to you personally." She exhales slowly, as if she's just as uncomfortable as I am. "Most of our graduating class knows what Roxanne does for a living, and while I respect what she's built all on her own, it certainly is a business that sends a shiver up my spine. She's always been stubborn, even ruthless. Had I known you were seeing her, and that she was lying about her occupation, I would have told you, Andries. I don't want you to think I'm complicit in her lies."

"It's okay. You wouldn't have known we had dated if it wasn't for that YouTuber."

"I realize that, but I just wanted to be completely honest with you. I feel like I've failed as a professor, letting someone I know take advantage of one of my students like that." Her tone is serious, her gaze unflinching.

"It was all consensual," I confess. "If it wasn't for her disgusting job and all the lies, we'd still be together now."

She raises her eyebrows. "Even with the age gap? I could see a fling between the two of you, but this great love affair that you seem to be stuck on just seems so odd to me. What do you two even have in common, besides being English majors?"

Feeling annoyed, I hand her the picture back, wishing I had the guts to take my own photo of it with my phone camera to look at later. "A lot more than you, or anyone else can understand. The age difference was a non-issue for us. But the sex work and the lies are an issue. Which is why we aren't together."

At this point, if she raises her eyebrows any higher, they'll be a part of her hairline. The professor looks endlessly skeptical about what I've just told her, but to her credit, she drops the subject, recognizing it as an argument she can't win.

She switches tactics, placing the photo back where it had been originally, and pulling a few flyers with business cards attached out of her desk. "Alright. Well, regardless, your class participation is suffering. You're clearly bored, tired, and obviously sleep deprived. I'm not a medical professional, but this wouldn't be the first time I've seen depression pop up in my young students."

"I'm not depressed," I insist.

"I can also smell the alcohol coming out of your pores, now that we're in this smaller room, so don't tell me that there isn't *something* going on with you." She slides the business cards toward me across the desk. "These are some resources for you, but the most important is the one on top. He's our school psychologist, and I think it'd really benefit you to at least talk to him."

Reluctantly, I take the flyers, leafing through them. Like she said, one is a psychologist, the other is an addiction counselor, and the third is a mental health support group. I know she won't let me leave them, so I tuck them into the side pocket of my backpack without a word.

"Also, and this one is a more personal suggestion, but you really do need to sleep. You're pale, and the circles under your eyes concern me. If you're struggling to sleep, marijuana is obviously legal, and there are plenty of things that could help you get some rest. I'd be happy to give you a few days leave from my class to sleep, if you want."

I shake my head. "I can't stop my forward momentum. If I stop to rest, then I might not get back up again."

She looks alarmed. "Andries, please call the psychologist."

I stand, gathering my things. "I'll consider it."

"...If Roxanne is bothering you, I can contact her and—"

I stop in my tracks and fix her with a firm glare. "Absolutely not, Professor, and I say that with the utmost respect. But I can't have my teachers calling my ex-girlfriend."

She sighs. "I suppose that is crossing the line. But I can't stress enough how concerned I am here."

"Like I said, I'll consider what you've said. See you in class tomorrow."

Closing the door behind me, I hurry back out into the main hall, blowing out a tense breath. That encounter was strange and uncomfortable. I just want everyone around me to stop pulling me aside and asking after my mental health with pity in their eyes. It's the last thing I want. Everyone, myself included, just needs to move on.

It's a short day for me, and while I'm not exactly looking forward to hiding in my apartment for the rest of the day, at least it's better than being around all these other students that seem to have their lives so much more together than mine. I consider picking up lunch before heading home, maybe calling Elise to join me, but my decision is made for me when my phone rings, and I see it's my mother.

"Hi, Mom," I say.

"Did you forget that we have a lunch date today, Andries?"

I groan internally. Yes, I had forgotten, and I really, *really* didn't want to go have lunch with my mother, who would be able to pick apart everything that was wrong while simultaneously making me feel guilty for being sad. Still, there is no way to avoid her, and I know it.

"No, I didn't forget. Can I just meet you there?"

Her voice brightens. "Yes, I'll see you soon! I've been looking forward to this all week."

"Me too," I lie, and Mom snorts.

"Sure you have, love. Anyway, I'll be there in twenty minutes."

I hang up, staring at my phone screen in denial about having to make such a public appearance in the state I'm in.

"Fuck," I mutter to myself, before opening the Uber app and ordering a car.

* * *

Outside of the restaurant, Mom looks like a drop of spring-time in the gray winter, her knit sweater is robin's egg blue with yellow on the collar and sleeves. I hug her obediently, wishing that being held by my mother offered any of the comfort that it used to when I was a boy.

She releases me first, holding my face in her hands to get a good look at me. I pull away quickly, but not before her happy grin becomes a frown.

"You look awful," she says, a note of alarm in her voice. "When is the last time you've eaten?"

Thinking about the piece of cold pizza I ate walking out the door this morning, I tell her, "Breakfast."

Her hands on my shoulders, she turns me this way and that, tutting in disapproval as she does so. "Well, I can't imagine it was a very good one. Are you sick? Or... this certainly isn't about all that Roxanne business still, is it?"

I clench my teeth against the judgmental sound of her tone. "It's a lot of things."

"Hmm. Sit down, let's get some nutrition in you before you collapse before my eyes, and then we can talk."

Predictably, she takes immediate control of the situation, ordering a green smoothie that tastes like grass and apples, insisting that it will help me feel better, because clearly I'm malnourished. I choke some of it down, unable to stop the sneer I make as it hits my tongue.

She orders lunch too, but I'm barely paying attention to whatever she's decided I'm eating. Anything to get this whole ordeal over sooner than later.

"I was hoping to catch up on everything you've been doing at school, love, but I think your personal life is a little more pressing. Tell me what's wrong."

"Mom, you know what it is." I rub my temples with my fingers, feeling stress building there rapidly. "I just need some more time, and some space to start over."

She sighs sadly, stirring her hot tea, the spoon clinking delicately against the ceramic mug. "She's just one woman, Andries. And not a very impressive one, at that. Do you think this is because she was your first love, or is there something else going on here that we aren't seeing?"

I know what she's getting at, even if it offends me. It's at my age that men start to show signs of mental illness, especially things like schizophrenia, and I guess I can't blame her for thinking it might be something more serious considering how long it was taking me to get over Roxanne. Still, though, I just wish she and everyone else could just accept that my heart is broken, and nothing more.

"We had basically moved in together and were never apart. I know it happened fast, and you and Dad don't approve of my partner or the speed with which we combined our lives, but it felt so right and real at the time. It still feels real now, which is why I'm taking so long to get over this, Mom. I'm not losing my mind."

"Oh, darling, I never said you were. It's just…" She grabs my hand, and squeezes. "I'm so worried about you. We all are."

I gently extricate my hand from hers and tuck them both under the table on my knees. "I just need time. More time."

"Drink your smoothie," she commands, and I obey. "I understand that time's supposed to heal everything, but I think we can speed up the timeline a little bit, don't you think?"

"Not really."

She huffs. "Okay, well. My mom told me she spoke to you about doing an internship at your dad's company. I think you should do it. You can still attend school part time, and the hands-on experience will be so valuable when you start looking for work in earnest. Or when you take over the family company." She winks at me, to which I only scowl. "You need something to keep you busy, and it might as well be something that will benefit you in the long run."

I could almost laugh. She has no idea that I'd be more than useless at a business internship. The only classes I've taken have been for English, and something tells me my dad doesn't need a poet on the payroll. But since she doesn't know of my major switch, I hold off on chuckling out loud.

"It's not for me, Mom. Give it to Elise."

She looks surprised. "To Elise? This is a very coveted position, and you're the eldest child. It's your position to lose, dear."

"Like I said, I don't want it. Elise will flourish though, I'm sure of it."

Mom isn't convinced. "This is a family business, and it's going to be passed down to our eldest, which is you. I can't force you to take the internship, but it'd be a stupid decision to let the opportunity pass you by."

"I'm just not interested," I say more forcefully.

The stubborn look on my mother's face lets me know that this fight isn't over, but she moves on and changes tactics, and for the second time in an hour I'm subjected to a lecture about how I need to go to therapy. Which, maybe I should, but it still isn't going to happen. My life is private. My heartbreak too. I'm not sharing it with any stranger.

"If you're not willing to be proactive about your future career, then you at least need to see a therapist for your mental state. Sitting around and ignoring it isn't going to help you heal."

"Mom, I don't have time for this nonsense. I have to study, I can't be doing a ton of extra stuff that is going to negatively affect my grades."

"It's just one appointment a week–" she insists, but I cut her off, which immediately makes her angry.

"I said no. I'm not going to reconsider. Please leave me alone about this so we can enjoy lunch together, Mom." I try to make my voice authoritative, but the bad thing about trying to tell my mom to stop doing something is that she's still seeing me as a little boy, not a full-grown man.

The server comes by, dropping the meals off in front of us. She's ordered me a salmon quinoa rice and veggie bowl, and I find myself really missing my cold pizza at the sight of it.

"Andries, your father and I are paying for your school and your very comfortable living space, so I'm going to have to insist on an ultimatum. Either you go to therapy, or you take the internship. It has to be one or the other."

Pushing around the food in the bowl, I try to formulate a response that will get her off my back as soon as possible. It's pointless, though, because I can feel her eyes locked onto me like lasers. Finally, I sigh, and drop my fork, knowing that there is no way out of this ultimatum for me.

"Fine. Fine! Can I at least have time to think about it?"

She hums in thought. "Okay, a few days, but nothing more."

"And I get to pick my own therapist," I add.

She shakes her head at this. "No. I have a very good one in mind that can even make house calls. If you decide on therapy, that's who you'll be using."

I get a sinister feeling from this statement. A therapist is definitely more palatable than taking on a business internship as an English major, but confidentiality would be a must, otherwise I'd just have to lie even more than I already am. If my mom is insisting I use *her* therapist, then that means the therapist would be compromised, and reporting everything back to her the moment I leave the office. I look up at my mom, feeling a sadness settle over me. It might be somewhat about my mental health, but this is also just another way for my mom to keep tabs on my life when she isn't around. And a way for her to discover my most private secrets.

I'm royally screwed. I can't believe she's doing this, but I shouldn't be surprised. The way everyone turned on me as fast as lightning once it came out that Roxanne was an escort has taught me that reputation matters more to some people than anything else in the world. My mom must want those secrets of mine so she can stop me from making another mistake that could potentially embarrass the family. She isn't worried about my heartbreak, and my depression. Only about the way it affects her reputation.

I stab my fork into my salmon with more force than I intend to when I answer her. "I'll let you know. It will probably be therapy, but give me some time to make up my mind for sure."

Having gotten her way, the sharp look leaves my mother's expression, and she goes back to eating her veggie bowl. "Wonderful. I'm positive this will help you. I know it sounds distasteful, but we all need someone to talk to sometimes, right?"

Out of words and energy for the moment, I simply nod. Mom accepts the short answer, and we eat in peace, changing the subject to more innocent topics like my young sisters and some of the plans for my father's birthday party. If the whole lunch was like this, then I wouldn't have dreaded it so much, but I knew from the moment she sat down that Mom was going to try to get something out of me.

And like the lioness she is, she succeeded, and I'm left here eating salmon as if I haven't been bested, talking to her like she hasn't just forced my hand yet again. How long will she refuse to let me live my own life, I wonder?

* * *

It's a little past 8 p.m. when the third woman of the day decides to come and harangue me, this time in my own home.

Elise hits the buzzer three times, even though she knows the code to enter, so at least I have the illusion of choosing whether to let her in or not. I know that she will just let herself in if I don't do it for her, so I pull myself up off my couch, scrape my forearm over my mouth, and let her in.

I'm not thinking clearly, because if I was, I would have at least hidden the whiskey bottle before doing so. Now, though, she pushes past me as soon as she comes in, plucking the nearly empty glass vessel, shaking it in front of me like you would a shoe to a dog that had torn it apart.

"Here on the orders of Mom, I'm assuming," I drawl.

"You're damn right I am, and now I can see why! You're drunker than a skunk, and you've drunk nearly an entire bottle of whiskey, Andries! How are you even upright?" Elise screeches.

I look at the bottle she's shaking in my face, somewhat relieved that I had at least picked up a midrange bottle of the stuff from the liquor store instead of more rotgut from the convenience store. It'd only add insult to injury to be busted drinking cheap booze.

"I've been nursing it for a whole week, calm down," I say dismissively, but Elise is having none of it.

I watch in mute shock as she goes to my garbage can, digging out a paper bag that had housed the whiskey bottle earlier, plucking off the receipt that was stapled to it before comparing the receipt with the bottle.

"All week, huh? Then why does this say you bought that exact bottle today, hm?"

I flop back onto the couch, knowing I'm already fucked. She will no doubt reveal this discovery to our mom, who will probably enroll me in both therapy and the internship immediately. "Great job, detective."

She puts the bottle in the sink, letting it drain as she walks over to sit next to me, pushing my legs out of the way despite my complaints. "I don't mind the sarcasm, Andries, but I'm worried about you."

I drape an arm over my eyes and close them. "You and everyone else I come into contact with, it seems."

She pats my calf as if she's comforting a dog, but I don't kick her like I really want to. She's trying to navigate this mess just like I am, but instead of feeling it all so intensely like I am, she's trying to keep my head above water while also living her own life. If I wasn't so trashed, it might make me sad, or thankful to have her beside me at least, but I'm numb right now.

"Let's go home for the weekend," she blurts out. "You don't want to admit it, but you're killing yourself being in here alone. If you're noticing everyone being concerned about you, it's because it's so obvious that you're breaking down. Let's both just go home, and you can detox from the alcohol while getting some much-needed space. What do you think?"

I don't love the idea of my dark bedroom back at the Van Den Bosch estate, but being fed quality food and not having to be alone constantly, even if I wanted to be most of the time, had its perks. And maybe if I can prove that I'm not having a mental break, Mom will drop the therapy or internship threat.

"Yeah, okay," I say, the world spinning even as I lie still with my eyes closed.

She lets out a relieved breath. "Good. Great. I'll call Mom when I leave and have them send a car for us, so you won't have to worry about it."

I wish I could sit up and properly thank her, but I'm fading into the less-than-restful blackout drunk sleep, and I can't manage to rise. So I just tell her, "Thanks, Elise," before becoming unconscious.

Right before I pass out completely, I can hear her opening my liquor cabinet and the sound of her pouring out all the bottles down the drain. I don't protest. I couldn't even if I wanted to.

CHAPTER 10

Knock, knock, knock. "Andries? Are you in there, dear?"

I pull the pillow over my head and groan, already regretting my decision to come back home for a few days to detox. It's been a constant parade of my younger sisters, my parents, and the household staff trying to get me to eat every thirty minutes, while being less than subtle about making sure I wasn't drinking.

Really, I wish I *was* drinking. I felt like shit when I was cycling between drunk and hungover, constantly in pain and barely able to keep my eyes open, but having it all leech out of my system slowly is almost even worse. I'm thankful I wasn't fully into alcohol addiction territory, because the small bouts of muscle spasms and cold sweats were some of the worst things I've experienced in my life.

I was a healthy kid, and a fit, strong adult. When I get sick, I'm only ever down and out for a day or two, but this detoxing bullshit is another animal altogether. It's like every cold I've had and the full body pain from working out too hard while being dehydrated, all rolled into one miserable package. And no one would leave me alone to just suffer, damn them.

"Yes, Mom, I'm here," I groan.

She enters as soon as I confirm, bustling over to hand me a small clear cup with three brown pills and a chilled bottle of sparkling water.

"Take these, drink, and get up. We're having a family dinner tonight."

I tap my phone screen to check the time. "Mom, it's noon."

She huffs. "Considering you're sweating out enough alcohol to start a brewery, and you look homeless, I figured you would need some extra time to make yourself presentable. Plus, your dad wants to speak to you before dinner."

"Great, another lecture about being a failure," I gripe.

She lightly slaps my shoulder, planting her hands on her hips as she looks down at me. "Not everyone in the world is here just to upset you, you know. I'm sure he just wants to have a nice father-son conversation, since the two of you see each other so little compared to how much you see the rest of us."

Dad and I have nothing in common, but I don't say that aloud. On some level, she must know already, but ignores the fact so she can pretend to have the perfect family. It isn't a point of contention between me and Dad, though. We still have a decent relationship, even if our interests don't align.

"I'll go see him once I'm presentable," I confirm to her, and she nods once, a self-satisfied smile on her face.

"Good! Casual dress for dinner tonight, but we'll have a few guests, so don't look too crazy, please. No sweatpants."

"It's like private school all over again," I grumble, watching my mom putter about my room, straightening things up and tidying as she goes, as if she doesn't have an entire staff to do these kinds of things. Not to mention that I'm an adult, perfectly capable of doing it myself. It must just be a mom thing, trying to help in any way she can.

"You complain a lot for a very privileged young man, Andries," she says breezily.

"So I've been told."

I sit all the way up and take the pills, washing them down with a hefty swig of the sparkling water, the fizziness filling up my empty stomach in odd ways. I can feel the layer of sweat on my skin, and the sudden craving for a shower is swift and absolute.

"Get out, Mom. I need to shower."

She hesitates on the threshold of my door, which tips me off that she has more to say. With a deep breath, I sit back down on my mattress and pat the space next to me. Mom comes over and sits, perfectly graceful as usual, hands folded in her lap.

"What is it?" I ask.

"Your landlord called this morning and said you're breaking your lease... Why, Andries? We worked hard to find that place for you."

She sounds hurt, and I hate it. "I just need a change of scenery, and someplace that no one can find me."

"Do you mean a place that Roxanne can't find you?" Her question is gentle.

"Yes, and no. She's part of the reason, but I had a weird encounter the other day with someone. When I got home, that journalist Kenneth that did the hit piece on you was waiting for me."

Mom's eyes go wide, and she lays a hand over her chest. "I can't believe it! After all this time, what is that toad doing crawling out of the woodwork to bother my son?"

"He knew my name, and I recognized him right away, which seemed to surprise him. He was asking questions about Roxanne, acting like he's doing a piece on her company, but considering his history with the family, I can't help but think it's about me too."

Even in the darkness of my room I can see Mom looks pale. "If that's true... then I can understand wanting to move. But there are other options. We could get security for you."

I shake my head. "I've already found a new place."

She looks at me for a long moment, in that probing way only mothers can manage. "You're not going to like what I have to say... but I think you should stay here for some time. It's all too easy to fall into old patterns like drinking, and you'll be safe from that journalist here too. In fact, I insist you stay."

I look at her like she's crazy. "Mother, school is an hour away. I'm not commuting that far."

"Our driver can take you and bring you back. You could even do homework in the car."

"*Mom*. I have a new flat to move into. I just told you that."

"You can sleep at your new flat when you're responsible enough, Andries. Until then, stay home, and recoup your sense and your health."

Her tone is stubborn, and I know I can't win, so I have to at least set some boundaries, so I'm not completely screwed by living here.

"I'll stay on the condition that I don't have to attend any social events that I don't want to be a part of," I counter.

She thinks it over, tapping her lips with a finger as she does so, and I can clearly see the judge in her wanting to break down my conditions into the very smallest pieces, but she refrains.

"Okay. That's acceptable."

I still don't like it, but it is what it is. "Great. Now, shower?"

She does as I ask, her passive-aggressive commentary continuing as she exits, only to return a second later with a pile of fluffy towels for me. This time when she goes out the door, I lock it for good measure, and take my towels and change of clothes to my ensuite bathroom.

I have every intention of showering, but when I lay my eyes on the large marble tub that I had all but forgotten about, I say fuck it, and run a bath instead. Not the most efficient way of cleansing myself, but I think a good soak will work wonders.

I find a bag of mint Epsom salts under the sink, some long-discarded part of a home spa package that some well-meaning distant relative had gifted us kids one holiday, and dump the entire package into the filling basin. The salt dissolves as soon as it hits the steaming water, and the room is filled with the scent of clean, crisp, brine and spearmint.

I shed my silk pajama pants, the only article of clothing I've been wearing while hiding in my bedroom, and lower myself into the bath with slow movements. It's too hot, but I don't care. The water envelops me, and I sigh in comfort, sinking as low as I can.

I stay there for way too long, my muscles finally relaxing, and the sweat being washed away to leave me feeling more like myself than I have in days. I ignore the messages coming in on my phone, the ticking of the clock, and the noises I hear coming from the rest of the house. I'm determined to soak here until I emerge as a new man.

At least an hour and a half later, I raise myself out of the water, toweling off and facing my reflection in full for the first time in days. I wince immediately and the scrubby stubble on my face and the sallow color of my skin. Tying the towel around my waist and beginning the tedious task of shaving.

Once I've finished, I check myself again. It's… a bit better, I guess, but I still look like shit. I pinch my cheeks to try to bring some color back, but when it doesn't work, I take more drastic measures, picking up my phone and texting Elise.

Andries: Hey, so never mention this again, but do you have some sort of face mask that will make me look less like a corpse? Mom said we have company tonight.

She answers immediately.

Elise: Oh, absolutely I do. Spa day!

Andries: No. No fucking spa day. If you can't take this seriously, then never mind.

Elise: Fine. You're no fun. I'll be right over.

I throw on a robe and wait for her. She's at my door in less than five minutes, a bowl in her hand filled with muddy green clay. I sit patiently as she paints it onto my face, and when she finishes and the clay begins to dry, my skin starts to heat up.

"It will increase blood flow to your face," she explains when I begin to complain. "You asked for this, so just be patient."

"So," I say. "Any idea who is coming to dinner tonight?"

"Your guess is as good as mine," she answers quickly. Maybe too quickly, as if she's lying, but I figure that it doesn't matter all that much.

I wash the clay mask off once it hardens, and my face is flushed bright red. Elise cackles, but assures me the redness will fade soon enough and I'll look a little more human. I thank her, maybe a little sarcastically, and send her on her way. I guess it's time to face my dad.

Sebastian Van Den Bosch spends a large portion of his life in his office, which is built and decorated to his exact specifications. There is no charming clutter like there is in Professor Josianne's, just a neat and meticulous arrangement of what he has designated as having a place in his most sacred room.

Everything is heavy, and antique, made by hand and not by machines. I lower myself into one of the dark red leather chairs when he waves me inside, and I sit in silence while he finishes up whatever it is that he's working on.

When my dad turns his attention to me, he seems happy to see me, a good-natured expression on his face. I favor my dad in height and the prominence of a lot of my features, but my mother's genetics are not going to take a backseat, so there is clearly a lot of her in my visage, too.

"I've barely seen you since New Year's Eve. How have you been?" he asks, voice loud and ebullient. I must look uncomfortable because he amends his question quickly. "I mean, besides the obvious unfortunate things that have occurred lately. Your mom did say you've been rather fond of the bottle lately. I hope that isn't going to be a continuing problem?"

"No, it won't be. I came home specifically to stop drinking. It was a temporary lapse in judgment when I couldn't deal with my own issues. It won't happen again."

He looks sad at the tense sound of my voice. "There's nothing wrong with having a drink from time to time to take the edge off, son, but when you're using it as a coping mechanism is when it becomes a problem. If you get past all this and think you're capable of having a libation every now and then, that's perfectly fine."

I want to tell him I don't need his permission, but I keep my mouth shut, just nodding in agreement.

"I have a confession to make, Andries," he says, sounding somber now. "A colleague of mine sent me a few YouTube videos featuring you. I guess his son is a content creator and recognized you. The one at your birthday is obviously distasteful, but the fight in your university cafeteria… Andries, that isn't acceptable behavior for a Van Den Bosch. Or anyone, for that matter. And with your sister right there!" He shakes his head, as if in disbelief, even though I'm sure he's practiced this speech multiple times before I came to chat.

"Another temporary lapse in judgment," I snap, feeling my temper rising. Why can't everyone just leave the past in the past?

"Is that what you're going to tell me when I say that nearly everyone I'm acquainted with knows that you were dating a hooker? And not only that, she seems to be the catalyst toward all of your other so-called 'lapses in judgment' that you've been experiencing lately."

I clench my jaw, but don't show any other outward emotion. "Everyone knows about Roxanne now, so what do I care if your friends know too?"

"You misunderstand me. My reputation is not something I worry about. I'm worried that your life is going to be harder with everyone on the planet knowing your private affairs. I just want to keep you safe. Your sister too, because I was hoping you'd be her guardian in Amsterdam, but apparently she is yours instead."

"Well," I don't want to find it amusing, but I do. "Elise can put almost anyone in their place, so I'm not surprised."

"Me either," Dad agrees, and we share an uncomfortable laugh.

"I never wanted to put Elise in any sort of dangerous position. If I could take that part back, I would," I admit. "There're a lot of things I'd take back if I could."

"Such as?"

I feel an almost overwhelming urge to tell him, right then, about my change of major. Being able to get it off my chest would be so freeing, and it would be one less thing I have to hide from everyone. He will lose his mind over it, but God, it would feel so good to be done with it all.

Dad hasn't been a dick like I expected he would. He's more worried than angry, and hell, if it was my son drinking himself to death and half-assing the college classes I was paying for, I'd be pissed. It makes me feel… vulnerable. Like I could share something as big as being an English major with him, and maybe even find acceptance.

"Dad," I hesitate, clearing my throat, but he waits patiently with his hands folded in front of him. "This whole business thing… the internship… I think you should give it to Elise."

It's obviously not what he expects me to say, and he blinks owlishly at me while he absorbs my words. "What brought that on?" he asks, bewildered. "If this is because you're in crisis mode right now, it's okay. I get it, and I don't want you to miss out just because you're working through some things. It'd be beneficial for us both to spend some time together, I think. I see so little of you anymore, I'd love to have you working beside me."

"No, you don't understand." I rake my hands through my still-damp hair, trying to figure out how to verbalize myself. "I know I'm supposed to follow in your footsteps. You might think it's the best for me or whatever, but I don't want to be an executive. I hate–" I chicken out at the last second, changing tactics from fessing up to already having changed majors to just telling him that I hate being a business major.

"I detest business school, Dad. I don't want to do it anymore. I feel like I'm wasting my life, my passion, and my talent. I want to be a writer. A poet."

Silence stretches between us, with Dad obviously being shocked, and my heart pounding as I wait for his response. His face goes through a range of emotions, while I sit frozen, but Dad finally sighs and pinches the bridge of his nose between his fingers. A gesture that I recognize that I've picked up from him.

"A… poet?" he says slowly.

"A published poet," I clarify.

"That's… well. That's something all right." He blows out a frustrated breath, and then, unexpectedly, he does the most painful thing possible.

He laughs. "You can't really expect to make a life out of poetry, son."

"I have no talent for business, Dad! Elise is the one to follow in your footsteps. I promise that if you force me into that position, you're going to be disappointed, and so is she. Elise can be everything you want in a future business heir."

"So, what? I give Elise the internship and you travel the world writing haikus about mountains and streams, while your sister stays here and works her ass off?" He laughs again, shaking his head. "No, Andries. I don't think so."

It's like a spear in my heart, even though I should have expected it. The only saving grace is that I didn't admit to not attending business school.

"I'm a grown man," I tell him hotly. "I can do what I want to do."

"Not on my dime, you can't," he replies. "Listen, let's just drop this now before it becomes more of a point of contention between us. We can revisit the internship conversation once you're feeling better and you don't have that hooker on your mind so much."

"What's the point of amassing all this wealth, if you can't even let your children follow their dreams!" I explode, feeling like I've been backed into a corner. "I'm not like you. And I never will be. I'm a writer."

He barks out a sarcastic laugh. "Really? You're really sure that's what you want to be? A poet? In a family of judges, industrialists, and politicians, you want to be the poet?"

"Yes," I say simply, tone even. "Yes, that's what I want."

He's not happy, and all the understanding he had tried to keep up for me during this conversation has run out. I can see the vein in his forehead, a clear indication he's pissed off, even if he isn't verbalizing it.

Even though I'm boiling inside with humiliated anger, I can appreciate how he grapples with his urge to just tell me to get out, and that I'm completely wrong. He knows I'm not in the best state of mind, and I guess he still loves me as his son enough to make the monumental effort to keep his cool when it appears like I'm pressing every one of his buttons.

"Andries," he sighs. "Poetry is a beautiful thing, and a fantastic hobby for someone like you to have, even if I don't really appreciate it. Hell, if you have a book explode in popularity, then I would say absolutely, try to make a career out of it, but in order to do that you need to have a proper job first. Otherwise, sitting in your flat and scribbling sonnets all day isn't a real job. It doesn't pay any bills, and it's just the same as being unemployed."

"So you're saying I should waste a sizable portion of my adult life working a job I hate while relegating the thing I do love to an after-work hobby, on the off chance that *maybe* I'll get a book deal?"

"I mean, that's a very simplified version of what it would really be like, but yes. That's what I'm saying. It's the most responsible way to go about it."

I stand, my heart in my throat. "Never mind, Dad. Listen, just give Elise the internship. You won't regret it."

He frowns. "But you'd regret not taking it once all this fog clears out of your mind."

"Trust me," I say with a sad laugh, opening his office door. "I won't."

* * *

"Andries, the dinner guests are here!" Mom says through my bedroom door, where I have gone to hide after my disastrous conversation with my dad.

"Can I just have dinner in my room?"

"Absolutely not. Everyone is sitting down now, so hurry up!" she demands.

Truth is, I'm already dressed and ready to go. I knew that she'd make me go, but it was worth a shot to try and skip. I open the bedroom door to greet Mom, who looks pleasantly surprised to see me already dressed for dinner.

"Oh good, you're already prepared. Let's go! I think you'll be pleasantly surprised at who has joined us for the evening."

"That sounds ominous," I say, more to myself than anyone else, but Mom laughs softly.

"It's not, I promise."

The trek from the wing of the house where my bedroom resides and the dining room take two or three minutes to clear, but Mom uses our alone time the best she can trying to suss out how my conversion with Dad had gone.

"So what did your father have to say?" she asks, overly casual.

I look at her out of the corner of my eye. "Don't act like he didn't already fill you in."

"Actually, he didn't. Which means he's either upset, or confused, and isn't sure what to make of it yet."

"Probably a little bit of both," I sigh. "I told him to give the internship to Elise."

Mom's steps stutter. "What! She's a year younger than you, Andries. The position is yours."

"I told Dad I didn't want it."

"But why in the world not? I'm sure he'll give you some more time to work through your personal issues before you start, but it's the perfect opportunity to work beside your father!" she exclaims. "Elise is perfectly content at school. She doesn't need the escape like you do."

"It wouldn't be an escape, Mom. It would be a prison."

"Well," she stumbles over her words. "Let's talk about this later, once dinner is done. But don't think this discussion is over."

"I'd never dream of it," I mumble.

She's right in the fact that I'm pleasantly surprised by our dinner guests. I had feared it'd be some of the higher ups in Dad's company, coming here to try and convince me to take the intern position, but instead I see Dan and Tatiana hop to their feet when I appear, Dan coming over to shake my hand and pull me into a back-thumping hug, while Flower Girl just smiles brightly and offers me a happy wave.

"You guys didn't have to drive all the way here," I tell them.

"We were worried about you, man," Dan says, his usually happy face somber. "I'm glad to see you looking more like yourself."

"Agreed," Tatiana says, her face almost painfully sweet with empathy.

It's an adults only dinner, for which I'm thankful, since Elise and Dan immediately start on each other when she arrives.

"Look what the cat dragged in," Elise coos as soon as she sees him.

"Don't talk about yourself like that," Dan quips right back.

My sister turns red, but doesn't miss a beat, turning to Mom. "So nice of you to invite the more unfortunate for dinner tonight. Who knows when the last time he had a hot meal was?"

"More recently than you, I'm sure. What do you weigh, seventy-five pounds soaking wet?"

They launch into what could easily be mistaken as a full-blown argument but is really just a battle of wits to see who has the quicker mind and mouth. Tatiana looks alarmed, but I catch her eye and give her the OK symbol. She relaxes, but still doesn't look entirely comfortable with the riposting between the two.

I'm actually thankful for it, because it means my parents can hardly get a word in edgewise, and we don't have to return to any uncomfortable subjects that I'd rather avoid. Neither of them seems to enjoy the sniping between Dan and Elise, but they don't interrupt, either.

Once everything calms down and we begin to eat, I can finally talk to my guests.

"Are you guys staying here or driving back to Amsterdam tonight?" I ask.

"Driving back," Dan answers. "Tatiana has class early tomorrow morning, otherwise I'd have stayed here. We could practice some fencing tomorrow and I could remind you how bad you are at it."

I snort, feeling lighter just having the two of them around. "Yeah, alright. I'll take you up on that challenge next time we have the chance."

Dinner goes well, and it's the first meal I haven't dreaded sharing with others. For a brief time, I can let Roxanne fade from the forefront of my mind and focus on other things. I still wish she was here with me right now, the way things were before I discovered her betrayal. She fit into my life so perfectly, that even the people who questioned our age gap had to admit we made a good couple. I miss her, and I can only hold it off for so long.

As the meal winds down, I excuse myself, heading out to the terrace where I hid on New Year's Eve, letting the cold air fill my lungs and soothe the tightness of my throat. The property is dark, unlike the night of the party, and it feels even more secluded. I need this time by myself, to wrestle the ache for a woman I can no longer have, and for the most part doesn't even exist, back into the depths of my heart so I can function. When people tell me that I just need time, these times are what makes me think they're full of shit. It still hurts just as bad as it always has. I've just found more creative ways to hide it.

My alone time is cut short when the terrace door opens, and I whip around to tell whatever relative has followed me outside to leave me be, but the protest dies in my throat when I see that it's Tatiana.

She looks happy to see me, but still nervous. "I'm not interrupting anything, am I?"

"No," I lie. "Just doing some brooding out here by myself."

She grins, walking over to me, a puffy jacket held close around her body. "Oh, well I can leave you to it, then."

"It's fine, the more the merrier."

We both look out at the night sky in silence for a few minutes. I hear her take a breath to steady herself before she speaks again.

"You're out here thinking about her, aren't you?"

I know exactly who she means because she's right. There's no reason to lie. "Yes."

"You still miss her?" she asks softly.

"Every second of every day," I admit. "But it doesn't matter. I need to move on, but I just can't bring myself to let her go."

"Do you really think it's over between the two of you? If you're still so in love, don't you hold out some sort of hope?"

I shake my head. "It's over. We are incompatible, and there is nothing to be done for it."

"Oh," Tatiana breathes, tucking a small lock of hair behind her ear. "She doesn't even know how lucky she is to have had your devotion like that. I mean… she's even lucky now, just because you're missing her."

Tatiana's words are so kind that it touches the most painful part of my soul, and for a brief flash of time, it feels better. "You're too good for this world, Tati."

She looks up at me, eyes soft and liquid. "Not good enough for—never mind."

I know what she was about to say, but I let the statement die, knowing it can only hurt us both. Instead, I put an arm around her shoulders and pull her close in a loose embrace. "You're a good friend, Tatiana. I can be nothing but a friend to you, but I'd love to spend more time together. You're good for my sour personality, Flower Girl."

She hugs me back, tighter. "I'd like that."

Holding her slight frame, I feel a rush of guilt at not being able to fall for her or have feelings for her. She deserves everything under the sun. Anything she wants.

"Thank you for your support," I tell her. "I know I don't deserve your friendship, but I'm going to take it anyway."

She giggles in my embrace before pulling away. "That's fine. It's freely given."

"Good," I say simply, and we go back to watching the stars on the horizon.

Meanwhile, the curtains move the slightest bit behind us, a small dot of light appearing before it disappears just as quickly, and everything goes still again.

CHAPTER 11

Amsterdam, January 16, 2022
Roxanne

I hate being back in Karl's house, but so far he has kept things completely professional, to the point that at first he acted like he hadn't tried to get me into his bed the last time we saw each other. But when he called asking for four girls, as well as a bonus to make up for how quickly he needed them, I couldn't say no. The girls would want the money, and frankly, so did I.

So without asking if I was invited, I brought the girls myself, and stayed close by the entire time while Karl's dinner-party raged on. Well, rage is a strong word. His parties are usually full of older men; business acquaintances that he's trying to impress, and what's more impressive than a beautiful, willing young woman? The partygoers aren't exactly party animals because of their age, but otherwise Karl's get-togethers are great for business, his and mine alike. The party started soon enough, around seven p.m., and the girls are being paid for four hours of service. So I'll be here with them until eleven.

As the night wore on, my previous client became more and more friendly with me. At first I spurned him completely, but eventually he had me laughing, and I let my guard down. Damn him. I don't know how I keep falling into this stupid trap, but I guess I'm just too curious to refuse a private meeting with him to hear about a peculiar business proposition he's got for me.

As I wait for Karl to join me into his study, I feel my phone vibrate in my clutch, and I pull it out. It's a message from... *Elise?*

I open the text out of curiosity, and the picture makes me flush angrily, while simultaneously fighting back the tears that are making themselves known in the corners of my eyes. It's a picture of Andries and Tatiana, embracing on the terrace at the Van Den Bosch estate.

Elise: Looks like he's found the perfect match, and to no one's surprise, it isn't you.

I could write a novel in response, tearing her down, but I don't. I just shove the phone back onto my clutch and click it shut, forcing myself to focus on the moment.

I perch on the corner of his desk in his office, my bare legs crossed when Karl finally comes in and sits on a leather loveseat, drink in hand.

"It's nice seeing you in here again, Roxie. Do you remember what we were doing last time you were in my office?"

"Paperwork?" I answer, knowing good and well it was something much more illicit.

"No, I had you bent—"

I cut him off with a snap of my fingers. "No! If you're going to get weird, I'm leaving. You said you wanted to talk about a business proposition, which is the only reason I followed you here. So talk."

"You grow less and less fun with age," he gripes, and I feel an incredible urge to slap him across the face, but I resist, waiting for him to get on with whatever business offer he has. Thanks to me, Karl had received a significant promotion, which meant his deep pockets had become even deeper. He was one of few clients that could drop sickening amounts of money on a whim, and when that whim happened to be a group of my escorts, my girls and I would profit greatly.

Which is why I let him sulk without laughing in his face, patiently bouncing my foot and watching him. Finally he relents, taking another deep drink and sitting the whiskey glass aside. Now I notice that he seems oddly nervous, which is bizarre. I sell sex for a living, and he's a repeat customer. What could possibly have him feeling awkward after all this time?

"I need a specific sort of escort for an upcoming dinner, Roxie, and I'm not sure if it's even something you can help me with."

I can't help but raise an eyebrow at his comment. My interest is immediately perked, though. "Try me," I drawl.

"Here's the thing. I want an eighteen-year-old...*virgin*. Not just a naive girl or one that looks eighteen but is actually twenty-five. I want an eighteen-year-old virgin that has never been an escort before."

His question throws me through a loop, and then another one for good measure. Horrified, I ask, "You're wanting to take her virginity?"

"No. It's just for a simple dinner, but I do want her to stay overnight with me. I won't fuck her, I promise, but she has to meet my parameters, or I'm not interested."

I blow out a shaky breath. "And what she would sleep on? Your couch or something?"

Karl sighs. "No, Roxanne. She'd sleep in bed with me. But that's all it will be. Sleeping."

"It makes no sense. If you don't want to fuck her, why does it matter that she's a virgin?"

His voice is steely and serious. "I'm a man who knows what he wants, and this is what I want. Can you do it or not?"

The idea of sending a virgin into the clutches of Karl makes me feel ill, especially one that has no idea how to escort, either. I don't believe for a second he won't want to fuck the girl, but maybe he's just trying to make her comfortable for another gig later. Or is he trying to find his new "girlfriend"? Someone he could replace me with? After all, when he was my client, he wouldn't book any other woman for himself—at least that I'm aware of.

For the first time in so long, I question what I'm doing. All the awful things Andries said about sex work come back to me. His critiques were like little knives in my ears back then, but hearing Karl ask for a virgin makes me see what exactly Andries is opposed to. This kind of debauchery even makes me uncomfortable.

"I want her to sleep back at her home," I tell him. "You can have a drink with her here at your place, but you'll definitely need to sign a non-sex agreement for me to even consider this."

"No problem," Karl agrees.

"How much are you willing to pay?"

"Seven thousand," he says matter-of-factly, but I laugh in his face.

"Double."

He smirks, and I hate knowing he was fine paying that amount all along. I should have asked for more. "Double, then. Do we have a deal?"

"I have to find a girl first, I'm not even sure I can. If I do, I'll contact you to come and sign the paperwork. I've never had a request like this before, so I'll have to draw a brand new one up."

"Perfect," Karl says, and I find his tone oddly slimy. "I have another request for this situation, but it isn't one that should cause any problems."

"Fine, out with it, then." I wave my hand at him to hurry. I don't want to talk about this anymore.

"I'll be going by Robert. I've already been in the press too much with my divorce, and this is a strange situation even for an escort agency, so I want to keep it under wraps if possible."

"Sure, whatever." I pause for a moment, gathering my thoughts together. "This is going to be a three hour contract, two for the dinner and one back at your place for a last drink. At ten o'clock, an Uber will take her back home, so I recommend starting at seven." I can see how displeased he is at the shortness of the gig, so I add, "I really don't want her sleeping here, but if by any chance she agrees to that part, we'll come back around to discuss compensation and rules then."

"I knew I could count on you," Karl chuckles, finishing his glass. "A true *madam*. You can do anything, can't you, Roxie?"

His words are like ants crawling on my skin, and I shiver, wanting so badly to be done with this conversation now. I hop down from the desk and smooth my dress out and grabbing my clutch, I say, "You'll be lucky if I don't cancel this entire thing in the morning. I better hear that my girls here tonight get some extra-large tips if you want to stay in my good graces."

Karl makes an appreciative noise in his throat as I pass him by. "You know, you could stay if you wanted. I can give you a nice big tip too."

"Go fuck yourself Karl," I hiss, continuing out of the office without looking back.

I bid my girls farewell, making sure they know to check in with me once they are home. I'm going to turn in early tonight. I've got too much on my mind to stay and play mysterious party guest anymore.

Outside, while I wait on my Uber, I pull out my phone again and even though I know it will hurt, I look at the picture again. Andries isn't holding her too close, but there is clear affection in his body language. Tatiana, who is easier to see, looks like the happiest girl in the world, and her eyes seem to be closed in ecstasy at being near him. They're beautiful together. A perfect fit, spending time together on that gorgeous estate, both of them looking like they could be carved from the finest marble.

And here I am on a street at night, brokering a deal to provide a virgin for an old man. What the fuck is wrong with this life of mine? I love running my business, but requests like Karl's make my skin crawl, and tonight, it makes me realize how far apart Andries and I really are. We exist in two completely different worlds, and much to my displeasure, Tatiana lives in his world with him.

He'll never want to be with me again. Why would he? I'm older, and an ex-escort. He has Tatiana, and now that I am able to see things more clearly, I have to agree with everyone else: They are completely perfect for one another.

The morning dawns bright and cold, and I've barely slept. With the heaviness of exhaustion and the increasingly un-comfortable memories of Karl's request rolling through me, I shower as fast as I can, get dressed, and all but run to my office. If I'm going to get this Karl thing done, I want to do it soon, so I can never think about it again.

My assistant Poppy finds me at my desk an hour later, flipping through pages and pages of the resumes of current escorts I have and ones that have left the company. Of course, none of them are virgins, and only one of them is under the age of twenty, and I have no idea where to start.

Poppy hands me one of the paper coffee cups she's holding, and I barely taste it, just happy to have the thick coffee concoction filling my hollow stomach.

"Thanks for this," I tell her. "I was dying here."

"When I pulled up I saw the lights were on, and I figured if you came in that early you were going to need some espresso," she says matter-of-factly.

"Smart girl," I chuckle. "You want to sit down and help me figure out an impossible puzzle?"

"Well, sure. You're the boss, after all."

I explain to Poppy what Karl requested the night before, and she wrinkles her pale nose in disgust, but she agrees that it's an idea we can entertain for as much as he's willing to pay. The difficult part is finding someone who meets all the requirements and also wants to be an escort. Sex work isn't usually on the agenda for virgins, so it's going to be like finding a needle in a haystack.

I have to keep pushing away the thoughts of how apoplectic this whole thing would make Andries. He isn't here, and he doesn't matter. I can't let him matter anymore.

Poppy taps a pen on the table as she thinks everything over. "We've got, what, five girls on the roster now that also go to the university?" I nod, and she continues. "Why don't we have them ask around their friend groups? If we are going to find an eighteen-year-old virgin, university is going to be our best bet. College kids tend to be poor, and too busy to be worrying about sex too much. Those variables might combine to make the perfect girl for us appear. What do you think?"

It's the perfect approach, and I tell her so emphatically. She drafts an email for all the escorts that go to university and sends it out, making sure that it lays out all the parameters in as clear of detail as possible. Karl doesn't have any preferences for hair, eye, or skin color; just that she's eighteen, not a current escort, and has never had sex before.

It's going to be a tricky thing, so I tell Poppy to add that the compensation will be €10,000 for a two-hour dinner with a client. No sex involved. Did I leave the hour at his place out on purpose? Yes, I'll get down to the gritty details later on.

Once the emails have been sent, I'm able to relax for a second while we wait for the girls to get back to us. I'm fully prepared to tell Karl to kick rocks if we can't find the perfect girl for him, but I'm conflicted on how I really want this to go. Do I want to be paid? Yes. Do I trust Karl? No. Not really. Whoever we hire will have to be smart and forward enough to make him back off if he tries anything out of line.

Poppy leaves to pick up our lunch, and I mull over the other big event of last night; the text from Elise. At first I was baffled about how she had gotten my number, but then I remembered we swapped them in Ghent. Back when she didn't think I was more worthless than the dirt on the bottom of her shoes.

After the way we argued when I went to Andries' apartment to get my things, it isn't a shock that she'd try to press my buttons, but I'm surprised she'd use her brother and her friend as ammunition to do so. She must really think that I'm a terrible choice for him, and wants me to stay away at all costs.

Well, if he's with Tatiana, Elise doesn't need to worry. I'd never come between a couple like that.

Impulsively, I send Dan a message, asking him outright if Tatiana and Andries are a couple. He takes a few minutes to message back, but he seems bewildered when he does.

Dan: No? I told you they weren't. What makes you ask that question?

Instead of explaining it, I just send him a screenshot of the text and picture. This time he answers right away.

Dan: Fucking Elise. I was there with all of them last night, and when they came in from the terrace, they were acting totally normal. I think that's a friend hug that Elise is trying to use to manipulate you. And them too, which is messed up.

Roxanne: Are you sure things just haven't changed between them, and you haven't noticed? Or maybe they're just taking things slow since she's so... you know. She's his 'Flower Girl,' remember?

Dan: Andries is too over the top and broody to hide a relationship. We all knew he was obsessed with you from the jump, so don't worry about it. They. Are. Just. Friends.

Roxanne: Okay. okay. Thanks, Dan. Really.

Dan: No prob. By the way, he seemed more like himself last night. I wouldn't be surprised if he reaches out to you soon.

Huh. I don't think he'll ever reach out to me again, especially if he hears about what I'm planning with Karl, so I don't even know what I'd say if he did call. Before he left for his family's estate, I had told him clearly that I wanted a second chance. If he accepted what I do for a living, would I try again?

Yeah, there was no doubt in my mind that I would.

CHAPTER 12

Amsterdam, January 31, 2022
Andries

The last two weeks have passed both faster than I could comprehend and, at the same time, at an excruciatingly slow pace. Commuting to class has been a pain, but I have to reluctantly admit that Mom was right; staying home meant I didn't drink nearly as much anymore. The added stress of having to drive back to Amsterdam almost daily certainly wasn't my favorite part of the day, but it did keep me busy enough that I was thinking about Roxanne less. Not much less, but anything was better than her occupying my every waking thought.

Distance also helped with the constant anticipation I had of seeing her. At home, there is never any fear that I'll leave the house and she'll be there; flawless, glowing, and utterly disturbing to me in so many ways. I hate her, and I hate that I still love her, but maybe this little bit of forward momentum I have made is a good sign. For the first time in so long I think I might have a chance of coming out of this entire thing without too much damage.

None of that means that I'm not still dreaming of her, to the point I'd wake up both completely erect, heartbroken, and pissed off. It's an extremely uncomfortable state to be in, as well as a confusing one. But if I can only see Roxanne in my dreams instead of every waking minute, then I guess that's better than I can have hoped for a few weeks ago.

Another perk of staying at home is that all the drama from the YouTube video has finally begun to die down as well. No longer was I the center of attention while also being oddly ostracized. I never wanted to be popular, or engage with a bunch of people at university, so that part didn't bother me, but the snorts and laughter when I passed by had gotten old pretty fast. I wanted to punch a lot more people than just the YouTuber at times, but I held both my tongue and my fists. It'd do me no good to be scrapping when I was also in the middle of trying to pull my grades up out of the hole I had allowed them to slip into.

Speaking of school, there is still one little issue: hiding the fact that I'm an English major from my parents while living under their roof. The house might be massive, but after all my issues, my family seems to always want to track me down and get into my business. I can't hide being an English student forever, but it's a problem I didn't need piled on top of all the other ones I'm fighting through. It might be a lie I tell myself to feel better, but I really do plan on coming clean, eventually. One day...

To be honest, I do miss my apartment, and all the things privacy has allowed me. I'm a solitary person so much of the time that being able to have my own space is something I value more than I realized until I was back in my crowded family home. I'm sad to see the apartment being emptied bit by bit, but moving out has already proven that a fresh start is what I need. It seems crazy that a place I lived for such a short amount of time can hold so many important memories, but it truly does. Good and bad...

After all, it's here that Roxanne and I had first made love, where I had first realized the depth of my feelings for her, and where we had behaved almost like a family until I had discovered the depths of her betrayal. Leaving behind the rooms where she had breathed soft sighs and laughter with me is sometimes so tragic that it makes my chest hurt, but I'm in the final stretch now. I'm almost free of all that tainted love.

This evening is the last one of packing up my apartment, and even though I'd have had more space to be creative and introspective if I did it alone, Dan and Elise had invited themselves in joining me to help. Plus, to top it all, I have to sleep in the apartment since the realtor will be coming so early to check the place and release the deposit. After so many weeks sleeping at home, I was dreading it, oddly enough. So maybe having my friend and my sister around for a large portion of the evening would make it less difficult to swallow.

Having them helping me also means I have to be two steps ahead of Elise at all times. Elise, the up-and-coming detective, is always on high alert, and truthfully, I have an embarrassing amount of poetry and narrative work about my ex. Dan knows my secrets well enough that he can also keep her at bay, but even he can't hide everything. Luckily, he also has the special talent of pissing her off like nothing else in the universe can, so that can buy me some time if I ever needed it.

Now, as we finish packing the last few boxes and bags, I'm fighting hard against feeling completely miserable. I don't want to stay here tonight—I know all the memories will come on full force, as well as the dreams that refuse to leave. The only thing I can think to do is stay up all night, but that has its own set of problems. What's better; being conscious of your own misery or having it haunt your unconscious mind?

It turns out I don't have as many possessions as I first thought, and most of my boxes are just heavy with books. I'm forever thankful for moving companies and interior designers that will put everything back together for me at my new apartment, but packing just feels so personal. It's a process of putting my entire life away bit by bit and holding it all in my hands so I can reminisce.

With all the boxes and bags lined up against the wall, there isn't much left to do. The appliances came with the apartment, so the kitchen is still usable, and if the sounds coming from Dan's stomach are of any indication, it's well past dinner time.

"I don't have much, mostly canned stuff," I tell the two of them, sweeping my slightly sweaty hair up and off my forehead. "But I can make us something, if you guys want to stay for dinner."

Elise, knowing how much I love to cook, smiles politely. "That sounds lovely."

Dan, on the other hand, is not convinced. "Screw that, let's order in. You know, you're supposed to pay your friends with pizza and beer for helping you move. At least that's what some exchange student told me one time."

Elise wrinkles her nose. "I don't want beer and pizza. Plus, Andries has stopped drinking for the most part."

"Alright," I say, pulling up my delivery app on my phone and tossing it to my sister. "Pick whatever you guys want. It's on me, apparently."

My sister looks ready to protest, but Dan rubs his hands together and plucks the phone from her grip. "Don't mind if I do!"

As expected, the two of them bicker over what we are ordering, but I'm busy taking in the setting sun over the river from the enormous windows. I heave a long sigh, knowing I'll miss this view terribly, but this is all for a good cause. I need to stay strong, or I'm going to be overcome with regrets.

Elise and Dan decide on Thai food, and I add an order of pineapple fried rice for myself before submitting the order. There are still stools at the breakfast bar, but being the fanciful person she is, Elise insists on us having dinner picnic style in the middle of the floor. She digs a blanket out from one of the boxes and spreads it wide, taking a seat at one corner with her legs crossed.

"This is stupid," Dan mutters, but he isn't put off by it as much as he lets on, because he follows suite, leaning back on his palms as he sits.

Since I apparently don't get an opinion, I join the two of them as soon as the food arrives, and we spread it out between us. It's immediately clear we had ordered an obscene amount of food, but my guests don't seem to mind, opening boxes and taking small pieces and servings from each.

After briefly wondering how expensive this order had been, I shrug, and do the same as them, gathering dumplings, wontons, and everything else before we all actually begin to eat. Conversation flows easily, and even though it's a melancholic evening for me, this part of it isn't so bad.

"Are you sure you don't want to just come back to the estate and drive back here in the morning?" Elise asks. "It's weird leaving you in this empty place."

I shake my head. "There's no way I can make it by nine a.m., when the realtor comes. This is just giving me a few extra hours of sleep."

There's more on Elise's mind, and after a few pointed looks from her, I give in. "What's wrong?"

She sits down her chopsticks and sighs heavily. "I just don't see why you have to even get another apartment. You've been doing so well at home…"

"Yeah, you would know, since you're constantly up my ass," I reply, causing Dan to laugh.

"I'm just worried, okay? It helps me be less anxious about you being out somewhere ruining your life if I can see you from time to time."

"Elise…" I blow out a breath. "The commute is bullshit, and I need to be independent. I'm an adult."

"I think you know why I'm so worried. You weren't exactly prepared properly for the real world."

This gives me pause. "Why do you say that? I lived abroad for a year."

My sister seems to be struggling to find the right words, wanting to explain herself while also not bad-mouthing our parents, but Dan saves her by interjecting.

"I think she's trying to say you weren't ready for the heartbreak that comes with it. In the real world, people lie, keep secrets, cheat, deceive, sell sex for money…"

Dan has a point. A really good one, actually. Of course, I knew about things like drug use and escorts when I moved here last year, but I wasn't ready for the lies and deceptions that came with my first relationship.

"You aren't wrong," I say grudgingly. "But I still think that's a problem with society itself, not in the way Elise and I were raised."

"I don't know," Dan replies. "Like I said, a lot of us love the city and all the gritty parts of it. We don't want something that has been scrubbed clean. The immoral side of it can be fun sometimes."

"I guess I'm just not a fun person, then."

"Yes," Dan laughs. "We already knew that."

I let it go, not wanting to get into this argument with Dan for what feels like the millionth time. I know I shouldn't care that he enjoys the seedier parts of the city, but I just wish I didn't have to know about it so much.

We continue eating, the food made better by the company I share, and it feels like the perfect send off for a space I wish hadn't become so irreparably tainted in such a short amount of time. Still, it'd be an enormous weight off my soul to never have to step foot in here again soon enough.

"Can you pass the—oh, hold on." Elise jumps up, grabbing her purse and sitting back down. I can hear her phone vibrating inside, and she pulls it out to read the text.

Her face goes through a range of emotions; shock, disgust, and then annoyance, obvious from her tightly pursed lips. I ignore it, figuring it is something going on with her friend group, but I see her eyes darting to me as she reads.

"What, Elise?" I ask in a groan.

"It's my friend Cassey. She just texted me something that I can't even wrap my head around. Do you remember Patricia, the girl that sent me the voice message?"

"Yeah."

"Well, Cassey just texted me because it seems like Patricia just took a job offer from the one and only Roxanne."

My world threatens to tilt on its axis at the name, but I keep my cool. "No way. Everyone you hang around is barely eighteen. Did Roxanne need a fucking receptionist or something?"

Elise leans in, appearing both scandalized but also excited to share such incredibly dramatic gossip. "No. As an escort! I guess she was offered €10k for only four hours of work! Can you believe that?"

Even Dan frowns. "But she's at least eighteen, right?"

"Yes," Elise confirms. "But like for a month or so."

"That's…" I shake my head, the convo we just had with Dan replaying in my mind. "That's disgusting."

"I'm going to text Patricia directly," Elise says, typing on her phone. "I have to know if it's true."

My appetite gone, I push my food away, clicking the to-go lid back into place on a few of the dishes. Dan is not fazed by the conversation, and continues eating, but Elise is so invested in her phone that she is letting her food go cold. I pack hers back up too.

My sister's phone vibrates again, and Elise gasps. "It's true! Oh my God!" She lets out a slightly hysterical giggle. "I can't believe she's going to go prostitute herself just for some money."

"I don't even know what to say." The emotions that cascade through me are overwhelming because there are so many variables to what is going on.

Elise's friend is a fool, and a naive one at that, but Roxanne stands out as such a predator that it makes me want to be sick. She's clearly recruiting young women, just as they become legal adults, and offering them a large sum of money to be escorts for her. These girls, some of them at least, could need money desperately, and the offers would be too good for someone to dismiss. It's such a simple first step into sex trade, but who knows how long they would stay?

"That's not all," Elise continues. "Patricia is being hired because she's a virgin, and a client of your ex requested an eighteen-year-old virgin for tomorrow night."

My stomach rolls and I stop in my tracks, staring dumfounded at my sister as she continues texting. "You have to be joking?"

Instead of responding, Elise turns her phone around and lets me read the text messages myself. Patricia had been approached by Cassey herself who explained the deal that Roxanne was offering to a single eighteen-year-old for a one-night gig. Once I finish, Elise takes her phone back, soaking up my reaction.

"I don't even know how she's going to do the deed, you know what I mean? Patricia is so anxious and shy. To think that she's going to have sex for the very first time with a stranger is so freaky!"

"Why don't you just ask her?" Dan chimes in. "Make sure she knows what she's getting herself into."

Elise does just that. To keep myself from losing my mind, I clean up the takeout, throwing it into the refrigerator even though I'll be out of the apartment tomorrow. Anything to keep myself busy. I try not to listen for the vibration of my sister's phone, signifying a reply, but I still notice it the moment it comes in.

"Oh. Well, that explains a lot," Elise says. "There's no sex going on, apparently. Roxanne made the guy sign a no-sex clause, or something."

I clench my teeth, taking a deep breath to try and center myself. "But that's bullshit, right? If the guy didn't plan on fucking her, then why would it matter she's a virgin or not? Roxanne could have sent an escort she already had on the payroll and just *lied* to the guy about it. She has to know the guy is going to try to pull something."

Elise shrugs. "I have no idea. Patricia seems pretty sure, though."

I can't help but shake my head. "She's just walking into the lion's den, and she doesn't even know it. Did you tell her she's being naive as fuck?"

"In not so many words, yes, but Patricia needs the money, so there's nothing I can say to talk her out of it, anyway."

I barely know the girl, having only talked to her once at my birthday when she was standing next to my sister and Elise decided to introduce me to her, but I feel almost absurdly upset about the situation she's putting herself into. It seems like she has no one there to protect her or explain how things would really be as an escort to her. Instead, Roxanne had found her, and her head was already being filled with these dreams of big paychecks, but in reality, she would just spend a bunch of time being used like a toy. There is no amount of money that could possibly be worth it, but

Roxanne apparently found an offer high enough to catch a few girls who don't know better.

It makes me think of Elise. If Roxanne and I had never met, then it could have easily been my own sister that Roxanne was trying to lure into escorting. Of course, Elise would never have fallen for such a farce, but this situation has made it terribly clear how close to my family Roxanne's horrifying business could get. I'm sure it isn't just Roxanne, either. There are dozens of businesses that provide girls for the red-light district, and the more those agency owners and pimps normalize and glamorize that lifestyle, the easier it will be to lure young women into.

"I need some space," I tell Elise and Dan. My sister looks mildly amused, but Dan looks annoyed. If I wasn't about to explode, I'd have stayed to see what's going on with him, but that just isn't an option right now.

It feels like miles that I have to walk before I can shut myself in my bedroom, and once I do, seeing nothing but my bed in the center of the room makes me even angrier. I was fleeing this apartment to get away from a woman who is so unbothered by our split that she's actively seeking out barely legal girls to escort for her. Roxanne herself might not be escorting anymore, but if this is what she's spending her time doing, it's even worse.

I had planned on just coming into this room to catch my breath and get my emotions under control, but my phone is weighing me down like a brick in my pocket. I'm just a few finger taps away from speaking to my ex herself and getting the answers that I want. Not only that, I can feel the words I want to say to her burning like acid on my tongue. I want to tear her down and make her feel like shit, just like I do right now. But if I call her, then she'll know how much she is bothering me, and how close she still is to the top of my mind.

To avoid calling, I grab a half-full notebook from one of the packed boxes and try to write. I'm going through so much with the move, my struggle to stop drinking, and my breakup, so I should be able to write about all those things I have to overcome. With all the chaos in my mind, writing should be a way for me to bleed some of that chaos out into something beautiful and meaningful. Instead, those terrible feelings aren't tangible to me. They are slimy and hard to grasp, and without being able to fully grasp my feeling, I just can't write them out. It's like trying to hold smoke.

I'm supposed to be a poet. Pain and heartache are supposed to be my bread and butter, the catalysts for brilliance, but everything I'm feeling seems so ugly that I don't want my hands to even shape the words. I hate this, and at the same time, it makes me hate myself.

"Fuck it," I breathe to no one but the room.

I toss the notebook aside and pull my phone out. After all this time I haven't fully blocked Roxanne's number, so it's easy to just open my contacts and call her. Doing so makes me feel just as dirty as sneaking a drink would, like I'm giving into my addiction while hiding it away from everyone else. I'm only human, though, and this would be a one-time mistake if I had anything to say about it.

I can't stop thinking about Patricia, and the problems that are sure to come if she follows through with the gig. I try to picture myself at eighteen, because imagining my own sister is too painful and unsettling, showing up to sleep with a total stranger. It makes me feel nauseous, and even panicked.

Patricia can't go through with this! She'll never be able to get back what she is potentially about to lose. Not just her physical virginity, either. She'd be giving up her dignity, self-respect, and innocence.

Roxanne had told me, after I confronted her, that there was no way I could understand what it was like being poor, or in need of money to live, and while I've never been in that situation personally, the answer to such a problem can't possibly be whoring yourself out.

I'm reaching the breaking point, and I know I have to do something, or I'll never be able to live with myself. There are two options in front of me: call Patricia and try to talk her out of everything, or call Roxanne and tell her to drop this whole virgin escort nonsense. I have a better chance of convincing Patricia, if she's really as timid and soft-spoken as Elise makes her out to be, but I also have the unfortunate personal connection with Roxanne that may give me some sway. If I had more time, I'd arrange a meetup with her for coffee or lunch, no matter how awful it would make me feel, just to be able to see her face to face and present my argument. I'd make that sacrifice for one of Elise's friends, no hesitation. But there is no time for that.

I barely know Patricia, so the obvious choice, no matter how distasteful, is to call Roxanne. I'm seething, and while tearing into her immediately might make me feel better in the moment, it won't solve any of the problems that need to be solved. I know she's probably still desperate to talk to me, so getting her to answer won't be a problem. It's just keeping my temper in check.

Mind made up, I pull up Roxanne's contact and call. It's almost comical that I'm doing so in the room where we first had sex, but there's basically nowhere in this apartment I can escape the memories of her anyway.

She answers after a few rings, and it's then I notice that I've broken out in a sweat.

"Andries...?" Her voice is soft, cautious, yet achingly hopeful.

"Roxanne," I respond, trying my damnedest to keep the emotions out of my own tone.

"It's...well, it's been awhile," she points out, her tone making my heart ache even more.

"It has," I agree, but I need to center myself and keep my focus. "Look, this isn't the social call you're hoping it is."

"Ah." She doesn't speak for a second, trying to suss out exactly what my reason for calling is. "Well, go ahead, then."

"Elise just got a message from a friend of hers about how Patricia has recently joined your team of escorts."

She huffs. "So? Patricia is an adult, she can make her own decisions, just like every other woman that works for me."

Upon hearing her answer, I can't hold my political correctness anymore and unleash immediately. "She just turned eighteen, Roxanne! She's an adult in the loosest sense of the word. How can you be so immoral as to hire someone like that? You're putting her in a vulnerable position that she can't even begin to comprehend!"

"From my perspective, you don't comprehend it either, Andries. I didn't seek Patricia out specifically. I put out some feelers for someone that had her specific... attributes, and she was the one who responded. There is never any pressure on my end."

I scoff at her cold and calculated tone. She's indeed a perfect madam. "Those attributes being her innocence and virginity, right? You disgust me, even more than the old decrepit man you're forcing this young woman to spend the evening with."

"What part of '*no pressure on my end*' are you not getting? No one is forcing anyone. Patricia was more than happy to spend time with this 'old man' for ten thousand euros. And if you or your nosy sister had actually talked to Patricia, then you probably know that she isn't even going to sleep with him," Roxanne spits out.

"There is no way in hell you're ever going to convince me that this man's end goal isn't to fuck Patricia, and you're just throwing her to the wolves."

"You're just too young to understand," she comments, before chuckling sardonically. "Too young, and too rich. You think I'm dirtying this girl for life, but she thinks I'm providing her with an amazing opportunity to make an enormous amount of money. You just can't see this through any other lens than the one you were born with."

"I'm not too young to see that you're dipping into my sister's pool of friends to find these girls, and that's a little too close to home for my taste! Why don't you go back to plucking trash out of the gutter to work for you and leave Elise's friends alone? Or was this just a tactic to get back at me one more time?"

"Actually, I didn't know that Patricia was Elise's friend. I never would have hired her had I known, but she's already signed the contract, and the gig is tomorrow, so it's too late to find someone else." She pauses, considering something for a few seconds. "From now on I'll look a bit deeper into who I'm hiring and make sure there aren't any... conflicts of interest, shall we say. That's all I can offer you at this point, Andries."

"That's a lie, because you can call this off at any time, you just don't want to," I bite back my more acidic words as they try to spill forward. "You truly are so different from the woman I fell in love with." My tone comes off more nostalgic than I expected, but I don't care, and tell her the rest. "The Roxanne I knew was an intellectual. She loved to sit at the bookshop with me and talk about the world, life, and everything in between. What did you even get out of living such a lie? How did you enjoy pretending to be someone else for so long?"

"Not that it matters, but that person *is* the real me. Just like this person is now. People have different facets, and they can be more than one thing." Roxanne sounds exhausted.

"There's no way the repulsive user of young women is in any way the woman I knew. I refuse to even consider that, but you can continue to lie to yourself if you want to," I sneer, unable to keep the venom out of my tone any longer. "And to think I spent so much of my time missing you…" I shake my head at my own naiveté. And there I was thinking Roxanne would've called this thing off for me. But no—she isn't gonna do shit. "Well, I'm done here. Goodbye, Roxanne."

"Andries, wait—" Roxanne starts to plead, but I've already hung up the phone.

The cruelest part is, had Roxanne acted horrified and had put things in motion to change the situation, it'd have undoubtedly softened my heart toward her. Instead, she continued to stick hard to the opinion that there is nothing wrong with what she's doing. It makes me wonder if who I was dating was nothing but a ghost, because at this point, she is basically dead and gone from my life.

I'm still fuming when Dan knocks once before entering the bedroom, looking worried.

"Hey, man. I'm leaving to take Elise home. Is everything okay in here?"

"Fine," I bite out as I rub my eyes tiredly.

Dan takes a few steps in to get a better look at me, and when he does, he flinches in sympathy. "You don't look fine. What's up?"

I take a few deep breaths, before telling him the truth. "I'm just so disgusted by the situation with Patricia. I called Roxanne to get the truth about it, hoping I was wrong about something, but all she did was double down and confirm everything I feared. I can't seem to escape her, Dan, and the horrible things she does with her life continue to taint mine."

Dan sighs in annoyance, crossing his arms. "Man, why do you even care so much about what these girls do in their spare time? It's really none of our business unless we're dating them. Patricia made a choice of her own accord, and it shouldn't matter what people like her do in private. You need to just let it go. It's fine to disapprove of something in your own life and not partake in it, like sex work, but nothing will ever come of judging other people for the way they want to live their lives and make their money."

"Money, money, money," I repeat, growing tired of the same shitty argument as I leave the bed and walk toward him. "Isn't that all it comes down to, time and time again? No, wait. This is Amsterdam, so it's money, sex, and drugs," I scoff. "The longer I live here, Dan, the more I lose faith in humanity."

Dan rolls his eyes, which hurts me a bit. It feels like he's dismissing what's bothering me, but as someone who approves of debauchery like what Roxanne does, it's not a surprise.

"The brooding poet is at it again I see." He chuckles, shaking his head in disapproval. "I'm out of here. Elise is ready to go. I'll talk to you soon."

I ignore him, and before long, I hear the door shut as he and my sister depart. The apartment is eerily silent, and I'm left with nothing but my own racing thoughts, and the disbelief that I had once loved someone who could act so callously without even thinking twice.

Out of options, I sit down on the bed and try to write again. The words come, stilted and rough, but at least it isn't a blank page.

CHAPTER 13

Amsterdam, February 2, 2022
Roxanne

I barely slept those past two nights, thinking about Patricia and wishing it was an event I could be there for her. I'm not usually so overbearing of a boss that I need to see everything that is going on, but the fact that she knows Elise and that Andries is so put off by her completing this job makes me want to crawl out of my skin.

Andries had voiced, out loud, the same concerns I had. Why was Karl so insistent that the escort be a virgin if he wasn't going to try and sleep with her? I didn't get too much detail about the event itself, so maybe having an eighteen-year-old virgin was just some sort of status symbol for older men like Karl, but that didn't make me feel any better.

If something went wrong...if Karl messed with that girl...it'd be very difficult for me to live it down in a professional sense. Not to mention, I don't know if I can ever forgive myself for taking such a risk when it's someone else's body at stake, not mine.

Escorting is a risky business, I just hadn't realized how much harder it would be working behind the scenes and not in the thick of it myself.

Once I get to the office this morning, I head straight to my desk, giving Poppy a brief wave. My stomach is churning, and I need to find out everything that happened once and for all. There had been no middle of the night calls from Karl or Patricia, and all my girls know they can call me any time of the day, so no unspeakable disasters had occurred. But that wasn't what I was worried about, anyway. I have no reason to ever think Karl would be physically violent with one of my escorts. It's the more insidious, lecherous problems that he can cause that I'm frightened of.

Being a man that had been pushy with me in the past, Karl may get mad when he's denied, but he knows that my wrath would know no bounds if he did something to my girls. While our meeting at Charlie's New Year party had ended tensely, he didn't chase me down or treat me badly afterwards, so I had been sure at the time that I was making the right decision with Patricia. Now, though, Andries had sowed doubts into me, and I can't seem to get rid of them.

My iPhone beeps with an SMS letting me know that I have received a new voicemail, and it's from Karl himself. Why am I so reluctant to listen? Is it because I'm afraid of what the potential bad news will put into motion?

I close my eyes and take a slow, steadying breath. *If Karl has hurt this girl in any way, I will do right by her. Legally, monetarily, emotionally... I will pay for whatever she needs. Lawyers, therapists...whatever. I'll do it.*

I'll have to take the hit, either to my business or to myself personally, but I have to maintain my integrity. If my other escorts see me let such a young, naive woman like Patricia suffer, I'll never have their full trust again. And, honestly, I shouldn't if I did something like that.

With my heart in my throat, I press the "play" button, and listen to the voicemail that comes through. It's from Karl, who seems pleased, if a bit vague. Nothing he says should set any alarm bells off, but something about it does anyway.

"*We had a better time than I could have hoped,*" he ends the message with. "*And I think she'll tell you the same. Thanks again Roxie.*"

Lips pursed, I go to delete the voicemail, but at the last second think better of it and save it instead. Just in case.

I try to focus on the rest of my daily work, but it's all just wasting time until Patricia arrives to give me all the information about her first gig from last night. Some girls think they're cut out for escort work, but once they actually try it for themselves they discover that it isn't something that they are comfortable with, or that they aren't able to separate sex from an emotional connection in their minds. I never have a single issue with new hires that don't want to stick with it, but it's always better to find these things out before they take more gigs that they aren't enthused about working. All that does is leave the woman feeling unsettled and her client frustrated that they paid for a warm companion but instead received an uncomfortable ice queen.

Patricia finally arrives about an hour after I do, looking fresh faced, but wearing a neutral expression, her blonde hair pushed in a high ponytail. I have her payment already written out, but I want to soothe my nerves and get a rundown of her experience before I send her on her way.

"Come in and sit down, Patricia," I tell her, waving her toward one of the chairs across from my desk. She sits with her back as straight as possible, but what sets off alarm bells in my head is the wince she does before sitting fully, as if she is sore.

Oh no, I think. *No, no, no.*

Keeping my expression blank, I ask her how everything went. Patricia is a small, fair blonde, and it's easy to see the slight blush on her cheeks.

"It went fine," she says simply.

I take her paycheck out of my desk and slide it across the glass surface toward her. She takes it with careful fingers, looking at it for a long moment before sliding it into her purse. She doesn't meet my gaze, or initiate conversation, so I press on.

"So you didn't have any problems with Robert, right?"

Patricia chews her bottom lip eyes darting around the room. I can feel my blood pressure rising. She looks ashamed, and I can't let her leave until I know the whole of the truth.

"Yeah, he was nice," she replies, twisting the hem of her shirt in her fingers.

I sigh heavily, rubbing my temples. "Patricia, I've been in this business long enough to know that something is bothering you. What's going on?"

She hesitates before shaking her head. "Really, it's nothing. Can I go home now?"

"If you just didn't enjoy the experience, that's completely fine. You never have to do it again. But I'm sensing that it's something more than that, and the second you signed that contract you were under the umbrella of my business. So, I'll ask again, and this time I want a real answer. Did you have any problems with Robert?"

"I don't want you to be mad at me," she admits meekly.

I soften my tone and look her directly in the eye. "I won't be mad at you, I swear. I just need to know what went on. I can't protect you or my other girls if clients are acting foolish and it's not being reported."

Like a puppet on strings, Patricia folds her body inward, burying her face in her hands. "Oh, I'm so sorry. I messed up."

I sit forward, pulse racing. "I need to know in detail, Patricia."

"He said I should keep it between me and him, that it's something that needs to be kept under wraps."

"There is nothing 'between you and a client' that goes on here. This is my agency, and anything that happens, good or bad, has to go through me first."

She looks like she wants to cry, but I'm a little proud of the eighteen-year-old when she tips her chin up bravely and fully admits to her mistakes. "We were drinking champagne, and I've only drank like one other time in my life. I got tipsy and...and..." She sniffles. "I went up to his apartment with him and we..." she swallows before her gaze drops to her lap. "We ended up having sex, and I spent the night there, since I passed out."

The silence in the room is deafening, pressing on my eardrums like water in a deep pool.

Patricia's eyes are red-ringed from crying, and how close she is to tears right now, where I can feel the blood draining from my face at her words.

I want to kill Karl with my bare hands. He had done everything he had promised me he wouldn't, and then had the audacity to leave me a voicemail about what a lovely night he had. Probably while she was still passed out in his bed! I'll never trust him as a client, or as a man, never ever again! This was his plan since the beginning—find a naive young woman, get her drunk to get rid of her inhibitions and then take full advantage of her.

I can't let Patricia sit here without saying anything, but my emotions are out of control. Nothing at this job has ever made me as angry as I'm right in this moment. Just like Andries said, Karl had just wanted to take the virginity of a girl that was barely legal. My stomach rolls and I have to force acid back down my throat.

I let this happen. I was supposed to keep her safe and I let this happen.

Just looking at her sitting across from me, her hands folded and held between her legs while she watches me with big, wet eyes, makes me want to scream. Nothing like this has ever happened at my agency, and hopefully the non-disclosure agreements both parties signed will keep my professional reputation safe, but it doesn't change the fact that I will know what happened forever.

"I told you not to drink if you can't handle alcohol, and I told you specifically not to drink more than a glass. You blatantly disregarded my directions..." I return to rubbing my temples, the headache building threatening to incapacitate me with its severity. "But regardless this is all on Robert. He took advantage of you and I'm going to handle this *right now*."

I grab my office phone and begin to type in his number when Patricia seems to snap out of her trance and surges forward, pushing the hang-up button.

"Don't!" she exclaims. "I was sending mixed signals. It isn't all Robert's fault!"

I throw her hand off the phone in misdirected anger. "I don't care if you told him outright that you wanted him to fuck you. He signed a no-sex agreement, and he broke that as soon as he brought you to his place. So whatever mistakes you made are vastly eclipsed by what he did. But just for curiosity's sake, why don't you lay out to me how this all went down, Patricia?"

She's full-on crying now and has to wipe her face before she can begin. "Well, we went to that dinner event, and it was such a fun time. Everyone there was drinking this expensive champagne, and they didn't seem affected by it at all, so when Robert offered me some I just took it."

I reach over and hand her a tissue. She gently blots her eyes before continuing. "I was only going to have one glass, but it was so good, and since no one else seemed drunk I figured it must have a really low alcohol content. So I drank more, and by the time the dinner was over, and I was supposed to go back to Robert's for the last hour, I was very tipsy."

"Did he notice you were tipsy?"

She nods. "Oh yes. He helped me to leave the restaurant and get into the car, but he wasn't mad about it! He just said I was adorable when I had been drinking. And, well, it was really nice to hear him say that. After spending all night around so many beautiful, wealthy people, the idea that he'd still be so intrigued by me made me want even more of his attention. It felt… good. It made me feel important."

As sick as her testimony makes me feel, I can't help but also feel a sense of understanding toward her. I had been that girl once, too, getting drunk on champagne I couldn't afford, and the attention of wealthy older men was very validating. It had given me a heady feeling of importance and self-worth, but when they eventually got tired of me I felt even more hollow than before.

"What happened next?" I ask.

Patricia takes a few breaths and ponders for a moment before she continues. "When we went upstairs he was showering me with compliments, saying how much he wished I could stay the night, and how lucky the first guy I'll sleep with will be. I remember hinting that it could be him if he really wanted but after that… I don't remember too much. I know he was gentle, and that I never said no, but I was so drunk at that point I had no idea what I really wanted."

"The most important instruction for the night was not to drink more than a single glass. And at my agency, an instruction is an *order* put in place to keep you safe. I can't keep my girls safe if they aren't following the rules I lay out." I exhale, leaning back in my chair and staring at the ceiling. "I think it's best we part ways, Patricia. Breaking the rules is a big no for me."

Her tears start to come hot and fast again, her bottom lip quivering. "This is all my fault, isn't it? I ruined this good thing I had going for myself and now all I have to show for losing my virginity is a check!"

I can't lie, I'm also angry at Patricia. I had tried my best to impart on her the importance of not drinking more than a glass and insisted that no matter how she felt the night of, she was never supposed to have sex with Robert. As soon as I let her out on her own, she broke all of my rules, and put me in this absolutely disastrous situation.

Still, my heart aches for her. She looks so young and vulnerable that I can't help coming around to her side of the desk, pulling up a chair in front of her, and taking both her hands in mine.

"Just because you made mistakes doesn't mean this was your fault. Robert knew the rules, he was sober, much older, and had signed numerous agreements put in place to keep you safe. It wasn't your fault, Patricia."

Through sniffles, she nods, squeezing my hands back. "I'm not even really mad at him. If I hadn't been paid to be there, he'd have been the perfect date, you know?"

"He's a very charming, convincing man, I'll agree, but in my opinion this still borders on assault." As I say the last word, a terrible thought comes into mind. "Patricia, did you tell anyone about this?"

She shakes her head immediately, but the way her eyes widened made me suspicious. I reach up and grab her chin between my thumb and forefinger, forcing her to look into my eyes.

"Patricia, this is important. Did. You. Tell. Anyone?"

She tries to shake her head in denial again, but it's like she's trying to convince herself, not me. Finally, she pulls away from me and buries her face in her hands again.

"Just one friend, and only in a joking way, since she was accusing me the night before of wanting to lose my V-card to

Robert and I told her I wasn't. I just admitted she was right, and I was wrong."

With the way the day is going so far, I know where this is leading, because any sort of good luck has vanished from my life long ago. "Is this friend you told in college with you?"

"Yeah." She sighs as she wipes her wet cheeks with her sleeves. "I don't have to tell you her name, do I? I want to keep my friends out of this mess as long as possible."

I'm already on my feet, grabbing my bag and my coat. "No, you don't. I have a sneaking suspicion that I know who it is anyway."

Patricia watches me leave, confusion on her face. I stop at Poppy's desk and tell her to keep an eye on Patricia and to call her an Uber if she decided she wanted to go home.

I didn't have any proof for my hypothesis about Patricia's friend, but I just feel in my gut that I know the answer. Andries had mentioned Elise finding out about Patricia's escorting through text, which meant Elise and Patricia are friends. If Patricia has told Elise about what happened, then I'm well and truly fucked, and will likely never be able to speak to Andries ever again. I don't know if I can manage to keep this under wraps, but I have to try.

I'm on the edge of my seat the whole way to Andries' apartment, calling him over and over to no avail. I know he's been ignoring me for weeks now, but I at least thought he would be more likely to answer since he called me himself a few nights ago. Of course, he sends me to voicemail every single time, until I have to sit the phone down to avoid throwing it out of the moving car.

When I finally arrive at his place, I have an odd feeling looking up at the apartment. It being dark isn't out of the ordinary, but there is this vague emptiness about the entire thing.

I park the car in a hurry and then hustle over to the keypad where I can buzz to be let into the apartment. I press the button over and over again, watching the window the whole time, and seeing nothing. Not even the flutter of curtains being moved away to check who is downstairs.

Now I know what the difference is. There are no more curtains! It's a sinking feeling to know that Andries might have actually moved away from this place that had been so special to us, and that I'd never even get to say goodbye to it. But the melancholy needed to be saved for later, because right now I have things that must be done.

After trying to get a hold of Andries a few more times, I give in and call Dan. Thankfully, Andries' friend has better social skills than he does, and he answers after a few rings.

"Hello?" he asks, a reluctance in his tone.

"Dan, it's Roxanne," I tell him straight away, and before giving him a chance to place another word, I add, "listen, this is going to sound crazy, but I *need* to find Andries. It isn't even about our fucked-up relationship situation. A client of mine–"

"Hey," Dan interrupts. "Roxie, he already knows. Patricia told Elise this morning that she was sexually assaulted, and Elise immediately told Andries."

It's all unraveling out of my control so quickly and it feels like it's impossible for me to stop. I want to sink down to my knees and weep, but there isn't any time to feel bad for myself. I swallow down my guilty nausea so I can speak again.

"It isn't how it sounds, and I'm going to do everything in my power to help Patricia. I just need to talk to Andries so he knows that too."

"He doesn't want to talk to you, though. Those were his very specific instructions, so I'm afraid I can't do anything to help you." Dan sounds like he's also a bit angry, or at least disappointed, and I can feel one of my biggest allies slipping through my fingers.

"Don't tell me you're turning against me too," I ask, voice quavering. "Dan, look—"

"Roxie," Dan interposes in a groan, cutting me off. "An eighteen-year-old giving her virginity up for cash is a little hard for even me to swallow. I just don't think she was old enough to make smart decisions, and she got taken advantage of. No hate to you or your field, but it's still a little much, you know?"

"Yes!" I say quickly. "I'm going to do things right by Patricia. I swear I didn't know what my client was up to. It was just an escorting gig, I swear. But I'm afraid Andries will never believe me if I don't tell him face to face." I pause for a moment to take a few deep breaths. "Please help me on this. Where is he?"

Dan doesn't answer immediately, and I hear nothing but silence on the other side of the line as he assesses my request, until he finally lowers his voice and says, "He's here at my place. He doesn't know I'm on the phone with you. But if you come, you have to act like you showed up on your own, not that I told you he was here."

"Okay, I can do that."

Hope swells in me no matter how hard I try to push it down. There is still a chance Andries could be convinced that I'm handling things correctly, and that I didn't set Patricia up. He doesn't have to like what I do for a living, but for some reason, I have to make it clear to him that I'm not using these girls.

Dan's house isn't far from Andries' old apartment, so I jump back into the car and waste no time in getting there.

Dan lives in a townhouse in front of the canals and I recognize immediately the façade as I drive down the street. After finding a miraculous space to park, I hurry myself and bound up the stairs, knocking on the door while I try to catch my breath. Dan answers, jerking his head to the side to indicate that I should follow him.

I don't waste any second as I step into the hallway and then into the living room but I stop right in my tracks when I find Andries there. As soon as he sees me, though, his features twist in disgust and he jumps out of the couch immediately.

"Why the fuck is she here?" he asks, his eyes on Dan.

Dan starts to answer, but I'm faster. "I had a hunch you'd be here since your apartment is empty. Andries, can we talk?"

He scoffs, barely looking at me as he does so. "The last thing I want to do is talk to you."

"I'm going to give you two some space," Dan mutters, heading down the hallway to his bedroom.

The tension in the air between the two of us is so thick it's almost visible. Andries watches Dan go with a look of betrayal in his eyes, before he tries to sweep past me and out of the living room.

Desperate, I grab his arm with my two hands, forcing him to stop. "Wait! Please hear me out. This isn't what you think."

He heaves a long sigh in annoyance, before turning around to face me. "You say that a lot, you know? When I found out you were a prostitute, you told me the same thing; that it isn't what I think because you're just the manager of a bunch of sex workers, not one yourself. And now here you are again this time to back track after Patricia being raped by your lovely client."

Raped? What a big word! "It's more nuanced than that," I tell him instead, putting on a softer tone. "You are much more upset than Patricia herself is. She seems more embarrassed than anything."

He shakes his head, disappointment lacing his features. "I knew you'd say that. You're lucky she signed that NDA and liability waiver, because Elise and I were all but begging her to go to the police and report that piece of shit you call a client. But she wouldn't because you made sure that she couldn't!"

What? The police? Is he crazy or what? I take a step back, blink a few times, my mouth gaping in shock as I process his comment. "I can't believe you'd do that, especially if Patricia didn't want to! Had she given in, she'd be in legal trouble, and it'd be *your* fault, not mine," I snap, unable to keep my indignation out of my tone.

He takes a few angry steps forward, closing the distance between us. "You know what I could do that would keep her out of legal trouble while also exposing what you and your nasty clients do?" he asks, his voice hoarse and threatening. My heart starts pounding fast inside my chest, but it's because of the closeness. "I was contacted by a reporter that is doing a hit piece on you, and he seemed desperate for information. The only reason I didn't give it to him was because he has a bad history with my family. But now—"

"Kenneth?" I ask, surprised. "Was his name Kenneth? He was harassing me at a party, but he was asking about you, not the other way around. I told him to fuck off."

A shadow of doubt passes over Andries' face, gone in an instant. "What? That doesn't make any sense."

"Those reporters lie! He knows we are split up and is hoping that, in our anger, we'll spill our guts to him just to hurt one another." I blow out a slow breath, my eyes dropping to the floor for a beat before meeting his gaze again. "I didn't tell him anything. Did you?"

"No. But now I regret that decision."

"You know that, even if I wouldn't pursue Patricia for breaking our binding agreement, the client himself would, if this story is allowed to hit the news. You'd be hurting me but ruining her in the process. It isn't worth it to you, I know that."

He pinches the bridge of his nose, shutting his eyes for a moment as he processes everything I just told him. He looks hurt, but mostly angry.

"I despise you," he growls, the disappointment in his voice catching me off guard. "It's you who put her in harm's way and now you've tied the hands of everyone who wants to expose you."

"Andries…" I sigh but keep my tone even. Screaming at him will only throw more gas to the fire. "These things are so incredibly rare that they're almost unheard of. Patricia is humiliated and angry at herself, but what she's most upset about is the fact that she can't take jobs at my agency anymore."

He physically recoils, his eyes widening at me. "She'd go back and do it again?"

I shrug one shoulder. "Like I said before, she made ten thousand euros in three hours. That might not be much in your eyes, but for a girl like Patricia, it's enough to come back for another taste." I shake my head, tired of the same argument replaying between us. "Look, for some women, prostitution is just work. Why don't you understand that?"

He gapes at me, and like a viper, suddenly strikes out and grabs my face in one of his large hands, squeezing tight. It hurts, but it's the shock that affects me more.

"If prostitution is just work, then why don't we have a course at the uni for girls like you and Patricia to become the best whores in town, huh? Maybe we should have a program teaching girls how to perform the best blowjob so they can put it on their resume? What do you think of that?" His hand continues squeezing my cheeks so hard that it makes my pulse steadily rise in anger. "You're the most immoral and disgusting bitch I've ever known," he hisses, his face inches from mine. "Don't ever try to talk to me again."

In a panic, I try to slap him away, shocked beyond recognition that he'd dare touch me like this. He dodges my flailing hands, pushing me back as he releases me, and before I can try and fight back he's stormed off down Dan's hallway and locked himself in another room.

I'm beyond startled as I rush out of the house, feeling my cheeks with my own hands. I open my front facing phone camera to look at my reflection, and besides some redness, there aren't any marks. It looks like the trauma of that terrifying moment will stay internal.

For me, the day is done. So many things are ruined beyond repair that I just want to go to bed and forget my interaction with Andries even happened. It isn't meant to be though, because before I can even get back to my car Poppy is calling me. As soon as she starts talking, she sounds worried and anxious.

"Uh, Roxanne? Karl is here, and he wants to talk to you right now. Can you come back?"

Wiping tears from my eyes, I mentally prepare myself for yet another battle. "I'm on my way."

* * *

"Hello, Karl. Or should I say *Robert*? You're awfully brave to show your face here after what you've done."

My fists are clenched at my sides, fingernails digging into my palm in my fury as I lay my eyes on the man who decided to betray my trust for good. Karl is with another man, who from the looks of it, seems to be his attorney, and my old client's face is steely.

"Roxanne," he starts, while I make way into my office and shut the door behind us. Once we hear the click of the door closing, Karl proceeds, and to my surprise, his tone is rather humble and genuine. "I want to apologize for everything that has happened. I got carried away. We both did. It was all too easy to forget she was someone I hired. We just meshed so well, and the sex was consensual. It was the natural ending to a night between two people who have chemistry."

"It can't be consensual if she's drunk, asshole!" I snap back.

"She was barely tipsy," Karl retorts immediately. "She knew what she was doing, and she even–"

The man beside Karl puts his hand on his arm and shakes his head, motioning Karl to stop talking. Karl just sighs in return, shoulders heaving with the force of it.

"I want to make this right," he says as if changing approaches. "But I also can't have word of something like this getting out. I know it wasn't an assault, and so did Patricia last night, but these things can balloon out of control so quickly, which is why I want to offer a settlement." Upon his announcement, the attorney steps forward and hands me a small stack of papers. "Split it however you want with the girl, whatever makes you happy."

I skim them quickly, not giving it my entire attention, until I see the numbers typed out. "A hundred thousand euros?" The shock in my voice resonates through the four walls, so I clean my throat, recenter myself, and regain my composure. "That's… acceptable."

"It's a reasonable amount for everyone to keep this hush hush." Karl grins, sounding quite sure of himself. "And you'll never have to see me darken your doorstep again."

That amount of money could do incredible things for me and my business. Before I realize it, I've picked a pen up, and the attorney is telling me where to sign. It'd be so easy, and if I gave just a portion to Patricia, she'd no doubt be fine keeping quiet too. But is this the right thing to do?

I look up at Karl, who looks smug with his arms crossed, and I hesitate. This isn't something that happened to me, it's something that happened to someone I was supposed to protect. It isn't my decision to make alone.

I sit the pen down on my desk beside the papers. "I can't sign this until I've talked to Patricia."

Karl barks out an astounded laugh. "What do you mean? Why bring the girl into this?"

The girl, he says. *He doesn't even use her name.* "Because she was the one assaulted, not me, and she deserves to know what's going on every step of the way. Now," I look between the two of them. "You may get the hell out of my office."

It's barely a thread of control over this whole debacle, but little by little, I swear I'll make this right.

CHAPTER 14

Amsterdam, February 3, 2022
Andries

When class lets out, I have some empty time in my schedule, but I don't want to go home just yet. The new apartment doesn't quite feel like it's mine, and it's a relief to know tomorrow I'm going back to the home estate for the weekend.

It's pretty cold outside, but the campus is lively. Small groups and couples are walking here and there, laughing and conversing like everything is right in the world for them. I had been on my way to feel normal again, too, until Roxanne had to fuck things up again like she always does. I haven't been able to get Patricia's incident off my mind.

If I'm being honest with myself, I'm also haunted by what I did to Roxanne, whether she deserved it or not. I moved in anger, but the fear and hurt on her face snapped me back into my normal headspace so quickly it could have given me whiplash. It was the first time I had touched her in so long, and that's how I had to go about it? In that moment, I had stooped just as low as all the other horrible people in this town and caused pain to someone I had once loved... and still do.

So that was the constant stream of thoughts processing in my mind. Guilt about Patricia, guilt about Roxanne, rotating over and over in my head until I couldn't take it anymore. I'm closer to drinking again than I ever wanted to be, which is another reason I'm so looking forward to going back to my family home. With everyone there to hold me accountable, I'm much more likely to keep my promise to myself and stay away from alcohol.

Watching the other students move through their day reminds me of how lonely I am, and it makes me think about the other invisible people hiding in their dorms and apartments, too afraid or tired to come out and join the rest of the world. I may be out here with everyone else, but I certainly am not a part of anything communal.

I need to do something to ease the melancholy inside of me, some sort of good deed to get my head back on straight, so I decide to go see Patricia. Elise told me she's been cagey and unresponsive to texts quite a lot, and even though no one knows about her assault, she doesn't want to leave her dorm room.

My sister is full of a fiery rage regarding her friend. The two of them hadn't been as close as say, she is with Tatiana, but the connection Patricia has with Roxanne and how it connects back to Elise and I is driving her crazy. Elise has moments of blaming me, and blaming herself for this happening to her friend, but at the end of the day I think we both realize that it's just a tragic coincidence. There's nothing either of us could have done once the events were set into motion.

I'm sure I'm not someone Patricia is particularly keen on seeing, either, but she needs to know that she has a bigger support system than she could ever know. I hardly know the girl, but if she called me up in the middle of the night needing help, I would go. Like I would for any of my sisters and brothers. That's just what you do to people; you help them in their times of need.

I arrive at Patricia's dorm and knock. From what I was told she doesn't have a roommate, so I know she's probably alone. After a second round of knocking, she opens the door just an inch or so, and when she sees it's me, she tells me to give her just a second to put some real clothes on.

I want to tell her it's her space and she can dress how she wants, but then I consider that she might not be comfortable being in any sort of state of undress after what had happened to her.

She lets me in, looking understandably confused about why I'm here. Patricia has put on an oversized hoodie with the university name emblazoned on it and a pair of black leggings. She looks cozy, and at the same time, achingly young and sweet. I hate that the world has already made a victim of this girl.

"It's nice to see you, Andries," she says shyly as she pulls her blonde hair into a messy bun. "So, um, what do you need?"

"I just wanted to come and check on you," I reply, shoving my hands in my pockets.

She fiddles with the strings on her sweatshirt, sitting down on her twin size bed. "I'm okay. Still sad sometimes, but okay. I told my student advocate that I had a death in the family, and they gave me some extra time on my assignments."

I almost sit next to her, thinking about hugging her to me like I would do one of my sisters, but I stop myself and choose her rolling desk chair instead, not wanting to crowd her. "That's good. I've had some emotional events happen myself and it definitely affected my grades, so it's nice to have some breathing room."

"Yeah…" she looks away from me and out the window. "You know, you and your sister don't have to worry so much. It's not like we hung out very much beforehand. As much as I appreciate your support, I also don't want you guys to pity me."

"No, no it's not pity!" I exclaim, quite surprised she'd even think of it in the first place. "It's genuine concern. We just want you to be well. I can't begin to imagine the trauma you've been put through."

Patricia frowns. "You know, I'm not even sad about the sex stuff. It's more that I had such a good opportunity with Roxanne's agency, and I screwed it up. She has such a good reputation for taking care of her girls and if I had just listened, I could've done other gigs. And after a few of those, I could have my own place, be out of this stupid dorm… it's just so much money."

I try to keep the shock from boiling over into my expression, but I can't. By the time she's done talking, I have to remind myself to close my mouth, since I'm so taken aback.

"You can't possibly mean that you would want to have sex for money again? After you were sexually assaulted?"

She sighs, her gaze dropping to the floor for a moment before she looks at me again. "It's so much more than that. I got tipsy, and I was all over him. Should he have been more conscious of my state of inebriation? Yes, sure. But in the moment I wanted it, and when we started having sex, I never tried to stop him. Had I been sober and given the opportunity to continue working with him through Roxanne, I'd have accepted it."

I lean forward, in disbelief at what she's saying. "This has to be some sort of trauma response. Can't you hear how crazy what you're saying sounds? This man took advantage of you, made sure you were tipsy enough, and then used you! I know you signed some paperwork, but you should really go to the police, Patricia. Ask them to keep your name anonymous and just make the report—"

"But I don't want to do that," she interposes, shaking her head. "It could ruin Robert's life, and cause trouble for Roxanne too, and she was only trying to protect me."

"If she was trying to protect you, she wouldn't have put you in that position in the first place," I point out, frowning.

"I think you've got this so mixed up because of how drastically Elise blew things out of proportion. There were definitely things wrong with what happened to me, yeah, but everyone keeps telling me I've been raped, and I just don't feel that way. Shouldn't I be the one that gets to decide how I feel about the whole thing?"

"Yes, but you're blinded by—"

We're both interrupted when Patricia's phone begins to ring. I can see that she's considering ignoring it, but at the last second, holds the screen up to show me who is calling.

It's Roxanne.

"Put it on speaker," I tell her as I bring my chair closer to her bed. "I won't make a sound."

Even though Patricia looks incredibly unhappy to do so, she answers the call on speaker, sitting back down on her bed.

"Hi, Roxanne."

"Patricia. I'm glad you picked up. How are you feeling?"

She laughs sadly. "Everyone seems to be asking me that constantly these days. I don't have cancer. I just slept with someone."

Roxanne exhales. "I don't mean to talk down to you like you're a little kid. I'm just worried. But I'm calling because, um, Robert came in yesterday with his attorney and they had some very interesting things to say."

Patricia sits up a little straighter. "Oh?"

"They want to offer you a settlement. It's… a hundred thousand euros. He said to split it between the two of us, but I can't help feel like I didn't prepare you well enough and that I should've been the one to personally drop you off and take you home. If I had been more involved, none of this would have happened."

"A hundred thousand euros!?" Patricia audibly gasps. "That's… that's an incredible amount of money. I can't take it all, though. You deserve—"

"We can talk about that later," Roxanne interrupts. "I also wanted to tell you that if you want to sue Robert or report him to the police that I'm behind you every step of the way. I'll front the lawyer fees and even get you set up with my own personal attorney. I want you to have every option at your disposal, should you so choose."

"But taking the settlement would mean less trouble for your agency too, right? If I accepted the proposal, could I still take gigs with you?" Patricia sounds hopeful, but Roxanne lets her down gently.

"I'm afraid not. I have very clear rules in place about drinking, and you were very quick to discard them. Plus, with that much money, I don't think you'd need to escort anyway." She tries to keep her tone light toward the end, but even I can see the disappointment on Patricia's face.

It just doesn't make sense why she'd be upset! There are so many different jobs she can take instead. They might not pay the outrageous amounts that Roxanne pays, but at least she won't be selling her body and her self-worth.

"I guess I need time to think," Patricia says finally. "Will you really support me if I were to report him?"

"Yes, dear," Roxanne's tone is kind and emphatic—and it comes as a surprise even to me. "It's something that you went through, and only you can decide how you want to handle it. I'll talk to you soon."

"Okay, thank you for calling." Patricia hangs up the phone and stares at it for a few long seconds.

This situation was complicated from the jump, but I certainly hadn't come to Patricia's dorm today expecting to feel a newly blossoming respect for Roxanne of all people. She had just paved the way for Patricia to press charges if she wanted, and she didn't try to lead her in one way or another. Roxanne would support her, even at a price to herself.

Fuck. I've judged her too harshly, it seems. When we were face to face, emotions ran so high that it's no surprise we ended up arguing. I wish I had all the information laid out clearly before. Then maybe the conversion would have played out differently.

"Do you know what are you going to do?" I ask Patricia, trying to pull myself out of the spiral of self-doubt that Roxanne had unknowingly thrown me into.

"You're not going to like this answer, I think, but I really want to take the settlement."

I wince, even though I knew it was coming. "I know you don't want to do it, but you need to report him to the police, Patricia. No matter what you think of this, if you were drunk, you couldn't consent to what he did. The settlement is to buy your silence."

She shakes her head in disapproval. "I already told you it doesn't feel that way to me!"

"Because he manipulated you," I tell her, my voice more serious and graver than before. "So much so that you didn't even notice it. But the reality is that he took complete and total advantage of you. If you don't report him to the police and get him arrested, he could easily go to a different escort agency and do the same thing to another young girl."

"I'm not a 'young girl,' Andries, I'm a grown woman. I don't need you or anyone else to tell me how I feel."

I want to argue that she just became an adult a month ago, but I know that it won't get me on her good side. "Next time it might not be a grown woman, though. You could stop this right here, right now. I'll take you to the police station if you want."

"But…that settlement money would change my life." I can see a sheen of tears in her eyes, and it twists my heart.

"If you sue him, you could get five times that, or even more. You'd never have to worry about money again, and you'd be doing the right thing in the long run to protect other girls."

Looking back down at her hands where she was twisting the hoodie fabric again and again, Patricia is quiet for a long time. Finally, I see her reach up and wipe her eyes with her sleeves before she meets my eyes again.

"Five times more you say?" she asks with a small voice, a pensive air lacing her features.

I'm a bit surprised at her question, but nod. "Yeah, maybe even more. God knows who that man is."

Patricia dips her eyes down to her lap again and remains quietly ruminating further for a few more instants.

All of a sudden, I hear her expelling a breath and she leaps off of bed. "Fine, let's go, then."

* * *

I call the most private driving company I know of, and after Patricia changes again into a pair of jeans, I direct the driver to take us to the police station. Patricia seems like she wants to bolt the entire time, and I know if I make one wrong move, she'll balk and refuse to report.

Her hesitation to report in the first place is making me feel torn. I'd been so angry that Roxanne had manipulated her, but if she didn't want to make the report, did that mean I was also manipulating her? I want to be positive that I'm just leading her in the right direction, but as always, anything to do with Roxanne leaves me feeling unsure. I had read many books about victims denying their own assault as a coping mechanism, and Patricia seems to be doing just that.

Still, I can't help but second guess the decision for a brief moment while we are on the back seats.

Once we reach the police department, Patricia looks seconds away from vomiting. I offer to go in with her, but that seems to make her feel even worse, so I let her go in alone, waiting patiently in the car while the poor girl goes to do what must be one of the most painful things of her life.

Nearly an hour later, she looks pale and drawn when she finally sits back beside me, answering my questions with short, one-word answers while keeping her eyes toward the window.

"You did well. I'm proud of you," I tell her, hoping to earn some sort of reply.

She mutters a vague, "Okay," not even looking back at me.

"Have I done something wrong?" I ask, confused at her attitude. "I'm trying to help you, but I feel like you're angry with me."

She doesn't look at me, continuing to stare out the window instead, before letting out a sigh in displeasure. "I just wish I had been able to decide what was right for me, on my own, but everyone was rushing me to make a decision."

"Time is of the essence with these sorts of things," I tell her. "If we had waited, he could have gotten wind of what you planned to do and try to make you sign that settlement, and then he'd never have to face punishment for what he did."

Patricia cocks her head to the side, pondering my observation. "Maybe."

She doesn't speak to me anymore, even as I walk her to her dorm, and she shuts the door in my face. I try not to take it personally, thinking that she's probably mentally exhausted.

The sun is setting as I leave her residence hall, and the concourse is nearly empty. I have this itching feeling that there is something I still need to do, someone I need to reconcile with, but I don't know if it's a mistake to do so. I need to talk to Roxanne, but if I do, then I'd have opened up communication between us again. It's a giant step back in the wrong direction.

But then, the image of me squeezing her scared face floats through my memories again, and I know I have no choice. I owe her an apology; maybe not for the breakup, but for the way I treated her the last time we were face to face.

I sit on one of the benches on the concourse, make sure I'm alone, and dial her number.

"Called to insult me some more? Or maybe you want to come and knock me round a little bit? I charge extra for that, you know."

I cringe. "Roxanne... ah, fuck. I'm sorry for grabbing you, okay? There's no excuse, but I'm still sorry."

"Oh," she chirps, clearly surprised. "I–well, thanks."

I clear my throat and roll my eyes to the stars. "I also wanted to tell you I took Patricia to the police station, and she filed a police report against Robert. I thought you'd want to be forewarned."

"Good for her. I just hope it helps her heal."

I drop my voice to nearly a whisper. "I heard what you offered to do for her. I have to say, I never expected that from you, but my respect for you has grown. Thank you for doing that for Patricia."

I hear her breathe on the other line, and the sound is achingly familiar. She lets out a breathy laugh after a few minutes. "I'm not as much of a monster as you always thought, huh?"

"I never thought you were a monster, Roxie. You just... you broke my heart."

"Roxie again, is it? I guess you really don't hate me too much anymore, then."

"Never hate. Angry, maybe. Frustrated, absolutely. But I could never hate you." My voice is thick with emotion.

Roxanne makes a vulnerable, small sound, and this little noise lights the smallest ember within me, deep in my soul where I was sure I had purged her. As it turns out, I can never truly remove her from within me.

"Do you want to go get dinner?" she asks, almost hesitantly. "We could go—"

"I'm sorry, Roxanne," I say, voice warmer than I had anticipated it to be. "Don't take it the wrong way, but..."

"I get it." Those three little words squeeze my heart so tight that I've got to shut my eyes to process the pain.

"I have to go. Have a good weekend," I find myself saying.

"You too, Andries. Goodbye." She sounds sad when she says the last word, but we hang up nearly at the same time, knowing this is the right thing to do. I remain sitting on the bench for a long time, iPhone in hand, thinking about what had just occurred. Nothing in my life has ever made me feel as weak as Roxanne does, but damn it all, when it came to her, I didn't mind being weak.

CHAPTER 15

Patricia has been initially standoffish, but as the weeks go on, she's started to warm up to us again, the emotional stress of having to file the police report finally starting to fade. Elise has been on edge about Patricia, so much so that I dared not tell her about my excessively amiable talk with Roxanne the night Patricia filed the report. Speaking of Roxanne, we haven't spoken again since that day and while I have been inclined to call her from time to time, I've managed to keep the temptation at bay.

Besides the crunch of having to get everything done in time school wise, it has been relatively peaceful these last few weeks. My new apartment is starting to feel more like someplace I belong as it accumulates the traces of my everyday life the longer I live in it.

Arriving back at my place for a quick break between lectures, I throw my bag aside on the floor and drop myself onto the couch. My phone has been off during class, so I turn it on and leave it on the low table in front of me, ready to go and pick a book to read. But almost immediately I realize that there is going to be no such activity for me.

I first see that I have eight missed calls from my dad, but before I can register anything else, my phone is ringing. Of course, it's Dad himself, and I pick up quickly, worried that the excessive calls are because someone is sick or hurt.

"Dad, is everyone okay?" I ask the moment the call connects.

"Oh, everyone is fine, except my company and the business I've spent my entire adult life keeping afloat. What have you done, Andries?!"

I freeze. "I have no idea what you're talking about."

"Let me refresh your memory," his voice is tight with barely controlled rage. "Someone got an escort from your ex's agency, fucked her when he wasn't supposed to, and now he has just been pulled out of our office building and was arrested! Something tells me this connection isn't exactly a coincidence!"

Bewildered, I sit up straight. "I helped a girl report an assault recently, and she also worked for Roxanne, but it couldn't be the same incident, because the man in that situation was named Robert."

"Wait until you hear about this part, son. Roxanne's agency is fully cooperating with the police, *and* they admitted Robert was just an alias for Karl!"

My head spins, thinking about how I had helped Karl get his promotion on Roxanne's request. It makes me feel awful, until I realize he'd have still wanted to victimize a young woman, promotion or not.

"You should be happy, Dad. That means they managed to save you the trouble of finding out Karl was a rapist further down the line."

He laughs cruelly. "You have no idea what you're talking about, son. The reputation damage that the company is going to suffer from this event will be astronomical. And how can he even be in trouble for fucking an escort? Isn't that exactly why you hire them?"

I grit my teeth at his refusal to see what a scumbag Karl is. "He took an eighteen-year-old's virginity after signing a contract that he wouldn't, that's the problem. He got her drunk and raped her."

"Sorry if I have a hard time believing an escort was a virgin. Although I'm surprised that you don't seem to be bothered by our family business being in jeopardy because of some stunt your ex is pulling." The disappointment in his voice hurts, even though I know I did the right thing. "I guess I shouldn't be surprised after the way you sulked around about her after the breakup, but I had hoped you'd have come to your senses by now."

"Dad," I say, keeping my tone firm. "This isn't about anything related to what I feel for Roxanne. This is about you calling me and being angry that I helped a victim go and make her statement to the police! It could have been any escort agency in town, and I'd have done the same thing. Plus, Roxanne isn't profiting off this in any way. All it's going to do is cause her legal trouble, but just like me taking Patricia to the police station, Roxanne is doing it because it's the right thing to do."

My dad lowers his voice to a quiet, furious hiss. "I don't give a fuck about what is going on in Amsterdam with hookers and their clients. Karl used an alias to keep our business separated from what he was doing on the side, but your ex had to go and expose him, which from what I understand, she and this Patricia both signed an NDA. Now I have the police barging into my place of business and arresting one of my top employees, *and* since he's a public figure due to his ex-wife's status, as soon as the news gets out people will be able to look up what he's done. I've never had a single incident like this before in the entire history of my career, but the second you get the chance to mess with my life's work in any way, you ruin it. Congratulations."

I huff a disbelieving laugh. "Correct me if I'm wrong, but it sounds like you're siding with Karl here, because you're quick to tell me what I've done wrong, as well as what Patricia and Roxanne have done wrong. But I feel like I detect some sympathy for that prick Karl."

"Do I agree with what he was out doing? No. But he hired this girl *legally* from an escort company and gave a fake name so it wouldn't affect our business in any way. So no, I can't fault him, because he isn't the one out there trying to ruin me and my reputation. That would be your acquaintance's job, Andries. Oh, and you too since you've admitted to encouraging that little escort to report him."

"I can't believe you're siding with a rapist because of image, Dad." I have to take a few deep breaths to center myself before continuing. "I'm beyond shocked."

"You are too young to understand the real world, Andries. I promise once you get to be my age that'll drop all this self-righteous nonsense. You're not a hero, and you never will be. Successful men make the tough choices to succeed. It's as simple as that."

"I hope you can sleep at night, knowing that you'd throw an innocent girl under the bus to save your employee."

"Goodbye, son," Dad says, sounding almost amused at this point, and he disconnects the call before I can utter another word.

The entire conversation leaves me reeling. Dad had been so angry, so full of vitriol, that I hadn't even had time to absorb the biggest shock of the conversation: Robert was Karl.

Roxanne might have called him a friend, and that had been enough for me to help push my Dad toward promoting him, but now that decision is biting me in the ass tenfold, because had Karl still been a lower-level employee, it wouldn't be such a hit for Van Den Bosch industries' reputation. Not only that, but I had to live with the fact that I stuck my neck out for a pervert that would take advantage of young girls when given the opportunity.

Poor Patricia. Poor Roxanne. Neither of them deserved this, no matter what bad choices they both made in their day-to-day lives. Patricia especially had just made a single mistake in taking that job and now she'd be front and center of a media storm against an employee of one of the biggest companies in the Netherlands. She might be able to line her pockets from it, but I know all too well that money doesn't take away the pain and humiliation of heartbreak and being taken advantage of.

Then again, had Roxanne not offered Patricia the job in the first place, none of this would have happened. Her friendship with Karl blinded her to what his real intentions were, even when outsiders like me and Elise could see clearly that he just wanted to take Patricia's virginity.

Roxanne... my beautiful, stubborn, powerful, flawed Roxanne. She's a dichotomy that threatens to tear me apart. Had her escort agency been something else like a modeling agency, she'd have been the perfect woman for me, but, alas, her agency goes against everything I believe in.

Fuck. This isn't going to get solved here sitting on my couch. I need to check if Elise and Patricia already know the truth too. I can't ever feel guilty for helping Patricia, but it doesn't necessarily mean I'm looking forward to the fallout it's about to cause.

She didn't even want to make the report. This is a problem of your own making, my subconscious reminds me, but I discard the thought immediately. Patricia is a victim, even if she doesn't want to admit it yet.

I check my watch and groan. I have one more class today, so I text my sister briefly as I head outside: *Let's meet up after class and check on Patricia.*

She replies a few seconds later. *Okay, I'll see you outside of your lecture hall.*

Once more I'm entering into a lecture with a head full of personal problems, which isn't exactly ideal for my education. Hopefully it will just be a recap day.

* * *

It was absolutely not a recap day, and my head feels like it's stuffed full to bursting with all the information that I've had to retain today. Luckily, after all the zoning out in class I had been doing right after my breakup, I had gotten into the habit of recording the lectures on my phone so I could listen back later.

Like clockwork, Elise is waiting for me outside of my lecture hall, a brown leather messenger bag slung across her body and a paper bag from the local bakery in her hand. "I thought we could bring Patricia some goodies. I have a class with her in the morning, and she wasn't looking so great today."

My stomach rumbles. "That's nice of you. Can I see?"

Elise hands me the bag and I pluck an orange cranberry scone out, biting the pastry before Elise can wrestle it away from me.

"Hey!" she yells, grabbing the bag out of my hands and holding it to her chest. "Those aren't for you! Glutton."

"What does Patricia need with a dozen pastries? I don't think she's going to miss one."

We walk together to Patricia's residence hall, but I can tell something is on Elise's mind besides scones. "You have something you want to share, little sister?"

"Yes, but I don't know if you're going to be mad or relieved when I do."

"I've had my share of shitty conversations today, so as long as you're not going to outright insult me, it'll be an improvement," I tell her with a chuckle.

"Okay." She takes a deep breath, amping herself up. "Dad called me and offered me the internship at the company."

She looks at me with wide worried eyes, and I wave my hand dismissively. "Go on."

"He, um, well, he also told me all about Karl, and the case against him." Elise frowns. "Had I known it was Karl who assaulted Patricia, I'd have still encouraged her to go to the police, but I'd have given Dad a heads up. I feel bad that we basically initiated a police raid at our family's company, you know?"

"Yeah, if Dad hadn't been such an asshole on the phone I'd feel more guilty, but he really tore me up when he called. I think he blames it all on me because I have the direct connection to Roxanne. And, well, because you're the favorite, of course."

She snorts, head shaking. "We both know Arthur is the favorite."

"Only because he's too small to get into scandals yet," I joke, and we both laugh, some of the tension easing. "Elise, I hope you know I had no idea Karl was Robert. I wouldn't have hidden something like that."

"I know," she says softly. "Dad will come to his senses in time, I'm sure. I'm going to talk to him when we get back home tomorrow, try to explain that he'd have done the same thing as you in your position, at least when he was younger. He'll come around."

"We'll see. But did you take the internship?"

"Yeah, I did." She searches my face as we walk for any anger or resentment, but there's none to be found. Secretly I'm thrilled, both for her and for the fact Dad won't ask me about it anymore.

"I know he's doing it as a PR stunt to get good press," Elise continues. "I can see the headlines now, 'Sebastian Van Den Bosch chooses eldest daughter for management internship, a triumph for women in the industry!'"

Elise is downplaying the news of her taking the internship, but I know deep down she's on top of the world. She has wanted this internship from the moment it became available. Her and Dad are like mirror images of one another. The position was made for her, she just doesn't realize it yet.

"You can be excited, Elise. I'm thrilled for you. Really."

"You're sure?" At that moment, she still sounds like a little girl, worried about losing her brother's favor.

"Positive. Give them hell."

We've reached Patricia's residence hall, and Elise is all smiles as we ascend the elevator, only taming her expression when we reach the other girl's door. Patricia is expecting us, and greets us warmly, but something about it is off.

Her expression is wooden, almost fake. She graciously takes the bag of pasties from Elise while I make sure to wipe any errant crumbs off myself before we all sit down to chat, Elise on the bed with Patricia, and me in the trusty old office chair that is two sizes too small for me.

Elise takes one of Patricia's hands. "How are you doing, love?"

"I know you two want me to be happy that Robert is arrested, but I just can't bring myself to be. I guess I should call him Karl now, though...." She looks between the two of us and seeing our confused faces wondering how she already knows his real identity, she pulls her hands out of Elise's grip, picks her phone, and shows us something on it. "Cassey sent me this."

I take her iPhone in hand and start checking the article more closely with Elise peering over me. There it is. The first hit piece reaching the media about Karl's arrest. There's even a picture of him at the headquarters of the Van Den Bosch Industries as the header. Of course—the whole thing had to be published by RTL, and not surprisingly, written by Kenneth himself.

"Karl wasn't a perfect man but I also don't think he's the villain we are making him out to be," Patricia continues while Elise and I are still processing the shock that his arrest went public so quickly.

"Don't worry," I assure her, giving her phone back. "Soon enough he'll go on trial, and you won't have to think about him anymore."

"You don't understand!" she exclaims, her tone growing irritated. "He was funny, charismatic, handsome." I see Elise wrinkle her nose, but Patricia isn't swayed. "We had real chemistry. I…I'd have liked to see him again, and now that's ruined."

I'm becoming annoyed with this back and forth with Patricia. If she didn't want to report him, why wasn't she more firm with me when I offered to drive her?

"You need to stop feeling guilty for a criminal that took advantage of you," I tell her, more firmly than I intend to.

"You just don't get it. I'm so terrified that my parents are gonna find out now, and they'll be so disappointed. They might even stop paying my tuition." She takes a shuddering breath. "I had no idea this would be such a media circus."

"Relax," Elise says, her tone soothing as she rubs her hand on her friend's back. "It's just one article. That's not a big deal."

Patricia sniffles, and I know from past experience that the tears are about to start. "I think I want to be alone, guys. Can we talk after the weekend?"

I stand, more than ready to be out of this dorm, but my sister seems hesitant.

"Are you sure?" Elise asks, looking at me before returning to Patricia. "I can make Andries leave and we can just have some girl time. Would that make you more comfortable?"

"No. I just want to be by myself, okay?"

"...Okay, if that's what you want."

The two girls hug awkwardly, and our elevator ride down to the main floor is much more subdued than the ride up. Elise looks upset, but I don't want to prod her, not when we have an hour drive to make together tomorrow evening.

"Do you think she's mad at us?" Her question breaks our comfortable silence and I find myself pondering longer than I should.

"I think she's a fickle girl who is confused about how she's feeling. I wouldn't take it personally."

She nods but doesn't look convinced. "Okay, okay. Well, see you tomorrow."

CHAPTER 16

Amsterdam, February 18, 2022
Andries

Dad doesn't waste time texting me a few news articles reporting about the arrest early the next morning. The incident seems to have blown up in the national press and every outlet was now reporting about it. Every news program and every paper reads, "KARL TOWNSEND ARRESTED FOR ALLEGED RAPE OF COLLEGE GIRL," or some variation thereof. I couldn't escape it if I tried, and since Dad is so connected to Karl, he told me he even had journalists calling and showing up in front of the headquarters. With Dad's birthday being tomorrow, the timing couldn't be worse.

Of course according to him, it's somehow my fault. There's no denying the small part I played in the whole ordeal, but for Dad to rest it solely on my shoulders isn't fair. I was helping someone who was vulnerable. It wasn't like I did it to instigate a smear campaign against my own family's business.

"You've got to fix this mess, Andries!" Dad demands over the phone. I knew I shouldn't have picked up his call.

"Me?" I snap back as I try to prepare myself some coffee. "What are you even talking about?"

"My birthday is tomorrow. If you want to be helpful, talk to that girl and make her sign that settlement once and for all."

I stop in my tracks, frowning and looking at my phone for a second. "How do you even know about that?"

"Because I just spoke to Karl," Dad explains. "The poor man just told me what happened. This is beyond ridiculous!"

"I can't do that," I tell him, putting the call on speakers while I start drinking my espresso. "Let him go to trial, it's a much better strategy."

"Better strategy? I want this mess to end now!" His anger is steadily rising, so I decide to put an end to this call before we both lose our temper.

I heave a long sigh in annoyance as I finish my coffee. *What a long weekend this is gonna be.*

* * *

It's dark when I pull the car into the round driveway in front of the family estate, and the valet comes out immediately to take my keys while other staff grab our bags. Elise has already unloaded hers, both of us used to doing things independently at college. It always takes a little while to readjust to living here, and then adjust yet again when we go back to school.

I'm actually looking forward to seeing Mom and having her embrace me in greeting. Even though I'm quite a bit taller than her now, I still always find comfort in that motherly gesture. She hugs me just as tightly whether I've been gone for a single day on a fencing trip or months away at school.

But Dad, on the other hand... I'd like some time for both of us to calm down before seeing him. But of course it's him in the foyer to greet us, and not Mom. I stop in my tracks while Elise rushes over to hug him.

"Arthur is sprouting more teeth and is grouchy, so your Mom is laying down with him," Dad explains.

I simply nod and move to walk past him and up to my room, but I stop when he holds out his hand for a handshake. Usually he'd embrace me in greeting too, albeit in a more back-slapping gesture than the warm way he hugs my sisters, so the handshake is new. A power move, and a way to let me know we aren't on good terms just yet.

I could ignore him, but while I knew it was because of pride, I know he'd think of it as petulant behavior. Reluctantly, I grab his hand and shake it firmly, our gazes locked together as if in combat.

He releases me, asking, "Don't you have anything to say to me?"

I frown at his question. "Not that I'm aware of."

"So you aren't going to apologize for your attitude this morning?"

"My attitude?" Then it hits me. He's referring to the phone call and how I went against his bullshit demands by hanging up on him.

"I've got homework to do," I tell him instead of starting yet another argument, this time, though, actually passing him fast enough that he can't stop me. To my surprise, Dad doesn't say anything or turn to watch me go, but when I take a last look over my shoulder, Elise is staring daggers at me.

Funny how she's my biggest ally until we're around Dad again. Then, it's easy to see where her loyalties really lie.

***

"Love, it's a family dinner. Even Aleida and Arthur are going to sit with us instead of eating in the nursery. Won't you please be with us?"

I roll my eyes at my Mom. "You're the only one that wants me there. Dad hates me right now, so why make both of our evenings miserable by forcing us to eat together?"

"He doesn't hate you, Andries! He's just under so much stress from work and all of the terrible things in the news about Karl. He isn't himself, but if he sees that you're willing to extend the olive branch first, he'll come around."

"No means no, Mom." At the pained look in her eyes, and the sheen of tears threatening to fall, I sigh heavily. "You want to take a walk around the grounds? Or a drive? Just mother and son stuff?"

Mom considers it, but shakes her head. "No, not today. I'd love to, but nothing sits right with me while you and your dad are at odds."

"Take it or leave it, Mom."

She blinks rapidly to clear away her misty eyes, tilts her chin up stubbornly, and storms out in the way only a Van Den Bosch woman can, slamming the door so hard some of my fencing trophies rattle.

I pull my headphones back over my ears and fall backward onto my bed.

With my dad's birthday party being so close, everyone in the house is getting tense about the cold silence between me and Dad. After all, family is coming from all over the world for the gathering, and we are supposed to be on our best behavior and looking as united as possible. It just isn't going to happen, though. I just need to be left alone.

I haven't talked to anyone back in Amsterdam, except for a few text exchanges with Dan, and I'm becoming more and more nervous that maybe Patricia is going to back out of the court case and withdraw her statement. I'm trying to put it out of my mind since there is nothing I can do while I'm here, but the thought continues to creep in.

Then there's Roxanne. Her agency hasn't been featured much in the news coverage, but there have been a few clips of her entering and exiting her office building, and it seems like she's instructed her escorts to arrive dressed in black with their faces completely covered to keep their identities private. Most of the time, no one would care who is an escort and who isn't, but with the media so hungry for anything to do with Karl, even the uninvolved escorts would be fair game for media scrutiny.

Roxanne, of course, goes bare faced for the world to see, drawing attention away from her employees. Doing her best to protect them, like she does everyone else in her life. Damn, I miss her. I miss that woman so much that is beyond ridiculous. It has been nearly two months since we broke up. How come I'm still missing her like this?

While scrolling through songs on my phone, an alternative rock playlist blaring from my headphones, Elise manages to enter my room without me noticing. I do notice her, though, when she yanks the headphones off of me and throws them onto the other side of the bed.

"Ow! What the fuck, Elise!" I yell, rubbing my abused ears.

She puts her hands on her hips and glares down at me. "You want to tell me why Mom is crying?"

"Menopause?"

She raises her hand as if she's going to slap me upside the head but thinks better of it at the last second. "Shut the fuck up, Andries. You're finished with this little act of defiance. You're coming to dinner and you're going to be part of this family, even if you have to fake it."

"You're sort of a bitch when we're back home, you know that?"

"And you're a coward. Come to dinner, or I will blow your cover about not being in business school."

I feel the blood drain from my face. "You wouldn't. There couldn't be a worse time than now. I'm already a pariah."

She huffs. "A pariah of your own making! Dinner is at seven p.m. Be there, showered and dressed, or I tell the truth to Mom and Dad. You hear me?"

I don't want to give in, but Elise is not a person who does things by small degrees. If she says she is going to out me, I believe her. "Fine. But if it's a shit show, you get to know that it's your doing."

She grins triumphantly, looking more like our father than ever. "Great. See you there, little brother."

***

Dinner starts tense, and by the time the salad comes out, everyone is on the edge of snapping.

The kids are unaware, Hanna chattering on and on about school, her tutors, and her piano recital coming up. She's sitting next to Elise, chair scooted almost hip to hip with her older sister, looking up at her periodically in awe. It's clear she misses having her around, and she takes full advantage of Elise's time at home.

Arthur is less impressed by me, blinking owlishly at me whenever I try to talk to him.

The kids are the only bright spot of this whole ordeal. Elise cuts her food while looking at me threateningly, as if she wants to use the knife elsewhere. My mother, bless her, tries to steer the conversation toward things everyone can relate to. Dad is stoically silent, to no one's surprise.

I take a long drink of my water, trying to scheme a way to excuse myself early. Mom had run out of generic topics, and, to my horror, I hear her change the subject to ask Dad about work.

"Are you excited for Elise to join you soon, Sebastian?" she asks cheerily.

Dad nods. "Yes. I'll need all the help I can get since I had to lay my best employee off."

Silence falls over the table, but Elise tries desperately to save the moment. "Don't worry, once you have me there you won't need anyone else."

He smiles at her in approval, but there is a cruel twist to his mouth. "Just don't do anything untoward around your brother or he'll have you arrested on the spot."

The quiet is deafening, but Dad isn't finished. He turns toward my mom to say, "Oh, Julia, did I tell you it's been officially confirmed that it was Karl that hired that escort? They were able to figure it out since the agency owner cooperated with police and turned over all the paperwork he filled out. The handwriting was an exact match. I'm sure she'll struggle to get clients into her whorehouse now that everyone knows she'll rat them out the moment trouble arises."

Mom's eyes widen, but she doesn't respond. I, on the other hand, can't hold my tongue any longer.

"She's doing it to protect Patricia, even though it's going to fuck up her business," I can't help but point out with a deep tone in my voice. "But you wouldn't know anything about choosing the right thing over your company, now would you, Dad? You'd keep Karl the rapist on payroll if given the choice."

Dad slams his fists down on the table, rattling the plates and glasses. Little Arthur starts to cry, clutching Mom's arm.

"For fuck's sake, Andries! After everything she did to you, you are still taking her side? When are you gonna grow a pair and forget that whore once and for all, huh?" Dad yells, veins sticking out on the side of his neck.

Fury rises in me, uncontrollable, and before I can stop myself I'm on my feet. I throw my glass of water over him, causing everyone else at the table to gasp or cry out, and in the ensuing chaos I turn on my heel and head back upstairs at a near-jog.

I have called Roxanne a number of disgusting things, but hearing Dad talk about her that way made something inside me snap. It shows me something that I don't want to admit to myself....

I still love her.

I run upstairs and lock my door behind me, ignoring it when Elise comes pounding at the door a few minutes later. Laying on my bed, pillow over my face, I could almost scream. Out of rage for how my dad has been behaving, and out of self-pitying sorrow for myself and the way I still feel about Roxanne.

I don't scream, though. I put my headphones back on, and when the urge has passed, I sit up, and start writing. No reason to waste good misery, they always say.

CHAPTER 17

V.D.B. estate, February 19, 2022
Andries

I slept like shit after the fight with Dad at dinner. I hate that I lost control like that, and I feel utterly guilt ridden about losing my temper in front of my younger siblings. Mom and Dad had never fought, not like Dad and I had, and it must have terrified them.

I don't dare leave my room to try and make amends, though. I'm convinced that Elise is crouched outside my room in camouflage, hunting knife in hand, ready to end me the moment I do. I had never heard my sister so angry as she was when she was pounding on my door, but it was the hint of sadness that scared me the most. I don't know if I can bear making both my sisters and my mom more disappointed in me.

I slept like shit, and I felt like shit. Still feel that way, actually.

When I woke up from my bothered, wretched sleep, I could already hear the house switching into high gear for the party. Dad's fifty-fifth birthday is to be the bash to end all bashes, and considering that it sounds like they are tearing the mansion down and rebuilding it from the ground up, it is certainly going to be something, to say the least.

And there is no way in hell I'm going.

Elise texts me first, telling me that we can all let bygones be bygones for the night so we can all celebrate Dad. I know that means she isn't letting me off the hook, but that nothing will be said about the dinner fight as long as I play my part at the birthday party.

Too bad for them. I'm going to stay in my bedroom until the next morning, even if I starve. I have a few things in a mini fridge on the other side of the room, so that'll have to do.

Determined to stick to my guns and skip the party, I shower, brush my teeth, put on a pair of sweats, grab reading and writing material, and throw my headphones on, cranking up the volume. If I don't hear what is happening, it won't bother me nearly as much.

Avoidance plan enacted, I open my notebook to write, and begin to whittle away the hours.

* * *

Once again, I'm reminded that wearing headphones in my room is a mistake, because it just leaves an open invitation for my family to harass me. To my humiliation, it's not just my mother who opens the door, either. She's followed by a young woman, whose long, bare legs and kind, open expression makes me frown in suspicion. This better not be a hookup attempt.

I jerk the headphones off and toss them aside, narrowing my eyes. "How dare you come into my room uninvited?"

Mom scowls, and I suddenly know for sure she's going to have a talk with me about manners next time we're alone. "It's almost time for dinner, why aren't you dressed?"

"Because part of the agreement for me living here so you can keep me under your thumb was that I didn't have to attend any of your asinine social functions," I remind her.

"It's a dinner in your own home. Your father's birthday dinner, might I add."

"Even more reason for me to not attend," I quip.

Mom stomps over to the light-switch and flips it on. I flinch, the light hurting my eyes after so long hiding in the dark. When my eyes adjust, I can see the young woman with my mother looking over me. It sets my teeth on edge at first, but I quickly realize it's nothing but polite curiosity in her face. No attraction or approval, just normal, harmless inquisitiveness.

She has the largest blue eyes I've ever seen, round and the color of cornflowers. Her skin is flawless, and she has a glow about her that I usually attribute to older women. This girl is still young, but she is content in a way most women my age aren't. She looks so familiar, but I can't place her.

Mom crosses her arms. "It's one dinner with your family. Get dressed, Andries."

"There are hundreds of people I have no interest in meeting," I inform her, reaching for my headphones. Mom plucks them out of my hand and tosses them into a nearby chair.

"You can at least say hello to Petra here. You haven't seen her since her and your Uncle Alex's wedding, and she's come all the way from New York to see us," she says, voice firm.

Petra? Oh! It's Uncle Alex's wife! That's where I know her from.

The relief that she isn't a potential date is swift, but I keep my expression neutral. "Yeah, I remember you now. What do you want?"

Petra opens her mouth to speak, but Mom cuts her off. "You and Petra are the same age, so I thought it might be nice to have someone you can relate to around." She loops an arm around Petra's shoulder and brings her forward a little more. "She's in college too. I bet you both have a ton in common."

I groan, closing my eyes. "Mom, you can't expect me to just become friends with—"

To my horror, Mom backs out of the room just as quickly as she entered. "You two just come down when you're ready! See you in a bit!" she chirps, shutting the door behind her.

What the fuck, I think, looking at Petra. She shrugs, and I wave her over to an empty chair, which she lowers herself into carefully.

"Sorry about this," she says, looking a bit awkward. "But your mom is worried about you. She thinks since we're peers, you might enjoy my company a little more than some of the dinosaurs downstairs." She grins at her own joke, but I can't bring myself to laugh. "So, uh…what are you writing in your notebook?"

I look down at the leather-bound notebook, and back up at Petra. "You don't have to pretend to care. I don't know why Mom brought you here, but seriously, you're wasting your time."

"Your mom told me your girlfriend broke up with you." She ignores my complaints, speaking to me in a rather soft tone. "I know how it feels to love someone and then to have that person break up with you. It's a pain like no other."

I laugh sardonically. "That's what Mom told you? Wow. Well, I'm the one who broke up with her if you must know. But it's fantastic that she can't bother to pay attention to the details of my relationship."

"Oh, you did?" Petra blinks a few times. "But why? Julia said you two were deeply in love."

"Because it's for the better," I tell her, my tone coming off more nostalgic than I aimed for.

Petra looks unsure, but circles back around to my writing. "What are you writing in there? Are you an aspiring author?"

I consider lying, but what's the point? "Sort of. Much to the disappointment of my parents." When my eyes scan my own words again, there is a lump in my throat, and I decide to tell her the truth. "I'm writing about how the woman I love above life itself broke my heart. Writing has therapeutic effects, or so I've been told."

"What did she do to break your heart? It has to be something terrible if you want nothing to do with her anymore."

"Oh, she was…" I stop myself, not wanting to reveal too much to this aunt I've met just once or twice before. "Whatever. I just want to write everything down, get her out of my system, and then move on. I was just a fucking idiot who believed she was the one."

Petra's eyes go wide. "The one!?" she repeats, visibly astonished. "You're not an idiot. The heart wants what the heart wants. Don't be surprised if just writing it out isn't enough to wash her from your system, though." I make a strangled noise, really hoping that she's wrong about this. "How long were you guys together?"

I search Petra's face, but I don't see any malice, or conniving motivations. Just genuine curiosity. She's probably just fishing information for my family, but I can share things they already know.

"Like three months, but I knew she was the one from the day I met her." I let out a self-deprecating chuckle. "You must think I'm crazy."

"Crazy? You?" she asks, shaking her head, a small smile spreading across her lips. "At seven I was already painting family portraits with your uncle and I and our two children, so I'll be the last person to judge."

I'm beyond shocked that she'd share something so damn personal, but I can't help laughing at her story. "Okay, that's even weirder than what I'm going through."

She laughs with me and the evening suddenly feels lighter. I might not know her much, but it's good to be around someone who isn't here to judge you about your past relationship.

"What's her name?"

"Roxanne," I tell her with an ounce of nostalgia in my tone. "Roxanne Feng."

"What a unique name. Did your mom meet her?" she inquires.

"Yeah, on my birthday." I chuckle, remembering the odd conversation about sex work we had on Christmas Day.

"Needless to say, Mom wasn't pleased even though she was feigning happiness the whole dinner."

"Why wasn't she pleased?" Petra continues.

Damn, she's quite curious. "Well for starters, she's thirty-five and Mom is forty-one," I tell her.

"Oh."

All of a sudden, she falls into an awkward silence as if I had said something wrong. "But I mean, you and my uncle are like twenty-three years apart, right?" I ask, since I fail to understand her sudden change. "And yet you seem to be doing okay."

"We are fine now," she responds cautiously. "But it wasn't always that way. I'll be completely honest with you... it wasn't always an easy road."

I shrug, falling back against the headboard. "I know, but even my parents have an age gap. Rules for thee, not for me."

Petra nods with understanding. "Yeah, it can be. Everyone older than you will always think they know better. But if you want them to respect your choices, you have to go toe to toe with them to prove you're capable. Not hide away and let them judge you."

I'm lost in thought, wondering if I'm going toe to toe with everyone or if I'm just running away, when Petra says quietly, "Come down to dinner with us, Andries. Your uncle would love to see you."

I don't say anything. Is this what she means, going toe to toe? Showing up at all the functions unafraid of judgment? I wish I could ask her if that's how she handled her own struggles.

When I don't answer for a few minutes, Petra stands up and adds, "I'll wait in the hallway for you to get changed."

Before I can object, she's gone. Staring at the empty door, I sigh heavily, and scrub my face with my hands. I guess I'm going to this fucking party. Thanks a lot, *Aunt* Petra.

***

"You wouldn't want your Uncle Alex to see you letting his beloved wife struggle down the stairs in her heels when his nephew could help her!" Petra giggles as she holds herself to my arm.

I huff in response, annoyed that I've been manipulated into coming down to this stupid party.

I'm hoping to see Uncle Alex first, to catch up with one of the relatives that doesn't see me as a pariah, but to my dismay, it's my dad who catches us at the bottom of the stairs.

"Andries!" he exclaims, as if we hadn't been screaming at each other last night. "Now that's a surprise!"

He tries to pat my shoulder jovially, but I dodge, pulling Petra with me. She stumbles the slightest bit and glares up at me, pinching my arm. "That was rude."

"It's a long story," I say tensely as we keep walking toward the dining room. "Don't ask."

I can tell she wants to anyway, but thankfully, she refrains.

As we enter the ballroom, I can't help but notice it's full of so many people it boggles my mind. It's decorated tastefully, and by the loud, carefree laughter floating over the crowd, it's clear the alcohol is flowing freely.

I could really use a drink.

Petra spots Alex first and drags me over to her husband. She releases me and stands tall to kiss him quickly, smiling.

"I've found your favorite nephew," she says cheerfully.

"Indeed you have," Alex rumbles in reply. He holds out his hand to mine, and I gladly shake it. As I stand in front of him, I realize we are about the same height, maybe I'm even an inch or two taller. Time truly flies.

Petra looks between the two of us and, content in the fact she has left me with someone acceptable, fades into the crowd.

"Look at you, Andries. You're a grown man now. I feel positively ancient," Alex jokes.

"Well, you don't look it. It's good to see you, Uncle."

His gaze follows to where Petra disappeared. "She keeps me young, I think. Other times it feels like she's killing me slowly but… that's love."

"Yeah," I hedge uncomfortably. "I guess it is."

"So!" Alex declares, grabbing a drink from a passing server's tray for each of us. He pushes one into my hand before I can protest. "I want to hear all about university," he looks around and lowers his voice conspiratorially. "Including any rogue classes you've picked up on your own. Your grandmother was furious when she found out how many random courses I had taken on the family dime."

Distracted from the unwanted alcohol by this statement, I grin. "Oh, you have no idea."

Without any hesitation, I launch into the conversation, and just like with Petra, having an interested, unbiased audience soothes my soul.

***

Dinner is fucking terrible, just like I thought it would be. Elise sits next to me, but we barely speak. I assume she's just here to make sure I don't bolt. Unfortunately, I'm a lot hungrier than I thought I was, and the food is fantastic, so I wouldn't have left anyway.

"Glad to see you join the land of the living," Elise whispers.

"Unwillingly," I gripe, and my sister rolls her eyes.

Everyone wants to talk to me, and I field what feels like a million questions with vague, short answers, but it's enough to keep Mom happy. The biggest dark spot is watching Mom be so affectionate with my dad, knowing that he had treated me so cruelly the night before, but there is nothing to be done about it. I just chew, swallow, and try my best to get through the painfully long meal.

Finally, it's over, and while Alex tries to convince me to join the men for port and cigars, I make an excuse about smoke sensitivity and slip away while no one is watching.

Just like New Year's Eve, the terrace is empty because of the cold, but there are a few radiant heaters scattered about to provide enough warmth to any intrepid outside adventurers. I lean against the railing, letting out a long sigh of relief at having survived the party for the most part. I still wouldn't have gone if I had my say in the matter, but now no one can blame me for not trying.

I get a few moments of peace before I hear the door open, and I turn, relaxing when I see it's only Petra.

"Hey, sorry," she gives me a small wave. "How are you doing?"

I shrug, turning back around as she joins me on the railing. "Fine, I guess. I just don't want to be surrounded by people right now. It's suffocating."

She nods understandingly. "Yeah. It's hard to tolerate these enormous groups when you're torn up inside."

I make a noise of agreement, but don't speak. Petra endures the quiet for a moment before she makes yet another question. This time though, it's even more personal. "You're still thinking about her, huh?"

And of course she's right. All night I've wanted Roxanne at my side. Between her and I there was no scheming plans or political intrigue. It was just love, and I missed it fiercely.

"It's hard not to," I admit. "The second time I ever met her was one this terrace."

Petra blinks in confusion. "Wait, she came here before you were even together?"

"Yep, she was the plus one of a guy that works at my dad's company." I exhale slowly, talking past the tightness in my throat. "The first time I met her was at the University of Amsterdam. I was lost, and she showed me the way. In those brief minutes we walked together, there was something between us. Something that told me I'd see her again."

"You seem to love her quite a bit," Petra breathes, caught up in the story. "Are you sure it's really over for good?"

It's the question I've been asking myself every waking moment it seems like, but hearing it said out loud by someone other than myself hits me like a ton of bricks.

"I do love her. To the point I have a hard time going through the motions of everyday life without thinking of her constantly. But I have to move on…" I swallow hard, humiliated at the impact my ex still has on me. "I just don't know how to… how to let her go."

I close my eyes tightly when they start to burn with tears and take a few deep breaths to refocus myself.

Petra quietly asks me, "Is it unforgivable?"

No, I think for the split of a second, but brush the thought immediately away. Since I take longer to respond, she adds, "What she did, that is?"

"She lied," I say, keeping it short. "Too much for me to be able to just let it go."

Petra winces in empathy. "Maybe she did it because she was afraid to lose you?" Her suggestion reminds me of what Dan told me. "Why don't you give her a second chance? She's just human, after all. We all make mistakes."

I smile wistfully at Petra. Throughout the night, I had realized what was going on with my mother forcing Petra's company on me and why she was making so many questions. After a brief Google search, it wasn't hard to find out why— according to a news article, she had successfully managed to find a partner for her best friend; some renowned Japanese artist, and knowing my mom as I do, she's probably hopeful Petra can do the same for me.

"I thought Mom sent you here to hook me up with some other perfect woman? She's been trying to dissuade me from even thinking about her." Petra's mouth opens in an 'o' of surprise, so I make up an explanation. "Everyone has heard about your friend Emma and that artist Shiori."

"Of course they have," Petra grumbles, sipping her glass of champagne. "Yeah, she brought me here to find you a partner, but I didn't know the details." She pauses, searching my eyes with her own. "Do you think she still loves you?"

"Yeah," I say immediately. To me, there is no doubt. I saw it in her eyes the last time we met. "She's been trying to reach out nonstop."

I drag a hand through my hair, frustration mounting. "I'm so damn confused. On one hand, I want to forgive her, but on the other…" I let my words trail off before letting out a breath. "My family is very much against me seeing her, and she works in an industry I'm fairly against, morally speaking."

"Can't she quit her job and do something else?" Petra asks, tilting her head to the side.

I laugh to hide the ugly truth. "I don't think so. She's a proud business owner."

"That sounds like a good thing. What kind of business?"

Annoyed that I can't explain without revealing Roxanne's actual occupation, I growl, "I can't tell you that. It's just…so fucking humiliating. But trust me when I say it's not good."

I can see the gears turning in Petra's head as she puts everything together. She's a smart, quick-witted woman, but if she's figured it out, she doesn't tell me. "Um, alright." She twists a lock of her hair around her finger as she talks. "Look, since I managed to find someone for my best friend, and God knows how high her standards are, maybe I can try and find someone else for you?"

I think immediately of Tatiana, all florals, bright white smiles, and perfume that smells like daisies. If I could fall for another woman, it'd have already been her. The kind, innocent, heartbreakingly honest Tatiana.

"I appreciate it, Petra, but I'm not interested in meeting anyone else."

She nods, seemingly having expected that answer from me anyway. "I understand. Don't tell your mother, but I promise not to force someone on you. I've been where you are," she confides.

We are both silent for some time. I can see on Petra's face that she's now distant, most likely thinking about her own love life; and all the things she and Alex went through in order to come out the other side. It's hard for me to believe this slight woman could not only weather that storm but also stand up against my own mother and grandmother.

If she can do what she had to do for love, so can you.

Petra stretches eventually, arms above her head. "Well, I'm going back inside. Don't be a stranger, Andries."

"I won't," I tell her as she pats me in the back in a comforting gesture. She and my uncle are the type of family I needed to be closer to, and I plan on making it happen. "Thank you for the chat."

"You're welcome," she says, smiling sweetly before disappearing back into the ballroom.

I stay outside longer than I should. Even with the heaters, my fingertips are beginning to tingle, but I just can't bring myself to go back into the party. Out here, I can miss Roxanne... heck, even love her from afar... in peace.

CHAPTER 18

V.D.B. estate, February 20, 2022
Andries

Just when I feel like the universe is doing everything it possibly can to make my life more difficult, it throws me a chance to escape and really think about things in a different perspective.

As a writer, being able to see things from every angle is imperative. I guess that's what makes it so odd that in my own world, my outlook is so stubborn and locked into place. Right now, I can't bear the thought of emerging from my room and facing the consequences of my escalating animosity with my dad. Our arguments and heated exchanges taint everything in the home, and I feel hopeless in wanting to escape it all.

Pacing the length of my room, I consider the best time to make my escape. I have to be able to get out without involving myself in any sort of conversation, which in this house, seems almost impossible. There is someone around every corner that wants to have a word or two with me.

I make the decision to leave once the sun sets, but then my phone rings. I figure it must be Dan, or Elise calling to scream at me from the other side of the house without debasing herself by walking to my room, but to my surprise it's an unknown American number.

Out of curiosity, and a touch of boredom, I answer.

"Hello?"

"Hey, this is Uncle Alex. Are you busy today, nephew?"

I blink a few times, slightly taken aback by this strange turn of events. "I'm not. Why?"

"I'd like you to join my family and I on a trip to the Van Gogh Museum. I hardly ever see you anymore and I've honestly felt pretty low seeing how you've turned into a man since the last time I saw you. I should be in your life more, kid." Alex coughs, maybe feeling that he had said too much. "Anyway, I'm taking my family since Petra is a painter and is dying to go. Would you do us the honor of coming along?"

I ponder for a moment. Alex and I barely know each other after so many years apart. But… It'd be a good way to pass the time until I'm ready to go to my new apartment.

"Uh, sure. I'd love to go."

"Good man. We'll be arriving around eleven a.m. The twins should be calm and well rested by then."

I chuckle. "Twins… I keep forgetting that you two have twins! How do you ever sleep?"

"A very expensive, but adept live-in nanny," he admits, his voice deadpan.

"I'll remember that if I ever have kids. I'll meet you all at eleven a.m."

"See you soon, Andries."

* * *

I don't know what I expected, but it wasn't this. The Van Gogh Museum is much, much different from I thought it would be. Outside, the enormous building is a circular layout split in half; one part stone, the other glass. It's attached to a more traditional-looking building, but the glass-and-stone motif remains.

Alex, Petra, and their children are waiting for me outside while other patrons flow around us like water. I pause when I see them, feeling the slightest pang of envy in my gut. They look so content, happy, and in love. As if the trappings of our excessive lifestyles have left Alex and Petra behind, and there is nothing left but the happiness their little family unit brings. Alex shakes my hand robustly. Petra gives me a quick embrace, and then the two of them introduce me to their children. The twins are in a double stroller, dressed in warm, puffy jumpers that squish their little cheeks up when they look around.

Their son, Jasper, is the larger of the two babies, and when I kneel down to speak to him, he just looks at me with enormous, round blue eyes. It's as if he's considering my every move and who I could possibly be.

Jasmine, the smaller twin, is not nearly as contained. She babbles loudly as I speak to her, grabbing at the collar of my shirt when I lean toward to give her soft, wispy hair a tussle.

The two babies are the perfect mix of Alex and Petra, and even though babies aren't my thing at this point in my life, these two were gracious enough to squeeze anyone's heart.

Petra pries Jasmine's hand off my shirt, laughing apologetically. "Leave your cousin alone, Jas," she scolds gently, to which the little girl howls in response.

Petra kisses Jasmine's face, and then Jasper's before standing back up, huffing but smiling. "Let's get inside before these two cause any more trouble."

I, like most people, know a passing amount about Vincent Van Gogh, but as soon as we step into the museum I know I'm going to leave today much more educated about the man and his life.

Entire rooms are dedicated to single paintings, with huge projections of them spread across the walls and floors wherever we move. Each room is its own painting, making it an immersive experience, and the perfectly coordinated music is the final touch to make it an exquisite display. I'm immediately impressed, but it's nothing compared to my aunt, who is absolutely agog. Alex smiles indulgently as we walk, and Petra is busy giving us a complex explanation and history of each painting and the meaning behind it. My uncle must be smug, seeing how much of a win this trip is for his wife.

I wish I had the chance to make someone that happy.

Eventually, Petra wants to linger at singular paintings, and Alex lets her know that he and I are going to peel off and explore a little on our own. We leave the twins with Petra, but they're so enamored by the lights and sounds that I'm sure they won't even know that their father has left.

"You have a beautiful family," I tell Alex, shoving my hands into my pockets as we walk.

"I do," he agrees. "It was hard to win it, mine and Petra's marriage, but now I can look at it and see the beauty too. Petra always knew, though. She always saw it that way."

"Seeing the two of you and comparing it to the way the story about the two of you is told throughout the family, really puts into perspective how much people will lie to get you to believe their point of view," I tell him.

Alex chuckles. "Well, she is quite a bit younger than me. I can see why some might not approve, but honestly, it's no one's business but our own."

We stop and take in the *Starry Night* exhibit, faces and bodies washed in blues, greens, and yellows as we move through the projections. "You and Dad were always good friends, though, right? He never had anything to say about you and Petra, really. If anything, it was mostly Mom."

"Tell me, Andries, you have a sister who is close to your age. Do you think she will still want to mettle in your business in fifteen years?"

I consider Elise, and snort. "Yes, absolutely."

"And there you see why my sister was so up in arms about whatever I was up to. But to answer your question; yes, Sebastian and I have been friends for a long time." He slides a glance over to me, and I know where the conversation is going in a snap. I want to kick myself for leading him right into it. "Your relationship with him is rather strained though, am I right?"

I scoff. "That's an understatement."

"It isn't worth holding a grudge over. You don't have to take my advice—" He holds up his hands when I start to protest. "But people don't live forever. You should make things right with Sebastian if you can."

"Why should I be the one taking the first step?" I ask, trying my best not to be too aggressive. "He's the one who called my ex a whore."

"I know, and that's what I told him," Alex says it so matter-of-factly, and I'm genuinely surprised he'd say that to my dad. "But his pride is blinding him, so maybe—just maybe—try talking to him. With the arrest of his best employee, giving him a word can go a long way."

"Is it possible you're saying this because he's your friend, not because you think it's actually what I need to do?"

He hesitates, considering his next words carefully. "My wife had a very strained relationship with her dad for a long time. As someone standing on the outside, I could see what they couldn't, and how if they had mended fences earlier, it would have saved them both some grief." Alex looks to me to make sure I'm paying attention. "Missing his daughter probably took years off Roy's life. I know he regrets the two of them being distant for so long. I know it's going the opposite way for you, but your dad loves you even if it doesn't feel that way. Don't wait until it's too late because who knows how many years you might waste?"

"I'll only talk to him if he apologizes," I say, but my voice is subdued. What Alex is saying is true, but I also can't just back down. "It's not my fault that his employee did what he did."

Alex hums in agreement, but then a thought comes over me like a bucket of cold water. "Wait, if you know about Karl then…" I close my eyes miserably, wanting to ignore the walls and walls of sunflowers that seem too bright and cheery for this talk. "I suppose he told you about Roxanne too, then?"

"He did," Alex responds, nonplussed. He notices me watching him, because I'm afraid he's going to call me a moron any moment or tell me how disgusting Roxanne's career is. Instead, Alex holds up his hands in front of him. "Hey, I don't care if she was a former escort or whatever. I care about you and your happiness."

I snort, but secretly I'm relieved to have someone in my corner. "You might be the only one in the family who feels that way."

"It's true. We might not see each other much, but I do want you to be happy and healthy, Andries. Which brings me to your, um, drinking habits…"

This time I motion for him to stop. "It was just at the beginning, after our breakup."

"A one-time coping habit can rapidly become a real habit," Alex points out. "Are you staying busy, so you don't dwell on this breakup? Roxanne seems to be occupying a lot of your mind, according to everyone in your family."

"Yes, I swear. Next week I will move to my new place and I'm even working on a memoir." It's a fancier way of saying it's a simple diary, but it's probably not necessary to dress it up for Alex. Something about the way he talks to me makes me feel like he doesn't judge me nearly as much as other family members.

Once we're done with the immersive part of the museum, we enter into the normal portion, passing numerous self-portraits of Van Gogh himself.

Maybe it's the tortured facade of the long dead, hopeless romantic artist that prompts Alex to ask, "Do you miss her?"

His question catches me by surprise, and I'm not sure what to make out of it. I start to lie but remember what I just told myself. Alex won't judge me, and it'd be nice to be real with someone for once. "Of course, I do," I sigh. "I thought what we had was... you know..."

"Forever?" he asks, still facing the wall of paintings.

I nod, speechless, and slightly embarrassed at the thought of it. Forever with an escort, what's wrong with me?

Alex isn't done, though. He continues to press. "And her? Did she think the same?"

"I think so," I sigh. "We were practically living together at my condo. It was all moving so fast, but we fit together so perfectly I hardly even noticed. When we broke up I had to pack up all her belongings and it was... painful to say the least."

We walk without speaking for some time more, all the while Roxanne and my love for her at the forefront of my mind. I think about her sleeping in my bed, waking and making us coffee in nothing but one of my shirts... and then I think of her betrayal, the humiliated rage on her face when I confronted her about her lie.

The taste of her. The sounds she made when I kissed her.

Alex startles me out of my self-indulgent pity party. "Your parents are gonna kill me for telling you this but..." he hesitates, rolling his eyes to the ceiling as if he still isn't sure he's saying the right thing. "Do you think giving her a second chance is totally out of the equation?"

My mouth falls open in shock. "Are you serious? She... she lied to me about her entire identity. Roxanne was selling sex during the day and then coming back to sleep beside me like it was no big deal."

"Maybe because she knew you would break up with her." He shrugs.

"Why are you taking her side all of a sudden?" I press, my eyes on his face.

"Because… as horrible as it seems, sometimes people lie when they are afraid of disappointing or losing the ones they love." Alex's tone is even and sure.

His words resonate through me, and I can't help but think about my English program and the fact I haven't told my parents about it. Does it make me a hypocrite to hate Roxanne for doing something similar? Her sins are much worse than mine, but still…. "Speaking from experience?" I ask, trying to turn the subject away from myself.

"Indeed," he admits readily. "And I was lucky enough to have someone who gave me a second chance."

"What do you mean?" I try to query, but my uncle just pats me on the back before leaving my side. I want to yell his name and make him explain how I was supposed to fix all of this while still sticking to my moral code, but he is walking toward his wife who has been standing in front of another piece of artwork for the last five minutes.

I stare at the four of them, and the easy, joyful love between them. I feel like Roxanne has cheated me out of that same kind of love, because she sold herself to me as someone she wasn't. Now, I stand here still in love with a person that isn't real, while a madam walks around wearing her face.

Even still, I want her back. I let Alex's advice roll through my mind, realizing that I would have to be the one to give Roxanne the second chance. Watching my uncle's family, it almost seems worth it to give in and welcome her back in my life, but there is no way my family would ever accept her now. I'd be a pariah.

Would I be able to live with being a pariah for Roxanne?

I won't be able to decide this afternoon, or maybe even this week. I need time and space to think. Shedding the worry for the moment, I approach them, greeting the twins with some tickles.

Before we leave, we take some pictures of the five of us, recruiting some other guests to snap the photos while we pose. I get to hold Jasmine and then Jasper and feel the weight of their little frames in my arms. All in all, it's a good day, and I feel better from it. Uncle Alex has given me so much to ponder and made the inevitability of my decisions all too clear.

* * *

"Did you have a nice time?" Mom asks, all but running down the hallway before I can close my bedroom door. She has spotted me, and now there is no escape.

"Actually, yes. The museum is amazing. You should go see it if you haven't. Goodnight, Mom."

I try to close the door, but she puts her foot in the way.

"Did you have some heart-to-heart talk with my brother?" she presses.

I shrug, not wanting to give her the satisfaction.

Mom sighs, her shoulders sagging. "Fine, don't talk to me if you don't want to. You're leaving tomorrow, right?"

I sigh. "Yes, Mom."

"Are you going to say anything to your father before you go?" She's trying to sound calm, but I can tell Mom is on edge.

I almost say yes. If I do, she'll cart me off to his office and shut me in so we can talk. I think about how Alex told me to mend things with my dad, but I'm just not ready. Maybe I'll take my uncle's advice after all, just going a little slower than recommended.

"I'll text him," I say. "I still need some time to calm down."

She wants to argue but holds her tongue. "That's better than never I guess. Now, give your mother a hug before bedtime."

It should feel childish, but there is a lot of love in her embrace that she doesn't show on the outside. I let her hug me close, even though I'm taller than her.

"Just be careful out there, my baby boy," she murmurs, squeezing me tighter.

"I'll try," I tell her honestly. "I'll really try."

CHAPTER 19

Amsterdam, February 24, 2022
Roxanne

Shuffling papers on my desk and glancing at the office phone —where the angry red light telling me of the many unheard messages blinks nonstop—I can't help but miss the old times when I could conquer problems day by day. Instead, I'm stuck in a quagmire of unending nonsense that I can't seem to escape.

The calls never stop coming in. Nervous clients, nosy tabloid journalists, and a strange influx of women curious about jobs, no doubt because of the ten thousand euros price tag that had been bandied around in the newspapers. I definitely wasn't hiring anyone, or taking any new clients, either. The agency is for now operating for current clients and escorts only. The potential leaks and problems are too many, and I'm drowning as it is.

I've had the same conversation over and over again the past few days, so many times that I could probably recite it in my sleep.

"No, there is no risk of this happening to you or any of my other clients. Yes, this was a case of extenuating circumstances gone awry, and our secrecy and discreteness remain intact."

If it was any other industry, I'd be worried about losing business, but the desire for sex never wavers. As long as there are men around Amsterdam, there'll be clients ready and willing to hire my girls, no matter the danger. I don't want just any men, though. I want the best for my girls—the wealthiest, the safest, and the most respectable that money can buy.

My voicemail box is full, and my email inbox is getting there, if such a thing is even possible. I had been walking the edges of high society my whole career with the brothel, but now that honest-to-God fame was knocking on my door, I wanted nothing to do with it. I just wanted to pull the curtains closed and ignore everything going on around me, but I'm a business owner. I have girls to take care of, and I don't want my company to go under. It's not an option.

With a sound like a blaring alarm, the phone rings yet again, startling me into dropping my pen. I'm ready to jerk the cord out of the back of the damned thing when I get the feeling that I should answer this call, even if it's just to tell the person on the other line to shut the hell up.

I pull the receiver off the cradle in a swift motion. "This is Roxanne."

"Ah, the beautiful madam Roxanne Feng, answering my calls herself! I feel like a celebrity."

In no mood to hear the oily voice on the other line, I sneer. "Should I hang up now, Kenneth, or do you have something constructive to say?"

"Wait, wait," he coos. His voice makes me see red. "I'm not calling to threaten you or anything like that. You've been doing a good job of getting yourself into the public eye all on your own. I was just going to offer you an opportunity."

Despite not liking Kenneth one tiny bit, I'm just too curious to decline. "...Go ahead."

"Well, I'm sure you know that I'm working on a piece involving Karl Townsend and all of his associated dramatics. From what I understand, he was both a business associate and friend of yours, so would you be interested in giving me a statement? It'd help you get ahead of the public opinion regarding your part in the whole debacle."

I laugh sardonically. "And here I thought you actually had something good to offer me. No, I'd rather tank my reputation all on my own than have some manipulative gossip columnist twisting my words for his own selfish needs."

"You know I'm an *investigative reporter*," he bristles. "This won't just be a single line in a 'gossip column' as you put it. This will be paragraphs upon paragraphs about your filthy business and who you associate yourself with."

His words make my stomach churn, but I power through, not wanting him to sense my uneasiness. "You can't possibly have anything to say about me that hasn't already been said."

"Oh, I don't know about that." In my mind, I can almost see him smiling devilishly as he leans back in his chair, maybe checking his fingernails as he does so. "Wouldn't it just be awful for all of those lovely ladies you employ to be named and dragged into this whole mess? Poor things. It isn't their fault, now is it?"

My uneasiness blooms into full blown anger. "Go fuck yourself, Kenneth."

Before he can say another word, I slam the receiver down. It's so much more satisfying than pushing a button on the cell phone screen, so I pick it up and slam it down again for good measure. If only the receiver had been Kenneth's head instead, then I really would feel better.

It was the truth when I told him that there wasn't any way he could shame me more than I already was, but I'm a phoenix; I'll always rise from the ashes. My girls, though... I want to keep their working environment as calm and collected as possible. I never want any of this nonsense with Karl and Patricia to bleed over into their lives. It was my mistake, and I was going to eat every morsel of it, no one else.

Rolling the thoughts of Kenneth's inevitable article around in my mind, I consider giving my own interview first before he is able to publish his. It'd no doubt infuriate him to have his scoop pulled out from under him, but as fun as the idea sounds, it's probably best to just lay low and let the idea of me and my brothel fade out of public consciousness. Sex work isn't all that interesting in Amsterdam; the draw of the story between Karl and the college girl is how high profile he is and how detestable the act was, but crazy things happen all the time in this city. The newest fascination would appear soon enough.

As I reply to what feels like the millionth email in the past hour, Poppy pokes her head into my office with an apologetic look on her face. "You've got someone here to see you."

I look up with a scowl. "I told you absolutely no visitors or appointments today."

"It's Patricia," she clarifies. Some of my annoyance fades.

"Send her in, then."

The petite, pale-haired girl enters the office, wearing a sweater that is two sizes too big with her hands tucked into the sleeves. She looks so young that I feel a pang of guilt for sending her on the assignment that is now causing the two of us so much trouble. She settles herself into the loveseat at the back of the office, looking everywhere but at me.

"Hello, Patricia," I start gently, leaning forward on my chair. "How are you feeling?"

She shrugs one thin shoulder. "Not great."

"What do you need?" I ask after a moment of her sitting in silence. It's like she wants to talk about something but is too nervous to do so.

"I'm just feeling all messed up inside," she elaborates. "I can't avoid all the news stuff about Karl, and every time I'm reminded of it, I feel more and more guilty."

"Guilty?" My interest is perked and I leap off of my chair, pacing slowly in her direction. "Why?"

She sinks lower on the sofa, looking miserable, and she heaves a long sigh. "I know he took advantage of me... somewhat, at least, but it wasn't like he was cruel. Now I'm hearing that he's probably going to lose his job and I just feel so awful." Patricia buries her face in her hands and groans. "I shouldn't have gone to the police. Everything is such a mess, and it's all my fault."

I take a few more steps and sit beside her, before putting an arm around her shoulders. The poor girl is stiff as a board, with soft sobs coming from between her fingers.

"He still crossed a line with you, after many, many guarantees that he wouldn't do so. You have nothing to feel guilty for, Patricia. He pushed you too far, even if he was kind about it."

"If I had just had better control over myself and the amount I drank, then we wouldn't even be having this discussion," she continues.

I can't help but feel sympathetic for her and her plight. After all, she's only a few months beyond seventeen, and trusted the client because she trusted me, but also because I realize how much it was my fault for putting her in a situation where she was such an easy target.

She lifts her head from her hands, wiping under her eyes with her fingers, and looking me in the eye, she says, "Karl's legal team reached out again and said the settlement is still on the table if I want to take it."

The announcement comes as a shock since I thought her decision to go to court was final. If Patricia signs the settlement, it'd definitely help to calm all this media frenzy about my agency sooner than later, but it'd also mean there would be no justice made and Karl would be a free man. For some reason, this bothers me more than I let on. "Are you going to sign it, though?"

"I don't know," she says, burying her face between her hands for a moment. "I'm so confused."

I pull her closer until our shoulders are touching in a quick hug before releasing her, pivoting on the loveseat to face her fully. "I know this is weighing on you, Patricia, but honestly, you've made your choice to report Karl and you need to follow that path to the end now. There is no way to make it go away except to finish what you've started," I find myself saying.

"My friends are so disappointed in what happened that I feel some sort of remorse about the whole thing, meaning I have to push it all down and hide it away," she fesses out. "It's like they want me to feel more like a victim than I do, and it makes me want to throw in the towel and be done with all of this."

"It's hard for a lot of people to understand the odd relationships that can form between escorts and clients." I bite my lip, considering how much I'm comfortable sharing with Patricia before I throw caution to the wind. "In fact, Karl was my first client, too." Patricia sits up straighter, obviously surprised by the news. "After a while, it became less like a client-escort agreement and more like a relationship. There was a time I'd have considered him my friend, but I'm so disappointed in his behavior now that any chance of friendship we ever had is dead and gone."

It doesn't seem possible, but Patricia looks even more miserable. "Just another thing I ruined."

I grab her hands and force her to give me her attention. "*No. No.* Karl did that all on his own. It could've been you or any of my other girls that this happened to, and his behavior would've never been acceptable."

"Okay…." She nods, wiping her eyes again, this time with the sleeve of her sweater. "I guess that makes sense. If he didn't do it to me, he'd have done it with some other girl."

Not if that other girl had listened to the rules, I think, but I don't say it out loud. "Exactly. Now go get your favorite takeout and get some rest today. Try to shed all this negativity if you can."

"Roxanne…" Patricia hesitates. "Do you think I could have another chance with the agency? I think I've learned enough from my mistakes that I could be a really good escort for you."

Ugh, this again. The poor girl has been obsessed with working at the agency more, but she's too much of a risk, even if she never made another mistake. Her reputation as a snitch would make it so no one would ever hire her, and she'd just be a drain on my payroll.

I shake my head and tucking a small lock of loose hair behind her ear, I say, "Focus on your studies and going to class. Once you graduate things will be easier."

"It'd be much easier *now* if I could make some extra money escorting," she insists.

"In a few years, we'll talk again," I say, more firmly this time.

She looks defeated, but eventually stands and bids me goodbye, her face sullen. It's incredible that this one girl has managed to create so much grief, but here we are. I hope the little problematic bomb that is Patricia will be out of my life sooner rather than later, but I also want her to be at peace with herself too.

* * *

It's almost time for me to leave the office when my iPhone rings. It's a nice change from the office phone that has been screaming at me all day, but when I see my sister's name on the screen, I have a moment of nervousness. I've been stressed about the news story about Karl and my agency affecting Lili and her bookstore, but nonetheless, I have to answer.

"Roxie," Lili blurts out as soon as the call connects. "Can you come to the bookstore? It's an emergency."

My skin prickles. "An emergency? What do you mean?"

"Just come on!" Lili insists. "I'll explain when you get here."

"Lili—" Before I can say anything the line goes dead. Angrily I toss my phone down on my desk and rub my temples, trying to dispel some of the tension that has been building all day.

I have no choice but to go, but it'd have been nice to know what kind of shit show I was walking into. With my nerves raw and my mind exhausted, I grab my bag and leave, telling Poppy to lock up on her way out.

I get to the bookshop in record time. From outside, nothing looks amiss. No reporters or journalists, no caution tape or fire trucks... nothing. It looks quiet, and that almost makes me more uneasy. Whatever is waiting for me inside is a complete mystery.

As I grab the handle of the door, it pushes open from inside, and Lili slides outs of the doorway, only opening it enough to fit her body out of the gap before shutting it again. I back up a few steps, crossing my arms when I notice the sheepish look on her face.

"What exactly is going on, Lili? What emergency?"

"You'll thank me later." She presses the keys to the store into my hands. "Just lock up when you're done, okay?"

Completely bewildered, I enter the dark bookshop. Instead of a fire, flood, or some other sort of disaster, there's a man waiting for me, tall and with his hands clasped behind his back. When he turns to me, my heartbeat kicks up into a gallop, and it feels like the floor has dropped out from underneath me.

"Andries," I breathe, my mouth suddenly dry. "Wh—what are you doing here?"

"I needed to talk to you in private," he explains, pacing slowly in my direction. "Somewhere neutral, so I asked your sister what she thought, and she suggested using the bookshop."

His expression is guarded, as if he expects me to just walk out the door without saying a single word. Maybe if I was tougher, I would, but there isn't an ounce of anger in him that I can detect, and that's a complete departure from our last face-to-face meeting.

"Okay," I acquiesce. "What did you want to talk about?"

The breath he lets out is enormous, his shoulders sinking with the size of it. "Ah, fuck, Roxie. Everything. Nothing. I don't even know." He clenches and unclenches his fists at his sides, like he doesn't know what to do with his hands.

Is Andries… Nervous?

After a minute, he seems to find his words, telling me, "I do want to thank you for everything that you've done with Patricia, encouraging her to make her own choice and backing her up. I know Karl was a friend of yours, or something along those lines." He looks uncomfortable at that thought but pushes through. "It couldn't have been easy to make the right choice, is all I'm saying."

"I'd have never left her to fight that fight alone, especially since I was the one that offered the job that made her vulnerable in the first place. I do have to admit I didn't think it'd blow up like this. But Karl burned his bridges with me way before this."

He frowns at my answer and I know in that moment, I might have said too much. "What do you mean?"

I cringe, not wanting to get into it, not when I have Andries right here in front of me and there are so many other things I want to talk to him about, and so many better ways we could spend this time together. "He just wasn't who I thought he was, that's all."

"Roxanne...."

"Fine," I blow a piece of hair out of my face, collecting my thoughts. "I cut him off when I started to think that something might happen between you and me, and he didn't take it well. After he figured out that complaining and trying to bribe me wasn't going to work, he went quiet. I should've expected something then, but at that point I still thought we could come out friends in the end, which was stupid of me. Long story short, he tried to buy this place," I motion around us at the bookshop. "He was offering way over what it was worth to the previous owner, but thank God I managed to get it back, and Karl then threatened me that Karma would get me." I conveniently leave the part where Karl was held hostage by a hitman until he accepted my terms.

Andries looks shocked. "That's such a scumbag move, trying to buy the place your family has spent their whole life working at."

"Tell me about it. Karl obviously didn't succeed and when I cut him off from my agency altogether he came back a lot more subdued. He approached me at a mutual acquaintance's party and apologized, telling me that a casual friendship and business relationship was better than nothing and that he wanted to reconcile," I explain. I'm not sure why, but it just feels so liberating telling Andries the whole story about Karl. "After hiring a few of my girls for successful, unproblematic events, he asked me about hiring a virgin escort. I had let my guard down, and it was fucking idiotic, but here we are." I roll my eyes to the ceiling, feeling sad about the false friendship I had lost and how I had been taken advantage of, which allowed someone else to also be victimized. "So, yeah, I'll never trust him again."

When Andries comes forward to take me into his arms in a comforting embrace, I don't stop him. Having him hold me makes something that had been pulled so tight that it was close to breaking finally relax, and I sigh.

"Thank you for being honest with me," he says in a whisper. "I've always wanted it to be like that between us. Open. Honest. No matter where we stand with each other." I nod against his shoulder. "If it'd have been like that in the beginning—"

"I know," I interject. "I fucked up." I pause, a gush of air rolling off my lips, before facing his cerulean eyes again. "By the time I realized how much I cared about you it was too late to tell you the truth without there being some sort of fallout. I couldn't stomach the thought of losing you, but that was such a short-sighted thought. You were always going to find out."

Andries sighs, his eyes locked with mine as he says, "I just wish I had heard it from you instead of some girl I barely knew."

"I'm sorry," I tell him, my voice thin. "Lying to keep you close is what ended up pushing you away from me. I–" I have to swallow past the lump in my throat before I can continue. "I wish I could've been braver when it came to you and me. Andries... I'd never had anything so precious as our relationship. It made me rash. I'm sorry."

To my surprise, he puts his hands on my shoulders and moves me away from him just the slightest bit, so there is enough room between us for him to lay a gentle kiss on my forehead. My eyes flutter closed, his breath mingling with mine. I savor it.

We don't separate. It's almost as if the moment we do, the magic will be broken, and we'll be back to being worlds apart. Looping my arms around his waist, I ask, "I can't believe you're even in town. I thought you were staying back at your family estate and commuting."

He tenses slightly. "I was, but mostly to... well... to detox." I frown at his words, and he unwillingly explains further. "I'd been drinking a lot." I move to pull away, ready to lecture him, but he tightens his hold on me. "No need to tear me apart, Roxie, everyone else already has. I'm fine now. It just depends on the day where I stay. I'm sure you can gather that my father and I are at odds with Karl getting arrested and me helping Patricia."

"I didn't even consider that," I admit, my mind already picturing the yelling and fights between him and his dad. "I'm sure he'll come around, Andries. You're his son."

He chuckles sadly. "You don't know my father very well, then."

I switch gears, wanting an answer to a question that had been plaguing me for a while. "It seems crazy to ask this right now, considering there isn't an inch of space to be found between us, but… are you seeing Tatiana? As more than a friend? I've heard rumors."

He groans. "I won't even ask how you heard rumors about *that*, but no. We are just friends," Andries hesitates. "I enjoy her company as such. She's a good person and respects my boundaries."

Despite our embrace, Andries and I are technically nothing to one another, so I have no right to feel jealous. But I do anyway. Tatiana is everything I'm not. Young, from a wealthy family, and an appropriate match for him. It'll be hard for me to ever see her as anything but competition.

"Okay," I say vaguely, but apparently there is enough annoyance in my voice that Andries picks up on it. He puts a finger under my chin and lifts my face up to look into his.

"She's my *friend*, Roxie, but you're something more. You two exist on completely different planes to me. Tatiana could never be you."

"What do you mean by that?"

Andries looks like he's going to answer, but with the quietest moan, he ducks his head down and captures my mouth with his instead. I'm shocked at first, but my body catches up quicker than my brain, and before I know it we're kissing passionately, like two lovers that have been separated for years.

His lips are just as soft as I remember, and his tongue sliding against mine suffuses me in shivers. Despite everything, despite all of the things between us, I still want him.

"Fuck," he growls, pulling away before I can stop him. Andries touches his lips with his fingers, and looking slightly embarrassed, he turns his body toward the exit.

"I'm sorry, that was—I've got to go," he stutters, but before he can make it outside, I grab him by the sleeve at the very last second. He freezes but doesn't turn to face me.

"What was that?" I demand. "Why did you kiss me?" In my heart, I know the answer, but I want to hear him say it out loud.

He huffs. "You know why."

"Tell me."

"Because despite everything that you've done to me, I still…" he sucks in a shuddering breath. "I still love you."

I release him then, my hand feeling numb. I can't believe this is really happening. I can't believe he said those words. It all feels like a dream.

Andries looks at me finally, "Thanks again for what you've done for Patricia. I'll talk to you later."

"Andries, wait—" I try to keep him here, maybe just for one more kiss, but he's gone before I can even finish the thought.

I'm alone again, but when I press my fingers to my mouth, I can still feel him there. A slow smile creeps over my lips, victory bells ringing in my head.

CHAPTER 20

Amsterdam, February 25, 2022
Andries

Some days, class is my escape from all the oddities of my everyday life. Today, though, it's dragging, and the reasoning is silly; the sooner I get out of here, the sooner I can continue daydreaming and working through what happened between Roxanne and I yesterday.

When I had called Lili to set up the meeting, I had told myself that, logically, it was to find some closure on the relationship between us. I had decided that since we seemed destined to run into each other again and again, it'd be a good idea to at least be able to see her here and there without it causing a torrent of emotions inside of me. I couldn't be her friend, but I had to be mature enough to be her acquaintance.

It'd all changed as soon as she walked in, though. Roxanne wasn't dressed to kill, and she certainly had no idea that she had been coming to meet me, but it was seeing her in her natural, everyday state that had really gotten me. She looked exactly like that when we were living together; her casual clothes, minimal makeup, and her hair swept away from her face. She wasn't some siren coming to drag me down to the depths or some stereotypical brothel madam in expensive silks and pearls. She was just... Roxie. The woman I had fallen for, who I had lived day to day with, who had held me during the night and shared my bed. It hit me, as soon as she opened that bookstore door with no idea of who was waiting to see her, that this woman was still the one I loved. She hadn't changed into a stranger like I had tried to tell myself for weeks now.

And that meant I was well and truly fucked.

I kept my distance from her at first, but as it always seemed to happen, we became closer and closer to one another until I was wrapping her slight frame into my arms and resting my head against the familiar scent of her hair. Now that there was no animosity between us, and the sharp, stinging feeling of her betrayal had all but gone, all that was left was the affection and magnetic attraction that had never left.

Of course, we had also kissed, completely destroying any boundaries I had set for myself. In the moment, it had been a rush of adrenaline like no other, but now, looking back, I can't help but see it was a moment of weakness—a moment where I was subconsciously toying with the idea of giving her a second chance like Uncle Alex and Aunt Petra advised so eagerly. Yeah, second chances are easy when the woman you love isn't a public figure known as a brothel keeper. Maybe I can't be Roxie's casual acquaintance, after all. Perhaps she's just too irresistible for me to coexist with. That certainly explains why she is occupying my every thought, even during class right now.

The last time she had haunted my every waking moment was when I was sure I hated her, and that obsession had driven me to drink. Now, though, it's that soft, sweet feeling building inside of me, like when she and I had first met, and I can't shake it. I want to see her again. In fact, I've been unconsciously planning how I can make that happen from the moment I woke up this morning.

I've gotten good at letting my body be present in class while my mind floats elsewhere, my hand scribbling across the notebook, making a list of everything that's going on in the lecture hall today so I could peruse it at my own pace once I had come down from the high of last night's kiss. I'm honestly a bit embarrassed at my lack of control, but also jubilant at how well the meeting went. One class of my head floating in the clouds wasn't going to fail me, I'm sure, especially if I was able to keep my head above water when I was struggling with my drinking problem.

Finally class ends, and I drag myself out of my seat and out into the main concourse. I forgot that Elise would be waiting for me, so when I see her I consider going the other direction to avoid conversation, but my sister seems to have a sixth sense that allows her to be extra observant, and she notices me before I can make the choice to flee or not.

She rushes over to me, hair pulled back from her face and free of makeup. She looks lower key than normal, which is odd, since Elsie never seems to be too overwhelmed to stay in complete control of her outward appearance.

Despite that, her smile is wide and glowing. "How was class?"

"Boring. You?"

"It was pretty average, but you know, it's strange that you go through all the trouble of having this secret major when you always tell me the classes are *boring*. Shouldn't something so scandalous at least be entertaining?"

"It's college. It's supposed to be boring, I think, no matter what the subject. But speaking of majors and business, how is the internship going? Is it everything you ever dreamed of, being Dad's right-hand puppet?"

She wrinkles her nose. "At first it was pretty obvious that he wished it was you there, but I think I've proven myself enough that he isn't missing his melancholy son anymore. Although, even without taking the job, you've influenced everything that goes on."

"How so?" I ask, looking at her quizzically.

She heaves a long sigh, her gaze dropping down for a moment. "All everyone can talk about is Karl this, Karl that, and while Dad hasn't made it public knowledge that you had anything to do with it, the fact that it was *me* that showed up for the internship and not you, like everyone expected, has all my co-workers speculating."

"Huh. I thought since Karl got fired that the gossip mill would sort of die down. At least that's what Mom told me would happen, just like with me here at school and the fight video."

"Well, about that…" Elise clears her throat, looking to the sky as if she's reluctant to tell me what she's about to say. "Karl isn't actually fired. He's just suspended. I guess since he hasn't been convicted yet, Dad intends to keep him on until he absolutely can't anymore."

My steps stutter to a halt. "No way? Doesn't he understand what the public opinion will be if they find out he's keeping a rapist on the payroll just in case the victim is lying?"

Elise shrugs, adjusting her bag on her shoulder. "He's damned if he does, damned if he doesn't. Karl has worked there for decades, as you know, and it makes him almost irreplaceable. He can either have Karl waiting in the wings in case it becomes appropriate to bring him back, which is the best-case scenario for Dad, or he can fire him and hire or promote a replacement, but the relationships Karl has developed over the years are indispensable. It'd be almost impossible to replicate them, and Dad doesn't want to start from the ground up, I guess."

"Wow." I can't help but shake my head. "Every day I'm more and more relieved I didn't go into business."

"You're telling me," she grumbles. "Now I have to deal with it all. But… I still like it. It's something new to conquer, and anything that makes me look like a better child than you is a plus."

I elbow her playfully, even though my mind is still reeling from the news about Karl. After his arrest I had been sure Dad had fired him immediately. I guess it wasn't so.

The conversation moves to more normal topics, like our plans for the weekend, when Elise seems to remember something with a gasp.

"Oh my God, I almost forgot to ask if you were coming to Dan's costume party tomorrow night! It's going to be such a good time and I think it'd really do you some good to let loose a little with your peers, if you know what I mean."

Dan had indeed told me about the party he's hosting, but I had brushed it off like I did almost every party invite. It just isn't my scene, and the longer I attended those reckless events, the more disengaged I became with people my age. It just isn't for me.

I don't tell Elise this, though. Instead, I just tell her, "No. I had forgotten until you just mentioned it. I was going to catch up on homework."

"Andries, come on!" she complains. "I really want you to go."

I look at her suspiciously. "No you don't. What's the real reason?"

A gush of air rolls of her lips. "If you must know, Tatiana doesn't have a companion for the night, and she was hoping her dear friend Andries could be her escort, or at least save her a few dances."

"There's always an ulterior motive with you. I don't like parties, and I don't care about Carnival, so it's still going to be a no. You can dance with Tatiana just fine. How about that?"

"Just some more of your slack I need to pick up I guess?" Her voice turns snarky. "Stop being such a weirdo and come to the masquerade. It's the perfect opportunity to show everyone that you've moved on from Roxanne and are nothing but your normal self again. You need this. You just don't know it."

I keep myself from outwardly cringing. I'm not really moving on from Roxanne if she and I are making out in bookshops in private, am I? Thankfully, no one knows about that but her and I.

"No means no, Elise." I can tell she wants to argue, so I make a show out of pulling my phone out and checking something. "Oh, hey, I've got somewhere I have to be, I'll talk to you tomorrow or something."

She sputters, but I make a break for it. We're skirting too close to the topic of Roxanne and the last thing I need is for Elise to know I'm still speaking to her. I can hear Elise yelling behind me, "I'll talk to you at the masquerade! You'd better be there!"

My poor sister. She's out of luck on that front.

Back in my apartment, I've given up any semblance of focusing on anything else but Roxie and our encounter the night before. I'm lying in bed, flipping through pictures of us together on my phone, reliving our time as a couple, photograph by photograph.

Maybe part of it had been a lie, but now that I'm not so angry at her anymore, I can see that our entire time together wasn't completely false. There had been something special between us, and it was undeniable.

I have so many pictures of us. I had wanted to capture every moment I spent with her at the time, not knowing then that I'd soon only have pictures of her and nothing else. Now, it gives me plenty to look at while reminiscing, but it's a double-edged sword. It also makes me miss her like hell.

Moving between photos of her sitting next to me on long drives and selfies taken of the two of us, I land on a video from my birthday, one that I didn't even remember taking of her in our room after the party. She's shimmying out of her dress and displaying her new set of lingerie for me, prancing across the floor like a model on a runway. She is, of course, devastatingly attractive, but it's her energy that draws me into the video too. Roxanne is happy, her smile and silly laughter as addicting as any other drug. We were happy, comfortable, free, and totally obsessed with each other.

Seeing her luminous skin against the lace of her sparse clothing has me harder than I can remember being in months. I sit the phone down the bed beside me and bite the inside of my mouth to try and make the erection go down, but it's no use. After the kiss, and now this rediscovered video, my body isn't going to be denied. I'll never stop wanting her it seems.

With a reluctant groan, I unzip my own fly, pushing my jeans down my hips with one hand and holding my phone, still playing the video, in the other. Once I'm free of my denim constraints, I wrap my member in my fist, hissing at the contact. It isn't her hand, or any other part of Roxie, but it'll have to suffice for the time being.

I pump myself in my fist, teeth clenched and breath coming hard through my nose. I can remember what happened after that video; our limbs tangled together, and the noises she made when she came apart for me. My cock pulses in my hand hard at that thought, and it's almost like I can hear her next to me, the way my name would spill between her lips driving me higher and higher.

I can feel my climax looming, just out of reach, when the video on the phone screen is interrupted as a call comes in. *Fuck!* I shove my cock back into my boxers as I read Dan's name on the screen, feeling uncomfortable at being exposed with my friend calling.

I was so fucking close. Goddamnit, Dan.

I answer, hoping that my voice is even. "What do you want, Dan?"

"Hello to you too, Andries," he grumps. "I'm just calling to remind my good friend about my costume party tomorrow night and confirm your attendance."

I pinch the bridge of my nose. "I already told Elise I'm not going. Carnival isn't my thing."

"Oh, you're going because it's *my party*, not because it's Carnival. I demand your attendance."

"Demand all you want. I'm not going."

Dan's voice becomes serious. "Either you show up at the party, or I'm coming to your house and dragging you there myself. Make sure you are wearing a mask, at the very least."

I can tell by his tone that there is no arguing, and it makes me want to snap my phone to pieces. There is nothing I want to do less than go to a Carnival party where both my sister and Tatiana will be. Not that their company is offensive, but in such a setting there will be no escaping the idea that I should be escorting Tatiana throughout the event.

"Fine," I grit out. "But I'm not staying the entire time."

"Whatever you say, Andries. Looking forward to seeing you tomorrow!"

I hang up without another word, throwing the phone down on the bed beside me and pressing the heels of my palms against my eyes. It seems like everyone I know is insisting on bothering me today, and the one person I wanted to hear from is silent.

I guess I'd better figure out something to wear to this damned masquerade.

CHAPTER 21

Amsterdam, February 26, 2022
Andries

It'd have been easier to just skip the whole ordeal and stay home, but I know if I do, Dan or Elise would show up at my doorstep in record time. I'm left with no choice but to attend Dan's damned party. If anyone asks, I plan on saying I'm dressed as a poet from the nineteenth century when in reality it's just the most convincing outfit I could put together from my current wardrobe without looking like a fool. I had only needed to purchase the mask; a black solid piece that covered everything from my eyebrows to the tops of my cheeks, to make the look work, so it wasn't as much of a pain in the ass as I had expected.

Paired with a white, tailored button-up shirt, black pants, and matching jacket, I realize that I look more like a secret agent, but it's only one night anyway. Elise had been right about one thing; making an appearance would help the rumor mill die down a little bit. I had to focus on that positive aspect if I was going to make it through the night without cursing my entire existence.

The party is everything I'd expect from an event thrown by the one and only Dan O'Brian. Lights are low, red and black scarves and tulle thrown over exposed lights and lit candles on numerous surfaces, casting the entire place in a sort of dreamy ambiance. I know that it's dark to help to obscure everyone's identities, but it also lent an intimate, romantic aura to the place that is hard to deny.

My plan is to greet Dan and Elise, hopefully avoid Tatiana, maybe have a drink, and then leave. I know my friend will be too busy playing host to keep tabs on me too closely, so a simple appearance should be enough to convince him that I had joined the gathering fully. I have no idea what anyone I know will be wearing, so all I can do is let them find me. I quickly see that I'm underdressed compared to most of the other guests who glitter in the low light. Some of them went as far as wearing full costumes, looking like regency aristocrats, others have more mystical attires like fairies, and there are even some who have come looking like gods and goddesses from various mythologies. The outfit that I had hoped would make me less noticeable will probably do the exact opposite here. I'm the outlier.

Oh well. There's nothing to be done for it now. I can't exactly transform myself into some prince or duke, so I'll have to make the best of my simpler ensemble. I order an Old Fashioned from the bartender, who is wearing a badger mask, and I sip it while leaning against the bar, watching the crowd. I just need to find Elise and Dan; then, I can be put out of my misery and leave.

My idea had been to blend in well enough, but to also be recognizable enough that the positives that Elise had mentioned would still benefit me. None of this mattered if no one knew who I was, so when I catch a few other students' eyes and get a familiar nod or handshake in return, I know I've walked that line perfectly.

My sister finds me first, and of course, she has Tatiana in tow. I curse inwardly, but this was to be expected. Elise wouldn't let the more nervous Tatiana brave this kind of gathering alone, but I had just hoped Tati would stay home since she didn't have an actual escort. No such luck, of course.

"Andries," Flower Girl breathes. "You look very nice."

"Underdressed compared to you," I respond, smiling as warmly as I can manage. It's not Tatiana's fault that her presence annoys me, that's all on me. "You both look lovely, of course."

That isn't a lie, either. Elise is dressed in sage dress with a matching mask. Embroidered silver leaves and vines coming from the bottom of her floor-length skirt and up to her chest lend at least a touch of costumed detail to her ensemble.

Tatiana, on the other hand, had taken more of an advantage, and is dressed head to toe like a fairy. Her long, soft hair is tightly coiled and pinned on the top of her head, huge, diaphanous wings extending from her back in glittering white and gold. Her dress looks like it's made of soft pink clouds, gathered at her waist, and spilling out from there. She's beautiful, young, and everything so many of the women here wished they could be. Once again, I feel a flash of frustration with myself. Why couldn't I have fallen for this girl, who would have made my life so much easier? Radiant Tatiana; innocent and well connected, would be my perfect social match. It's too bad that I find her endearing, but not at all someone who sparks my interest. I guess I just love to make things harder on myself.

This close, I can see the heavy highlight on both girls faces, like the softest sheen of frost. Tatiana smiles happily at my praise, holding up her hand so I can dutifully kiss her knuckles before releasing her. Elise looks less than thrilled, waving me away when I go to embrace her.

"No thank you, Andries," Elise says diplomatically. "I can't have everyone knowing that we are related. It'll ruin my mystique."

I roll my eyes, and Tatiana laughs. It's light, like the tinkling of bells, and I can't help but to notice the way her body sways toward me when she does so. If I hang around these two for too long, I know I won't be able to get rid of her. As much as I like Tatiana's companionship, a setting like this is bound to give the crowd the wrong impression of our relationship. The masks, the music, the dark atmosphere; it all lends itself to something seductive and romantic, and that is everything I wanted to avoid with Tati. The fewer mixed signals the better.

I keep the conversation light between the two of us, keeping everything as surface level as I can while scanning the crowd for anyone that might get me out of this situation. Some of the party guests are dressed up so extravagantly that it's almost impossible for me to tell who they are, but there is one distantly familiar face across the bar: Paul Erickson, a published author who lives in the area. He and I had been introduced at Dan's red-light party last year. I remember how he'd encouraged me to stick with my craft, saying that it was better to pursue it while I was young and still passionate about writing. I wouldn't consider us friends, but he'll work well enough as an excuse to ditch my sister and Tatiana.

I excuse myself, and I can see the disappointment on Tatiana's face. I try my best to not let it get to me, but I can't help it. I wish there was someone else for her I knew would treat her right, so she wouldn't have to pine after me for so long. I know a lot of it is my sister's doing, but there is genuine affection from Tatiana too.

I slide through the crowd until I'm beside Paul, who is dressed in a falcon half-mask. There's no recognition on his face at first, but it quickly clears, and he shakes my hand enthusiastically.

"Andries! What a surprise," he booms over the noise of the crowd. "How are you, friend?"

"I'll be better when I'm done playing dress up," I admit. "But otherwise I'm well. Besides the media dust ups that I'm sure you've heard about, of course."

Paul shakes his head. "I don't pay much attention to that sort of thing. It clogs my mind up."

"Good, then I certainly won't fill you in," I comment, and Paul chuckles. "How's your writing going?"

"It's going as well as can be hoped, I guess. I think I need to travel some. Just get away somewhere new and clear my head. Everything just tends to become gray and melancholy when I write these days."

"I understand that," I commiserate. "I'm working on a memoir of my own, but there have been quite a few moments of upheaval in my life lately making things more difficult, and it always seems to stop my writing in its tracks. I'm finally at a good pace now, though, so I hope I'll be finished sooner rather than later."

"You seem to live such an interesting life for someone so young. I guess that's the reason why all these gossip rags are so obsessed with your family. Here," he reaches into his pocket and pulls out a business card, pressing it into my hand. "This is my agent's number. I'm sure a memoir of yours would sell well among those who are fascinated by your life and the lives of your family. Give him a call once you finish edits."

Feeling a rush of adrenaline from the idea of being published, I grin widely; the movement pushing my mask up just slightly. "Thank you, Paul. I really appreciate it. I'll definitely be in contact."

"Good luck. It'd be great to have someone that wasn't older than sin on the label with me."

We talk more, mostly about what Paul hopes to do once he finds a source of inspiration again, but I can't help but look for Dan as we do so. Showing up here was pointless if he didn't see me, and I know he will never take my word for it. I have to see him, or this was just a waste of an evening.

Finally, I spot him in a shimmery green suit jacket and scaled mask reminiscent of a dragon. He's deep in conversation with someone, but I can't see who it is until the crowd shifts slightly. When I see who his conversation partner is, my breath catches in my throat.

There has never been a moment when I haven't found Roxanne beautiful, but tonight she has ascended into something indescribable. It could have been because I missed her so much, or because she had been all I've been able to think about for days, but whatever it is, I'm helpless. I can't look away.

Her dress is a rich carmine that hugs her body from her chest down. It hangs off the shoulders, and the edges of the neckline and the bottom of the skirt, which brushes the floor, is trimmed in black fur. The outside is completed with elbow-length black gloves and a thin black mask that leaves much of her perfect face bare. Her lips are the same red as her dress, and they are tilted up in a smile as she laughs at whatever Dan is saying. Involuntarily, I feel a rush of jealousy that is quickly eased when I remember that it's just Dan, and that he has no interest in Roxanne that way. Plus, I have no right in feeling any sort of jealousy over her since she and I aren't even together.

Moving toward them isn't a choice. Like so many things with Roxanne, walking toward her and Dan is an unconscious thing, and before I know it, I'm standing in front of them with my hand on Dan's shoulder. Roxanne takes as second to recognize me, but when she does, her mouth opens in an "o" of surprise.

"Can I talk to you, Dan?" I ask, voice tense.

He nods, but only takes us a step away from Roxie before he crosses his arms and says, "What?"

It's low enough that I know she can't hear us, but she's watching, nonetheless. It makes me uncomfortable, but I don't want to hesitate too long and cause her to leave. "Why the hell would you invite Roxanne?"

"A couple of reasons. For one, you insisted you weren't coming, so… hello, Andries! So nice to see you. I hope you're enjoying yourself. Second, I figured if you did come, this would be the perfect opportunity for the both of you to reconnect with a little bit of anonymity."

"There are no second chances," I lie, knowing that Roxie and I are right on the brink of one. "So you wasted your time."

"Look at her, man," Dan insists, and I can't help but to shoot my gaze over to her like he says. "She's a smoke show, and we both know that she's just here for you. Loosen up. Live a little," he leans closer to me to talk quieter. "My bedroom's available for the two of you; the key is on the door."

My mouth hangs open at his words, I want to argue, but he cuts me off before I can even open my mouth. "Just thank me later," he says before the upbeat, plucky music coming from the string quartet slows and lowers into something dark and romantic. Dan's eyes leave me, and he looks around the ballroom. "Well, I'm going to find Jessica so I can enjoy a moment of romance myself instead of playing matchmaker for you two crazy kids."

I open my mouth to complain, but he pats me on the shoulder a few times and disappears into the crowd. Roxanne is still watching me, her eyes in the shadow cast from her mask. She looks mysterious and dark, the epitome of all my fantasies, her gown skirting the line between formal wear and a silken bedroom robe that she might slip over her shoulders after making love.

After touching myself last night and being interrupted before I could find my release, I hadn't felt any need to resume my solo pleasure-seeking actions, but seeing the shape of Roxanne's body as she walks toward me has me sorely wishing I had finished myself off at least once before coming out tonight. I can feel the blood rushing from my head to my groin, and I know I'm in trouble.

Her expression makes me think that she can already read my thoughts, which doesn't help my issue any, and by the time she's right in front of me I swear I'm half erect.

"Andries," she purrs, all of her professional and natural allure on full display, unlike the more human woman I had met at the bookshop so recently. "Dan wasn't sure if you would be here. I'm glad to see you are."

"Would you have dressed that way if you knew I wasn't coming?" I ask, hating that everyone here could see how irresistible she looks.

"There's not an inch of inappropriate skin showing, Andries, so I don't know what you're talking about," her voice is amused.

She isn't wrong, either. Her neckline is low, but not obscenely so, and while there is a long slit up her skirt, it ends at her thighs, and only one bare leg shows when her skirt swings aside a certain way. Roxanne's dressed in a publicly acceptable way, so maybe it's just the fact that I know so intimately what's underneath all that red silky fabric that is leaving me uneasy.

"Okay, let me rephrase that, then. Would you have come at all if you thought I wouldn't be here?"

She gives me a knowing smile. "I'd have, but only on the slim hope that you might eventually show. If not, at least someone would tell you I was here and what you missed out on it. But I assume that means you like my costume?"

"Like isn't strong enough of a word," I admit, leaning closer to her neck. "You look... fuck, Roxanne. You know how you look, I don't need to tell you."

She laughs, her hand fluttering around her throat. "Only you could refuse to give me a compliment and still end up giving me the nicest compliment of all. To be fair, you look nice too. Very brooding, starving artist of you."

There's something buzzing between us, some sort of undeniable energy, that has us moving closer and closer together as if magnetized. "I'm glad you approve. At least my presence wasn't wasted."

The string music continues to drone over the crowd, couples spinning across the floor in circles. I know Roxanne and I should talk about what happened at the bookstore, and how we will navigate things going forward, but I don't get a chance to. Over her shoulder, the light catches on two outstretched gossamer wings, glittering and unmistakable. It's Tatiana, without Elise this time, craning her neck as she looks about for what I can only assume is a dance partner. She has to be looking for me, and I can't think of anything that would ruin this moment with Roxanne than being forced to dance with Tatiana.

On a whim, I take Roxanne's gloved hand and pull her out onto the dance floor with me, right into the center of the crowd. She stumbles once but catches her balance as I swing her into position, my hand on her hip as I pull her close. Roxie is annoyed at first, and I can tell she's ready to scold me, but the magic of being out on the dance floor together, close enough to share breath, washes over her and I both. There is no anger or annoyance, just one another.

"You could have asked," she murmurs. "I'd have danced with you either way."

"It was an emergency."

"A *dance* emergency?" she sounds disbelieving, but she doesn't tense in my arms, only teasing.

I don't want her to know the truth of it all, but I can still see the tips of the wings Tatiana is wearing bouncing in the air on the edges of the crowd. I guess my eyes must land on her for a brief second, because Roxanne looks in the same direction, and gets a peek at the younger woman between the bodies of the other guests before she is obscured again.

"Ahh," Roxanne breathes. "That makes more sense. You didn't want to dance with your flower girl tonight?"

"All it'd take is one dance for it to be all over the tabloids that I'm courting her. My family is waiting with bated breath for me to date her, but they're out of luck. Plus, it isn't fair to give her the wrong idea about our friendship."

"*Friendship*," Roxie repeats, not sounding convinced.

"Yes, friendship," I say, looking her in the eye, my tone serious. "That's all it's ever been, and all it'll ever be."

The music swells and dips, giving me the opportunity to pull her even closer. With our bodies pressed together the way we are, there's no way she can't feel my growing erection, but even if it's madness, I don't care. I want her to feel how she affects me.

I've missed this. Painfully so. Maybe even more than the sex. Being this connected to Roxanne is everything I've ever wanted in a relationship, and even knowing what I do about her now, it hasn't changed the connection between us. Or how good it feels to have her in my arms and against my body.

She shifts her hips and lets out a wordless exclamation. "Andries, surely you aren't...."

"Only for you," I tell her, our eyes locking for a moment. "No one else could get me this hard just with a dance."

"I didn't mean to make your night uncomfortable," her voice is low and seductive.

I lower my head so I can rumble into her ear, "On the contrary, Roxanne, you're the only thing making this party worthwhile."

She shivers, and I feel a rush of inexplicable pride. Even with both of us wearing masks, we can read each other so clearly. I'm falling into her eyes, hypnotized by the curve of her lips, and totally ignorant to the fact that more and more couples are turning to watch us.

It's when I hear both of our names whispered quietly around us, the only words I can pick out, a shiver of unease runs down my spine. I don't want to lose what is happening between us, but the last thing I need is my sister to come charging out after us. I can't let Roxanne know, either, because I don't want her to second guess what is going on.

It's a wild thought, but an idea skitters across my mind, both scandalous and too attractive to ignore. "Do you want to go somewhere a little more private?" I ask her.

She hesitates, but I can see the moment she makes up her mind to take what she wants without overthinking it. My brave, rash Roxanne. "Yes."

My hand lowers from the middle of her back to the very top of the swell of her ass. I grind her body against mine. She gasps.

"Go to the bar and wait for me. I'll text you where to go in a few minutes. I don't want us to be caught and interrupted," I explain, not wanting her to think I'm embarrassed to be leaving the party with her, but also nervous about what would happen if we were spotted exiting hand in hand.

Luckily, the heat of the moment makes her more agreeable, and she nods. Once the dance is over, we separate, with me leaving through the back of the crowd and her pushing through to go to the bar. I keep my head down and my shoulders hunched, not wanting to be stopped for a chat or recognized by anymore. I know exactly where I'm going, and I smile while Dan's words replay in my mind.

My friend's bedroom isn't as neat as I'd have hoped, but the bed is made, albeit sloppily, and most importantly of all, there's a lock on the door. It's at the far end of the house, away from the ballroom, and I hope it'll give me the privacy I so desperately need for what is to happen next.

I send Roxanne the text explaining where I am, with some rough directions, and then there is nothing to do but wait. I take my mask and jacket off, and set it on the nightstand, resisting the urge to palm my erection through my pants while I'm waiting. If I had the time I'd jerk off, giving myself some much-needed self-control when I could finally touch her, but it wasn't meant to be. She would just have to receive me at my most feral. It has been much too long.

When she arrives, her mask is already in her hands, her face bare and open for me. We exchange no words as I rush forward, Roxanne closing the door behind her right before I crush her against it, my mouth on hers. I take both of her thin wrists in mine and pin them against the door above her head, my lips moving over hers frantically, as if we only have moments before we will be parted again. She makes a needy noise in her throat when my tongue delves into her mouth, and I swear I'm lost.

Roxanne tastes like champagne; she must have been drinking, and even with her hands pinned, she's as desperate for this as I am, writhing against me like she can't get enough. After seeing her and kissing her in the bookstore, it was like my mind had been wiped of any reason why I had left her in the first place. The same mind threatens to go completely blank when she snakes one leg around my waist, and I release her hands, hoisting her up with my hands around her waist.

I kiss her top lip before sucking the bottom one between my teeth and nipping gently. Then she's burying a hand in my hair and tilting my head to the side so she can kiss and lick up the column of my neck and the line of my jaw before her mouth is on mine again. We are reacquainting ourselves with each other; it's heady and disorienting. I have no control over myself.

I want to strip her bare and once more memorize every inch of her pale skin, but time is short, and both of our needs are off the charts. I can't make slow, involved love to Roxanne on Dan's sheets, but there isn't any timeline where she and I leave this room without having fucked. It's inevitable.

Roxanne doesn't fight it as I lift her. She wraps both legs around me now, and I place her on the dresser, right below a wall mirror. I can only see my own reflection as I gather her skirts up in my fist, pulling her dress up while my mouth descends to the swell of her breasts. I can't get her out of the bodice and have to settle for palming the globes of them through the red fabric, pinching her nipples until she cries out.

She strips her own underwear off, and it's nothing but her bare core pressing against me now. We're almost at the point of no return, and as much as I'm happy to jump off the edge, I have to make sure she feels the same, even if my cock is ready to explode out of my pants from how hard I am.

"You want this?" I ask simply, not able to form any other complex thoughts.

"Please, Andries," she begs. "Yes, yes I want it."

When I dip my hand between her legs, I find that she is ready for me, almost dripping with need. It takes all my willpower to summon the motor skills that allow me to undo my pants, pushing them and my boxers to my ankles. My manhood springs forth but is only subjected to the chill air of the room for a moment before I'm working myself between her folds.

Words of praise spill from Roxanne's lips as I clutch her legs, feeling them tremble around me. I take as much time as I can, not slamming into her the way I want, but something tells me she would take whatever I give her with gusto. Once I'm finally seated in her to the hilt, I begin to move, almost breathless from how good she feels. Tight, hot, and welcoming.

"Touch yourself," I growl. "I won't last long like this."
Roxanne doesn't question my commands, her snaking between us to rub quick circles around her clit with her fingers as I thrust into her without ceasing. I can't believe I ever thought I could let this go... live without this. I can't. Not ever again.

Her legs are shaking like she might break, her channel tightening with the combination of her own touch and my fucking her. Our movements have the dresser rattling, but I don't care. There is no one in this wing to hear us, anyway.

It's a good thing, too, because when I hear the thread of desperation in her moans, I push into her even more frantically. The mirror hits that wall, *bang, bang, bang,* but it's not a distraction to me, more like the pulse of her and I becoming one.

The color is high on Roxanne's cheeks, a sheen of sweat covering us both, still almost fully clothed but exposed just enough to fuck each other senseless. She keeps one hand between her legs, just like I told her to, while the other grips my upper arm for support. Her breaths are hitches between sounds of pleasure, while mine hiss between my teeth.

She throws her head back and I take the opportunity to kiss her neck, tasting the salt of her skin as I bite at the tendon running to her shoulder, causing her to shudder against me and her channel tightens in one sharp grasp. I fix my eyes on the ceiling, exhaling slowly, trying desperately to keep control of myself. Every cell in my body is screaming at me to fill her with my seed, but she has to come first.

Without ceasing my thrusts, I pull her legs up higher where they are wrapped around my hips until they sit closer to the bottom of my ribcage, letting the head of my cock hit her inner walls with each push.

"Andries," she keens, and I can't help the feral grin that blooms across my face.

"What, baby?"

"Don't you fucking stop," she nearly sobs.

"I'm not," I assure her, both with my words and the push and pull of my cock into her. "Not until you come for me."

The walls of her pussy start to flutter just as I feel something ready to burst within me, a concentrated ball of pleasure at the base of my spine. I can feel her arching her back as she starts to come, right before she clenches down on me like a vice. Her only anchor is her single hand on my arm, and I can feel the press of her nails through my sleeve. Roxanne pants my name as I gather her close for the few last strokes before I lose myself inside of her. When she sinks her teeth into my shoulder, overcome by her climax, it's over for me. I come so hard inside of her that it feels like my soul is leaving me, pouring into her with abandon. She rides her orgasm, and mine, out longer than I'm able too, writhing and grinding with me still inside of her until she has milked every ounce of pleasure out.

When she relaxes in my arms, I'm reluctant to pull out of her and break the spell of what just happened. We hadn't spoken a single sentence to one another, but even in silence, we knew what the other wanted... what they needed. Our connection is unmatched.

"Come home with me," she whispers in my ear, breaking the silence. "I want to spend the night with you. The weekend even."

I shouldn't. I have to study, and I can't just jump back into staying together all the time without working some things out first. Still... It was a night of decadence. Why shouldn't I take this thing that I want so badly?

"Yes," I tell her simply, and her face lights up. "You leave first, and I'll meet you there. Just text me the address."

Roxie kisses me again sweetly, before she goes and puts her panties back on, and she then takes her mask on the way out. I try not to think about how she's going to walk all the way down to her ride with my cum running down her thighs, because if I focus on it too much, I'll be hard all over again.

I clean myself up in the bathroom to waste some time, figuring that we'd share a shower at her place. Once it's been long enough, I exit the room, straightening up Dan's dresser a touch before I do so. All I have to do is make it through the hallway and reach the exit without being caught, and I would be home free.

I'm nearly reaching the front door when a hand grabs me by the arm. Annoyed, I spin around to see Elise, who must have been skulking around the door like security to have caught me so quickly.

"Why did I just see Roxanne leave, and now you're leaving too? Don't tell me you were going home with her, Andries!"

I don't think she can tell what I've just been doing; I fixed my hair and straightened my clothes, but I feel humiliated to be caught, nonetheless. My sister is scowling up at me, and I know if I leave now she will just have me tailed to find out the truth. Roxanne and I still have nothing concrete, just this tenuous newborn connection, and I don't want to ruin it with Elise following me to her home.

Already mourning the loss of the weekend that is now slipping through my fingers, I shake my head. "Don't be ridiculous. I was just going for some fresh air."

"Well, you've had enough," she sniffs. "Let's go back in. Tatiana is waiting to dance with you."

My heart plummets as Elise drags me back to the dance floor, but I know if I resist she'll catch me right away with Roxanne. Feeling like an utter fool, I manage to send her a text that just reads, *Sorry, got caught up at the party. I'll catch you later on.*

She replies back, almost immediately: *That's okay, we can catch another day. Enjoy the party. X*

Her reply causes a pang to my heart, but before I can even send another text, Elise is pushing me toward Tatiana, who is smiling shyly. The poor thing has no idea what I was doing less than twenty minutes ago, and it seems disingenuous to take her hand for a dance now.

But what choice do I have? Disgruntled, I take her outstretched palm, and guide her stiffly to the dance floor.

CHAPTER 22

Amsterdam, February 28, 2022
Andries

Rolling over, I check the time on my phone and immediately decide it's much too early for anyone to be knocking on my door. As the pounding continues, I have to come to terms with the fact that it isn't part of my dream and that there is actually someone wanting my attention at the obnoxious hour of eight a.m. on a Monday. I don't have class for over two hours, so I can't figure out why I must be bothered.

Whoever it is, is relentless, and with a muttered curse, I throw my blankets off, pull a black robe hanging on my door frame on, and stomp blurry eyed to the front door. I throw it open to Dan's widely grinning face, and consider slamming it again, until he holds up the drink carrier containing two cardboard coffee cups in front of my face.

"Good morning, sleeping beauty," he says with a teasing voice.

I frown, but step aside, and he enters with an infuriating spring in his step.

Dan also has a paper bag, which he takes to my breakfast bar and starts unloading. There are cream cheese bagels and two coffees. Once I snatch the one with my name out of the drink holder and take a swig, I decide not to murder him here and now. It's a double shot latte with heavy cream and a touch of hazelnut. It's almost worth being woken up for.

After a second drink, I manage to use my words. "Why the fuck are you here, Dan?"

"I just wanted to be the first one to show you this!" he crows. I hadn't noticed, but there is a magazine rolled into a tube and crammed into his back pocket. As I sit on a stool and spread a copious amount of cream cheese on my bagel, Dan slaps it down on the table in front of me. The cover is some of the usual nonsense about A-list celebrities, but when I look up questioningly, Dan motions for me to open the magazine. I flip through the pages, Dan watching me like a kid on Christmas. There is nothing of interest until....

In the middle of the magazine there is a feature titled 'Masquerade Madness?', and the grainy pictures featured are clearly from Dan's party. The biggest and clearest picture makes my heart drop; it's a shot of Roxanne and I dancing, not an ounce of air between us, her looking up into my face and me gazing down at her in adoration. Our masks hide our identities somewhat, but her blond, swept back hair makes her almost instantly recognizable. I skim the article, heart hammering in anxiety, but after a few paragraphs speculating about whether the couple pictured was indeed Roxie and I, it moves on to other, smaller drama. Dan watches me read, not even touching his food as he takes in the moment fully.

"Why do you look so thrilled?" I ask, annoyed.

"Because my party made the news! Thanks in no small part to you and Roxanne, I'm sure, but it credits the masquerade to me and everything."

"Glad that I could help you out, because this has the potential to be disastrous for me." I tear the bagel apart with my fingers, feeling frustrated and a touch violent at this outcome. I couldn't have one night, not even one small dance with my ex-girlfriend without the whole world noticing, it seems. At least our bedroom tryst had gone unnoticed, for now.

"Why? They don't even positively identify you."

"It's pretty clear it's us, Dan," I gripe. "And the last thing I want is for my family to know Roxanne and I reconnected in any way, shape, or form. I'm already on the outs with my dad over everything with Patricia; if I'm seen dating her again, it's all going to blow up in my face spectacularly."

"Andries, you're a grown man. You've been making decisions that your family doesn't agree with for years now. Why hide Roxanne? And for that matter, why continue to lie about your major?" He seems baffled, and frustrated just like I am. "Do you actually want to date her or are you just stuck on her because she's your first love?"

"I'm going to be honest with you, Dan." I sit my food down, dragging a hand through my hair. "I want to be with her more than anything. I'm tired of pretending like I don't. But she still runs that agency, and that makes things more complicated, especially to my family, who wants to maintain a squeaky clean image above all else. Even if I wanted to shirk all of my family ties and live a life that is completely true to what I want, I can never shed that connection fully. I'm a Van Den Bosch for better or for worse, and I have to consider that when I make my decisions. Dating a former prostitute and a current brothel keeper, simply won't fly with my family. Ever. It disgusts them."

"You have to stop letting your family and their approval dictate your life," Dan's tone is serious; a rare thing for him. "They live in the past, man. Step into the future and do what makes you happy. Be with Roxanne if that's what you want."

"It's not only them. I don't think I could live with her running that business. If we got back together, she'd have to consider selling it. I can't live, and maybe even raise children, with someone who is in the sex trade. That's a boundary I won't cross."

"Being so biased like that is going to make your life harder in the long run. If you would take a step back and just consider her a successful entrepreneur, it wouldn't be nearly as hard on you."

I shake my head. "I can't help the way I feel, Dan. And my partner for the rest of my life can't sell sex for a living. It just goes against my core sense of self."

I can tell he's annoyed with me, but we're both interrupted as I get a text. It's from Roxanne, and it's too long to be read in the alerts bar, so I unlock the phone to read the entire thing.

Andries, my PA just showed me the magazine. I'm so sorry. If I had known there would be paparazzi, I'd have covered my face completely. I know your family is going through some hardships in the media and I never wanted to add to them. I never intended to make a public scene. Please believe me.

I frown as I read it, feeling guilty that she'd ever think I would blame her for something like this. After the way we broke up, and some of the harsh things I said to her, it's no surprise she feels the need to walk on eggshells around me. I can only hope that it won't be that way forever.

You have nothing to be sorry about, I reply. *I pulled you onto the dance floor, not the other way around. I took the risk and I take the blame, okay? Don't beat yourself up. Someone must have sold that picture to the magazine anonymously because it isn't credited. There is nothing we could have done to stop that.*

"She's upset about the magazine," I muse to Dan out loud. "That makes two of us, I guess."

Dan rolls his eyes. "You can't let me enjoy anything exciting that happens to me, can you?"

My phone goes off again, this time with a call. I hold up the phone so Dan can see the screen, emblazoned with a picture of my sister. "This is exactly why. If your exciting moments get me chewed out by members of my family then no, I'm not going to let you enjoy them."

He grumbles to himself and eats his bagel while I answer reluctantly. I can almost hear how quickly Elise is breathing the moment the call connects, and it makes me want to both laugh and cry at the same time. She is really feeling some strong feelings, and I'm likely going to bear the brunt of them.

"How could you!?" she screeches. "Is this why you were ghosting Tatiana all night? You gave her one measly dance, with your hands on her shoulders like a freaking high schooler would do, but you had time to dry hump your ex in the middle of the dance floor!? You swore you were done with her!"

"Good morning, Elise," I deadpan. "Nice to hear from you too, dear sister."

"I'm in no mood! Tatiana just called me in tears, and I had to walk down to the convenience store and buy a magazine before even getting breakfast! Just answer my damn question!"

"It was just a dance. Nothing more, nothing less," I lie through my teeth, trying to banish the memories of Roxanne with her legs wrapped around my bare waist.

Her temper cools, but only by a degree or two. "You shouldn't be interacting with her at all. Anything between the two of you is going to have the tabloids all abuzz, just like they are now. You need to pretend like she doesn't exist."

"I only danced with her to thank her for helping Patricia." *Lie, lie, lie.* "I haven't seen her in person since, or even spoken to her on the phone, so calm down please."

Knowing Elise, calming down is the last thing she wants to do, but it's a school day for her too, and neither of us can afford to have a huge fight. "Fine. But I'm still pissed about this, and poor Tatiana is heartbroken."

"Stop lying, Elise. Tatiana is just a friend, and she knows that," I insist, fighting the urge to grind my teeth. The idea that Tatiana and I are getting together is so played out by my sister that it makes me cringe every time she mentions it.

"Whatever. We'll see. I better not hear about you being around Roxanne anymore. You've caused us enough worry through your breakup."

Elise hangs up without another word. I hold the phone away from my face but notice there is an unread message from Roxanne. To my surprise, it isn't more apologies or talk about the tabloid. Instead, her message reads, *We should talk. Are you free tonight?*

I must read it eight or so times before Dan clears his throat. I turn to him, and he asks, "What is so interesting?"

I'm tired of lying about Roxanne, and Dan is maybe the only person I can be honest with regarding her. I decide to come out with it and tell him the truth. "Roxanne wants to meet up. I literally just told Elise I wasn't seeing her anymore, and it feels wrong to go against my word immediately like that."

"Elise is only worried about Elise, and Elise's public image. If you want to see her, then go."

Despite Dan's advice, I almost tell her no. I want her in my life, yes, but I just don't know how she's supposed to fit. Being together as a couple will be impossible without putting my entire family against me… But then I think about my uncle Alex, and his insistence that I should give Roxanne another chance, and how he and Aunt Petra had to try multiple times before their marriage actually succeeded. Alex had insisted he had always known Petra was the one, he just had to open up and let her in. Maybe… maybe that's what I need to do with Roxanne.

Yes, what do you have in mind? I answer finally, still unsure whether I'm doing the right thing or not.

A few seconds later, my phone beeps with her answer:

Meeting up at my place like we were supposed to Saturday night. I'll send you my address.

CHAPTER 23

Amsterdam, February 28, 2022
Roxanne

He had class. He is still coming, he's not avoiding you.

I repeat the mantra in my head again and again as I wait on Andries, twisting the fabric of my kimono shrug between my fingers as I pace. I worked for a few hours before coming home to prepare something for us to eat and make the penthouse more welcoming, but even that hadn't kept me occupied enough to not think about him constantly.

Andries had accepted my invitation this morning, and that was the last thing I'd heard from him. Now I feel stupid for not asking what time he would come over. I had wanted to seem like I was playing it cool and casual, but right now I feel anything but.

At the party, we had sex. I've had to come to terms with that fact over and over again yesterday. I hadn't meant for things to go like that. In fact, I had hoped we could talk about our possible future together, as friends or otherwise, but Andries had been hard from the moment he tugged me onto the dance floor. Feeling that visceral reminder of what I did to him, and how much he wanted me, made all rational thought flee my mind. Then he kissed me, and there was very little intelligent thinking between the two of us from that moment on.

It had been so long that I had started to question whether the physical attraction between Andries and I had just been the rosy tint of my memory and not reality, but when I came apart in his arms just a two nights ago, it had cemented what I had been trying to deny for weeks: sex with Andries is unlike anything I had experienced in my whole life. We are a perfect, flawless match in bed. Now, if we could just figure out how to coexist happily at all other times, we might have a chance.

It's almost six p.m. when I hear the doorbell buzzing. My heart leaps, and I all but run to the front door to let him in. When I open the door to his tall figure, I swear I run through an enormous array of emotions in a single second: love, relief, excitement, trepidation, and lust. I've never had any men come here, let alone an open invitation to stay however long they wanted.

He smiles at me, the expression slightly uncomfortable. "Shall I come in?"

"Sorry, of course," I step aside, and he walks slowly past me, taking in the space. "It's just such a shock to see you here. I hardly let *anyone* in my apartment. It's my sanctuary."

He pauses in the middle of the hallway, looking at me, a bit confused. "Do you want me to leave? We could get a hotel room or something."

"No, no," I say quickly, then I shut the door behind us and go back and take his hand on mine. "I want you here. I swear."

Andries relaxes and I decide to give him a full tour of my place. It really is my sanctuary; that description is not an exaggeration. Showing him the living room, his eyes go up to where the ceilings curve upwards at an angle, the crystalline light fixtures hanging down on long chains. The front part of the penthouse's walls are painted in light pastels, large bookshelves full of the pieces of literature I have loved over the years stand in front. Decorations consist of soft watercolors in pale gold frames, and the centerpiece of the sitting area is an oversized cream-colored velour couch. I lead Andries to the back where my bedroom is, and the difference is stark. Here the walls are a dark turquoise, and there are diaphanous jewel-toned curtains covering the windows instead of proper shades. My king-sized bed is piled high with several pillows, a dark purple velvet blanket spread neatly underneath them.

The master bath follows the vintage theme, with my oversized soaking tub resting on four clawed feet and a ring of lights around two identical round mirrors hanging over decoratively tarnished brass sinks. A lot of the windows are wide, single paned, older-styled windows that always reminded me of the posh apartments seen in black and white films. It's a mix of ultra-modern paired with vintage pieces, but it's undoubtedly welcoming and cozy at the same time. I had worked hard to make it so, and it gives me a rush of pleasure to see how much Andries appreciates it.

"You are stamped all over every inch of this place," he comments with a chuckle. "If I'd have known you lived somewhere like this, I'd have moved in with you instead of the other way around."

"It's not too late," I say slowly, and Andries smirks.

"Don't get ahead of yourself, Roxie."

Before letting any uncomfortable silence to settle in, I lead him back into the living. "Can I get you something to drink?"

"Whatever you are drinking," he answers, his tone even.

While Andries sits on the couch, I head to the kitchen and pour us both a glass of chilled white wine and bring it to the living room with me. He takes it graciously, reclining on the couch with a sigh.

"Long day?" I ask, sinking down on the sofa next to him and braving a quick kiss on his temple. He doesn't object, just smiles warmly.

"It was longer once I knew I was seeing you this evening," he says, causing my heart to flutter in response. "Despite having a few interesting classes, the day seemed to drag on and on."

"It was the same for me," I confess, taking a sip of my wine. "I was so distracted at work that I took a half day instead. I think my assistant was actually glad to be rid of my nervous energy."

His face darkens at the mention of my job, but as much as I change the subject, it isn't something we can really avoid. Andries, though, has other plans, asking questions about the penthouse.

"I can't get over how much this space suits you. You know, you really have an eye for design. I can't believe we spent all that time in my cold, boring apartment when we could have been here."

"This isn't the kind of place a librarian can afford, though," I tell him, sounding more nostalgic than I wanted. "I knew you'd have found it suspicious and most likely you'd have asked me how I could afford it," I blurt out, and he tenses once more. I want to attack the subject of my escort business and be done with it, but I also don't want to ruin the night.

"Speaking of which," he says stiffly. "Do you want to share with me how everything started? Like how you got into... that line of work?"

My eyes widen in shock at his question. "Do you really want to know?" I ask, surprised. "Like, for real?"

"Sort of," he admits. "This is such a big part of your life that I know nothing about."

"Fine," I take a hefty drink and exhale. Then I tuck my legs under myself, getting comfortable for the long story ahead. It feels bizarre to actually be talking about this with him now, after hiding that part of my life for so long, but I know we need a clean slate. I'm fine with that if it'll help him forgive me.

So that's where I start; my beginning as an escort. "As you know, I've never been wealthy. Money had been beyond tight, especially when I went to college. Karl was my first client; I met him at a bar, and he offered me money to go on a date with him. He was younger at the time, so the age gap wasn't so startlingly obvious. His pockets were deep, and he always took me along to all the events that his lifestyle afforded him. During the hours I spent with him I would rise high above my station, and when it was over, I was quite a bit richer for it."

Andries listens carefully, but I still feel like there's no way for him to understand the lack of money; not with the way he grew up, and still lives, for that matter. It's so frustrating to think that if I could just get that point through his head that he'd finally see why I lived my life the way I did. Maybe that ability to see things from the perspective of others would come with age. He's a caring, empathic man, but I can't forget how young he still is. He has a lot of learning to do still. "And while escorting was never supposed to be a permanent solution to my problems, the money was too great that I got immediately addicted in a way. The work ranged from mediocre to awful, but I was able to fund a better life for Mama and Lili."

I explain how, once I graduated, I took an internship at a big-name publishing house, letting escorting fade into my past. It was supposed to be the defining moment that jump started my career, but to my horror, I found that the pay didn't even allow me to cover rent and food.

"Karl hired me the very evening I quit my job," I tell Andries. If we want a clean start, then I suppose he needs to know the impact that man had on my life. "He sent a tailored Dior gown and a pair of Jimmy Choo pumps directly to my door a few hours before. He wanted me to look my best, and he insisted I keep the dress once the night was over. It cemented my opinion that escorting was the right path for me during that point in my life."

"So why did you start an agency?" he asks, sounding attentive and curious.

"My bank account and my schedule grew and grew throughout my twenties, but as thirty rapidly approached, I started to feel tired of escorting and I wanted to eventually retire. That's when I decided to start the agency, keeping only my three best clients on my personal schedule. The rest of the time, I hired girls to work for me, and organized work for them, taking a cut for myself. It seemed that working on the front lines had made me especially suited for managing such a business, and it flourished." I pause, noticing how his gaze drops for a moment as he processes everything I just said. "There was one thing that always ate at me, though, and it was that from the moment Mama discovered what I did for a living, she stopped talking to me. I miss her more than anything in the world, and while our relationship is finally starting to heal, I want it to be faster. I want my mom back in my life."

Escorting had saved me, but it had also taken from me. It had taken my mother, and more recently, taken Andries from me. That, and my own lies.

Once I'm done, we both sit in the pressing silence with each other, my history spilled out before us like a tapestry to be examined. Andries looks conflicted, like he's having trouble swallowing what I've said, but eventually he nods once.

"Thank you for being so honest with me. I know it wasn't easy to talk about your past like that." He gives another gulp while considering me. "I need to be honest with you, though," his tone has become more serious and my heart skips a beat in anticipation for his next set of words. "I'm still uncomfortable with you being in the industry. I don't think anything can change that, but my thoughts are clearer now that I know the entire truth."

"What will you do now?" I ask, voice quivering with nerves.

"I don't know if I'm being honest. I have such a strong moral objection with sex work that it's hard for me to come to terms with someone I love being involved in it."

"Andries… It's valid for you to not want to be with a sex worker, but why are you so vehemently opposed to it as a profession overall?"

"It's a long story," he exhales through his nose, sinking further into the couch. "I spent some time in Medellín, Colombia, and while I was never a fan of that industry, living there truly cemented my dislike for it. Women lined the streets both day and night, selling their bodies just to feed their families. The worst part was…" He clenches his jaw for a moment, as if he's reliving something almost too painful to name. "The worst part was the mothers that were out there selling their daughter's virginities to the highest bidder, as if it was the most natural thing in the world. Just business as usual. Most of them weren't even eighteen. It was disgusting, devastating…."

Shocked, I can't help but say, "That's why you had such a problem with the Patricia situation?"

He ignores me and keeps speaking. I wonder if he's afraid that if he stops, he won't be able to finish. "I bought food for dozens of them, night after night, just so they could go home to their families and not stand out there on the street corner. The misery was emotionally ruining me, and I had to leave. I went to Tibet and spent the rest of my year there."

"That clears things up a lot, and I'm sorry you had to go through that. It isn't the same as what's going on here, where it's legal and regulated, but I can understand that it's too close for comfort." I try to come off as comforting, knowing that what he's just shared is hurting him. I feel a flush of affection when he reaches over and squeezes my hand in his in response.

With my heart full, I decide to tell him something I never did before. "I know we didn't start out in the best of circumstances, but I really think there is something special between us." I pause, observing the small smile playing at the corner of his lips. "And I want you to know that I'll do anything to assure we can have a future together."

He turns his body fully in my direction, giving me his full attention. "Would you stop running the agency for me? Between the money you've earned, and the bookshop, you should have enough to invest in something else, right?"

I knew it was coming, but the question is still a punch to the gut. Before Andries, this business I had built was sort of my first love. Now, my actual true love is asking me to give it all up. "Some of those girls have kids and are counting on that money to live, I can't simply close shop and leave them jobless."

"I'm not saying you have to close up shop," Andries insists. "Can't you just sell the business to someone else?"

"I…." Nothing comes to my mind. I just don't have an answer to give him.

"Look, I've thought about us a lot, and I can look past the lies and what you did to get where you are today, but you and I together like before while you are still running that place is not something I'm comfortable with."

What hurts the most is that I know he's being fully honest with me. This isn't about a preference, or about Andries getting his way no matter what. Escorting and sex work is a real hard limit of his, and we won't make it if I refuse to give it up. There is no easy way out of this for me.

"This agency is more than just a way to make money," I say desperately. "I look after those girls to make sure no one hurts them or takes advantage of them. It's not as black or white as it seems."

"I know that," Andries replies, exasperated. "Which is why I understand it might take some time to find the right person to take over, and I can wait for the day you turn the page on that chapter of your life and move on from it once and for all."

He must be able to see the conflicted feelings on my face because he draws me into his arms, gathering me to his body. I take the offered comfort, nuzzling my face into his neck and letting my stress flow away for the time being. He knows I need time to think, there's no reason to say so out loud, but for now we are together, and the air has finally been cleared. For that at least, I'm thankful.

"I want to show you something," he says in a whisper, close enough to the shell of my ear. My interest is perked and when he looks me in the eye, he then adds, "I, um, I wrote a few poems since the last notebook I gave you." He goes to his backpack and takes from there the leather carmine notebook I offered him for his birthday. My stomach flutters at the idea he never threw it away, but instead kept it to write his heart out. "While I'm sure some are terrible, you might find others more interesting." He hands me the notebook and I can't help but remain staring at him with parted lips. "Here."

Swallowing past the lump in my throat, I start flickering through the pages, my heartbeat steadily rising in excitement. "Do you mind if I look at them now?"

"By all, means…" he answers, running a hand on his hair, his face softening with a smile.

The first poem I lay eyes on has been written back in January, and my smile falls as I start reading it:

My mind has difficulty to comprehend
Why you felt the need to pretend

My heart is shattered and broken
All because you left the truth unspoken

The feeling of betrayal I cannot explain
Confused, hurt, and no longer feel sane

My adoration for you used to travel far
But all you left me with is a love scar

Andries peers over to check which one I'm reading and immediately then says, "Oh, that one was during our breakup, it's bad, I know, I was mostly drunk, and…very heartbroken."

Despite his comment, my eyes remain pinned on the page, the poem causing a pang to my heart. I can't help but feel guilty and so damn bad at everything he went through because of my lies. In my world, lying and keeping secrets is just part of the job, but for him, it's total betrayal.

"I'm so sorry for all you went through," I tell him sincerely, my eyes going up to meet his. "If I could go back in time—"

"It belongs to the past," he interposes, patting me softly on the arm. "I want us to move on." Our eyes are locked for a moment and I find myself smiling at him. "Speaking of which…" He cuts eyes contact, taking the notebook from my hands and starts flickering through the pages until he finds the one he wants. "Look at this one."

"Would you read it out loud for me?" I ask him, seeing he never read his poetry to me.

Andries seems slightly taken aback by my request, but finally obliges. "Um, okay, sure…" He takes a few deep breaths and holding the notebook between his hands, he clears his throat and puts on a more solemn voice.

"*What you did to me truly cut deep,*

"*You were my dream yet I could no longer sleep*

"*But I realized it came from fear*

"*The truth was a distance you thought would keep me near*

"*You deserve a second chance*

"*After everything you still make my heart dance*

"*Forgiven but not forgotten is the thought*

"*Because I still love you, a lot.*"

He shuts the book, his eyes now pinned on me, and I find myself totally lost for words as I digest the poem he just read.

"This is so beautiful," I say as we embrace each other in a tight hug. "I never in my entire life thought I'd meet someone so precious like you. Thank you for writing this."

"Glad you liked it," I hear him saying. We remain quiet for a moment, enjoying the comfortable silence.

"I made some dinner," I tell him softly. "It's in the kitchen."

I'm reluctant to let him go, but our talk from earlier and the poems we just read has zapped a lot of my energy, and dinner is a must. I follow him into the kitchen, toasting some bread to go with our pasta, and we have an achingly domestic meal together over wine and conversation about anything but my job.

Andries would be content to talk poetry with me for hours, but after discussing so many emotionally draining subjects I feel more tired than I thought I was. We rinse the dishes together, load the dishwasher, and make our way into the bathroom, both of us loose and sleepy from the wine.

I run us a bath in my enormous soaking tub, one of my favorite purchases that I ever made for the penthouse. Andries settles into the water first, stripping his clothes off and laying them in a neat pile by the door. He's so beautiful that it almost hurts. I had no chance of staying away from him after our first time together... I know that now. Somehow our lives will have to find a way to come together, even if I'm not sure how yet.

After climbing into the bath, my back to his chest, we relax in the steaming water for a long while, speaking of light and happy things while Andries lazily runs his hands over my entire body. It's clear when the intention changes from affection to seduction, his hands skimming over my nipples and dipping between my legs, and it isn't long until I've rotated to face him, guiding his hard cock into me with a helping hand.

We both moan as we are joined, and from there the lovemaking is slow and unhurried, water sloshing at the side of the tub. There is none of the frantic energy of our encounter at the party, just a deep need for us to connect on this most basic level.

Once he's inside me, we don't move at first, at least not where we are connected. In the low light of my bathroom, I lean back, letting Andries have full access to my body. He skims his hands up my ribs, fingers stroking over my shoulder blades before sweeping back down again, under the water and against the bones of my hips.

It tickles, making me twitch. Andries makes a hissing noise, and then chuckles. "You get tighter when I do that."

He repeats the caress, and I jolt again. I can see the white of Andries' teeth as he grins, but before I can scold him for wasting time on games, he touches me where I've been aching for him.

Andries cups my breasts reverently in his palms, squeezing gently before his thumbs flick over my nipples. I exhale, and I move my hips unconsciously with him still seated deep inside me. The pleasure from his touch is shivery, but as he rolls his thumbs over my hard nipples again and again, I start to feel needy, getting wetter and more swollen.

To my annoyance, although my body seems to think differently, Andries touches me in an achingly slow matter. After what seems like the thousandth pass of his thumbs over my hard peaks, he pinches them between his fingers, sending a rush of arousal from my chest to my pussy.

I open my mouth to complain about his slow pace, but he surges forward and kisses me instead, his tongue darting into my mouth with a swiftness unlike the slow crawl of all his other touches. My eyes flutter closed as I kiss him back, his hands still teasing my breasts and nipples at a pace that becomes more and more desperate as we kiss deeply.

With a groan, he pulls away, moving his lips and tongue across my jawline and down my neck, his hands coaxing me to lean back even further in his lap. I grind against him, his cock pulsing inside of me, but I let him push me back just enough so he can fasten his mouth over one of my hard, aching nipples. He licks and sucks until I bury my wet hands in his hair, pulling until he moves to the other peak.

I can't take much more, and as blissful as his clever tongue on my nipples is, I need more, telling him so with another movement of my hips. I pull him away again until he looks in my eyes. I start a patient, rolling pace, fucking Andries in a way that I feel the hard length of him stroking the most sensitive parts inside of me with each movement. There is no hurry, but it is still devastating, especially for Andries, who groans from deep in his chest with each stroke. Feeling the way his body tenses under mine, and the coiling of need between my legs, I know it won't be long.

Andries finishes first, his body curling upward toward me as he does, and the desperate uttering of my name combined with his hard upstrokes are the last thing I need to finish, too, in a shuddering wave. We spend almost as long in the afterglow, just holding each other, before the water chills enough that we have to seek the warmth of the shower.

"Stay the night," I tell him, washing his broad back under the shower water. "Don't go."

"I'm glad you offered before I had to ask," he chuckles.

As we crawl under the blankets together and fall into slumber wrapped up in one another, the only thought on my mind is how hard it is going to be to separate myself from my job, because I don't think I can give this thing with Andries up again. I just have to find the cleanest way to pull myself apart.

CHAPTER 24

Amsterdam, March 1, 2022
Andries

I'm a fairly early riser, and as such, I always set my room up to brighten with the sun as it rises. Roxanne, though, has blackout curtains that block her entire bedroom windows, so when I wake up, the room is dark and sepia tinged.

There is a small alarm on the nightstand that reads 10:02 a.m., much later than I should be up. I can't bring myself to feel bad about it though. I swing my arm over to embrace Roxanne, but I find an empty space instead. My hand lands on something that crinkles, which turns out to be a note that she has left me. It reads:

You were sleeping like an angel, so I didn't want to wake you up. There's a coffee and a croissant on the table.

I'm disappointed that she didn't wait for me to wake up, but I suppose her job, however distasteful, still requires her to keep a professional schedule. I slide out of bed and stretch, my muscles stiff from the unfamiliar bed and the awkward position of our bathtub sex last night, but despite all of that,

I am content. We haven't solved all our issues, but we are well on our way. At least I hope so.

Roxie's whole apartment has the same softly lit aura to it that the bedroom does, only a touch brighter. I pull open the gauzy window coverings in the living room, looking down at Dam Square and all the people gathering there, heading to work and classes or simply seeing the sights. Amsterdam is not a city that I want to spend my life in, but there is a certain old beauty to it that is undeniable.

My coffee is lukewarm; it's 10 a.m., after all, but it's enjoyable enough paired with the croissant and the view. It isn't until I decide to check my phone that the real dramatics of my life are able to take hold.

The messages roll in quickly. First is Elise, asking, *Where are you?*

This is followed by Dan's more specific, *Are you home? Elise and I wanted to surprise you! I hope you are good! Gimme a call if you need someone to talk to.*

My decision to ignore my sister and call Dan instead is easy. I don't plan on telling either of them what is actually happening, but if one of them figures it out, I'd much rather it be Dan than Elise. He answers brightly, his chipper tone slightly annoying.

"Hey buddy! What's up? Elise and I went to your apartment this morning to try and take you out for breakfast, but you didn't answer the door. Everything okay?"

"Fine," I tell him. "I just wasn't home, that's all. Nothing to worry about."

"That's weird, because we came by at eight a.m. since your sister had a nine a.m. class. You were out that early?" His tone is cheery, but there is a hint of suspicion in it.

I know immediately that I'm caught, but I don't want to make it easy on him. "I might have stayed out all night."

Dan continues to press. "Really? And may I know where? You know you can tell me anything."

"It's none of your damn business, man," I snap, but Dan laughs uproariously.

"You do realize just by your tone you gave away the answer, right? I *knew* it! You were with Roxie, weren't you? Oh man, Elise is going to be pissed when she finds out."

"Promise me right now that you won't tell her," I demand. "It'll immediately get out to the rest of my family and be an enormous mess. We need some space to breathe if we're going to work things out."

"So that's what you're doing? You two are trying to make a relationship work again? But on the down low, like secret lovers or something?"

I pinch the bridge of my nose and exhale slowly. "Yeah, something like that I guess. We need to be able to do it alone, though, without the influence of everyone else."

"Don't worry about my influence. I'm really happy for you, man. People like Roxanne shake our lives up and make us see the world in a different way. You need this."

The sincerity in his voice is actually touching, and I find myself feeling a surge of affection toward my stalwart friend. "Thanks, Dan. But seriously, don't tell Elise."

He laughs. "I wouldn't dream of it, but you need to call her and convince her that you were sleeping off a hangover or something. She was already starting to suspect you had spent the night with someone."

Once I get off the phone with Dan, there's no point in wasting any time, so I call my nosy sister right away to clear everything up the best I can. I hate that I have to lie to my sister so much, especially when she is right about a lot of things and only wants the best for me, but there is no way she will ever understand what Roxie and I have.

She answers just as quickly as Dan, but her tone is much more accusatory. "Where the hell were you this morning?"

"Sleeping. I had a late night. Don't worry about it."

I keep everything short and succinct, hoping she'll lose interest quickly. It seems to work at first, but quickly backfires.

"Okay, whatever you say. What are you doing this afternoon? You want to get lunch?"

Elise knows I don't have class at lunchtime, so I can't lie. With an internal sigh, I tell her, "Sure, sounds good."

"Great!" she chirps, and I'm automatically suspicious about how low key she's being about everything. She gives me the name and address of a local farm-to-table cafe, and we agree to meet right after her afternoon class.

I feel like I've been caught in a whirlwind. One single night with Roxanne and everyone seems to be up in arms about where I'm at and what I'm doing. How could I keep her a secret if everyone is so nosy about my personal life? What should have been a calm, slow start to the morning has turned into calamity, but there is no escaping it now.

With a steadying breath to get my annoyance in check, I finish my coffee, grab the croissant, and get ready for class.

* * *

Elise is waiting at the cafe just like she said, and I give her a wave that's cut short when the other person at the table stands up. I stop in my tracks and consider leaving right then and there. I did not want to deal with this today. Or ever, really.

My sister has brought my dad to lunch with her. He and I haven't really spoken since the outburst the night before his party, and things had been inescapably tense ever since. It's so obviously a setup that I can't wait to have Elise alone to give her a piece of my mind. But I'm here now, and I might as well face Dad. I had already dealt with the tough discussion with Roxanne last night, why not just clear everything up in the shortest amount of time possible? Who cares about my sanity, anyway?

"Elise," I deadpan. "Dad, I suppose I can't say something has come up and I have to leave?"

"He just wants to talk to you, Andries," my sister blurts out. "I'm going to go. Call me later."

"Elise," I hiss again, but she's gone in a flutter of skirts, and I'm left standing awkwardly at the small cafe table with Sebastian Van Den Bosch.

It doesn't look like the best place for a talk like this. The restaurant is small and open concept, the size more similar to a coffee shop than a real dining destination, with dried herbs hanging on the walls and vases of fresh flowers on every table. I lower myself into one of the small chairs and Dad does the same, neither of us speaking.

It isn't until the server drops off two lemon waters that Dad clears his throat to speak. "You look healthy, son. I suppose you're staying out of your cups?"

"Just a glass of wine here and there," I admit, thinking about the half bottle I had shared with Roxanne the night before.

"That's great. I hope you know I didn't tell your sister to bolt like that. From what I understood I was having lunch with you both."

I laugh sarcastically. "I guess we both should have seen through her machinations, but it's too late now. I'm sure that cutthroat attitude is serving her well at the company, though."

"She's… she's doing far better than I expected. I know I said you were my first choice, but I can admit when I am wrong."

I sit my fork down from where I had been pushing my spinach salad around on my plate. "You can admit when you're wrong, huh?"

He makes a sour face, but to my surprise, answers honestly. "Yes, and that means I also want to say that I'm sorry for calling your ex a whore. I had no idea what kind of terms the two of you were on and it wasn't fair for me to do that. I just had some… actually, *a lot* of lingering animosity toward her for letting Karl hire that Patricia girl. But the truth is even if you weren't around at all it probably would have happened the same way."

It's so unexpected for him to apologize like this that I don't know what to say at first. Dad watches me for a moment, giving me a chance to speak, but when I don't, he continues.

"I never wanted to think my best employee could do something like that. It's so shameful. You were absolutely in the right to get that Patricia girl the help she needed and to take her to the police. I just couldn't see that through my own selfish worries."

"Thank you, Dad. Really," I manage to say. "I know apologizing isn't a skill that runs in this family after all."

He smiles, thankful for the levity I assume. "You're correct about that. We are a prideful sort." The smile fades and he shakes his head. "I just don't understand why these college girls would put themselves into this mess. It baffles the mind."

I have a little more insight after talking to Roxanne, but I still agree with my dad quite a bit. "Well, it's easy money and they get to enjoy the finest things in life. Nothing new under the sun, really. Have you spoken to Karl since he was arrested?"

Dad shrugs between bites. "Not much from him directly. I've been talking to his legal team, though. I've heard that the prosecutor might drop the charges."

My mouth hangs open for a moment before I can snap it shut, the shock running through me real and tangible. "Why in the hell would he drop the charges?"

"Well, it seems like the girl gave Karl mixed signals, she went to his apartment, took her clothes off, and—"

I can't hold my tongue, causing me to interrupt him and say, "She was drunk, Dad. Drunk!"

Dad looks around nervously when I raise my voice, noticing a few heads turning our way. "Andries, please. Calm down."

I want to tell him to fuck off, but he isn't wrong about everyone looking our way. A vision of the tabloid picture flashes through my mind, and I know I don't want to draw any more unnecessary attention to myself. I bite my tongue, and try to continue eating, even though I'm fuming.

I can't keep it down, though. The food sours in my stomach, compacting into a hard ball until I can't stomach anything more. Dad seems on edge, but not nearly as bothered as I am, asking me simple questions that I answer in as few words as possible. All the while my temper is boiling beneath my skin, thinking about how much trouble I had gone through to help Patricia, how much sleep I had lost over the whole thing, and how it had strained any chance of fixing my relationship with Roxanne to the max. How could Patricia be willing to throw all of that away? Surely, the prosecutor will only withdraw the charges if she stops cooperating.

An awful thought floats to the forefront of my mind. Why would my dad be talking to Karl's legal team if he wasn't involved himself in this somehow? The thought is almost too much to bear, but I force myself to ask, "Dad... did you ask them to try and convince Patricia to sign the settlement?"

His fork freezes mid-stab, but he shakes off the stillness quickly, like it never happened. "I had nothing to do with it, son."

"Okay," I say simply, but I don't believe him at all. We had been getting somewhere, Dad and I, but he just couldn't stop himself from lying to me. It hurts more than I thought it would.

Everything rolls downhill from there, and when I bid him goodbye, it's with a cold handshake and zero eye contact. The entire lunch has drained me, and I want to throw in the towel and call it a day. The idea of Patricia letting the charges be dropped won't leave me alone, though, and I make the quick decision to go and see her to try and figure out why this is happening.

I should call her first, but I don't, and I bike straight back to campus. I text her once I'm outside her dorm building, and after a few minutes, she comes down to let me in. Patricia looks much better than the last time I saw her, with a little bit of color in her cheeks and hair clean and braided. We make small talk on the elevator ride up to her room, but once we're inside, she looks at me knowingly.

"You want to talk about the case, right?"

Well, if she's going to get right into it, so am I. "Why are you backtracking, Patricia?"

She plops down on her twin sized bed, clasping her hands together. "Andries, I'm on the cusp of being poor. Karl's lawyer contacted me and offered me fifty thousand euros to drop the case. That's more money than I've ever had at one time. If I go to court, I might lose and then end up with nothing. It's a better deal than I ever could have hoped for."

"I don't understand. Patricia. To Karl, fifty thousand is nothing. Plus this isn't just about money, anyway. You're doing it so things like this don't happen to any other girls."

"I know, I know, but I also have to look out for myself." She pauses as she thinks something through before her attention returns on me. "Why do you care so much about this, anyway?"

I hate having to talk about this for the second time in twenty-four hours, but there is no help for it. "Because not too long ago, I was visiting a country where sexual survivors didn't matter. Here your voice counts, so you have to use it."

Patricia looks stricken, her eyes misting over. She quickly looks away from me and out the dorm window, most likely ruminating over my words, but she purses her lips and shakes her head. "I don't have a choice, Andries."

"Fine," I sigh. "I'll pay you the fifty thousand."

She jerks her gaze back to me, and I can tell she doesn't believe me until she sees the sincerity in my gaze. "You're serious?"

I nod. "What happened to you could happen to any other girl. I want to stop that if I can."

"I…" she lets her words trail off, collecting her thoughts. "I never would have expected this. If I want to take your deal, what do I need to do?"

"Just call your lawyer and tell him you want to go through with the case."

As if on autopilot, she pulls her phone out and makes the call on speakerphone. The lawyer answers, sounding glad to hear from her, until she tells him why she's calling, causing him to bluster in disbelief.

"Patricia, that settlement is an extraordinarily generous offer! You should accept it."

"I know," she says quietly. "But I have to do what's right."

He still sounds flabbergasted, but the lawyer quickly collects himself. "Mr. Townsend wants this case gone more than anything. I'm confident I could get double the offer. Would you drop it for a hundred thousand?"

Patricia's glance flicks over to me and then back to her phone screen. "Hold on one second," she tells the lawyer, hitting mute so he won't be able to hear the two of us.

"Can you do a hundred thousand?" she asks bluntly. The words could have knocked me out of my chair. They shocked me so much.

I can't say anything at first. This entire time, Patricia had been purely a victim in my mind, but with this one question, she has telegraphed that she values money over justice... even when it's justice for herself. Suddenly, I can see why she'd have taken that escort job and asked for more. For her, it's money above all and I was just too naive to see it through.

Still, what choice do I have? Karl being put in jail means the safety of countless other women, which means I have to support Patricia and her case no matter what. Stomach churning, I nod. "I can, but you have to do something for me."

She looks bewildered. "What?"

The idea had been in the back of my mind for a while as a last-ditch effort, but now that she was going to try and manipulate me even when I wanted to do the right thing, I decide that I can push her a little further.

"I want you to do a TV interview with a reporter I know. About the dark side of escorting. What do you think?"

She chews on her lip while she considers it. "Going on TV, might open some doors," I add.

Finally, she nods once. "Okay, fine."

I explain that she'll get twenty-five thousand from me after she signs a contract drawn up by my own lawyer that guarantees she won't back out, another twenty-five thousand once the interview is finished, and the rest once the case is settled. She agrees, bringing her phone back up to her mouth and turning the mute off.

"It's non-negotiable. I want to go through with the trial."

The lawyer, clearly pissed about being left on hold for so long and being dragged around by Patricia's mercurial wants and needs, is short with her. Once she's off the phone, Patricia looks shell-shocked, but also excited. It's easy to see why; after a single phone call, she had guaranteed herself double the money she had been previously expecting.

I feel ill as I leave her dorm, questioning everything from Patricia's intentions to the thing I'm about to do. Nothing can ever be easy or consistent. It always has to be as complicated as possible, and I feel like I'll never have any peace from all of this.

My phone feels like a grenade in my hand, and once I make this call, the pin will have been pulled. Still, what else can I do? Following my plan, I'll not only get Karl on trial, but I'll also expose the dark side of escorting to the world like I've always wanted. It had to be done.

I dial Kenneth the journalist, pulling out the crumpled business card from my wallet for the number. I have physically threatened this man multiple times, so I half expect him not to answer. To my surprise, he does, and even seems happy to hear from me. I know he thinks I'm calling about Roxanne, so I take some satisfaction in his surprise once I tell him that I have the interview of the century up for grabs.

"I can get you the escort involved with Karl Townsend," I tell him.

"Karl Townsend?" Kenneth repeats in surprise. "But I heard the escort he hired had signed a settlement."

"She didn't. She was about to, but she retracted at the last minute. I happen to know her personally, and she's agreed to do the interview."

"What do you want in exchange for that?" he demands. I can tell he's interested. Desperate, even, for this scoop, but he keeps his cool. He knows he isn't getting this from me for free.

"Simple. All I ask is that you leave me and Roxanne in peace. No more coverage about us or my family."

"What does your family include? Parents and siblings?" He is astute, leaving no stone unturned. I can admire that, as much as I hate the man. Still, I want more.

"Can't you extend it to my mom's family? Her siblings and parents, too?"

"That's a lot of people..." He chuckles, as if I'm a little kid he's talking to. "For just one interview, I can't sacrifice an entire decade of content, but I can keep your parents, your girlfriend, and your siblings out."

"Fine," I snap, sounding more annoyed than I actually am. In one fell swoop I have accomplished a number of my goals, all by manipulating the people around me and not raising a finger on my own.

I'd be safe, and Roxanne would be safe. Best of all, we'd be at peace to be together. Even as I end the call with Kenneth, the pride of my own scheming is building in me. This is everything I wanted, even if it has to come in a more complicated package than previously thought. I could handle it, though. No problem.

CHAPTER 25

Amsterdam, March 1, 2022
Roxanne

I've tried to keep everything Andries said off of my mind but being at work here at the agency makes it impossible to forget. From the moment I unlocked the door and walked into my office, I had been filled with a sense of grief, maybe my days here are truly numbered.

Andries staying with me last night, and how wonderful it had been, made it all too clear that he was going to be my first priority after all. I had promised myself my entire career of owning the agency that a man would never come between me and this place I had created, but now, things were different. I loved Andries, and I wanted to be with him. If he couldn't stomach the agency... I had to figure something else out, or this was going to drive me crazy.

Poppy, her bright red hair piled on top of her head, is typing away at the front desk. I can see her through the crack in the door, and I feel even worse, thinking about how my most trusted employee who, after all these years, was a close friend, too, would be left adrift if I sold the place. There was so much more to consider besides how I felt about Andries. I need to tread as carefully as I can.

It isn't about the money anymore, either. It's because this agency was precious to me, a passion project that had become so much more, and because it gave me a hands-on way to protect the girls who worked for me that might otherwise work in less than savory conditions.

I can't make a choice without knowing all my options, though, so with a lump in my throat I call Poppy into my office. She sits down daintily in the chair across from me, her expression bright and happy. "What's up, boss?"

"Off the top of your head, can you think of any good replacements for the agency?"

She looks bewildered. "A good replacement? For who exactly?"

I swallow hard. "For me."

I can tell she's shocked, her cherry-colored lips parting and her eyes going wide. "For you? You want to leave the agency?"

"I don't *want* to," I admit. "But I think it's time for me to move on."

My heart shatters when I see Poppy sniffle subtly, tapping her eye with a fingertip to avoid tears. "I don't understand. Is this because of the thing with Karl? We are still getting and doing great business, Roxie, I swear."

"No, no," I sigh, knowing I have to be honest. "Andries wants to give us another chance, but if we do, I have to sell the agency."

Her demeanor changes almost instantly. "You would sell your own business for a *man*? Roxanne, you can't settle for someone that can't accept you and what you do. You are a success story… an entrepreneur! Almost any other man would be honored to have your attention. You don't need to do this."

"Andries is someone who has seen the darkest side of what we do, and I want to give our relationship a shot. I've been in this industry for fifteen years now…" I shake my head sadly. "That's a long time for this kind of work, Poppy."

"I get it, but still… This agency is your baby, someone that loves you should understand that. They should love you *and* your agency."

"Okay, Poppy." I sigh, exasperated. "Until then, can you give me a list of our competition and see if they would like to acquire us?"

She looks conflicted, but at the end of the day, she is my PA and I'm her boss. Poppy nods tightly and leaves my office. Her shoulders are stiff, and I know she wants to talk more, but there is no point. I have to see everything clearly if I'm going to be confident in my decision. Maybe I would never be happy about it, so confidence would have to be enough.

Just like yesterday, I can't settle. There is too much in my mind and body for me to be content sitting here all day making schedules and calculating time sheets. Frustrated, I close the window I'm working on and stand, pacing to the floor-to-ceiling window and staring outside, hoping the wider view would give me a little more space to think.

It's a beautiful day out, only a few white, fat clouds floating across the sun breaking up the light every now and then. If I sell the agency, I'd have more time to be outside on days like this, feeling the sunshine on my skin and breathing in fresh air. An early retirement wouldn't be all bad I guess, but there is still a part of me that would rather be working here instead of tanning on some distant beach. Here I was the boss. Here I was in control, and as I know all too well, control isn't a sure thing anywhere else in the world.

I'm lost in thought when my phone rings. It's my cell, not the office phone, and the screen indicates it's my sister calling. I answer gladly, realizing that we never discussed her setting Andries and I up and the bookstore.

"I can't believe you haven't called to chew me out already," Lili jokes first thing.

"I would have… except, your little scheme worked out pretty well. He kissed me."

"What!" she gasps. "Tell me everything!"

So I do. I know she meant everything about that night at the bookstore, but I tell her everything else, too. The bookshop, the masquerade, Andries sleeping over… everything. I crave her advice on the issue with selling the agency, so I tell her that as well, asking her what she thinks. I never hesitate to tell my sister anything. Her opinion matters more to me than anyone else's.

"So are you really going to step down?" she asks, incredulously.

"I'm considering it… It's complicated. I understand where Andries is coming from, and I really do want a second chance at this relationship, but on the other hand, I don't think it's fair that he can't accept me as a whole, agency and all."

Lili is quiet for a moment. "You might not like to hear this, but I'm on Andries' side about this. You aren't running a modeling agency or anything like that. Amsterdam is one of the few places your business would even be legal. There's a reason it is banned in other parts of the world."

"I know, I know. Trust me. But the agency is just such a big part of my life, and it's hard to let it go. It feels like giving up something I've crafted with my own two hands for so much of my life."

"I understand that part, too, Roxie, I promise I do. Only you can make the right choice for you. If you let anyone else talk you into a choice, you'll question whether it was the right one for the rest of your life. This is all you, dear sister."

After we hang up, I grip the phone in my hand and consider Lili's words. She's right that, no matter how much advice I get, I can't make any other decision than the one that feels right for me. I've only ever followed my own gut, and I'll have to continue to do so from here on out.

I sit back down at my desk, intending on getting some real work done, but before I can put my phone in my desk drawer it pings. It isn't my sister this time, though. It's Karl.

The girl declined the settlement again. No idea why. Something's off. Call me when you can.

The more interesting part of this text is that Karl somehow believes I want Patricia to sign it. For me, whether she goes to court or not, is the same, but I'm too curious to get to know more about Karl's scheming, that I decide to call him, nevertheless.

"What do you mean she declined the offer?" I ask in disbelief when he answers, feigning indignation. "It's so much money. I never would have dreamed she'd turn it down."

"Me either," he replies, sounding equally confused. "Her lawyer called mine and said she's not taking it. As of yesterday she was about to sign, so I have no idea what happened. Roxanne…" He sighs. "Can you call her on my behalf? She might listen to you."

"You must be joking," I blurt out upon hearing his request. "You know I'm supposed to be on her side for the trial."

He pauses before asking, "Are you, Roxie? On her side?"

I laugh sardonically. "Don't ask me that, you asshole. I'm still so angry with you."

"Can't you just call her and try to catch up? See if she'll drop some information? I'm sure you'd rather be up to date on what's going on instead of in the dark. She trusts you. I bet she'll talk."

It's so wrong, but… he's also right. I don't like to be kept in the dark. "Fine. I'll see what I can do."

Before my moral compass can stop me, I dial Patricia's number and wait for her to answer, trying to think of the best way to go about this without sounding like I'm prying into her business. She picks up, sounding apprehensive, so I start out gently.

I ask her how she is, and if she's feeling okay. Patricia loosens up slowly, obviously happy to have someone to talk to, so I press my luck and invite her out for coffee. Maybe in person she'd be more down for gossiping.

"Oh, uh. No thanks, Roxanne. I've got a lot of stuff to do for school, and I'm trying to avoid being out in public as much as possible."

"I understand," I reply lightly. "I just thought you might want to do something more normal. I'm sure you've been spending a lot of time alone."

"Yeah, I have. But what else is there for me to do besides go to school…?" She sounds so down that it makes me feel guilty, and I know I have to get to the bottom of this conversation before I chicken out.

"That's… unfortunate. Have you heard from Karl lately? I heard that he wanted you to sign a settlement. I bet you're relieved if that's the case since this will all be over soon."

"Yeah I, um, I didn't sign it."

I'm glad she can't see the cringe that overtakes me hearing her say it out loud. Karl was right. "Oh…may I ask why? It would definitely make things simpler for you."

"I want justice, and that settlement was just a way to silence me." Patricia tries to put some bravery in her voice, but to me it just rings false.

"Wow," I laugh awkwardly. "For someone who didn't even want to file a police report, you've taken quite a U-turn. Was the settlement not good enough?"

Patricia makes an odd noise, one that sounds strangely regretful. "It was great, but money is not everything in life. I realized there's enough evidence to convict him and I want to go down that road."

What? That doesn't make sense! I remember Patricia telling me not so long ago how she felt guilty about Karl's arrest. Multiple times she has told me that she enjoyed his company and that he had been kind to her. She had been so reluctant to go to the police, and now she's adamant on going to court and getting justice? It just isn't adding up. Something is clearly off.

"You know, if there's something you want to tell me," I tell her slowly. "I can help you navigate this whole situation…."

Patricia's voice takes on a stubborn tone, and it's clear she's done with the subject. "I'm good. I've got a great lawyer and friends."

"I'm sure you do. I just wanted to offer you a helping hand if you needed it," I assure her.

"Well, I don't. Thanks for calling though. Bye, Roxanne."

"Bye…." I hang up and sit the phone on my desk, rubbing my eyes with the heels of my hands.

I know that someone is pulling Patricia's strings behind the scenes, I just can't figure out who. It isn't her defense, since her lawyer had wanted her to take the settlement, so it has to be someone with a grudge toward either Karl, or myself.

There's only one person I know that has direct animosity toward me, and that's Elise Van Den Bosch. She's also Patricia's friend, so it would make sense she'd worry more about some false justice instead of money.

With a heavy sigh, and feeling like I'm consorting with the enemy, I call Karl again, guilt churning in my gut the moment he picks up.

"I think it's Elise prodding her to continue the court case. You need to speak to Sebastian and see if he can get his daughter under control."

CHAPTER 26

It's been a painfully long day, and the idea of going home to be alone is almost too much to bear. I make my way back to my apartment, going back and forth in my mind about whether I should invite Andries over again already, especially after outing his sister to Karl, but in the end my desire to be with him wins out.

I miss you, I text him. *I've been thinking about you all day.*

Oh? he replies. *How so?*

Well, I thought about you the most when I started to look for buyers for the agency. Hard not to think about you while doing that.

It takes him some time to respond, and I worry that I have upset him with the slightly snarky part of the message.

To my relief, he finally replies, *Are you serious? If so, I'm really proud of you! That's such a big step.*

Kicking my feet up on the sofa, I grin, and hold the phone to my chest with happiness. When I go to answer back, I see he's texted me again.

Remember when we spoke about going to Paris with your mom and sister?

Confused, I text, *Yes...and?*

When you step down from the agency, I'd love for us to go there and celebrate.

The fact that he remembered that little detail about my life makes me love him even more. I have to see him tonight!

I think that's a great idea, I tell him. *Why don't you come over and we can discuss it further?*

I can't, Roxie. I've got homework.

I huff at his reply, texting him back, *Just do it here! I graduated from that same program, remember? Maybe I can help.*

Three dots emerge on the screen for a moment. It seems Andries is unsure at first, but I know he misses me just as much as I do him, and eventually he relents. I tidy up and pour us some wine; a deep, dark merlot this time, and change into a long, silk, cream-colored nightgown.

I go and open the door when I hear the sound of the elevator arriving. Once Andries lets himself in, I waste no time in greeting him properly with my mouth on his. He jolts when I kiss him immediately, no words shared between us, but after a heartbeat or two he melts into the embrace and returns my kiss with gusto. I feel his hands slide down my back to palm my ass, but he stops after he gets a handful, groaning as he pulls away.

"You missed me that much?" He laughs, running a hand through his tousled hair. I nod, and his smile is almost enough to make me jump on him again. Unfortunately for me, he holds his backpack up, shaking it. "I told you I have to finish my homework, Roxie, so let me at least get started."

I give him an exaggerated pout, but he ignores me, settling in the couch of the living room to do his studies. He's such a multi-faceted person, and despite my minor complaints, I actually love to watch him work. He draws his eyebrows together just slightly as he does so, a small wrinkle of concentration forming on his forehead. In these moments it's easy to see what an incredible author he will be once he graduates; he puts his heart and soul into everything that has to do with literature, from his own writings to things as minor as a bit of homework.

Since it probably isn't great for him to drink while studying, I lay a napkin over his glass of wine and bring him a chilled bottle of sparkling water instead before curling up on the couch with a book of my own, a used copy of Murakami's *Norwegian Wood* my sister had taken in from a seller recently. I tuck my legs under myself, pulling the throw blanket off the back of the sofa and around my shoulders, trying to relax. It's difficult, though, with Andries right there. His mere presence makes me fidgety.

I snap a few pictures of him on my phone when he isn't paying attention. His scholarly focus is just too adorable, and I want to keep the photos for myself when I am missing him. I deleted so many in anger when he broke up with me that I needed to start replacing them when I could, and candid is always best.

I manage to become absorbed in my own book when I notice Andries shifting in his seat. When I turn my attention to him, I can see he's frowning, that concentration wrinkle between his eyes deeper and more pronounced, like he's struggling with something.

"What are you studying?" I ask him.

"English Linguistics Three," he mumbles distractedly.

"I remember that course. Very tedious."

He looks up at me, surprised. "How do I keep forgetting that you took the same courses as me?" His attention switches back to his homework. "Can you help me with a question?"

I dog ear *Norwegian Wood*, sitting it down on the sofa next to me. "Of course."

He sighs unhappily, like asking me for help annoys him, but he quickly clarifies, "I know it's wrong of me, but I feel like being so tedious about the grammatical parts of language takes some of the creativity out of writing."

I consider the thought. "I can see what you mean, but just ask me the question so you can move past it."

"It says, '*What is a morpheme?*'"

"Easy," I say, scooting closer so we are shoulder to shoulder, and I can see his paper. "A morpheme is a word or part of a word that has meaning and cannot be broken down into smaller meaningful segments."

Andries looks skeptical but writes down the answer anyway.

"I can explain further if you want," I tell him, snuggling close and sitting my chin on his shoulder. "I think I got a B in that class."

He snaps his notebook shut and shakes his head. "No, I'm done for now. I'm hoping this won't be something that we spend a lot of time on, but if it is, I might need more study help."

"Well," I say, swinging one leg over his hip until I'm straddling him, "I suppose I should have some kind of reward for helping you…"

He raises his eyebrows but doesn't protest, helping me settle on his lap with his hands on my hips. "And what kind of reward are you looking for, Ms. Feng?"

With a growing smile on my lips, I take control of the situation, pushing my hands up and under his shirt and along the ridges of his bare chest before pulling the shirt off completely. He slides the straps of my gown down over my shoulders, pushing the top half of the garment down until it's around my stomach and my breasts are bare. It takes me effort to undo his belt, and he has to help me in removing his pants while I sit up, balancing with my hands on his shoulders, but eventually his pants are around his ankles, my dress is bunched up above my thighs, and we are both more or less naked.

Both of us are breathing raggedly. Andries teases and plucks my nipples with the lightest touch while I grind my wet core along the length of his cock. I haven't taken him inside me yet, sitting far enough back that it juts between us, and I can tilt my hips forward and slide the length of it over my clit again and again. Kissing the column of his neck, I sink my teeth gently into the tendon that sticks out there as Andries gets more and more tense, all the while covering my body in goosebumps with the sensations his fingers on my nipple are creating.

"Were you," Andries grits out between his teeth, "waiting for me with no panties on?"

"You caught me," I confirm, my voice needy.

"Fuck," he gasps. "I need you now, Roxie."

I grind my mound over his cock a few more times, loving the sharp shocks of pleasure as the tip of him glides over that little bundle of nerves, but I don't want to wait any longer, either. I lift up just enough for Andries to reach down and guide himself to my opening, the thick head of his member giving me a delicious preview of what's to come.

As he slides deep, I cup his face in my hands, setting a slow, devastating pace while keeping our faces intimately close. I kiss his full lips, rolling my body so his cock presses against the sensitive front of my inner walls with each movement. I don't want to pull back. I want to take in the subtle changes in his expression and the tiny gasps and moans spilling from his mouth.

We stay connected that way, exchanging searing kisses while I drive the both of us higher and higher. Andries touches me all over, his fingertips pressing into my skin. He and I are like one living thing, sharing both a heartbeat and breaths.

My need takes on a desperate edge, and I have to push against more, roll against him further, to get that last little push toward my climax. It's been building this entire time slowly but powerfully like drops of water into a cup, but now it's about to spill out of me, if only I can tip it over.

With my orgasm hovering just out of my reach, I have the sudden urge to crush my lips to his. I do so, kissing his plush, full lips with such delirious need that it's almost bruising, our teeth clicking together. I make Andries drink my moans as they pour out of my throat, and he rewards me with the undeniably male sound of a growl rising from his chest.

He pulls his mouth away just long enough to grit out, "Easy, love," before I'm on him again, the silky rolling motion of my hips becoming tumultuous and unhinged. I want to come… I want to come so badly, and I'm so close that it's driving me mad.

Andries steadies me, moving his hands from my breasts and moving them to my hips, keeping my body steady while he takes just the smallest bit of control from me. He's fucking me in even strokes upward and into my pussy, the firm grip keeping me right where he needs me to fill me deliciously with his cock again and again.

Combined with the way I writhe forward, forcing the thick head of his member against my g-spot, Andries gives me just enough to push me over the edge and into the climax I've been chasing. Almost without warning, I'm swept away by a deep, shuddering orgasm, hands clutching his shoulders for dear life.

When Andries comes, he sucks in a breath sharply, burying his face against my neck and locking his teeth into my shoulder with just enough pressure to sting, his thrusts becoming uneven until he finally stills against me.

The heat of his cum sets off little aftershocks in me. I ride the last of them out, laying my forehead against his and whispering, "I love you, Andries. I love you."

He nuzzles my neck and jaw in lazy, ardent kisses as we both wind down. I know it's just an excuse to stay inside of me, but I want the same thing, so I let him take his time. It should be too hot, both of us slicked with sweat and pressed together with not even air between our bodies, but the heat is almost intoxicating. I want Andries just like this, every night, forever. Even if it costs me so much, he's worth that and more.

His arms lock around me like a vice, as if he's just as unwilling as I am to separate. "Are you really going to step down from the agency?" he asks, catching me off guard.

"Yes. I'm trying," I promise, kissing the corner of his mouth. "I want to be back together like before, and I know that you aren't comfortable with my job. Just be patient with me."

"For you," he says huskily, "I could wait for eternity."

CHAPTER 27

Amsterdam, March 4, 2022
Andries

I didn't think I would be as nervous as I'm to go through with the interview tonight, but I can't help the tapping of my foot or the clenching and unclenching of my fists as my lawyer draws up the agreement for Patricia. I'm not even the one giving the interview, but it's impossible to deny that I was now the key orchestrator of Patricia going up against Karl.

Patricia looks beautiful tonight; I'm sure it's because she knows she'll be all over the local news within a few days, but she also looks startlingly young in her mauve sweater, pearl necklace, and matching pearl earrings. It'd certainly shock everyone to see someone so innocent looking decrying the sins of escorting to the world.

She keeps looking up at me from where she is seated in front of my lawyer's desk, smiling excitedly. I suppose it must be a totally new experience for her, and she was also minutes away from getting a twenty-five thousand euro check from me too. That would excite anyone.

Signing without an ounce of hesitation, Patricia plucks the neatly written check out of my hand with glee, looking it over with sparkling eyes before carefully tucking it into her clutch purse.

"Are you ready now?" I ask, trying to ignore the feeling that I'm being used and focus on the good that will come out of this.

"As ready as I'll ever be," she confirms, wringing her hands as we exit the office and walk toward my car. To keep everything as private as possible, I had decided to drive her myself. Everyone would know the truth soon enough, but it would undermine this whole deal if someone else got wind of what Patricia and I were doing this night.

To further ensure that the interview is kept secret, we decide to do it under the cover of night. I keep glancing over at Patricia as we drive, the streetlights illuminating her face in waves. I have been through so much to make things right for this girl, so why am I now feeling this bitter animosity toward her? Not much of it, but enough to notice.

It's especially obvious when I see her keep checking the inside of her clutch and feeling the check with her fingers, assuring herself it's still there.

RTL studios is mostly dark this late, but there are a few windows in the pale rectangular building lit up. Media never sleeps, I guess.

I keep close to Patricia as we walk in, and she keeps her head down. She invokes so many feelings in me; pity, protectiveness, and the aforementioned bitterness all at once. I'm looking forward to lessening our interactions once this is all over with. Her true anxiousness begins to show once we are inside RTL, and everything becomes real to her. Patricia's hand shoots out and grabs mine almost involuntarily and I let her, cupping her palm while not interlacing our fingers as I take her to the elevator. It feels wrong, but I have to keep telling myself that she needs a friend right now.

"Am I doing the right thing?" she asks quietly as the elevator descends to the basement studio.

"Absolutely, yes," I reply. What I don't say is that it's too late to back out now, anyway. She already signed the contract.

The studio Kenneth has brought us to is bland but comfortable, the walls painted a diluted burnt orange, a bevy of different lights and mics hanging on the ceiling, and in the center of the area underneath it all is a dark brown loveseat directly across from a matching cozy chair. It's all meant to put the interviewee at ease enough to open up while still being basic enough to work for all genres of pieces that might have need of an interview. The seats are surrounded by multiple cameras, and once we enter the room, the employees milling around begin the soundcheck.

Kenneth isn't wearing his unassuming college gear that he had sported when confronting me the first time outside my apartment. Instead he looks slick and professional, having traded his thick-rimmed glasses for sharp, thin metal ones and his curly dark hair perfectly combed back. Just like the room, he has some touches that make him more approachable; his white linen button up has the sleeves rolled up to his elbows and the top button undone, giving his appearance just enough softness that Patricia wouldn't feel like she was being interrogated. It strikes me that he might be a much more impressive adversary than I had first anticipated. He obviously seems like a capable man. I'll try and keep him on my good side.

Kenneth nods briefly to me, but after that all his attention goes to Patricia, who positively blooms under Kenneth's praise for her bravery. There's a blush of red around her hairline and neck as he leads her to her seat and sinks down into the chair across from her.

"Do you need any water or anything else before we start, Patricia?" he asks politely, and she shakes her head.

"No. I'm ready."

"If you need anything, it's just beside you on the table," Kenneth proceeds.

I stay in the back for the whole ordeal. The last thing I want is to be on camera. Kenneth starts by looking directly at the camera behind Patricia's shoulder and begins the monologue.

"Good evening. Tonight we will hear from a very special guest, my friend Patricia, who is here to tell us all about the dark side of escorting in Amsterdam, and how the practice, while legal, preys on unsuspecting women and girls. Patricia has experienced firsthand how it feels to be taken advantage of by a client, who was none less than the current Head of Global sales at Van Den Bosch Industries, Mr. Karl Townsend, all in the name of making money for an escort agency, and she's here tonight to explain all about how this has affected her, and what we can do to prevent his tragedy from happening to other girls just like her. Patricia, thank you for being here."

She looks at the camera behind Kenneth, giving it a quick wave. "Thanks for having me."

Kenneth leans forward. "Patricia, how old are you?"

"Eighteen."

"What would bring someone who has just turned eighteen to begin escorting?"

"I had a friend who was working as an escort during the weekends. She was represented by a local agency and the money was better than most salaries, even at C-levels. So one day I got in touch with the agency owner, and she booked me my first client. With class I didn't even have time for a part-time job, so this seemed like the perfect way to earn some money while going to school."

"And that client was Karl Townsend?"

Patricia nods. "Yes, it was. He went by an alias, though."

"So your evening with Mr. Townsend didn't go as planned from what I understand. Can you tell me a little bit about that?"

I can see Patricia swallow, and her hands start to fidget. "The idea was that I was supposed to go with him to an event and dinner, but that was it."

"And that's not what happened?" Kenneth presses.

"No…" She looks down at her feet. "I drank a few glasses of champagne, and Karl was always refilling my empty glass and making me feel special and good. After the dinner, I was feeling dizzy and drunk, and Karl took me back to his home and he… he continued to compliment my appearance, then he started kissing me, and he even said how lucky the guy who would have sex with me for the first time would be…."

I don't think Patricia notices it, but there is some shock and disgust in Kenneth's eyes. He laces his fingers together and schools his face to look calm and understanding but his questions are anything but. Kenneth makes more questions about the evening and Patricia willingly speaks and answers all of them, but I'm getting more tense by the second, checking my watch as the minutes tick by and the interview goes deeper and deeper into detail. I really want to be finished with this. Kenneth promised not to talk about Roxanne, but I'm ready to step in the minute he decides to go against his word.

Finally, it ends, and Kenneth stands, giving Patricia a quick hug before he turns to me and offers his hand. I shake it, and he pulls me closer to pat me on the arm in a friendly manner.

"This is going to be a big deal, Andries," he says, and I nod.

"I'm aware, trust me," I tell him. "Thank you for your services."

"I'll be in touch, and you do the same if you decide you want to share anything else, okay?"

"I won't, but I'll keep it in mind just in case. Have a good night."

"The same to you both," Kenneth replies.

I gather Patricia, letting her link her arm through mine. My stomach sinks when I feel that she's shaking, but I don't ask if it's adrenaline or fear. All I can do is pat her arm and tell her that it's over and she can relax now.

She's quiet in the car, more so than she was on the way here, although she does open her clutch to look at her check a few times. We're halfway back when her phone rings. She digs it out of her clutch and pauses.

"It's Elise," she tells me, sounding confused. "Did you tell her about this?"

"I haven't told anyone. Go ahead and answer it."

Patricia puts the call on speaker, and at first, it sounds like my sister is just calling to check on her friend, and I relax. Patricia doesn't tell her that she is with me, thankfully, but it doesn't take long for the call to take a weird turn.

"So, Patricia, I don't want to pry, but people at work have been saying that you might not take the settlement?"

Patricia inhales sharply. "Uh, yeah. That's right. I'm weighing my options."

"Personally, I think you should settle. It was a good plan to confront him, and you should get a decent compensation, but dragging it out is bringing a lot of unwanted media attention both your way and to my dad's company, since Karl still technically works there. I work there now, too, and it's affecting me as well. It'd really be a big help for all of us if you would sign."

My hands clench on the steering wheel, and it takes all of my willpower not to exclaim in shock. I'd have *never* thought Elise would take Karl's side, even just enough to get Patricia to settle out of court! Patricia also seems frozen, taking a long time to respond.

"I... no, Elise. My decision is firm, actually. I'm not going to sign."

Elise huffs, "How has your opinion changed so drastically? At first you didn't even want to press charges at all and now you want to take it as far as it will go?"

Patricia looks at me desperately, and I'm torn. Not knowing what else to do, and aware that it will be public knowledge that Patricia did the interview soon anyway, I motion for her to hand me the phone. I click it off speaker and hold it to my ear.

"So you were the one persuading Patricia to accept the deal?"

"Andries!?" she sputters, before gaining control of herself again. "I should have known. You and your history of bad decisions. Look, I'm an intern at Dad's company now, so his problems kind of become my problems, too."

"Ha! No, Elise, they don't. This is Dad's way to manipulate you into doing what he wants. Look, Karl is a piece of shit and needs to go."

"You don't get it," she snaps. "He's an integral part of the company. He's also the best performing employee and—"

"Elise!" I yell, cutting her off. I see Patricia jump in the seat beside me. "You're becoming exactly like Dad, and it isn't good."

"Patricia isn't even your friend. Why are you so bothered about this?"

"Because she's *your* friend. You should care more about her than Dad's company, Elise. Think about that."

I hang up the phone, tossing the phone into Patricia's lap. I'm fuming, and I cut off any attempts she makes at talking. Once we pull up in front of her dormitory, I pull my checkbook out of my backpack and write her the next check for twenty-five thousand euros. Patricia takes it with more hesitation this time, and I know she's feeling conflicted about everything. She looks down at the slip of paper, and back up at me, sheepishly saying, "You're really awesome, Andries. Roxanne was really lucky to have you."

With that she leaves. I only watch her go for a second before I call Roxanne myself. Now that she's on my mind, I have to see her. I need something positive, and she's the brightest thing in my life.

"Hello?"

"Do you have plans tonight?" I ask bluntly. She laughs softly.

"Actually, yes."

"With who?" I ask, bewildered and annoyed that she might not have time for me.

"You."

I relax and chuckle. "You're funny. Should we meet at your place?"

"How about we have dinner someplace? I haven't eaten yet."

I hesitate, not wanting to upset her. "Let me cook for you instead."

"...Still not comfortable being seen out with me, huh?"

I exhale slowly. "I just want to keep us out of the spotlight, that's all. What if I spend the weekend at your place? Will that make up for it? We can order in if you want."

"Fineee," she drawls. "You win. Come over."

I consider picking up flowers, or wine for her, but my heart is telling me to get to Roxanne as quickly as I can. I forgo the elevator in the lobby of her building, not wanting to wait, and even though I'm winded when I reach her floor, I know I made the right choice.

Roxanne is waiting for me, and before I can open the door she does instead, standing there in nothing but a black silk robe and lace panties. All the blood rushes to my head, pulse pounding in my ears, before a large portion falls away again and shoots to my groin.

Sometimes with the two of us, words aren't needed, and that's what is happening right now. I rush forward, slamming my mouth to her until her tongue is sliding over mine before descending her body with my lips and teeth, covering every inch of her in my affection, heedless that we're still in the hall. I reach her belly button when I hear her throaty laugh and she runs her fingers through my hair, grabbing and pulling me up.

"Let's finish this inside," she purrs, pulling me into the apartment.

I go in without complaint. I'd have to be a mad man not to.

CHAPTER 28

Amsterdam, March 5, 2022
Roxanne

There isn't much better than coffee on my terrace with a soft blanket around my shoulders. Two things are making it even better today, though; the hazelnut creamer I had bought on a whim, and Andries spending the weekend with me.

It's early, and Dam Square is quiet for the time being. It will explode with activity in no time, but for right now, it's just me, my coffee, and the sunrise.

It isn't long before Andries opens the terrace door and joins me, his flannel sleep pants and university sweatshirt making him look oh so domestic. Him staying all weekend almost makes it feel like we are back to normal, even though I'm aware there are still issues between us to hammer out.

I smile distractedly as he kisses me on the top of my hair, then he sits in the chair next to mine, watching my face and not the Square, before his curiosity gets the better of him.

"Is everything okay?" he asks carefully.

"We should go ice skating," I tell him, just like that.

He blinks, totally taken aback. "Ice skating?"

I turn toward him, grinning. "Yes! Lili's date took her yesterday, and she had an amazing time apparently. We should go too. It's been so long since we've done something spontaneous."

"Your sister had a date?" Andries is still a few steps behind. I blame it on the early hour.

"Yes, she's been seeing someone. So… ice skating?"

He frowns, turning to Dam Square now to avoid my gaze. I know why he doesn't want to go, but I want him to say it out loud so I can shoot his pathetic excuse down. I won't hide in my apartment with him forever, no matter how good the sex is.

"Roxie…" he starts. "Those places are always packed this time of year."

"Exactly my point," I snap immediately. "No one will recognize us in the crowd."

He pinches his nose and closes his eyes. "We already spoke about this…."

"Are you ashamed to be seen with me?" I know that isn't it, really, but I can't help the hurt in my voice.

He doesn't look up, just sighs in displeasure at the confrontation. "You know it's not that. I don't want my parents or Elise finding out, that's all. I have to be the one to tell them."

"Oh, come on, Andries, let's be real." Now my tone is sarcastic, maybe more so than I intended, but oh well. "Your family doesn't go skating at a crowded public venue. You guys probably rent a pristine mountain lake and helicopter in or something." He scowls, his expression sour, and I chuckle. "Don't give me that face. You know it's true."

He doesn't respond, just crosses his arms, and continues to look out at the Square. Finally, I've had enough. I stand in a huff, pulling my blanket around me and grabbing my empty coffee mug. "Fine! I'll go alone. I need to get some fresh air. I'll see you later."

Opening the terrace door, I step one foot over the threshold when I feel a tug on my blanket. I turn, and Andries has it clenched in his fist, looking at me in disbelief.

"You're really going ice skating without me?"

"If you aren't coming, then yes," I tell him, trying to contain my amusement of seeing his sad puppy face. "Now let go of my blanket."

Andries stands slowly, every movement full of reluctance. "Fine Roxie. You win. If we see anyone, though, we're leaving immediately."

I bounce on my toes, kissing him swiftly before pulling him inside with me. "Agreed! Now let's go!"

* * *

We got to Jaap Edenbaan later than I'd intended, since Andries and I might have taken a bit longer in the shower than planned.

After he has a moment of distraction at how nice my butt looks in my jeans, I finally get us out the door and on our way. There isn't a cloud in the sky, and with the whole day in front of us, I'm happier than I've been in weeks.

Jaap Edenbaan is enormous, looking more like a racetrack than an ice-skating rink, since it's also used for speed skating. Today, though, it's open to the public, and the long oval track is full of everyone from couples to little children holding on to their parents' hands. There is grass in the center, and there are skaters sitting there, laughing about their falls or just giving their feet a much-needed break.

Andries and I have spent many dates dressed impeccably and, mingling with people just like his family among the glitz and glamor. This time is different. It's real, slightly messy, silly, and wholesome. It seems so much more genuine than anything else.

"I'm so excited," I breathe, more to myself than Andries, but he slips an arm around my shoulders anyway. We're standing in line to get our skates, and to me, it doesn't matter who sees us. We aren't any different from anyone else. Andries is wearing a forest green fisherman's sweater and dark wash jeans, his only caveat for the extra chill of the ice rink is a pair of leather gloves. He looks every bit of the old money heir that he is, but at the same time, he doesn't look out of place here with me either. I think it's his demeanor, which has lightened bit by bit over the past hour as we made our way here. Once we are on the ice, rented skates on our feet, he's laughing out loud as we try to find our footing.

"I haven't done this in years," he admits, his long legs unsteady on the slick ground.

"Me either! That's why it's fun."

There are plenty of things that could make the morning and afternoon frustrating; the rough ice, the rather large crowds, or even the uncomfortable rented skates, but none of it matters since we are together.

Andries holds my hand as we skate, just two faces among hundreds, and the opportunity to be just another couple makes us both let go in a way we haven't in so long. Once we figure out what we are doing, we race. Andries catches me easily and spins me around the ice while I squeal in laughter. I kiss his cheeks, rosy from the cold, and he does the same for the tip of my nose.

I take dozens of pictures once I know he won't object. Shots of Andries skating alone, as many selfies as he will allow, full of joyful, goofy grins, and a few artful frames of our clasped hands and our shadows on the ground.

Once both our feet are aching, we give up the ghost and leave the ice oval. I moan as I slide the skates off, flexing my feet up and down to relieve the pain.

"This was your idea," he points out, wincing as he takes off his own skate.

"It was totally worth it," I insist.

Before we leave, we stop at the cafe and get hot chocolates, drinking them sitting hip to hip as we watch the other patrons skate. I sigh, letting my head rest on his shoulder. I feel him let out a long breath, and his free arm loop over my shoulder. He kisses my hair, just like he did early this morning, not even minding that it's such a mess from wearing a beanie all afternoon. I'm pleasantly tired, sore, and full of joy.

"You're right," he tells me softly, his breath flowing over my face. "This was worth it."

I turn and kiss him gently on the mouth, both of us tasting of hot chocolate. "When will you learn, Andries, that I'm always right?"

CHAPTER 29

Amsterdam, March 9, 2022
Roxanne

I wish I could have held on to those warm, fuzzy feelings from the ice-skating date for longer, but I only have a few days to bask in it.

Poppy yells for me to come to the front desk, and I can immediately see that her complexion is washed out under her makeup, her lips pale.

"You have to watch this," she blurts out, waving me over to watch her computer screen over her shoulder.

On the screen is Patricia, sitting in what looks like a professional news studio, and my stomach sinks. Oh, this is bad. Really bad. Poppy clutches my arm as we watch the younger woman tell the interviewer anything and everything about her time with Karl and how he had plied her with alcohol and taken her virginity. Both of us are agape as we take it all in, and I feel like I could vomit. She's going to destroy my entire business, one acerbic word at a time!

All of that shock and grief transforms into rage as soon as the camera cuts to the man asking the questions. I knew I had recognized the voice, but it doesn't click into place until I see his slimy face.

"It's fucking Kenneth," I hiss.

"The journalist from the party?" Poppy asks.

"Yes. That fucker."

I feel like I could burst into flames on the spot, I'm so angry. I'm contemplating how I'm going to handle all of this, and how I'll possibly assure all my clients that this will never happen to them when my iPhone rings.

I pull myself away from watching the interview to take the call in private. I'm not surprised that it's Karl, but what does take me off guard is how pissed off he is.

"Hel–"

"You knew Kenneth!" he spits out, not even letting me finish. "You set up this fucking interview, didn't you?"

I blink a few times, my racing mind taking a second to catch up. "What? No! Of course I didn't! Why would I tank my own business?"

"I don't know, but you're the only person I know who also knows Kenneth," he bites out, not convinced.

"I told her time and time again that I wanted her to settle, just like everyone else. I have no idea who could have possibly wanted to change her mind. Maybe it's Elise. Have you spoken to her or her dad about it?" I ask him, trying to calm ourselves.

"I'll ask them, but call Kenneth too and see if he can tell you who brought the girl to the interview," Karl demands.

"But—"

"You have his number, right?" he interjects again, his voice so loud that I flinch and hold the phone away from my ear. "Then call him! Now!"

I can feel tears of frustration pricking the corner of my eyes, and it makes me glad we aren't having this fight in person.

"Fuck you, Karl!" I yell right back, hanging up right before a single sob escapes my throat.

I hear Poppy softly asking if I'm alright, but I have tunnel vision, and I slam my office door in her face so I can be alone. My breaths are ragged as I sit down, holding my head in my hands and trying to compose myself. This isn't happening. This *can't* be happening.

But it is, and if I don't want to lose my agency before I even have the chance to sell it, I need to act now.

Kenneth's business card is buried deep in my desk, but I find it after some time. I would have sworn yesterday that I would never dare to call him, but now I don't have much of a choice. I dial on the office phone, holding it between my ear and shoulder.

He must be able to see my business name on his caller ID, because as soon as he answers he sounds smug.

"Are you calling me to congratulate me on my biggest interview yet? I'm ready to hear it if so."

"Who the fuck set that interview up, Kenneth?"

"Oh, you don't know who it was?" he chuckles to himself, and I can feel my blood pressure rising. "Well, that's quite interesting."

"What do you mean?" I demand, reclining on my chair as I hold the phone to my cheek. "Why would I know who set it up? Is it someone I know?"

"Yes, actually, you know them very, very well."

I fly through everyone I know that could also know Patricia, and no one fits. "Was it Elise? My PA, Poppy?"

He hums. "No, no. It isn't anyone at your agency, rest assured."

I slam my fist down on my desk, wishing that it was Kenneth's face. "Tell me who it is, dammit!"

"Have a good day, Ms. Feng," Kenneth quips, hanging up before I can say another word.

I shoot up from my seat, pacing the floor, so full of anxious energy that I don't know what to do with myself. In the space of less than an hour, I have seen Patricia blow everything about my agency out of the water and then been blamed for the entire ordeal by Karl who, for all intents and purposes, is the actual source of the problem! I have done everything he asked; found an escort, a virgin one at that, and trusted him with her. He had fucked everything up, and now had the nerve to blame it all on me. It's inconceivable.

There is a soft knock on my office door followed by Poppy peeking her head in, her expression guarded. "Is everything okay?"

"No, Poppy. Nothing is okay." I let myself fall back into my chair, throwing my head back in misery. "Someone I know did this to screw over both Karl and my agency at the same time. I made this one single mistake with Patricia, and now it feels like my world is falling apart."

She comes behind me and puts her hands on my shoulders, rubbing gently to ease the tension there. "It will be okay, Roxanne. The interview won't hurt anything. All the men who come here know what hiring an escort entails… Some negative press isn't going to be the end for us."

"You don't understand. Clients will stop booking our girls if they know the girls can just break NDA's like they are nothing. Especially if they go to the media. We need to keep our VIP list happy. They count on our discretion."

"I'm sure they'll understand that it's an isolated situation. Our clients know that. They have to!"

"Yeah, maybe some of them will understand, or consider it worth the risk, but Karl isn't happy, and he knows a lot of my other clients. What if that means he'll scare the hell out of them, so they don't book?" I shrug my shoulders to brush her off, and dejected, she takes a few steps back, clearly uncertain of how to comfort me. "Someone had to set this up, Poppy. Someone I know."

As if the universe has heard me, my phone pings. I lift it and unlock the screen, seeing that it's a message from Karl. My pulse kicks up as I read it:

I know who did it. My boss's daughter told us. Call me back.

CHAPTER 30

Amsterdam, March 9, 2022
Andries

The lecture hall is buzzing as I take my seat, and I'm afraid I know why. As soon as it was confirmed that Patricia is a student here, the entire school wanted to see the interview, and now it's all anyone can talk about.

No one knows my part in it, at least not yet, although some of my classmates that had seen me with Patricia and Elise around campus did ask me if I had any idea about her escorting incident. Of all the scandals I have been a part of at this school so far, this one eclipses anything else by far. There's no escaping it.

Professor Josianne comes in the side door on the floor of the hall, and her frame shifts the moment she hears how distracted the class is. She has to know the reasoning, but I'm sure she was hoping that she could get through the lesson without having to acknowledge it.

I watch as she takes a deep breath and squares her shoulders, walking to the middle of the floor and waving her hand in the air for silence. Eventually, the room settles, and we all wait quietly to see what is on the agenda today. I've got everything out for taking notes, but something tells me it isn't going to be the normal lesson.

"I'm going to keep class short today, since it's clear our minds are elsewhere," Professor Josianne begins. "I've already been briefed, like all the staff has, about one of your fellow classmates being interviewed about a negative experience she had, and it is my understanding that the interview has recently aired. It's impossible for me to tell you to forget about the whole thing and move on, so I want to address it all here and now so next class we can continue with our forward momentum."

She clasps her hands in front of her, turning her head to take all of us in. The room is quiet, respectfully waiting for her to continue. I'm on the edge of my seat about what she is going to say, and I'm positive I'm not the only one.

"Your fellow student, who I won't name, unfortunately fell into the trap that is escorting, being tempted with the promise of easy money. With this city's reputation for being a place that sex can be bought and sold like any other product, it isn't surprising that a number of students have turned to escorting to make some money. From what I understand, the hours are low, and the pay is high. As a young person, that's about as good as it can get."

She takes a deep breath before continuing, as if the subject makes her uneasy. "The problem is that unlike other jobs, escorting leaves a mark on every person that partakes in it, whether it be just a tiny bit of uneasiness or the loss of self-worth. It may fill your pockets, but your body will remember the things that you had to give up to earn that pay. Escorting is not a job that you can keep for a long period of time, and by partaking in it at all, you run the risk of not having any other marketable skills once you want to stop. All I'm trying to say is that all of you need to be careful. There's no glamor in being a college-aged escort and servicing old men who look at you as nothing more than a product to be consumed. That student took the risk, and is paying for it now. Let her story be a cautionary tale for you all. Stay safe, please."

Everyone around me murmurs to one another, but I'm feeling the first stirrings of victory in my chest. If a professor feels this way, then there's a good chance some of the students do too. If I can keep just one student from falling into the trap of escorting, then this will all have been worth it.

Professor Josianne dismisses class early like she promised, offering a willing ear if any of us had any more questions about the risks of that industry. Cleaning up my desk, I check my phone for the time, only to see I have a few messages.

The first is from Elise, filled with an unsurprising amount of vitriol: *Congrats on your shitty move! Dad's furious for what you did, you fucking moron.*

It hurts, like I knew it would, but I had already been expecting this reaction from my sister.

I did what I had to do, I reply simply.

Fuck off! she retorts.

I type up a few paragraphs but end up erasing them all in the end. I'll let Elise stew in her negativity for a while, and I'll talk to her once she's calmed down. In my heart, I know I did the right thing. I helped someone that wasn't able to help themselves, and it'd help save other girls from the same fate that had befallen Patricia.

My second text is much more pleasant, and it's from Roxanne: *Are we having dinner tonight?*

I'm glad to tell her yes. I know Roxie must have seen the interview by now. Hell, I think the whole country has seen it at this point, but I haven't dealt with the fallout yet when it comes to her. Patricia and Kenneth both played by my rules and didn't mention Roxanne specifically, but it was a fool's errand to think that she wouldn't be affected in one way or the other. I'll just have to see how the cards fall. As of right now, she isn't scolding me or telling me not to come over tonight, so that's a good sign, at least.

* * *

I don't make it over to Roxie's until after class, and I'm exhausted by then. It has been a long day, and while Professor Josianne tackled the Patricia issue head on, none of the other professors chose to do the same. That meant I was forced to slog through those classes even though it was abundantly clear that no one was really engaged in the lessons. Patricia, as expected, wasn't to be seen around campus, so I didn't even get to see how she felt about the whole thing. Oh well, I guess I can always call her later.

Roxanne isn't waiting at the door for me in lingerie this time. In fact, she isn't waiting for me at all, and after pushing the open door and making my way in, I find her curled up under a blanket on her velour sofa, reading. She barely looks up as I walk in, depositing my backpack on the floor.

"There's wine in the fridge," she tells me absentmindedly, turning a page without acknowledging me anymore.

Feeling spurned, I take her up on the offer of wine, bringing two glasses back with me. She holds her hand out and I hand her the glass, and after a long sip of the Pinot Grigio, she marks her book and closes it.

For the first time since I walked in, she gives me her full attention. "Why didn't you tell me you were the one who set up that interview?"

I sit down next to her and am hurt when she subtly moves further away. "After you gave her permission and support to go to the police, I figured you were done helping Patricia and weren't interested in her case anymore," I tell her, my tone even. "It felt like a nonissue."

She purses her lips at me, looking both annoyed and upset. "Of course I was still helping her, Andries. What happened to her was horrible. The thing is… I didn't even know you were involved. All this time I thought it was your sister sticking her nose where it didn't belong. Meanwhile, I'm sleeping next to you at night, and I have no idea what's going on."

"I tried to separate myself after she initially pressed charges, but you are right about Elise fucking with things. She and my Dad were trying to get Patricia to drop the charges in exchange for money. I did what I had to do. What I thought was right."

"Oh," she says quietly, swirling her wine in her glass. "Is that so?"

"Yes," I huff, feeling like she's being intentionally dense. "She was about to sign the settlement, so I told her I'd pay her instead to go ahead with the case, as long as she agreed to also do the interview."

Roxanne looks taken aback, opening and closing her mouth a few times as if she can't figure out what to say. She's looking at me with wide, incredulous eyes, and it's starting to make me uncomfortable.

"Why are you looking at me like that?" I ask finally. "You were onboard with her going ahead with the case, weren't you?"

"Yes, with the case!" she exclaims. "Not with that interview! I really thought you would have given me a heads up about a hit piece that talks shit about my agency."

I had hoped it would be different, but now I see that this is where this conversation was headed from the start. Not about Patricia, or even me, but about Roxanne's agency. Everything always comes back to that fucking agency.

"Seriously? That's all that matters to you, isn't it? That girl was raped, and you're still worried about your brothel."

"I'm the fucking owner, Andries!" Roxanne yells as she throws her hands up in exasperation.

"Then *stop*. You said you were looking for a buyer. Sell the fucking thing already and be done with it."

She pauses, cocking her head to one side as she examines me. When she speaks, her voice is calmer, but at the same time, more vulnerable. "That's why you set up that interview, isn't it? You wanted to make my line of work look bad in the hope that I'd quit faster."

"No, that wasn't my intention," I insist, blood starting to pound in my head. "I wanted to help Patricia and at the same time raise awareness about the dangers of prostitution. That's all. It's nothing about you."

Roxanne shoots to her feet, still clutching the blanket around her as she does. "Liar! You just wanted to shame me."

"Roxie, you're being ridiculous. Your name wasn't even mentioned." I can tell my voice is bordering on sarcastic, but this conversation just seems so crazy to me, I can't help it.

I feel like shit now, though, seeing the sheen of tears in her eyes. "I thought we had an honest and transparent relationship. You said that's what you wanted. This is the exact opposite of honest and transparent."

This is a real fight between us now, and I hate it so much that I have to resist the urge not to grab my things and leave. It was never supposed to be like this between us again. Looking at her, passionate and sad, I just want to hold her in my arms and tell her to forget any of this ever happened. But this is the real world, and these things have to be resolved.

When I don't answer, she quickly wipes the unfallen tears away, sniffling. "Maybe Poppy was right—I should be with someone who is proud of my business instead of asking me to get rid of it."

I guffaw. "Proud of you for selling *sex*? Aside from your faithful customers, and the likes of Karl, I don't see why any man would be proud of it."

She huffs, head shaking at my comment. "I don't need a congratulations card or a party to celebrate me or anything like that, Andries. I just want to be loved *and* respected, both in equal amounts." She bends over slightly to retrieve her book and wine.

Without another word she leaves for the terrace, shutting the door hard behind her. I can hear her shuddering breaths right before the door is totally shut, and I know she's going outside to decompress and gather her thoughts. It's tempting to follow her right away, but I force myself to give her some space for the time being.

Here, surrounded by her and all her things, it's impossible to make my thoughts go elsewhere. It's less than ten minutes before I'm pulling the terrace door open and going outside to join her. I hope this brief reprieve has been enough for her.

Again, she doesn't look up from her book, but still manages to ask, "You're still here?"

"I'm not leaving until you tell me to," I inform her, taking the other seat.

Roxanne crosses her arms and fixes her eyes on Dam Square, talking to me while facing away so I can't see her emotions flit across her face. "It isn't fair that I have to sell the agency to be with you. I love it."

"It's only because you lied to me in the beginning. If you had been honest, I never would have fallen for you. Wait," I rub the back of my neck, thinking over my words. "Actually, I'd still have fallen for you, but I never would have let it show. I never would have pursued you if I knew you were selling sex, but by the time I found out, I was already in a relationship with you. *You* took my right to choose away by lying to me."

She doesn't say anything, never taking her eye off the square. Waiting for more from me, so I continue, "Look, I want to give us a second chance, which is what I'm trying to do. I don't think I'm being unreasonable."

"But what if we split up and I've already sold the agency?" she asks, her voice thin, her eyes finally on me.

"We won't break up," I point out.

"Are you sure? I'm turning thirty-six next month, Andries, and you're barely twenty! What if one day you wake up, roll over, and see that you're living with an old harpy while there are so many women your age out there you could be with instead?"

Roxanne is bleeding vulnerability as if she's been stabbed, and her pain hurts me too. This fear that she's too old for me has haunted her for a while now, and no matter what I do I feel like I can't fully assuage it.

Still, I have to try. I take her face in my hands and look her straight in the eye, enjoying her soft skin against my hands. "I love you. And despite everything we went through, I'm still here. What I said at Christmas was serious; I'm in this for the long run."

"Oh, Andries," she breathes, words catching in her throat.

"I'm just as scared as you are that one day you won't be interested in me. All I can do is hope that day never comes."

Her eyelids flutter closed when I lean down, kissing her with aching softness to punctuate how serious I am about my words. I drag my lips over hers, as light as air, before kissing her in earnest again. She hums against my mouth, and it wrecks my concentration.

"Can I ask you something?" I manage to say, pulling her into a tight embrace just to feel her pulse next to mine.

"Sure," she sighs.

I try to speak, but nothing comes out. I lick my lips, swallow, and try again. Still… nothing. I'm so anxious that the words seem to be trapped in my throat, and try as I might, I can't unstick them. If I ask her this, then there is no turning back. Soon I will have to come clean to my parents and sister, and deal with whatever they throw at me. One look at my Roxanne, though, lets me know I'm making the right choice. She's more than worth it.

"What are your views on marriage?" I manage to choke out.

Roxie sucks in a breath, surprised. "Marriage?" she squeaks. "Well, um, I don't know. I never thought about it before."

"But what are your views?" I ask again, feeling the pressure mounting by the second.

"I think it's a beautiful and very noble commitment," she says nervously. "What about you?"

I clear my throat, and to my horror, I can feel a blush running up my neck. "Actually, I, um... I like the idea of being married to you."

"Oh," she gasps. "Have you been thinking about it?"

"A bit, yeah. I know my parents would kill me if we got married, especially if we were to elope, but..." I reach over, brushing a strand of blond hair behind her delicate ear. "It's a risk worth taking."

Roxie grasps my hand when I finish tucking her hair away, kissing my palm before lacing our fingers together. She looks like she's just been told something profound, something she never thought to hear with her own two ears.

"That changes my perspective on a lot of things," she admits quietly. "If you're willing to risk your relationship with your family for me, then... yeah. It really changes my perspective."

"Come here," I tell her, my voice husky. She does as I say, folding her legs as she sits on my lap and wraps her arms around my neck. She smells like sunshine and night-blooming jasmine. "One thing I can tell you, Roxie, is you'll never regret selling the agency."

She searches my eyes with hers, and in slow motion, she lowers her mouth to mine. We kiss slowly, exploring each other's mouths at leisure, tongues dancing across teeth, until we both pull away breathless.

"Can I ask you something?"

"Sure," I say.

She nuzzles her nose against mine, kissing the corner of my lips and whispering against my skin. "Can you spend the night here?"

CHAPTER 31

Despite being in my office, I find myself constantly drifting in my thoughts to moments I've had with Andries, causing my heart to race in excitement and pleasure. There have been times when I try to analyze and understand how deep his roots have been planted in me, still a little puzzled how I became so attached to him. One thing is certain, he has made me a changed woman, taking his rightful place over what meant the most to me—my agency. The thought of another chance with him is overwhelming and I'm not quite sure if it was happiness or peace or a combination of both when we had come to the conclusion that being together would require compromise from the both of us—from him by being openly with me no matter what his family thinks, and from me by distancing myself from the business that has been the source of our separation in the first place. But I must say I was quite surprised at him talking about marriage.

After all, Andries knows the implications of our age gap. Not only this but my unwavering position on the matter of marriage is making me drown in an infinite abyss of thoughts. It's scary, maybe a bit crazy, to think about walking the aisle to him. His fearlessness and willingness to overlook how this will tarnish his family's image goes beyond anything I had thought.

Sitting up in my office and interlocking my fingers on the desk, I wonder if marriage would be a stretch above my expectations. Of course, I want to spend the rest of my life with him, but I haven't considered the reality of becoming wedded to him. And I think it makes sense that he has decided to bring it up of his own volition. If it had been based on my desperation to be eternally entwined with him, I'd have mingled with a bit of guilt. I love him, of course, but maybe I'm a bit more realistic with my expectation, unlike his. Maybe I've been afraid of losing my agency because of the prospect of losing Andries in the future. There would always be some new troubles in the offing, but marriage, I believe, definitely gives some assurances. It gives clarity and indicates an unmistakable willingness to interminably pursue his love for me.

"I like the idea of being married to you."

Thinking about his comment about marriage brings a smile to my face; I've been many things, but becoming huddled up with him in a passionate, longstanding marriage ranks above everything I'd have achieved. And it isn't just considering my marriage to him, it's mostly about the standards and traditions we'd be defying. I'd actually be with a man willing to go against his powerful family to be married to me. It gets crazier every time I think about it. And it reinforces my desire to abandon my role in the escort industry. It now makes more sense to make such a sacrifice considering the things Andries intends to barter for my sake —his entire life.

A knock comes at the door of my office, jolting me from my introspection. I turn to the door, wearing a smile on my face. The thought of becoming his wife adds a sparkle to my responsiveness to the day.

Poppy looks slightly nervous, though, clasping her hands behind her as she walks into my office. She swivels left and right, heaving a heavy sigh.

"Karl is outside with his lawyers. He really wants to see you," she informs me in a soft, calm voice.

I'm actually not surprised about her announcement. I knew sooner or later Karl would come to my office for yet another face-to-face. "Let them in."

I sit back in the chair, keeping a clear head. Moments later, Karl walks in, obviously exasperated. He has a miserable look, losing the shine that previously announced his appearances.

"Did you see the interview? Did you see what that silly girl did on TV?" he asks, storming into my office like it belongs to him. "Aren't you supposed to have an agreement with your girls to keep their dealings private?" He presses his hands against my desk, leaning forward. He's sniffling, heartbroken, and distraught. His lawyers drop down in the adjoined chairs overlooking my position.

"You broke the agreement, Karl. You made the situation difficult to control," I reply.

Karl is gritting his teeth as he leans forward. A pulse taps away on his wrists. He looks to be trembling from a combination of fear and anger. He inhales deeply and pulls away from the desk, dropping one nervous hand on his brow. The lawyers remain behind him, patient, quiet, and attentive.

After a spell of tapping his brow, Karl turns toward me, staring deep into my eyes. There is a slight hint in the look in his eyes that he is equally angry with me. Perhaps he thinks I could have handled the situation better in spite of his indiscretions.

"Have you spoken to Andries? Have you found out the motivation of the girl? How could she just change her position all of a sudden?" Karl asks, tapping his temple with a forefinger.

"Okay. You have to calm down." After a few seconds of silence and Karl finally beginning to breathe, I then tell him the truth. "Yes, I have spoken to him."

"And?" he asks immediately, dropping his hands on the desk again. "Does he have a hand in her decision or not?"

"Yes, unfortunately he does," I answer, my tone low. "Andries advised her to do the interview and decline your settlement."

"That piece of shit. That fucking piece of shit," Karl spits out, backing away from the desk. His lips quiver, and the pulsing movement on his wrists intensifies.

"Hey! Don't talk about him like that," I retort angrily. I spring from the chair, glaring at him. I understand Karl is in a deep mess, but insulting Andries is totally out of the question.

He starts roaming around my office, taking heavy breaths, obviously shocked by my stance. His eyes continue to shimmer with a wet glint. I can see he wants to say something else but just opens his mouth and closes it back immediately. He looks from one lawyer to the other before turning back to me.

"After everything he's been doing to me, heck, even to you and your business, you are still taking his side?" he asks in a gruff, sad tone. He squints his eyes before covering them with one palm, obviously overwhelmed by the rush of events in his life.

A transient moment of silence comes between us. It's easy to see the immense influence of Andries on my responsiveness to things. Defending him comes naturally to me, and although Karl looks miserable, I'm still a little miffed at his choice of words in describing his stance on the man I love.

"Speaking of my business..." I swallow past the lump in my throat and take a few deep breaths, before finishing my sentence. "I'm likely going to sell the agency," I tell him, dropping back down in my chair. "So, if you know anyone interested, let me know."

Karl takes his hand from his face and gawks at me. Today, it seems, is replete with news that leave him floundered and shocked. He moves forward, exuding a disappointed look. He leans against the desk, finding a bit of equanimity as he stares into my eyes.

"You want to sell it? You really want to give this up after so long?" he asks in a hushed tone.

"Yes. Poppy has been in touch with a few of our competitors to see if they would like to merge."

"But this is your whole life!" he barks, pulling away from the table. "What has come over you?"

I knew Karl wouldn't understand my decision, and it's pointless explaining it to him. So I just exhale loudly and tell him once and for all what he dreads the most, "It's time to turn the page. I'm sorry I can't be more useful, but you're going to have to go on trial."

Karl heaves a long sigh and dips one hand in his pocket. He pulls out an empty chair and drops down between his lawyers. The lawyer at his right side sits up, seizing the ensuing moment of silence.

"This is exactly what we wanted to talk about," he says solemnly. "If Mr. Townsend is going on trial, are you going to testify in favor of or against him?"

"I haven't decided yet," I retort.

Karl taps the lawyer on his right side, impelling him to sit back in his chair. He leans toward him and whispers in his ear. Karl swivels at me, exuding a faint smile.

"Roxie, we've known each other for fifteen years. I've always helped you out. You are where you are today because of me. I took a chance with you when you desperately needed help. Can't you at least do this for me? Can't you do this for the sake of our history?" Karl pleads. He looks regretful, but I'm hardly touched by the look on his face. If anything, he is simply taking up the appropriate mien for this situation.

"You took advantage of one of my girls, thinking you could get away with it. You are the one who put yourself in this situation, Karl. You only have yourself to blame," I remind him just as fast.

Karl sits up, clasping his hands together. Instantly, he loses the remorseful look on his face, taking a more calculated expression and tilts his face upward. For a moment, it feels like he is considering moving toward my desk and get closer to me, but instead, he just says, "You were not there, Roxanne. You didn't really see what happened. It all happened so quickly. I thought she wanted it just as much as I did. She's even the one that started undressing without me saying a word."

While he is speaking, Andries' harsh critiques about Karl comes to the fore of my mind, and I must say, it's hard to see him in a good light after everything he has done.

"What happened to you? You know perfectly well that you have more to gain being on my side than hers," Karl proceeds, raising his voice slightly and snapping me from my thoughts.

"That's your opinion," I say, springing up from my chair. "I have to leave now. I'll see what I can do," I inform, already grabbing my coat to make my way out.

"What if I help you find a buyer for the agency? I know a lot of people who'd be interested," Karl suggests, wringing himself from his chair and walking in my direction.

He suggestion makes me pause. I know Karl is in a great position to find a good buyer for my agency, but I also know in exchange, he'll want my testimony to be a positive one on his trial, which makes it hard to accept. There is no way I can testify in his favor without hurting Andries, whose welfare has become a priority in my life.

Unwilling to dwell too much on this thought, I move from my position, adjusting toward him.

"Bring me a good deal, and we can talk further," I tell him, leaving him slightly impressed.

***

An hour later, I'm in a café, sitting before Lili, who is obviously excited. We are both having grilled salmon with potatoes and lemonade. Lili is quite beautiful today; I can see how she's been deliberate about her outfit, make-up, and fragrance and it's not hard to find out why.

"I think Robin is a really great guy. Mama was right," my sister comments, keeping her eyes on her plate. Her voice is hushed, creating the impression that her utterance is simply an extension of her prevailing thought. She looks up at me, exuding a faint smile.

"Who is Robin?" I ask since his name doesn't ring a bell.

She drops the half-eaten potato back on the plate and adjusts forward. "The guy I met at Christmas," she replies, her tone softer than usual. "The doctor Mama wanted to introduce me to. I told you about him. We went ice-skating together."

"Oh, right," I mumble, composing a smile. "Good for you. I'm happy to see you're finally enjoying yourself." A short silence ensues before I switch topics. "How about Mama? How's she doing?"

Lili shrugs. "Mama is fine. She's feeling much better now. She can walk without a problem. She's even doing aqua gym classes and helps at the bookshop every few days," Lili replies, taking a sip of her lemonade.

"Don't you think it's too much to let her work at the bookshop? Wouldn't that be a burden to her?" I ask, an ounce of concern lacing my tone.

"Well, it was her idea. I think she wants to contribute in some way. She doesn't simply want to be a burden. The most important thing is to make her happy," Lili replies, before forking the rest of her potato into her mouth.

My eyes return to my plate, and while I'm cutting another bite of salmon, my mind starts wandering toward Andries and his plans for the rest of our lives. His words replay again like a melody, instilling an ineffable sense of happiness inside me. Somehow, it feels like a fantasy. It's crazy how I hadn't yet seen myself married to him until the conversation last night. And in some sense, it continues to feel surreal. After all, he's only nineteen. Does he understand the implications of getting married at such a young age?

Lili taps the table, ripping me from my thoughts. I take a bite from my salmon, masticating without a sound, but Lili has her eyes on me, staring studiously.

"What are you thinking about this time? You seem far away," she points out. "Let me guess, Andries again?"

"Well, actually...," I realize at this precise moment that Lili knows nothing about my latest conversation with Andries, so I remain silent for a moment pondering the best way to tell her the news. "We are considering getting married. It's crazy, isn't it?"

All of a sudden, my sister drops her glass of lemonade at the same time as her mouth, and she blinks twice, looking at me with deep astonishment in her gaze. "What? How? When did you guys get back together? And what happened to him? Has he really decided to overlook your occupation?" Her tone is rushed, and I can see how confused she is.

"No, he still hates it. It's a bit complicated because of his family. But he has assured me he'd go against them and be with me if I sell the agency," I tell her. I sneak a sip from my glass of lemonade, capturing the befuddled expression on my sister's face.

"Really?" she asks, flabbergasted. "So you're really going to step down?"

I know how much she disapproves of my business, so it comes as no surprise that she's happy at the news. "Yep, I'm already looking for a buyer. I'm going to do this for him since he's also sacrificing his relationship with his family to be with me."

"Wow. This is getting serious," Lili says, dragging her chair forward. It's a slightly strange move, but keeping her chair close to the table allows her to adjust her face forward. She pushes away the plate and cup of lemonade before her. Apparently, the conversation has really piqued her interest.

"I'm so proud you're doing this, Roxie. I thought you'd never walk away from that line of work. If Andries managed to convince you to sell the agency, then he's truly a blessing in your life." She pauses, pondering her words for a moment. "And what are you going to do next?" Lili finally asks, her tone filled with curiosity. There's suddenly no desire left to entertain the meal before her.

"Well, I don't know what I'd do next. I have never thought about leaving until now. I guess I could focus on my first love and invest in literature," I say, before finishing the rest of my food.

My sister nods as if thinking something through. "How about a memoir?" she asks out of nowhere, a glint in her eyes. "You can write about your life and reveal the inside-out of what you used to do. Your contribution would likely reduce the number of college students venturing into this trade. Don't you think?"

Poor Lili… I can almost taste her inching desire to be fully involved in my gravitation toward a more harmonious, moral life.

I take a gulp of lemonade, pondering her words. "Sex work is and will always be linked to poverty and lack of good opportunities. If a college student or someone who just graduated can't find a job with a decent wage, she'll find it in escorting. To reduce sex work, other jobs need to stop exploiting people and pay them better. Sadly, I don't think this is going to happen any time soon," I tell her as candidly as I can.

"That's exactly why you should focus on changing things. You have to speak about it. This could be your calling. You could even advise lawmakers." A smile spreads across my lips at how eager my sister is. "I just feel you'd do a great job if you follow this path. You're confident. You're brave. You have experienced this firsthand. There's no one better placed to change the narrative."

All of a sudden, my phone beeps—a welcomed distraction from the intense brainstorming we were having. I pick up my phone from the table and thumb on it. It's a text from Andries, and his question brings a smile to my face: *Hey, just wanted to confirm if we are still good for this weekend?*

I look from my screen up to Lili and study her face for a moment. There are still perceivable inklings of curiosity in her eyes, and I'm pretty sure she's yearning for more details about my future plans than what I just gave her.

An idea starts forming in my head, and leaning forward, I ask, "Would you be available Saturday night for dinner with Andries and I? You can bring Robin, if you want."

"Oh." Lili can't hide the astonishment settling on her face. "Yeah, sure, sounds great."

I turn to my phone, thumbing back a reply to Andries:

Yes, but only if we can go and have dinner Saturday night with my sister and the guy she's been seeing.

He responds almost immediately: *Oh! Okay. Deal!*

CHAPTER 32

Amsterdam, March 11, 2022
Andries

After school, I'm back home stuffing my luggage with the required clothes for the weekend. Thinking of which, I can't help but marvel at the changes in my life—ever since I reconnected with Roxanne, everything has become different. I feel like I have been freed from the shackles that held my heart bound, but it makes me also wonder how my parents will feel about my new relationship with her. After all, to my family, it's no news that I have become an enigma, a mere shadow of my previous self, because of my breakup. But how far will they go to express their disapproval once they know we are back together?

I don't regret giving her a second chance, but at the same time, I'm not sure if I'd be willing to cope with a life where I'm hated by every member of my family for being in love with her. It's surely not the life I had imagined for myself, but I'm relieved to have acted on my own accord.

Moments later, I walk to the kitchen and help myself to a cup of coffee, knowing that my evening will be long. It's black and bitter, just as I like it. I'm slouched against the cabinet and taking measured sips, my mind visualizing the way things would go down this weekend, when the sound of my phone ringing pulls me out of my thoughts. It must be Roxie who wants to know at what time I'll be arriving. Perhaps she's already eager to have me over. Perhaps she misses me as much as I have missed her. I hurry down to my bedroom and pick up my phone. But my excitement is short lived when I see who's calling. It's none other than Elise herself. Seeing her name on my phone screen sends sticky flushes down my stomach. Elise always smells like trouble, and her knack for being a nosy sister seems to increase day by day. Reluctantly, I take the call, resorting to silence as I place the phone against my ear.

"Hello, brother," she greets with that little, innocent tone she usually does when she's fishing for info. I remain standing on the other side, totally quiet. "I can hear you breathing, Andries. What are you up to?"

I frown at the question, my eyes falling on the luggage resting in front of me, and I wonder if she's calling me because she knows something about my weekend. "What do you mean?"

"Are you going back home this weekend?"

Her new question makes me pause and I swallow the lump past my throat at it. Does she already know the answer and is just testing my honesty? "No. I'm staying in Amsterdam." Technically that's not a lie either.

"Doing what?" she presses on.

I heave a tired sigh at her little inquisition, ready to hang up on her. "None of your damn business."

I'm about to finish the call, when she makes a question that leaves me speechless. "You're seeing Roxanne again, aren't you?"

Fuck! I freeze on the spot, unable to say a word. I take a few deep breaths, trying not to let my astonishment get the best of me. "Um, no, I'm going to hang out with Dan," I say instead.

"Dan is spending the weekend in London," she retorts. Her response sends a frown on my face. What is it about my life that gets Elise so interested? I struggle to find a response to her statement.

"I bet you didn't think I knew Dan's schedule, huh?" she continues, and I can sense the tinge of victory in her tone.

"Oh! He must have forgotten to reschedule," I offer, halfheartedly. There is a pause from her side as if she's assessing my answer.

"Look," she begins, her tone even. "I have no idea how you managed to forgive your ex after what she did to you, but as your sister, I'm left with no choice but to ask you to put an end to that affair once and for all."

"What?" I utter in shock, my jaw gasping at her audacity. "Who you think you are? Stay out of my fucking life!"

"Sorry, bro, not as long as we share the same family name," she replies, sounding more like an enemy than my sister. "Either you break up with her yourself, or I'll tell Mom and Pops about it."

Her words are like a knife perforating my chest. I can't believe it! My own sister is threatening me? I chuckle at the whole thing and start walking around my room, processing what's happening. It feels like she enjoys tormenting me and gaining some sort of control over me.

"Fine, go ahead," I tell her, after careful consideration. "You have no proof anyway."

"I've got the tabloid picture. You're lucky our parents don't check those magazines," she says, sounding quite sure of herself.

"Goodbye, Elise," I reply, hanging up.

For a moment, I'm impelled to fling the phone away, but I manage to hold myself back, inundated by the bickering of my sister. She continues to set herself as an irremovable thorn in my side.

* * *

I find reprieve from seeing Roxanne again. I'm finally back in her penthouse, and her arms are wrapped around my waist as she continues to hug me tight. Then she looks at me, her succulent, kissable lips inches away from mine, making it incredibly hard to focus on anything else. But I do take a moment to contemplate her beautiful face. She looks so happy to see me again, her lips twist into one of those mesmerizing smiles that warm my heart. I instinctively run my fingers over her cheeks, brushing her smooth skin until I pull her closer for a lingering kiss. The taste of her lips reminds me how much I had missed her. No matter how much I have tried to stay away from her, she's my home. Despite what my family thinks of her, Roxie makes my world goes round, and I know how lucky I'm to have her in my life. When our lips part, she smiles at me in the most alluring manner as if she knows what I'm thinking. She brings her right hand to my hair, brushing it backward and caressing my cheeks. "Welcome back home," she says in a whisper, her breath brushing my skin.

I place a gentle kiss on her forehead, grinning.

"You are definitely home to me," I tell her, pressing my lips against hers once more.

She wraps her arms around my neck as I revel in her warmth and deepens our kiss, her tongue dancing with mine and letting me know how much she wants me.

When she pulls away, there's a beam of satisfaction playing at the corner of her lips. "Always so poetic."

I try to smile at her words, but the confrontation with Elise from earlier comes back to the forefront and replays in my mind. Roxanne must have noticed a change in my expression as she brings both her hands to my cheeks, forcing me to look her in eye.

"Are you okay?" she asks in a slightly pained voice. "Did I say something wrong, or are you having a change of heart?"

"Oh, no," I reply immediately. "I'm not having a change of heart, not at all. It's just..." I cut eye contact for a moment as I think of the best way to tell her the truth. "I'm just worried about my sister. Elise has been really intrusive recently," I say, trying not to sound too alarmist.

"Elise really needs to focus on her life and not yours," Roxanne rebukes, before releasing an exasperated breath. She shakes her head, her mind drifting away for a beat. "Does she know about us?" she looks me in the eye with intense curiosity, as if trying to find the answer in my gaze.

"Judging by my last phone call with her, I think not only she does, but she's also planning on telling my parents about us," I admit. It's pointless to lie about something like this.

After all, Roxanne knows very well what my family thinks of her.

She pulls away from me, bringing her hands back to her side, and I instantly feel colder at the lack of her touch.

"Would telling your parents the truth be an issue?" she asks, her tone more worried than before.

I ponder for a minute her question, wanting to reassure her, but also, at the same, share my concerns with her. "I honestly have no idea. I couldn't care less about what they think, but knowing my parents as I do, they aren't going to be happy about it."

Truthfully, I'm worried about what they are capable of and if they'd go as far as to do something to her, but maybe I'm just overthinking.

At first, Roxie is silent. Her face is void of any expression, and her eyes are empty as she processes what I just told her. But I keep calm. I have to, even though her lack of reaction to what I've said about my parents confuses me.

Damn it. I shouldn't have told her about my personal problems or brought up my family. She's quiet for quite some time, while I remain standing in front of her and waiting for her to say something. Maybe I'm overreacting, or perhaps I've ruined the atmosphere for what was supposed to be a romantic weekend for the both of us.

She seems distant, engrossed in her own thoughts, when she moves further away from me. But I close the distance between us just as fast. If there's even a single bit of doubt in her heart about us, I'll put it out.

She continues to back away until she's standing against the sidewall. Without a word, she turns away from me, goes to the kitchen, opens the refrigerator, and grabs a bottle of

Krug Clos d'Ambonnay. My lips twist into a smile as I recall the last time we drank one of those bottles. She's up to something, I can tell.

This time, I lean against the wall and keep quiet while observing her. She opens the bottle, picks up two flutes, and then fills them halfway. With the two glasses in hand, she walks back toward me and, without saying a word, hands me one of the glasses.

Slowly enough, she leans forward until her soft lips are pinned against mine for a kiss.

When we break apart to catch our breath, she presses her forehead to mine, and in a quiet voice, she says, "I know your family. I know how powerful they are. But here, when you're with me, I don't want you to worry about them. I don't want us to ruin our weekend with any of this. We should be creating memories, not destroying them."

I find myself nodding at her words and she raises her glass to mine.

"I'm proposing a toast to us, to our beautiful weekend and the memories we'll create."

Roxanne's confidence and strength are one of the things that made me fall for her. I can't contain my excitement, so I grin, my pulse quickening as I picture the rest of the evening. She clinks her glass to mine, and we both take a sip.

"Wanna see a movie?" Roxanne asks, winking.

I can definitely tell we'll be seeing more than movies tonight.

CHAPTER 33

Amsterdam, March 12, 2022
Roxanne

With Andries spending the afternoon at the gym downstairs, I read Poppy's text message from earlier again, and go to the living room, sit on the soft parlor couch, and turn on the TV —only to be met with news of Karl's trial. I carefully listen to what the journalists say, consciously trying not to get disappointed by how biased they sound. As Poppy mentioned over her SMS, they are trying to paint a positive image of Karl, given the fact that he's a powerful and successful man, but it's too sickening to watch the extent they'd go to clear his name. Patricia, on the other hand, has been made to look a lot less than a victim, and much more like a calculated manipulative professional escort who set him up for personal gains. It's upsetting to say the least.

A part of me is happy Andries is not here to witness the unfortunate state of the news coverage. On the other hand, though, if he'd have been here, he could have finally understood why it'd have been a much easier choice for

Patricia to have accepted the settlement. Nonetheless, I keep my eyes on the TV, watching how helpless and naive Patricia appears in front of the judge. All of a sudden, though, my landline phone starts ringing. I answer quickly once I figure it's from the reception.

"Hello?"

"Good afternoon, Ms. Feng," the young man greets, his tone always so friendly. "There's a woman here who'd like to come upstairs and speak to you."

A woman? My brows crease immediately at his words. "Who's she?" I ask.

"A certain, um, Julia Van Den Bosch."

Holy fuck! The phone slips from my grip as grim flushes run up my spine. I'm utterly shocked that Julia has found out where I live. My heart is in my throat and I can't help but shiver at the thought of having her here in my apartment.

"Hello? Are you still there, ma'am?" I hear the receptionist asking from the other side of the line.

Quickly, I pick up the phone and put it back up against my cheek.

"Yes," I reply, sensing the touches of anxiety in my voice. "Um, that's fine, let her in."

Right after hanging up, I put a call through to Andries. He doesn't take the call, and my heartbeat quickens knowing that Julia is coming upstairs in a few minutes. Fuck! Fuck! And fuck! It'd be crazy to have Andries run into her while she is here. As I hold this thought, I thumb on my iPhone, sending him a text: *Your mom is at the reception desk. Stay at the gym until I get back to you.*

A gush of air rolls off my lips after sending the text, hoping he'll see it before leaving the gym. I start roaming through the living room, hiding Andries' belongings and removing anything that could give her any indication he's spending the weekend here. I'm simultaneously afflicted with a mix of fear and trepidation. A rash of gooseflesh sweeps through my arms as I wait for the arrival of his mom. Only, the longer I think about it, the more I realize there is nothing I can do to change how she regards me. Julia will always see me as someone unsuitable for her son. What is there to prove?

All of a sudden, though, a knock pervades the living room. Despite my effort to calm myself, I'm still slightly shaken by the sound of the knock. A mix of acids sweep through my stomach, weakening my resolve. The knock comes again, compelling me to move from where I am. I'm suddenly lumbering like an old woman suffering from severe arthritis. Mercifully, my phone beeps as I was about to give the first step toward the door. And thank God, it's Andries: *Fuck. Elise didn't waste time. Tell her I'm not here.*

I take several deep breaths, shutting my eyes for a brief moment as I try to recenter myself. A knock comes at the door again. This time, though, I try to be more emboldened. I leave the living room, reach the foyer, and finally move to the door. I open it, and my eyes lay on the intimidating frame of none less than Julia herself who stands tall in front of me. She might exude elegance thanks to her formal knee-length dress and high heels, but she greets me with nothing more than a wry, disdainful smile. She nudges my shoulder and storms into my place, uninvited. She then crosses the hallway, looking right and left, until she makes her way to the living room, obviously in search for her son.

I shut the door as she trudges inside, and, after following her back inside the living room, I say, "Good afternoon to you too, Julia."

Julia just ignores me as her eyes scan around the open layout. It's clear she simply wants to take her son from the house of the woman who'll always be a whore in her eyes.

"Where is he?" Her high-pitched question resonates through the walls, and I can't help but smile at her annoyance for not finding him.

I remain a few steps behind her, watching Julia proceed toward the TV, the biased discussions about the case still airing. She takes a perfunctory look at the screen first before she turns her attention back to me.

"How did you find my address?" I ask, keeping my tone under control.

The disdain in her eyes hasn't changed a bit, and I can see a smirk spreading across her lips.

"I'm a judge. A well connected one at that. Surely you're not that dumb." Standing inches from me, she looks me right in the eyes and repeats the same question, her tone more threatening than before. "Where is my son, Roxanne?"

I hold her gaze, keeping my chin high, and I savor the silence between us while her distress keeps growing.

"You won't tell me where he is, will you?" Julia asks as if reading the answer in my gaze.

"He isn't here," I lie, dropping my face.

"Fine," she spits out. "I'll just sit here and wait for him, then."

Before she can do so, I step in and say, "Julia, your son knows that you're here. He isn't going to come back until you leave."

She stops at the side of the couch, her eyes widening in shock at the news. Despite her best attempt to hide her astonishment, her face is contorted, and her lips are pressed together in perceivable fury. Her right hand convulses to a fist, and she inhales deeply, sucking in her breath.

I can hear the sound of her heel hitting the tiled floor as she starts walking back in my direction. "Look, I'll be very frank with you; for your own good, you better leave my son alone once and for all."

The seriousness in her tone makes me snort, and I can't help but shake my head in dismissal. "Or else what?"

She gives a few more steps forward until standing inches from me. She then leans down to my ear and says, "Or else I'll make sure to find a way to close down your business for good."

"You don't have to bother yourself with my agency, Julia." I pause, observing the frown forming on her face. "I'm selling it. In fact, I'm turning the page, and I'm doing it for Andries." Despite the tension between us, I can't forget she's just trying to protect her son, so I decide to open up and tell her the truth. "I never wanted to hurt him, I swear. I made a mistake, but I intended to tell him the truth about my business."

Her stern expression remains just the same. "I know exactly what you are doing," she says, sounding dismissive. "You have power over him and you're unwilling to let it go."

My brows crease together in confusion. "What are you talking about?"

"You've been in this business long enough to know exactly what you're doing to him," she says, looking at me with the same judgmental eyes as her daughter. "He's the catch of the century for you, but guess what? Being with someone out of your league won't erase your shitty past."

I drop my gaze to the floor, heaving a sad sigh. I'm trying to keep myself composed and calm, but I think Julia is deliberately poised to push me to the edge. "Julia, everyone deserves a second chance in life. I'm trying to move on. I'm trying to—"

"Not with my son!" she snaps, her loud voice startling me. "Do whatever *you* want, but don't involve my son. He deserves so much better," she adds, causing a pang to my heart.

"We've even talked about marriage. Our feelings are—"

"Oh, just shut up," Julia barks, storming out of the living room and back to the hallway. "He's nineteen years old for fuck's sake."

I follow her, hurrying myself before she can reach the door. "Julia, listen!"

She stops in her tracks, turning around slowly, her eyes staring at me like they could shoot daggers. "As long as I'm alive, you can be sure he'll never marry you." Her harsh words have managed to paralyze me. If I thought Elise was cruel, I can now see where she got it from. Julia charges down to the door, exuding anger in her stride. After opening the door herself, I'm convinced she's gonna leave, but she turns one more time, a pensive look on her face. "You may tell Andries we're cutting him off until he stops this silly affair with you."

I frown at her statement. "Cutting him off?"

"Yes, no more allowances and no more bills paid on his behalf," she explains. "There's no point for him to come back home either. He'll be totally on his own. You should let him know what he's getting himself into."

Before I can even say anything in return, Julia shuts the door behind her, leaving me staring at the empty foyer. Fuck! I run a hand through my forehead as I heave a long exasperated breath.

I fall down next to the refrigerator, disillusioned and crestfallen. Julia's remarks have left a gaping hole in my heart. There's no way I'll ever gain redemption in her eyes. After a few moments, I help myself to a glass of wine and head back to the couch, dropping down. I pick up the TV remote and switch off the TV in desperate need for silence. Will Andries accept being disowned like that by his family just to be with me? He's so young! What if he stops loving me in a few months and realize he made a mistake? What if he misses his family to the point he will choose them over me? I can't imagine him being cut off by his family like this—I don't think I'll be able to live with the guilt if he does. I take two quick gulps from the wine, dialing the reception.

"Reception, how may I help you?"

"Has Julia left the building?" I ask, my heartbeat quickening at the simple mention of her name.

"Yes, ma'am, she actually just left."

"Thanks."

After hanging up, I call Andries, and I'm positively surprised at how quick he answers me this time.

"Hey! Is everything alright?" he asks, his tone softer than usual.

"Not really," I fess up, unable to lie. "Your mom just left the building, you can come up."

"What happened?" he asks, sounding worried.

"We'll talk when you come back," I tell him, before I hang up and drop the phone on the couch.

I had never dealt with so much disrespect and humiliation than with my last interaction with Julia. Maybe she's right—maybe he needs protection from me. My heart is heavy and I'm beyond lost at what I should do next. I sit back on the couch, mingling with gloom, her words replaying in my mind. I know she's not bluffing. I know she and the rest of his family truly intend to disown him. But how can Andries possibly handle this situation?

Moments later, I hear the creaking sound of the door opening. But I'm just too shaken by the whole incident to go and greet him so I just remain on the couch, listening to the sound of his footsteps as he heads to the living room. When he finally comes around, a concerned look on his face, his eyes travel from the empty glass of wine to me. He moves closer, dropping down beside me. Then, without a word, he curls an arm around my shoulder and leans closer, pinning a quick kiss on my cheek. We remain like this for a moment, neither of us finding the will to talk. It's a comforting silence, but he needs to know the truth. I need to find the will to tell it to him.

"Did my mom say anything horrible?" he wonders, nearly in a whisper.

Tears start trickling down my eyes. I never minded people not liking me, or even despising me, but when it comes to the mother of the man I love, it's a different story.

Her words take a domineering hold on my mind, weakening my resolve, and when I turn to Andries, intending to tell him about her disturbing utterances, I can't find the will to speak. I take a few deep breaths, trying to compose myself, but it's harder than I thought.

"Baby, what happened?" His soft voice makes my heart ache, and he starts rubbing my back in a failed attempt to soothe me.

Oh gosh! What have I done?

"What did my mom say to you?" he asks again, pinning short kisses on my head.

"She, um…" I sniffle my tears back and try to find the courage to tell him the rest. "Your family will be disowning you if you don't let go of me. She was pretty serious."

Andries immediately withdraws his arm from my shoulder, dropping one hand on his brow. He looks speechless and utterly shocked by my revelation. His new lost expression leaves me fraught with fright. I imagine this would be the end. It has to be. Andries won't just lose his family for me. That would be overreaching.

"I have enjoyed every moment with you, Andries," I tell him as I lay my hand on his. "You have taught me how to love. You've made me realize the importance of love in making the world a better place. If this is how our relationship ends, I want to let you know that it has been a great ride. I have enjoyed every bit of it, and I totally understand if you want to break up," I say, exuding a sad smile. He turns toward me, his brows creasing in confusion.

"What are you talking about? I'm not going to break up with you. That's out of the question." He leans forward, just enough to plant a chaste kiss on my forehead. "We're both making sacrifices for this to work. Since you're giving up your agency for me, I don't mind giving up my family for you. I knew this would happen sooner or later." I blink twice, my lips parting at his words. "My parents are stressing out because they can't control me anymore. That's all."

I never expected he would be so chill about this whole situation. I study his expression attentively, but he seems quite sure of himself. "Do you need help with your rent? I can help out. I can pay your rent until you figure out what to do next," I suggest.

"Don't worry about that. I have been receiving a monthly allowance from my parents since I was born. I have enough savings to last me for the next decade at least," he says, adjusting his face toward mine. "Everything will be alright." He presses his lips against mine, and sucks on my bottom lip, dispelling the inklings of gloom in my heart. "Now, shouldn't we go get dressed for the dinner with your sister and her date? What's his name again?"

"Um, Robin, I think." I know he's just switching subjects to push the talk of his disowning behind, and honesty, so do I. "Oh, I talked to Lili about selling my agency, by the way," I tell him, playing along. "She thinks I should write a memoir and speak about my experience as an agency owner."

"I think it suits you," Andries says, exuding a smile I hadn't seen in a long time. More precisely, since the day I told him I had bought the bookshop.

CHAPTER 34

Amsterdam, March 14, 2022
Andries

There are no words to describe the pain I feel for being disowned by my own family. Even though I knew it was bound to happen eventually, it still hurts like hell. From my current standpoint, my family has never been able to accept me, as silly as it sounds. But despite the harsh reality, my mother's attitude has been the most upsetting. Just a few weeks ago, she wanted me to stay at the house and now she kicks me from the family altogether like I'm nothing more than dirt under her shoes. And all of that is thanks to Elise...

Speaking of which, I'm standing outside her lecture hall, perfectly aware she'll walk out of that door in a few minutes. I have full intention of confronting her about what she did. She's always been the perfect daughter, loyal to the bone to our parents and their aspiration and the whole thing makes me want to puke. She has no desire to live in a real way, to explore the limitless possibilities that exist out of this mapped-out life.

And maybe it's a good thing—maybe it makes her trustworthy and typical. But for me, there's no fun in living a life drawn like an architectural design.

Moments later, throngs of students troop out of the lecture hall. They are mostly engrossed in conversations, pervading the ambiance with a distinct cacophonous sound. I watch Elise from afar as she walks alone, minding her own business, in direction to the exit of the building. I follow her, speeding up my pace fast enough to catch her arm, and make her stop.

Before she sees it's me, her immediate response is to jerk my hand away.

"We need to talk," I demand.

She gasps in surprise upon seeing me. "What the fuck are you doing here?"

"Let's go somewhere quieter," I say, grabbing her hand again.

"No way! Leave me alone." She throws my hand down, shrugging me off entirely.

"You owe me an answer, Elise," I snap back.

Despite her attitude, I take her hand once again and drag her with me across the hallway, sneaking a few glances at her as we drift away from the crowd, and head to an empty lecture hall.

Once we are finally alone, I close the door behind us and without wasting any second, ask, "You know Mom came to Roxanne's place, don't you?"

"Of course I do," she says without an ounce of shame or bother. "I spoke to Dad, and he told Mom." Before I can even say another word, she takes a step closer and with a more serious tone, she continues, "Listen, I have done everything I did because I wanted to help you. You're not just screwing yourself here; you're screwing our entire family name by associating yourself with that woman."

Fuck! She's batshit crazy! I huff at her words, losing any remaining empathy I had for her. "You're aware they cut me off too, aren't you?" As I observe the expression on her face, it's clear that the answer is yes. *What a fucking bitch!* "You know what? Now I've got nothing else to lose, but you do!" I snap, pointing a finger at her.

"You're going to run out of money sooner or later," she interposes before I could align a few threats about her and her precious reputation. "And then what? You think a woman like Roxanne who was only having sex with men for money is going to help you out? You're so fucking delusional." She puffs, head shaking for a moment. "When money stops, your relationship is going to stop just as fast," she says, her tone rising, either in anger or distress.

"You don't know her," I growl back. "In fact, you know absolutely nothing about her! You don't know what she's sacrificing for my sake."

"Listen, I know how women who get into prostitution think. I've got a few friends who went into it. Remember? And let me tell you, they aren't going to stick around only for love. You better believe me on this."

"She's selling her agency," I announce, causing Elise's mouth to gap and her eyes to widen in surprise. "And once that's done, I'll propose."

Elise adjusts backward, drawing apart from my side. She stares at me with desperate contempt, gritting her teeth in suppressed anger.

"Are you fucking insane? What the fuck is wrong with you? You want them to disown you forever just because of some whore that slept with you?"

I close my hands in fists, but I keep my cool despite her language. "You're fucking crossing the line here."

"That's the truth, Andries! She's one, or at least *was*. You're the only one that can't see her for what she is. And you know what? Maybe I should go tell Mom and Dad you've never attended any business courses. I'm sure Dad is going to find it very amusing."

"Why the fuck are you doing this?" I ask, hollering. "You're my sister! I trusted you!"

"To see if you wake up once and for all from this absurd relationship!" she shouts at me, her hands on my arms as she shakes me back and forth. "It's so fucked up, don't you see it? You, Andries Van Den Bosch, marrying a former prostitute? This is beyond humiliating for us all."

I'd never seen my sister behaving like this before, and I'm beyond disappointed at her. "What's humiliating is your attitude, Elise," I tell her once she has regained her composure. "You're becoming just like our parents—which isn't a compliment."

She shakes her head for a moment, descending into a brief routine of huffing and puffing.

"Andries, in a few years, you're going to be broke. Roxanne expects a certain lifestyle. If the money isn't coming in, you're going to be in big trouble and no one in our family is going to help you out, believe me. They were dead serious when they suggested cutting you off," she warns, sticking to the position she has taken throughout our conversation. It's clear this discussion isn't going anywhere.

"You know what? I think I'm better off without you all," I say, storming away from the room.

"Andries! You have to listen to me!" I hear her shouting behind me when I'm already in the hallway, heading to the exit of the building.

After stepping outside, my eyes lay on none other than Dan himself, which is weird since he doesn't have class in this building from what I can remember. I brush the thought just as fast when he approaches me.

"Hey!" he greets, his face beaming at me. Unfortunately, I'm unable to reciprocate. "Is everything okay?"

"Fine, just some shitty stuff going on with Elise and my parents," I growl, not wanting to dwell further into it. "How was London?"

"It was good, I had a birthday I had to attend to," he replies, his eyes observing me attentively. "Do you want to talk about what happened?"

"Nope," I tell him. "That's alright."

"Alright, then…" He pauses, looks at me with a frown and drops one arm around my shoulder, before asking, "I'm going to a fencing class. You want to join me?"

I shrug. "I don't have my equipment with me."

"We can go to your place to grab it first if you want."

Well, I haven't gone to a fencing class for a long time, so why not?

* * *

Since we are the last ones arriving for the class, Dan is slated to be my adversary. With everything going on in my mind, I don't trust my fencing abilities one tiny bit. Coach Edgar is going to be greatly disappointed if he expects to see my usual performance. But I do notice something strange today, as I walk through the gym, it seems like the rest of the lads are particularly interested in me. Is it because I didn't show up since last year? I don't know, and I'm not supposed to care about the whispers that begin to spread through the studio room, but my ears perk up when I hear someone mumbling my name out loud.

Dan looks at me, his shoulders slumped. It's obvious he heard it too. I see a group of three guys, standing not far from us, where the voices are coming from, and I can hear bits of their conversations—all of them about me. When they burst out laughing, I turn toward one of the lads, who seems to be the main bull-thrower.

"Excuse me," I say, poking on his shoulder. Laughter instantly vanishes when everyone lays their eyes on me. "Any interesting stories to share?"

The group suddenly goes quiet, turning their attention between me and the big-eyed guy who was jovially making everyone laugh just seconds ago.

"Well, since you insist," he snorts, feigning confidence.

I cross my arms, waiting for him to finish but strangely he hesitates for a moment. "So?"

"Is it true that your girlfriend was a prostitute?" someone else behind him asks.

Everyone starts snorting at the question, and before I can take care of that motherfucker, Dan steps in.

"Alright, that's enough," he says, curling an arm around my shoulder to drag me away from them before I lose my temper. "Let's go over there to practice."

We might go to the other side of the gym to start the class, but with everyone knowing about my personal life, I can't concentrate anymore on the practice.

Heck, now I can't stop thinking about the question that guy asked me. He reminds me of what Elise said just an hour ago. *It's so fucked up, don't you see it? You, Andries Van Den Bosch, marrying a former prostitute? This is beyond humiliating for all of us.*

"You aren't paying attention to your opponent," Coach Edgar yells.

He's talking to me, but I barely hear him. I can't seem to focus at all. The question still hovers around my head. It's like that bull-thrower has reminded me of how people now perceive me. Do they think I suffer from low self-esteem which is why I'm with her? And somehow, I continue to think about Elise and everything else she said. *When money stops, your relationship is going to stop just as fast!*

Fuck. Would Roxanne really leave me if everything turns sour and I go broke? Would that really happen? I mean, she's well-off and lives in a superb penthouse. Plus, she'll become even wealthier once she sells the agency. Surely, she won't behave like that if I face financial difficulty. Would she?

My mind is a ticking time bomb waiting to explode as I replay Elise's remarks in my head. As much as they hurt, I try to ignore them. I love Roxanne, and nothing can change that. Since I can't focus at all, I stop the practice, give a word to Dan, and leave for the locker rooms.

There, I start changing back into my casual clothes until Dan comes in moments later.

"Hey, bud. Are you okay?" Dan asks, sounding more worried than earlier.

I nod a reply because I'm not sure how I'll sound if I say something.

"Okay, maybe fencing wasn't a good idea." He pauses for a moment, sits beside me and starts taking off his gear too. Once we are both ready to leave, he stands before me and asks, "Why don't we go get something to eat?"

I like the idea better. "Alright," I mutter pensively as we make our way out. I can tell he's worried, especially given the fact I didn't tell him what happened.

We walk to a restaurant not too far from the gym studio and sit at one of the tables near the big floor-to-ceiling window. After ordering, I remain just as quiet, so Dan starts rambling on about something, but I'm not sure what it is because I can't bring myself to pay attention.

Once our meal comes in, I start picking at the mashed potatoes with my fork, waiting for my appetite to return. Dan on the other side has already attacked his poor chicken like he hasn't seen food in days. I only realize how hungry I'm after I finally dig a bite into my mouth. The steak is tender and juicy and my stomach growls in thanks. Dan and I don't say anything to each other as we eat, but his company is comforting on its own.

When the waitress comes back to take our empty plates, Dan orders a crème brûlée while I just lean back, feeling full but also much better than when I came in.

"There's something I have to tell you," I announce.

Dan looks at me, his brows rising in surprise, and he leans forward, resting his forearms on the table. "Finally!" he blurts out in a snort. "So, what happened?"

I heave a long sigh, getting myself ready, before I finally blurt out, "I've been disowned by my parents."

"Holy shit," he exclaims, his eyes widening in shock and his mouth hangs open for an instant. "Is this for real?"

"Yeah, unfortunately," I say, leaning forward again so we are closer. "Elise told my parents that Roxanne and I are back together, so they're cutting me out completely."

"Fuck! That's so disgusting!" A gush of air rolls off his lips as he processes the news. "Have you spoken to your dad about all of this?" he inquires, and I can see the anger and disgust laced in his eyes.

"No, I didn't," I tell him. "But I'm pretty sure it was his idea and Mom's just supporting him. What an asshole...."

"Fuck. So now you are on your own?" The waitress comes over to give Dan his dessert so I keep quiet until she leaves our table.

"Yes, completely," I sigh.

Dan turns to his crème brûlée, taking a spoon full of it, and putting it into his mouth with an agreeable moan, which I pretend not to hear.

"Can I ask you something?" he continues, looking at me with a more serious expression than before. "How long would your savings last you?"

I pause, pondering his question for a moment. "If we only count what I have in the bank, I'd say three to four years without adjusting my lifestyle," I answer truthfully. "But once I finish college, I don't see where I'll be able to make the same amount as the allowance I was receiving. At least not an entry-level job from an English degree."

"Oh, forget it," Dan blurts out. "There's no job out there that is gonna pay you that well." I nod, knowing this all too well. "Have you spoken about this to anyone else?"

"Not yet," I tell him. Then as I think something through, I turn toward him and say, "Dan, I need you to do me a favor." His attention shifts from the dessert to me. "I want you to try and convince Elise to keep her mouth shut about me being in the English program. She wants to tell our parents I'm not doing business school."

He shoots me an arched eyebrow. "Does it make any difference at this point?"

"They are already disappointed enough in my life's choices, let's not make it worse."

"Alright, I'll call her after dinner," he says in a reassuring manner.

"Thanks." I give him a quick pat on the arm.

"What are you going to do now? Are you going to speak to your dad to see if he can stop this madness?"

Speaking to my dad is like the last thing I want to do, but unfortunately, if I want to get my allowance back I've got the feeling it's the only solution.

"I'm going to have to," I reply, while Dan is shoveling yet another spoon full of crème brûlée into his mouth.

* * *

On my way home, I notice I've a missed call from Roxanne. When I call her back, we catch up about my fight with Elise, and I tell her about my meeting with Dan. I leave out the parts about the fencing class from earlier today, not wanting to dwell on it any longer.

"Are you going to be alright?" she asks, her lovely voice laced with concern.

"Yeah, don't worry, I'll manage."

Just as I turn the corner to my building, my eyes lay on none less than Karl himself standing right in front of my front door, dressed in a pair of jogging pants and a hoodie. What a big contrast compared to his usual perfectly tailored suits. But what the fuck is he doing here? I stop in my tracks, looking at him with a frown.

"Um, babe? I'll call you right back. Someone's at my door," I say before hanging up.

His lips form a slow smirk as if he enjoyed catching me off guard.

"What are you doing here?" I snap at him, keeping some distance.

He paces in my direction, his demeanor giving way to a more humble expression. "I just want to talk," he says, sounding more desperate than I thought.

"Not interested." I turn my back on him, and make my way toward the door, keys in hand.

"Please," he says, reaching for my arm in a desperate attempt to catch my attention. When I turn, ready to shove him away, I can't help but notice how his face has become as sad and pitiful as a beaten puppy. "Andries, listen, I have lost so much. I already lost more than half of everything I owned from the divorce. I don't want to go on trial. I don't want to lose my job. I barely have anything left."

I snort at his observation. "Don't worry. You'll likely keep your job since my dad likes you more than his own son," I point out.

Karl frowns in confusion, squinting his eyes at me. "Why do you say that?"

"Why don't you ask him?" I retort.

"Listen, man. I'm not here to make any trouble. I have learned my lesson. I just want this to be over. I'll pay you whatever you want if you can get Patricia to back off," he says.

"Whatever I want?" I repeat, surprised. "You told me you had barely anything left."

"I'm borrowing right and left." It sounds mostly like a lie, but I brush it aside.

The money is tempting, and given my current situation, I actually consider it for a second, but decide against it anyway.

"I don't need your money, Karl. I just need justice," I reply, turning back to the door, then I put the key into the locker but when I'm about to enter inside, Karl grabs my hand. His eyes are pleading with me. I pull my hand quickly from his grip and in the blink of an eye, sneak into the lobby. I don't bother to spare him a glance as I shut and lock the door behind me.

Once I'm safely inside my own apartment, I call Roxanne again. I tell her about Karl's sudden arrival at my place and she gives me a few updates about his trial. Apparently, despite all the positive media coverage he's got, it's not looking so great for him. Good.

"Are you going to testify against him?" I ask her as I make my way to my bedroom.

She pauses for a second and then says, "I don't know. I'm a bit conflicted. Karl helped me get on my feet. He helped me get my life together at some point. I don't know if testifying against him would be betrayal."

I stop immediately in my tracks, caught totally off guard at her revelation. "You have to tell the truth," I remind her.

"Especially since you are the one who connected Patricia to him. This could be good for your public image if you side with her."

I hear nothing but an exasperated breath from the other side of the line. "I think you're right. I'll contact Patricia's lawyer and see what I can do." I smile, proud of her for making such a decision. "Also, I want you to know that I love you... so much." My heart does a little somersault in response and my smile keeps growing. "Whatever problem your family has with you will come to an end in time. I'm sure it's not going to last forever."

"Thanks," I reply, my tone barely audible. "I love you too."

I don't voice my opinion to Roxanne, but I don't think my problems with my family will easily fizzle out. Not with such a prideful and stubborn father as mine. But I do need to give it a try and face him once and for all.

CHAPTER 35

Amsterdam, March 15, 2022
Andries

There's a certain element of dread that washes over me as I walk into my dad's office. While he might have agreed to meet me, it isn't a good look to be cut off from the family, and dealing with him when it comes to finances makes a really horrible taste appear in my mouth. Especially because it's all due for my choosing to be with the woman I love, and it's only my decisions that left me in this situation in the first place. No matter how I decide to live my life, though, I need to get my allowance back. Being in school I have no way of making the same amount of money than what I was receiving from the trust fund. My parents had no right to remove me as one of the beneficiaries since that fund was created generations ago—way before them and it has accumulated generational wealth, so it's not really up to them to cut someone out at their own whim.

I know why they did that, though—they want to humiliate me. They want to force my hand and make me bow to their demands. But that's not going to happen.

I look behind the imposing desk as I walk into his office and find Dad on the phone, waving at a chair for me to sit. I choose to stand instead, looking out of the floor-to-ceiling windows that overlook the canal.

While Dad continues on the phone, my eyes keep appreciating the view that stands before me. The city is gorgeous after all, but I've got to admit, the view is more impressive from Roxanne's penthouse. As I come to think of it, once she sells the agency we will finally settle into life together and I might even be living there permanently.

What does the future hold for me? I have no idea, but I do know that she's a part of it and something that I need to pursue. Dad pauses as he hangs up the phone and turns around, looking at me. "You can sit down, you know." I remain standing in front of the window, ignoring his nasty tone. "Although if you're enjoying the view that's fine." Silence settles between the two of us for a moment, until he finally adds, "It could be yours one day."

I can't help but frown at his comment. Well, that is an odd way to start a conversation. "What do you mean?" I ask, my gaze turning to him. "I thought we were here to talk about you cutting me off."

"We are." He steeples his hands, leaning back on his chair as he considers me. "But we're also here to talk about your future. After all, you're my son and you're a smart man." He pauses for a beat, heaving a sigh. "Smart enough to know that the future with an ex-hooker isn't the way to go. You know that, right?"

Despite his harsh language, I remain calm and unmoved, letting myself just to take a deep breath in and out. "Don't talk about Roxanne like that," I tell him, keeping my tone even. After all, I didn't come here to have yet another fight with him, but to build a bridge between us. So turning to face him, I say, "I love her, Dad. You're going to have to get used to that." I decide to hold off on telling him that I'm going to propose her. After all, it's none of his business to know what I have in mind. "She's done what she had to do in order to make ends meet and survive."

Dad chuckles, head shaking in amusement. "I can't believe this…." Suddenly, he leaps off of his chair and paces in my direction, carrying a pensive expression on his face. "You're seriously standing here telling me you're in love with a woman who got Karl in trouble and has almost brought down the reputation of our company?" he asks, mere inches from my face. "We've been dragged through the mud thanks to her."

"Actually, that was thanks to your perverted employee." It's a legitimate shot, and his eyes narrow. "He's the one that sexually assaulted a young woman while she was drunk."

"The case isn't over. We'll see when the verdict comes."

I know it's pointless arguing about the case with him. He must be the one financing that media campaign on Karl's behalf. His opinion isn't going to change any time soon, so I refocus myself and continue, "Like I said before, I love Roxanne and she's going to be part of my life whether you like it or not."

Dad doesn't say anything in return. Instead, his attention goes to the view, and with a stoic expression plastered on his face, he remains observing it in silence for a moment.

"I had a meeting with the board yesterday," he announces out of the blue, disregarding my statement. Typical. "I'll need to step down in about ten years." The revelation surprises me to the point of being stunned. "As my son, this company is your legacy. And it's only natural that you are the one that takes over." There's the trace of a smile gracing his lips, his eyes even hold a glint of pride, but I've got no idea why. "I've spent decades expanding the company and I know you'll be more than ready to take over when the time comes."

There's never been any indication before that he wanted me to take over. Sure, he's always wanted for Elise and I to go to business school, but taking his place? That's a whole different story!

"What about Elise?" I ask immediately.

"Elise is a smart woman, but she's not the face of this company. I'll give her some other chief role once she's ready. But you're the legacy we need."

Legacy. It's the first time I've ever heard him refer to me in that way. Like an actual son rather than an afterthought. "So, you're offering me…becoming the next CEO?" he turns to me, and his smile gets broader. Like the shark who suddenly sees a treat dangling in front of him. He's already got it all planned out, I know that.

"You can join the team, be an intern, and we'll work together until you're ready. Just imagine me being your mentor." He puts his hands on my shoulders, trying to make me feel the same excitement as he feels. "Plus some of the best minds around helping you out. Then I retire officially, and you take over." Since I remain completely silent and expressionless, Dad continues his pitch. "And I don't have to tell you that you'll never have to worry about money again.

This company is very profitable and will continue to be for the foreseeable future."

I know this sounds like the dream for so many people, but doing such a deal with my dad feels like selling my soul to the devil. "And what do you want in exchange? You want me to break up with Roxanne? Kiss your feet?"

He laughed at the last part, but his answer actually surprises me to the point I almost get startled. "Nothing, son. This comes with no strings attached." I can't help but not believe him, and I think he knows that. "You can even stay in your relationship with that woman." What? I freeze, totally baffled at his statement. I search his eyes for any hint of malice or that he is trying to pull a fast one. But I can't see any of it.

"Are you serious? You'd even accept Roxanne as my girlfriend?"

He nods once. There has to be some kind of motive for this, and it's hard to figure out what it might be.

"Think about it; unlimited resources and wealth. You at the helm of something your great-great-grandfather started and Roxanne by your side. Wouldn't it be a great life path?" he asks, turning back to the window.

I know exactly what that means though—being his new puppet and renounce once and for all to my dream of becoming a published poet. The money would be great, yes, but what good is money if you can't follow your passion? Being CEO isn't the job for me. And he needs to know that. So it's a pretty easy decision to make, really.

"Dad. It's very hard to tell you this, but this whole thing, this legacy… it isn't what I want. In fact, it's pretty much the opposite. I need to break free from it, not to dive in and become a part of it." It takes quite the effort to be so blunt and direct with him, but satisfaction and relief flows right through me afterwards.

"Break free from it?" His expression turns cloudy, and he sounds beyond offended. "You want to break free from what has provided you with every opportunity and resource you could possibly ever want?" He shakes his head in displeasure. "You're crazy. This is the opportunity of a lifetime and you're throwing it all back in my face? Do you know how many people would kill to be in your position?"

"Crazy?" Now I'm the one being offended. "Crazy for not wanting your life? Imagine that, the entire legacy that's turned you into a bitter, old man who can't accept his son has got other aspirations." I can see that one hits a nerve, especially when his expression darkens even more. "I don't know how to be clearer about this, but I don't want your life, I want to follow my own path." His eyes narrow and I can see how hard he's trying to keep his composure.

"Fine," he says curtly. "If you want so badly to go your own way then I guess you can do it without me. And without my money." His tone has become arrogant and his lips twist into a smirk that irks the heck out of me. "Which means…"

"I already know what it means," I say, cutting him off. "You aren't giving me my allowance back, right? That's fine," I lie, but I'm just too vexed to convince him otherwise. "I'll figure it out."

When I'm about to walk past him, he reaches out and holds my arm with a tight grip.

"You really want a sad, pathetic life, don't you?" he asks with venom in his voice. "It's absolutely astounding. I think that woman has really messed with your head. When you get it together and start making the right decisions, you can come back anytime." He finally lets off of me and leaves my side, returning to his desk. "Until then, don't bother asking me for anything again." I'm stunned into silence as I watch him sitting back on his chair with a cold, stern expression. "Maybe your girlfriend can start to give you an allowance, huh?" he spits as he picks a few papers up which sit in front of him and starts focusing on them. "After all, she's used to people paying her for this type of arrangements, so it'll just be her doing the same."

His words hit me like a slap in the face. He doesn't care about me, and his statement about being okay with Roxanne was obviously just a farce to get his way.

So the offer had come with strings. He just thought that his strings didn't apply because of who he is, and the fact he was offering me his job. Whatever, I'll be able to make it work somehow.

Without another word I turn and leave his office, not even hearing a voice behind me. Part of me hopes that he'd call me back, that he'd change his mind somehow. But when it comes to money and pride, my dad has no equal for stubbornness.

I'm walking away not only from him, but from the life he wanted to impose on me. Although I'm terrified of the future, it also feels strangely liberating. There are other people in my family I can turn to. Grandma has always been the most supportive one, and I feel like I need advice from someone who is wise enough not to turn their back on family for such a petty reason. Plus, she's always been here for me, and I know once she's heard what's going on, at the very least I'll be taken care of.

Once I step out of the headquarters, I pick my phone and decide to give her a call.

When she picks up the phone her voice sounds quite happy. "Andries! What a nice surprise! And it isn't even my birthday." *Touché*. Normally it's a quick text once in a while to check in, but calling is imperative in my present state.

"Hi Oma, It's good to hear your voice. Things have been a bit, um, weird lately."

"Oh, my dear. That's pretty normal in our lives, isn't it?" She makes her usual clucking noise into the phone. "But I'm sure you're not calling just to hear my voice. Are you?"

Does she already know what my parents did to me? Of course she does!

"You know me well," I say, amid a quick snort. "I really need to talk to you. Face to face, I mean. Are you free?"

"Of course! Come by the estate for lunch. In about, what, an hour?"

"Perfect. See you then. And thanks." Making my way back to my car I'm still processing everything that happened with my father. The shameless way he tried to buy my loyalty by offering me his job, just to keep me under his thumb is beyond revolting. It hurts to think he'd rather cut ties with me than accepting the life I want for myself. But I guess only time will tell if he truly meant it.

* * *

The drive helps me to cool down and get my head together. After all, there's nothing better than leaving the city to the country side. Grandma lives in the middle of nowhere, close to a small town called Dieren. Her estate is one of the originals in the family and is a wide sweeping area that encompasses several acres of land in the country. As I drive through the gates, after being allowed entrance, I'm swept away by childhood memories of Elise and I playing in the gardens with Grandma. It was such a fun and careless time.

Once the car is parked, I head to the front doors, but before I can even knock, someone opens the door from the other side.

"It's great to see you back, Andries!" Stuart, the butler who's been with the family for decades, greets me. "Lady Margaret is in the petit salon," he informs while helping me to take my coat off.

"Thank you, Stuart."

Walking through the opulent house always brings back good memories. Elise and I getting lost in the massive rooms and playing on the gigantic lawn both front and back. It's a little kids' hide and seek paradise.

I find Grandma standing straight by the window as I step into the petit salon, the logs in the fireplace crackling as they warm up the room. She turns around, her lips twisting into a gracious smile. "That was a quick drive," she points out, pacing in my direction, sporting a black turtle neck with a beige cashmere stole draped around her arms.

"Thank you for having me for lunch." After greeting her, we exchange a quick hug. As much as she's a healthy woman, her body feels quite frail in my embrace. But her eyes are sharp as tacks as usual, and she scans my face attentively. "I take it things didn't go well with your dad."

A quick snort rolls out of my mouth. "Wow, you're on the ball today." She grimaces and then points to the sofa.

"Sit. We obviously have a lot to catch up on and I think maybe you're here for some venting. Or is it advice?" Always so straight to the point. As we sit beside each other, Oma leans back against the couch and considering me for a moment, she then asks, "What did your lovely dad have to say?" I know her opinion about my dad isn't the best, and as much as he garners respect for his business acumen and nobility title, Oma also knows that he's about as warm as a December morning. "It couldn't have been good if you're here to see me."

I take a deep breath, pondering the best way to start. "I suppose you already know my parents disowned me?"

"I do, yes," she answers, her tone even.

I remain silent, waiting for her to tell me who gave her the info, but it seems like she isn't going to dwell into further details, so I proceed. "Dad offered me his job, I mean, in like ten years or so, but I turned it down. It's just not for me and what I want for myself and my future." The way I say future obviously gives her something to think about because her eyebrow raises.

"Well, my dear. You know that as long as I'm alive you definitely don't have to worry about anything. As the young kids say these days, I've got you." Her eyes twinkle as she says it and again I have to stifle a bout of laughter. "And frankly, I think my daughter needs a bit of a talking to. Just because she married your father doesn't mean she's got to go along with all his decisions."

"The thing is, I'm not sure if this wasn't her idea in the first place," I lament. "She's the one who went to Roxanne's place and told her I was going to be disowned."

Grandma leans slightly closer to me, and lowering her voice, she says, "Trust me, dear, it was your dad's idea." Ah, she finally admitted it.

Stuart walks into the salon, so we keep quiet as he approaches us. "Ma'am, lunch is served."

Grandma smiles at him and nods, before her attention returns to me and she pats me on the arm. "Let's talk as we eat, you must be starving."

As we walk into the dining room, I notice the table is exquisitely decorated, like it's for some sort of celebration, except it's just for the two of us. Still, it makes me smile seeing the fine porcelain and the bouquet as a centerpiece. I wonder if in a few years maybe there would be young children running around the table like my sister and I used to. I should come here more often.

We're served some lamb loin, accompanied by green onion purée, I can't help but salivate as I take my first bite. It's delicious as always. There's one more thing I want to bring up, and while we munch away I figure this is as good a time as any. "There's something else I wanted to talk to you about," I say, breaking our comfortable silence. "I know Mom had a few properties that she wanted to pass onto me when I turned eighteen." Oma puts her cutlery down, her interest piqued. "But since I was abroad, I'm not sure if she managed to transfer the ownership or not."

She nods, before her gaze returns to her plate. "Yes, I remember when she talked to me about it. There were four units, all part of the same building, if I recall properly."

"Would you mind checking to see if I own them?" I ask as she focuses on cutting her food. "You have access to all the properties the family office manages, right?"

"I suppose." Some silence settles while she finishes to eat, but my eyes remain pinned on her. After drinking some water, she finally heaves a sigh, and says, "Fine, I'll check that for you."

"If those buildings have been transferred to my name, can you change the banking details accordingly?" I press on, causing her to stare at me slightly perplexed. "After all, I should be the one receiving the income that comes from the properties I own, not my parents."

"I can do that, yes, but I hope you'll give me a bit more details from your side as to why you have been disowned. Your mom didn't tell me much."

I can't help but wonder if Mom was just too ashamed to tell Oma the truth, but I brush the thought aside as soon as it came. "Roxanne and I are back together," I announce, which makes her frown in confusion. "For good. And my parents don't like the idea of it." Again, her eyebrow twitches and I know she's intrigued.

"You've decided to give her another chance? Even after everything that has happened?" I know the question is coming from a good place, not a bad one. She's not demeaning Roxanne, but it's legitimate to have concerns, since my grandmother knows the type of business she is involved with like everyone else does now.

"She's trying to find a buyer for her business. Selling it is a big step in the right direction," I tell her and take another bite of my purée with some lamb on it.

"Selling?" Oma repeats, her tone laced with surprise. "So she's looking for a buyer right now?"

I nod while chewing and she looks away, as if thinking something through. "That's an interesting take. Do you know a bit more about her business?"

"More than just a bit, yeah," I answer, quite amused at her question. "It's actually pretty impressive when you look at the whole operation and how she manages things."

"That's what I'm curious about. I'd imagine that she owns the client roster and then simply outsources her… talents?"

"I know she has got a few women on the payroll," I divulge. "I can't tell you for sure how many, but she's got a whole team to take care of the bookings and management of the girls."

"Do you know anything about the way the fees and transactions are structured?" Now that question gives me pause and causes me to raise my eyebrow a bit.

"I actually don't. That would be something you would have to ask Roxanne herself." As I come to think of it, I can't help but look her in the eye and ask, "Why are you asking these questions, anyway? Are you interested in buying her agency or something?" Thinking about my grandmother actually owning an escort service, even one slated for only the best of customers is kind of funny in my mind. A madam that would be old enough to be the mother of the customers and the grandmother to the girls.

"I didn't know she was such a savvy businesswoman, that's all," she says quickly and picks up her fork to take a bite of her purée. Just as quickly the subject is changed, but it still makes me wonder. The idea of Roxanne being able to sell her business would only make things better for both of us. On

447

top of that, if I can get ahold of the properties that I'm entitled to, we can both have a nice jumping point to move forward with and I can start to really think about the future. In the back of my mind, I make a mental note to remind Grandma to approach Roxanne if she wants to know further about her agency as we move on to other topics of conversation.

It was definitely the right choice to come out here, and I know that it always will be. As much as my father might want me to suffer or be under his thumb, it's good to know that one side of the family would rather see me thrive instead of descend into trouble.

CHAPTER 36

Amsterdam, March 24, 2022
Roxanne

The trial of Karl Townsend has been the talk of the town—especially for those we wanted to sell the agency to. They have perceived the case as a weakness and tried to devalue my agency and its worth. Regardless, I'm confident about my price tag, and I have no intention of selling it for less. As we finish yet another phone call without closing any deal, Poppy returns to her desk with a semblance of disappointment plastered on her lovely face. On my side, I take this moment of solitude to text Andries and check on him. It's been nearly a week since Julia came to my penthouse to threaten me and her son, and yet, I can't seem to stop thinking about it. Andries might not have said a word about it since then, but I know him all too well. The disowning of his parents is impacting him much more than he lets on. I wish I could do something for him. But what?

Not even ten minutes after Poppy leaves, I hear a few knocks on my office door.

"Roxanne?" Poppy asks, peering in the doorway. "There's someone who would like to talk to you," she says.

"Oh," I utter, given the fact I had an hour without any appointment. "Who?"

I can see Poppy hesitating before blurting out softly, "Andries' grandmother."

My eyes widen immediately in surprise, and I leap off of my chair just as fast, smoothing my dress at the same time. "Of course, let her in."

I see Poppy stepping aside and give space for a tall white-haired woman to walk past her.

"Good afternoon, Ms. Feng," she greets, her elegant fragrance permeating the room the second she walks in. "I presume you must be surprised by my visit, but your PA told me you were at the office the whole afternoon, so I thought to stop by," she says politely. "I hope you don't mind."

"Well, um, not at all." I'm still so stunned by her presence in my modest office, that is actually hard to even articulate. "Um, please, come on in," I tell her, trying to compose myself. "Can I get you something? Water, coffee, tea—"

"I'm good, thank you," she says, her eyes lingering around the room.

"And your name is? I don't recall Poppy telling me," I say.

"Margaret," she responds, her lips curving up and displaying perfectly aligned white teeth. "I'm Julia's mother."

My heart squeezes at the last part, but I keep my uneasiness to myself. "Well, Margaret, very nice meeting you. Please have a seat." I gesture to the white leather couch in the sitting area and Margaret follows me through.

"This is a beautiful office you have here," she points out as she sits.

"Thank you." I can't help but feel a tad anxious of having her here. After all, it's not every day that I have a noble lady paying me a visit.

"I suppose having an agency consisting of a bunch of high-end ladies pays rather well," she says as she continues to scan around, her eyes taking in every little thing.

"It does, yes," I reply, not sure why she made that comment in the first place. "Are you here because of what your daughter did?"

"No, dear." Her attention returns to me, and I find her bright blue eyes glowing when she says, "I'm here because I heard you are searching for someone to take over."

My eyes widen in surprise, and I find myself speechless for a moment. "Oh, Andries told you?"

"He did, yes." She smiles at me, reveling in my shock.

I'm still confused as to what she wants exactly, but I decide to be honest and tell her the truth. "Yes, I'm trying to sell it."

"May I know how much you are asking for?" she asks suddenly. I freeze for a second but then put myself together again almost immediately.

"Six million," I disclose. "This is what the agency was able to make in the last two years in net profit." I go to my desk and take from there a file which I hand to Margaret, before returning to sit beside her.

She puts a pair of reading glasses on, giving her an air even more aristocratic, and she stares, carefully scrutinizing the first few pages. "That's quite impressive." She looks up at me and I smile in return. "And you started this agency just five years ago?"

"That's correct. We have a total of a hundred girls currently. Some make more than others, but our top ten bring us in around a hundred thousand per month in fees," I explain while she continues perusing the company details.

"You charge how much? Thirty percent?" She asks, her eyes returning on me.

"Yes, and the agency takes care of everything, from finding high-end clients to matching them with the right girl," I tell her, my heart bouncing in excitement at her strange interest. "The girlfriend experience is what most men are after."

"That I don't doubt," she comments, her tone filled with amusement. "Do you have the financial statement and balance sheet for your company?" she asks as she continues to flip through the document.

"Sure. It's on page twenty," I say in a heartbeat, helping her locate the proper page.

We keep quiet for a moment while Margaret reads everything through.

"Apart from Mr. Townsend, I assume you must have a lot of influential clients who seek the companionship of your girls, no?" she asks, her eyes drifting back to me.

"We do, yes. Karl is likely the *least* influential of them all," I tell her. The amusement must be evident on my face because Margaret laughs as well.

"Who else do you have coming here?" she continues.

I feel torn whether or not I should disclose something so private with her, but she's Andries' grandmother, after all, and she seems fairly interested in the agency, so I decide to give her the name of one my former personal clients. "Um, Charlie Polinski."

She doesn't even look surprised when hearing his name. "The retired CEO of Polinski Bank?" I nod, a small smile playing at the corner of my lips. Somehow, I had figured out that she was a well-connected woman. "Oh, I always felt something was off with him. Who else?"

"A few deputies, former ministers, businessmen, athletes, and financiers," I reply without batting an eye.

"Those men must be doing some serious pillow talk with your girls," Margaret suggests.

I let out a quick chuckle. She's so right, though.

"They do, yes. After a few sessions with them, they become more comfortable and open up like a shell about everything—marriage, business, politics… the works."

"Well, I can see why my daughter doesn't like you at all." She shuts the document close, putting it on her lap. "But I, on the other hand, am delighted to have met you, Roxanne," she says, looking at me like I'm something to be admired.

"Really?" My voice quivers a bit in excitement, but I proceed, "In all honesty, I thought you'd be like your daughter and come here to try and convince me to leave Andries or something like that."

Her lips curve up in understanding. "My daughter is a bit less… business-oriented, to say the least. She is a judge, after all. Sebastian would have been easier to get on your side if you didn't let his favorite employee become disgraced with that court case."

"Andries was against it," I tell her. "There was nothing I could have done to prevent that trial from happening."

She sighs, her gaze dropping to her lap for a moment, before returning to me. "I understand. That wasn't an easy position to be in. You did well to side with Andries. My grandson is one of a kind. His ideas and values are totally over the top." There's a flicker of pride in her eyes when she speaks of Andries.

"He's pure and kindhearted. I have never met someone like him before," I disclose. I'm not sure why, but I feel much more comfortable around this woman than anyone else in Andries' family. Maybe it's because of how wise and down-to-earth she is, and staring her in the eye, I say, "He's the only reason why I'm willing to sell the agency and do something else with my career. He's worth it."

She nods in understanding, her expression softening with a smile. "He's always been different," she says, shifting in her seat to a more comfortable position. "Quiet and reserved, with his nose always in books." I listen as she speaks, some nostalgia lacing her tone. Her gaze drops to her lap for a second as she considers her next set of words. "Sebastian never had a good relationship with his son. He wanted to mold him into his image, like the perfect heir of the family. Alas, Andries couldn't be more different." There's a distant look in her eyes as she tells me all of this.

"Was it hard for him to grow up with a father like Sebastian?" I ask her, curiosity getting the better of me.

She frowns. "Oh, it was. Let me tell you a story…" We adjust ourselves in our respective seats, leaning forward to get closer to each other. "Sebastian loves hunting, and he couldn't wait to share his passion with his son. The boy was only twelve at the time, but he took him on a hunting trip and forced him to shoot at the deer that was their target."

My mouth hangs open at the revelation, and I can't help but ask, "Did Andries do it?"

"He did. And the poor boy cried all the way back home. He has hated his father ever since," she admits, letting her head drop down.

My whole body hurts as I picture the cruelty of the whole thing and I feel tears forming at the corner of my eyes as if I could feel Andries' pain. "That is horrible."

"It is. Andries was clearly not interested in hunting by any means, but Sebastian was convinced his son could learn to enjoy it." She lets out a sigh, trying not to let the gloomy memory get the best of her.

"Some men are like that," I murmur, causing Margaret to chuckle in agreement. "Which is why I thought I'd never marry."

"Julia told me you had never had any serious boyfriends. Outside of work, I mean. Is it true?"

Her new question takes me off guard, but I realize we have entered into the confession territory so I keep my head high and say, "It is. I don't like men in general. I just like having clients."

"That's a good way to look at it," she answers, before leaning back against the couch, a comfortable silence settling between us while Margaret seems to be ruminating something through. "I understand why Andries loves you," she declares out of the blue, causing a flutter in my stomach. "You are street smart and bold... all while looking like a delicate daisy."

I let out a chuckle, quite flattered by her words. "A delicate daisy, huh? I can see who Andries got his poetic side from."

She smiles, considering me for a moment. "When shall we proceed with the signing for the agency?"

WHAT! I nearly jump off of my seat, and even stutter as I ask, "You're going to buy it? I couldn't accept that."

She blinks twice, visibly surprised. "You can't?"

"Not from you," I tell her. "Andries will be mad at me for selling my agency to his grandmother."

"It'd have been a fun story," she says with a smile as she thinks about it. "But no, don't worry, the cheque is not coming from me."

I frown upon hearing her last sentence, and Margaret seems to revel in the moment.

"It's coming from Beate Uhse AG—a German adult entertainment group in which my family office owns a minority stake," she informs me, her tone more serious than before.

I blink a few times, totally taken aback at the revelation. Just a few minutes ago we were talking about Andries' childhood and now she's telling me her family office owns a minority stake in an adult entertainment group? Wow. It seems too good to be true. "Really?" I ask, unable to contain the curiosity from my tone. Margaret nods, her expression just as stoic as before. "That's huge. I mean, they are the biggest group in Germany."

"And they are the ones buying the agency," she reminds me. "I had a meeting with the board recently and this acquisition would fit nicely into their growth strategy."

"But... How did you convince them without even checking my financials?" I ask her, partly confused and partly overwhelmed with joy.

"I know how to be convincing," she says, as I realize she had already done the pitch on my behalf.

"So," she continues, crossing a leg over the other as she takes a leather notebook and a pen out of her purse. "Should we do the signing Friday, April eighth?"

I look at her and at her open notebook—which seems to be a calendar—and my heart jumps in excitement at the realization this is really happening. *Holy shit! I'm really doing this!* "Sure, that works, fine," I blurt the words out.

"Great, they will send you the purchase agreement to your email in the next few days." While Margaret is speaking about the next steps for the purchase of the agency, I'm still totally shocked, unable to digest the news. It feels too surreal to be true, too easy. I don't know much about Andrics' maternal side of the family, but Margaret seems to be one of those persons that you better not have as an enemy. "I've made sure that your staff keep their jobs and I also have found a few potential candidates to become the next managing director."

"When it comes to the next manager," I begin. "I want her to have experience as an escort too and to always put the safety of the girls first. Those are my only requests."

Her lips curve up with a smile. "They seem reasonable."

"Thank you for everything," I say as we stand up. "I don't know how I'll ever be able to pay you back for this."

She looks me in the eye with a soft stern. "Just take good care of my Andries. That's all I ask in exchange."

CHAPTER 37

Amsterdam, March 25, 2022
Roxanne

The Italian restaurant where I'm meeting Andries for dinner isn't too far from my agency, so I get there in no time. After the meeting with his grandmother yesterday, I figured I should tell him the news in a more romantic setting. Plus, now that his parents have disowned him, he's no longer been apprehensive of being seen with me in public.

Reaching the block of the restaurant, I can't help but smile up to my ears when my eyes lay on a tall young man, blue eyes, wide shoulders, sporting an open dark blue trench waiting for me outside. Once I get out of the car, I walk in his direction, my heart fluttering in excitement.

"No longer afraid to meet me in the public, huh?" I tease Andries as I clasp my arms around his neck.

He chuckles at my joke, wets his lips, and gives me one of his irresistible smiles. "Meeting you in public was never the problem; what my family could do to us if they knew we were together was."

"Well, they haven't done anything we can't get through," I tell him, before I lean in to kiss him.

We shut our eyes when our lips touch, letting ourselves revel in the moment.

Once our lips part, we make our way into the restaurant and are immediately greeted by a hostess who leads us to our table. I'm pleased to see we're sitting at a corner table by the window. The table is cozy, lit by a floating candle in a bowl with two roses as a centerpiece. It's perfect!

After giving us the menus, she serves us champagne and breadsticks as our starters. I nibble on one of the breadsticks as I take Andries in. He's removed his trench coat, and is now rolling up his sleeves to his elbows, some strand of hair has fallen on his brow, and I find the all combination absolutely mesmerizing. He tries to brush them aside, but to no avail.

"Is there something wrong?" he asks, noticing me staring at him for a bit too long.

I clear my throat, cutting eye contact for a brief second. "Not at all," I say, regaining my composure. "In fact, I have good news."

"Ah, that's something I want to hear." He pauses, taking a sip of his champagne, before giving me all his attention. "Tell me what it is."

"Well, your grandmother came to my agency yesterday afternoon," I announce, causing him to gape at me.

"She did?"

I nod, reveling myself in his astonishment. "And not only that, but she found a German company interested in acquiring my agency. Isn't that amazing?"

"She found you a buyer?" I can't help but snort at how stunned he is. "I can't believe it," he says, visibly confused at the revelation. "That's something I never thought she'd do."

"I received the purchase agreement today and our legal teams are finalizing the last details," I proceed, my tone coming across even more excited than before. "The signing will be on Friday, April eighth, and they'll be hosting a cocktail party with dinner afterwards—which you are obviously invited to."

"Now, that's…" Andries lets his words trail off as he tries to find the right thing to say. "Absolutely incredible. I'm so damn happy." His eyes hold a glow that wasn't there a few seconds ago, and when he looks me in the eye again, he says, "Thank you so much for doing this for me."

"I'm not doing it for *you*," I tell him, causing Andries to crease his brows in confusion. "I'm doing it for *us*." His expression softens with a smile, and he leans forward just enough to give me a quick peck on the lips. "She also told me about your childhood and, um, about that hunting trip with your father."

His eyes widen in surprise but he tries to play it off by taking a sip of his water. "Well, that's…"

"I'm not here to judge or anything," I add just as fast. "I want you know I'm here for you if you want to vent about him."

He snorts at my reply, shaking his head. "That's okay. I gave up the idea of having a healthy relationship with my dad a long time ago." Somehow his words carry a heaviness that squeezes my heart. "He wanted me to be just like him, but I couldn't be anymore different. I think deep down that fills him with a mix of anger and sadness, but I cannot change who I am."

I can't help but lean closer to him and rub my hand on his back in understanding. "I'm sure one day he will realize how amazing you are," I say in a low voice, my mouth close enough to his.

"Thanks," he answers, before planting a soft kiss on my lips. Then he takes his glass of champagne and raises it slightly in the air. "To us."

I do the same and clink my glass to his in a toast. "To us."

After scanning over the menu, Andries asks for lasagne, and I order some spaghetti Bolognese. We eat while talking about lighter subjects, and his mood is much more jovial than before. All of a sudden though, I feel my iPhone vibrating inside my clutch. At first, I ignore it, but curiosity getting the best of me, I decide to discreetly pull the phone out when Andries is focused on his lasagne, only to find out it's a text from his sister herself. What the heck? What would Elise want from me?

I take the moment to pull out my phone and read it:

Hey, Roxanne. It's Elise. I need to talk to you face to face. Are you available Monday at around 9 AM? It's quite important. Thanks.

It's brief, but it stuns me nonetheless. What could she possibly want to talk about on Monday? As I come to think of it, that's the day I'm testifying at Karl's trial. I sigh heavily. She probably wants to beg on her dad's behalf that I don't testify against his favorite employee. Well, I've already made up my mind on the subject, but I accept the invitation anyway. It's always a good idea to meet with his sister and try to reconnect with her.

"Is everything okay?" Andries asks, most likely noticing the astonishment on my face.

I lock the phone and put it back on my clutch, before returning my attention to him. "I'm fine," I tell him, my lips curving into a smile. Noticing he's already finished his dish, I take the menu again and ask, "Do you want some dessert?"

A naughty smirk that is all too familiar starts forming across his lips, and he leans closer to my ear as he whispers, "I'm only hungry for one thing… And I'm certain it's not on the menu." He nibbles the shell of my ear lightly, driving his point home.

My heart pounds, prickly heat coats my arm, and I'm sure my blood pressure is steadily rising. I wet my lips as I picture what we'll do once we reach home. Andries calls for the waitress, gesturing for the check as I try to contain myself until we're in private.

After we pay, we walk out of the restaurant hand in hand, our stomachs full and our minds already elsewhere, making our way to the parking lot. Reaching my car, Andries presses me against it, and, holding my face between his hands, he suddenly comes down on my mouth, hard and intense, kissing me with so much fervor that I feel a rush of wetness coating the fabric of my panties. His tongue dives in, fondling mine, and I moan at the connection, my clit throbbing with need. He rolls his hips into me, pressing his erection against my core, causing me to gasp.

"You've no idea how much I missed you," he growls against my mouth, when our lips part just for a brief moment. He holds me captive by the fingertips and the air grows almost too thick to breathe. But I need more, so I shut the small gap between us and kiss him back, slipping my tongue past his lips, moaning and tasting him until he groans with pleasure in my mouth.

"Let's go home," he says in a quick, short breath. "Or else I'm gonna have you here."

I gasp immediately at his words. "Are you serious?" My eyes start scanning through the parking lot, and even though it's nearly pitch dark, there are a few passers-by walking not too far from us. When I look back at Andries, he's got that devilish smirk on his face and I know if we don't leave right now, I'll be in trouble. I manage to walk past him and go around the car to the driver's seat.

I open the door and lower myself, realizing it's the first time he's going to be a passenger.

"You look like you're at the helm of a pirate ship and not a car. So smug and mischievous," Andries quips. "Almost like you have something naughty in mind."

"Not at all, you just have your mind in the gutter," I respond tartly, but I know he can see the quirk of my lips and the amusement I'm feeling.

"It's only there because my girlfriend insists on parading herself around without a bra," he rumbles. I feel his fingers on my upper thighs then, just a shadow of a touch, but it makes me shiver.

I pull out into traffic, but the roads aren't as busy as they usually are, so instead of swatting his hand away I let Andries touch me to his heart's content. It starts with just fingers and palms on my upper thighs, hips, and belly, stroking along my ribs like he's memorizing me through touch. I keep my eyes on the road and my muscles loose—that is, until his wandering hands make their way to the underside of my breasts, bare under just the thin layer of fabric, and I'm keenly aware that this isn't going to stop at just some flirtatious caresses.

My grip tightens on the steering wheel as Andries' fingers find my nipples, tracing tight circles around them before pinching lightly. I make a small yelp of a noise, and he chuckles darkly.

"Look how hard your nipples are," he says roughly. "If we were still at the restaurant, everyone would see how hot I make you."

I can only spare him a quick glance while driving, but when he tugs one of my hands off the wheel, I let him, starting to lose my senses in the haze of arousal. When he presses it over the hard length of his cock, that arousal spikes sharply.

At first, Andries guides my movements, his big palm wrapped around my wrist as he shows me just how he wants me to stroke him. I can feel the heat of him through his pants, and the way he gets harder and harder for me, until Andries finally lets me set the pace.

He folds his arms behind his head, and my nipples tingle at the loss of his touch. It doesn't matter, though. This is all about him now.

"You like it when I touch you like this?" I ask, squeezing his cock. "You like getting jerked off in the car, Andries? Cumming in your pants for me?"

"God, I love your filthy mouth," he groans.

"I love yours too," I admit. "Especially when it's between my legs."

"Fuck–" he hisses, bucking against my hand, but I don't let up, relentlessly stroking him.

"If I let you come, are you still going to be able to fuck me when we get home?"

Andries blows out a breath slowly, his body started to push against my hand. "Roxie, I could fuck through a brick wall right now. There is no way in hell I'm not going to be inside you tonight."

"Good," I say with a wicked grin, sliding him another quick look. "Then come for me, Andries."

He gets almost impossibly hard under my grip before his hips buck and he grabs my wrist again, forcing my pace faster and harder for only a few seconds before I feel a rush of wet heat against my palm. Andries moans shamelessly, throwing his head side to side as he spills himself for me.

Any other time, I'd sit back and take pride in being able to make him come from so little, but tonight is different. I'm swollen and needy between my legs, and no matter how I shift myself in the seat I can't find any relief. Knowing that he's so responsive to me, and wants me so badly, has me more turned on than I can handle.

Andries relaxes in his seat, eyes closed as he catches his breath for some time, but as we approach my apartment building, he rouses himself enough to look over at me. He takes in my still-hard nipples, the goosebumps on my arms, and my flushed cheeks, and I just know he's aware of how much I want him.

"I see why you had that caveat about me still being able to fuck you," he says, wetting his lips with his tongue where they had dried out from all his open-mouthed breathing. "You're about to burst into flames."

I don't answer verbally, just giving him a tight nod as I park the car. Once it's shut off, he leans over long enough to kiss me, one quick press of lips, before he's walking around the driver's side to help me out of the vehicle.

"I'm going to have you drive more often," he laughs, linking his hand with mine.

"Or you can just return the favor," I offer.

The walk through the lobby and into the elevator feels like I'm under water. Everything is going so slowly, taking so much time, when all I want to do is to be in my penthouse and shed the clothes that are now driving me crazy. Nothing would settle me down until his skin was on mine.

My apartment door clicks shut behind Andries with a decisive sound, and we look at each other for a long moment. God, he's so gorgeous; tall, his clothes fitting him like a second skin, they're so perfectly tailored, his brown hair only slightly mussed from our car escapes. He has his hands in his pockets, and I hold back a giggle, thinking he's lucky he wore dark pants, otherwise his dashing appearance would be ruined by the stain that must be on the front of his pants.

I can't laugh, though; not with the serious, almost feral look in his eyes. It makes me feel like a prey animal... like Andries is ready to devour me.

"Undress," he says simply. "I know you want to be fucked, nice and hard, right? Take your clothes off and bend over the arm of the couch."

I swallow hard, nodding as I slip my clothes off in just a few smooth, sultry movements. He didn't ask for a show, but I'm giving him one anyway. I turn my back to him as I slide my panties down my legs, bending at the waist so he gets a full view of my ass and my pussy peeking out from between my legs. I hear his sharp intake of breath, but he doesn't move, waiting for me to finish his command.

I can feel my pulse in my ears, and between my legs. Like Andries said, I feel like I could catch on fire, the lust is burning so brightly within me. I slink to the couch, my movements feline, and I bend over the velour arm just like he told me to. I'm almost shaking with anticipation, but when I crane my neck to look back at him, he's already right behind me.

Andries unbuttons his shirt in mechanical movements, doing the same for his pants. He can't take his eyes off me, gaze flickering up and down my bare form as he undresses. As in control as he's trying to act, I know this man, and how young he is. It makes him overeager sometimes, but I really love when he loses himself with me.

"Look at you," he says, voice thick as he slides his hand between my legs. "You're so ready for me."

He pushes two fingers into my channel, pumping them in and out, awakening my nerves for him. Pulling out, he slides the slick digits over my clit, causing a burst of sensation before dipping them back into me.

Andries pulls his hand away, and my body immediately mourns the loss of him. The next thing I feel is his grip on both of my ass cheeks, and the thick head of his cock pushing between my folds.

"Do you think you can take it all like this, Roxie?"

"Yes. Yes. Give it to me, Andries. Fill me up."

He doesn't need any more coaxing, but as he thrusts into me slowly, I can see why he gave me the warning. I should have expected it, but my mind is so lost in the mists of my arousal that I didn't even pause to think about how different his cock would feel in this position. The angle of our bodies has me tighter than I'm used to, and when he snakes an arm under my hips and pulls me upward onto my tiptoes, the effect is even more pronounced. He has to work his cock into my channel, inch by devastating inch, and I can feel my pussy stretching to accommodate him. It's almost a burning sensation, but one that feels so, so good.

The noises I'm making are high and helpless. Andries peppers kisses along my spine as he fills me up, whispering, "You can take it, Roxie, I know you can," into my ear. His words bring on another rush of wetness, and then, he's finally all the way in.

"You're so fucking tight," he groans, pulling out just slightly before slamming back in, jolting me to where I needed to grab onto the cushions in front on me.

The way he has me lines his cock up with my g-spot perfectly, like an arrow to a target, and when he thrusts home, a wave of pleasure hits me bone-deep. The moan I let out must clue Andries in, because he laughs knowingly, only the smallest hint that he's as turned on as I am apparent in his voice.

"Right there," I confirm. "Don't change a fucking thing,"

I can barely keep my feet on the ground as he fucks me, and the long minutes of being desperate for his touch in the car is all paying off. Andries thrusts into me with abandon, his hands cupping and kneading my ass before grabbing my hips and using the grip to keep me right where he wants me. The push and pull of him inside of me, coupled with the rough drag of my nipples against the velvet sofa, and the inescapable sounds of his hips slapping against my ass cheeks are a heady concoction.

And then there is the feeling of him hitting that secret place inside me, again and again and again. It's a deep, dark sort of pleasure, coiling in my core like a snake about to strike.

"Don't stop," I beg. Thank goodness, he doesn't.

As we both get closer to the edge, he leans over me, the almost stifling heat of his body covering my back as he kisses the back of my neck, nipping between thrusts. I feel pinned, cornered, like there is no choice but for me to take his cock and let him fuck me.

I dig my nails into the couch cushions, breath coming raggedly. I can feel every place his fingertips are pressing into my flesh, every breath he breathes out on the back of my neck, and all of the sudden, it's just too much. I can't hold on any longer.

"I'm coming," I gasp. "Oh fuck, Andries, I'm coming."

He only grunts in response, giving me no space, staying on me as I come. There is no snapping explosion this time, but a whole-body wave that threatens to drown me. I feel my orgasm in my fingers, my toes, my chest, and especially, my core, where my pussy grips Andries cock like a vice.

His strokes stutter before he slams into me harder than ever. I'm lost, floating up us both as my orgasm wracks me, but I can still feel the heat of his seed filling me up for what seems like whole minutes. Andries lifts off me, his hands gripping my ass again as he throws his head back and almost roars his release. I can already feel it dripping down my legs.

Once the last shudder of my climax dissipates, I feel boneless; exhausted. I'll find it silly later, but as I slide down the arm of the couch onto the floor, desperate to lay down, Andries follows me, and it doesn't seem odd at all.

We tangle up with each other there on the floor, all long limbs and sweat, letting out bodies come down from their high. It feels so perfect and natural, that an errant through springs to my mind, now that my lust is spent.

"Can I ask you something?" I murmur against the skin of his shoulder. "Why don't you live here with me?"

He tenses. "What do you mean?"

"You know, like when we were together?" He doesn't answer, or relax, so I quickly add, "That doesn't mean you don't get to keep your own place, but…why not spend every night here with me?"

It takes him a long time to respond, so long that I begin to feel nervous, but finally he says, "Do you really want me here every single night?"

Andries sounds so hopeful, so vulnerable, that it makes my heart ache. "Every night, always."

His muscles finally loosen, and he curls into me even closer, letting out a relieved laugh. "Well, I think I can manage that."

CHAPTER 38

Amsterdam, March 28, 2022
Roxanne

When Elise walks into the café with her haughty air around her, I know exactly what she is here for. She almost flounces like she is trying to be a supermodel even though she is just another spoiled brat—a part of Andries' family. The smile on her face looks like a viper approaching my table and when she sits down without being invited, it's definitely with an air that she isn't going to take any crap.

"Hello, Elise. So good to see you again." I try to make the words as dry as possible coming out of my mouth. "Please, sit down," I say, as if she hasn't already done so. There is definitely some bitterness still coming through my body after everything that has happened. But Elise still holds the upper hand with everything. She knows about the only thing that can tear Andries away from me.

"Thank you," she says, sounding proper. As the waiter comes by she orders a fancy whatever and then quickly gets down to business. "So," she begins, before leaning forward on the table. "Do you know why I asked you to meet up?"

"Yes, I assume your father is sending you to do his dirty work." The blow has teeth, and the look that quickly flashes across her face tells me it has done the job. I sip on my drink as smoke almost curls out of her ears.

"I don't know what you mean. All we are looking for is that whatever testimony you decide to give in a few hours, that it doesn't reflect too badly on Karl. There's a lot at stake for my dad and Andries—as well as his possible future."

I bristle at the idea that she cares anything about Andries and his future, especially because she has no idea what is going on behind the scenes and the fact that I am changing my entire life for him. Not that somebody like her would probably care unless it affected her allowance.

"I think that it's none of your damn business what I'm gonna say about Karl." Her expression doesn't change as the waiter puts down her drink and she takes a sip.

"Listen. I know that it doesn't help anyone involved if you eviscerate him on the stand and tell the world about all the things he's done. After all…" She looks at me up and down again. "It's just a business transaction, right?"

I know what those words imply, and it almost makes me see red, so I take a deep breath and just bite my tongue. "That's right," I finally tell her. "Just business."

"Then we are all on the same page. I think it's just good to make sure things don't get blown out of proportion," she says. "And I also know that Dad would really appreciate it. That could go a long way for Andries. And you do care about him, right?" Again, it's hard not to grind my teeth about what she says. Like she is accusing me of feelings that I don't have or making it seem like I don't care for him as much as I do.

"I'll see you later, Elise," I say. "Feel free to keep tabs on what happens during the trial." Without another word I stand up and walk out of the coffee shop, leaving her with her stupid mouth hanging open. God, as much as I love Andries, his sister is going to be a real handful to deal with if we ever get married.

* * *

The trial, at least the portion I am to attend, is set to begin in an hour, and I have to mull over what Elise has said. She is right in the fact there is no need for me to completely destroy Karl's life. After all, he simply made a request, and I fulfilled it. What Patricia went through is something that was out of my control, and she has admitted herself that she broke the rules I had set. I'll be as impartial as I can, but to avoid further trouble with Sebastian, I won't go to the point of destroying his best employee by revealing things that aren't relevant to the case.

Giving my deposition is actually quite easy. The prosecutor tries very hard to get me to say things that aren't a hundred percent true. Leading me with questions is obviously the best way to get Karl to pay for what he has done, but I stand my ground firmly and simply state the facts. Like Elise has said, there is no need to embellish even though I'm furious with Karl for what he did by taking advantage of the situation.

Now it is down to between him and Patricia, and my agency is simply the provider for what has occurred, which is completely legal. Two adults can hash things out in court if they wanted to. For my part, I'm done with everything and want to move on from the situation. My testimony definitely wouldn't support Karl, but it certainly doesn't acquit him either. That is up to his lawyers to figure out if they can.

Walking out of the courtroom, I'm thankful that I'm free from my side of things and I can now focus solely on selling my business. The fact it is thanks to Andries' grandmother that I'm finally selling it is like the icing on the cake. His mom might hate me, but her family office will actually have a minority stake of my business thanks to their own shares of Beate Uhse AG. How ironic. In a few days, the deal will be signed, and Andries and I will finally live our lives like we please.

My iPhone rings in my hand and as I turn it face up, I notice it's a text message from my sister: *How did it go? Are you on the way?*

It went very well, I text back. I*'m coming soon. So excited for our shopping session! I really want to get a new dress to celebrate the sale.*

The last time I went shopping with Lili at De Bijenkorf was for Christmas, so I'm beyond excited to finally go back with her. It's also a great opportunity to spoil her a bit. I head to my favorite department store, reminding myself that growing up we never had been able to even think going near it.

Walking into a couple of high-end boutiques with Lili by my side, it doesn't take long before we find a couple of perfect dresses for the signing event and the cocktail celebration that will ensue. Business casual, not too provocative, just as I like.

We walk further down the mall and suddenly there is a Cartier store looming beside us. On an impulse, Lili grabs my arm, pushing me back closer to her, so we can stand in front of the store. "Look, at those earrings," she says, pointing out to a rose gold pairing. "They'd look exquisite for the signing event."

The glass display cases are of course right behind a glowering security guard, and everything is locked up tight. No way a couple of innocent women could get into the cases and make off with what is inside. And the nice thing is, we don't even need to.

Lili looks through the display cases and when she sees some of the prices her eyes go wide, and she gasps immediately. I knew that it is a bit of a step up from what we are used to. The fact that I can bring my family into the world that Andries is a part of, and especially because it is my money that is going to be the catalyst, and not his, is even more satisfying. Six million minus some legal fees, is definitely going to make a great difference. Plus that is on top of what I've already saved up over these last five years.

"True, let's go inside so you can try them on," I tell her, and when she turns her head, she almost looks shocked. It's hard not to laugh when I see her expression, but it isn't her fault that she has no idea about things that cost so much. Mama has given us lives of relative frugality and frugal habits die hard.

Because their lives have changed so much along with mine, I want to give my sister everything. "C'mon, let's go in."

Despite her reluctance, I finally manage to drag her inside, and a store clerk immediately comes by with a welcoming smile. Lili looks closer at a few of the items and then points. "That one is really nice." And then another, "And that one."

"Excuse me," I say, turning toward the store clerk. "Can she try on those earrings, please?"

"Of course." The gloved lady comes over, and delicately takes her rose gold earrings outside of the case, inviting Lili to go face the mirror to put them on.

I stand behind my sister, and then lean forward just enough to see my reflection and hers in the mirror. "Look at you!" I say, her smile rising with pride as she turns right and left to contemplate herself. "They look wonderful on you, Lili."

"Have you seen the price, though?" she asks in a whisper. "It's seven thousand euros for a freaking pair of earrings."

"It's my gift to you." And before my sister can protest, I turn around to find the store clerk and say, "She's taking them."

While the clerk is sorting out her earrings, I pace around the store, my eyes scanning across the marvelous jewelry in the displays. All of a sudden, I instinctively stop in my tracks when my eyes lay on the section of engagement rings and I can't help wondering if Andries will propose with one of those. Not that it matters of course, I'm a big girl and can afford one of those rings myself, but it'd be a nice gesture, nevertheless.

"Any that you like in particular?" Lili asks, sneaking in beside me.

"That one is beautiful, actually," I point at a platinum and emerald-cut diamond solitaire.

"Can she try it on?" Lili is already asking to the lady and I feel a pang of embarrassment for her unapologetic request. I guess it's just pay back from earlier on.

"Of course." The clerk is smiling up to her ears when she takes the ring out with her gloved hands. "May I?" she asks, taking delicately my left hand.

I nod once, and she places the diamond ring on my finger.

"Look at that! How beautiful!" Lili exclaims and my heart does a little somersault in response. "Let me take a few shots for you." She grabs her iPhone and starts taking pictures of myself with the ring on. It is indeed a very beautiful ring. But as I sneak at the price tag, even I can't help but gasp. Six figures for a ring is beyond outrageous!

When I notice Lili typing something on her phone, my interest is suddenly perked. "What are you doing?"

"Nothing, just texting Robin..." After a few more seconds, her attention returns to me and she plugs her phone back into her purse. "Well, shall we?"

* * *

My adrenaline is already pumping at the thought of Andries having already arrived at my place. While he still has his apartment with his books, clothes, and other belongings, he's been sleeping with me nearly every night—just like before. When I get into the living room, my eyes lay on him sitting on the couch, his eyes focused on a book. I'm not sure if it's for college or not, but I take a moment and stand by the doorway to observe him, letting myself revel in how hand-some he is. Jeez. I can't help but think about that ring I tried earlier at the shop and how after selling my agency, he could become my fiancé... After everything we went through this year, it feels like the worst is finally behind us.

"How was your day?" he asks, when he finally lifts his head to look at me, while I'm still leaning against the doorway. "Is everything okay?" He shuts his book and rises from his seat, pacing in my direction. When he stands in front of me, he leans down just enough to kiss me, sending a thrill up my spine.

"It was great. I went to do some shopping with Lili, and I even ended up getting her a pair of earrings for the cocktail party. She was so happy." There is just enough of a playful lilt to my words to cause him to smile, except he doesn't. He remains thoughtfully looking at me.

"I heard that you went pretty soft on Karl?" Suddenly my amusement dissipates and I swallow past the lump in my throat when I meet with his inquiring gaze. "Was that on purpose?"

"I didn't go easy on him I was just... normal. He's just a distant memory that I want to resolve and get rid of, nothing more. After all..." I close the short distance between us, wet my lips, and take a hold of his chest, letting my hands drift across the surface of his sweater. "We have so much to look forward to. The sale is going through, and once we can figure all that out then our problems are done and over with. We can move on together...." When I look up into his cerulean eyes, I know that I've made the right decision.

While he remains undecided for a moment, he eventually leans in and kisses me gently, and what is a soft kiss becomes harder at every passing second, and I find myself breathing hard with my body responding to his touch.

CHAPTER 39

Amsterdam, April 2, 2022
Andries

My grandmother is always the type of person who wants to be the peacemaker and make sure everyone in the family gets along. I have no idea how she even gets along with my dad since they are quite the opposite. His version of keeping the peace is to disrupt the entire world it seems, at least by making the world succumb to his own ideals.

Meanwhile his mother-in-law has always been a strategic partner. As she sits here discussing the case with me, her lips sip at her glass like they always have, with a dainty air. She's asked me to come over, and that can only mean one thing. She might want to fish for more info about Roxanne before getting the executives at Beate Uhse AG to officially acquire the company... or she's got news about my properties. But somehow we started talking about the trial first. There's a bit more testimony and then the judge will start deliberating.

"You need to manage your expectations when it comes to the verdict, Andries," she finally says, observing me. "Even if he gets a fine, it'll be considered a victory. It means the man was convicted of his crime and he's receiving at least some sort of punishment for what he did." I know she's right, even though that would be a laughable sentence.

"I know." I sigh. "It just feels like justice isn't going to be done unless he goes away for a long time." Thinking about what Karl did still makes me feel sick. I find myself indulging in a small sip of wine, trying to ease my thoughts with some alcohol.

She nods and purses her lips. "Very true. But what has happened in the past is in the past and it's all up to the court now to figure it out." Once that has been said, she moves on to another subject: my life. "Have you thought about what you're going to do after everything has been settled? I mean, once the sale goes through."

I take a deep breath. This is something that nobody knows about yet, but Oma is someone I know I can trust to keep her mouth shut. Plus, she is probably the only one that will be happy to hear the news once it is revealed. "Well, I'm going to take Roxanne and her family to Paris for some time away to celebrate the deal… and to propose."

When I say the word *propose* I can see her eyes twitch and she even chokes on her drink. My grandmother isn't one to show emotion, so it's quite funny to see her reaction. "Really, Andries? It feels so…" her eyes narrow as she thinks something through, "…sudden." It's a good word to use when I think what she really wants to say is ludicrous or something the equivalent.

"We've spoken about it already." And not only that but we are also somewhat already living together—not sure if she needs to know that though. "She's selling something she's *very* attached to, so it's only fair to show how committed I am to the relationship."

A brief flash of a smile dances over her lips this time, and it's funny to see her trying to reign in emotions. "You are definitely one of a kind, my dear. That is a grand gesture like no other." She takes another sip of her drink, considering me. "Do you have a ring already? I think that's probably a silly question."

Now it's my turn to almost laugh. She knows me pretty well. "I actually do. When she went shopping with her sister, she picked one out and her sister sent me pictures of it. It was easy to head over the next day and buy it for her."

I'm wondering why her demeanor seems to have changed a bit. Oma seems on edge, and if anything we should be celebrating the fact that Roxanne is selling her company.

When there's a ring at the doorbell a sudden shudder goes through me and I'm wondering if there's something up. Like she's going to pull a fast one and suddenly tell me that a lawyer's coming in to force me to sign some kind of agreement with my dad if I want the deal of Roxanne's agency goes through. But when I see Mom sweeping into the petit salon and greeting each other with big smiles, I know exactly what is going on. She must be here to try to convince me that being with Roxanne is a bad idea and that I'm throwing my life away.

"Hi Mom," I mutter, between clenched teeth, trying to keep my cool despite her presence making me feel quite uncomfortable. There's no need for air kisses or any of that crap.

"Andries," she greets, her tone prime and proper as she sits right in front of me. To my surprise, Mom's holding a portfolio in her hand, and something tells me they contain the properties I told Oma about.

Speaking of which, my grandmother seems to feel rather uneasy between the two of us. "I think I'll go and check out the garden. My rose bushes have been doing terrible this year." It's so obvious she just wants to leave us alone that I almost want to laugh out loud.

Once there's only the two of us in the petit salon, I can't help but turn to my mom and ask, "Let me guess, you're here as a last ditch effort to get me to leave my girlfriend?" Her face doesn't even flinch as she continues staring at me behind her long eyelashes. "You should already know that's a waste of time."

"First things first," she begins as she extends a hand to give me the portfolio. Too curious to decline, I take it in my hands and continue to listen. "Your grandmother had the amiability to inform me that she changed the banking details for the rent of a few apartments that you happened to become the owner of last year." While I'm feeling euphoric at the news, Mom doesn't seem to share the same feeling. "Since you were in Tibet, or God knows where, I had forgotten to let you know about it."

As soon as she finishes talking, my body gets a thrill. I open the case and quickly go through the paperwork. It's all there, and now I can breathe a sigh of relief knowing that the group of locations, which all have decent tenants will start to flow income into my bank account next month. The timing couldn't be better.

"Forgot?" I repeat, raising an eyebrow at her chosen word. "You mean you held a grudge against me because I left home for a year going against you and Dad's plan?"

Mom heaves a long sigh in annoyance, averting her gaze as she processes my question. "Fine, I'm sorry," she replies, her eyes meeting mine again. Yet she seems rather vexed than sorry. "I wanted to tell you about it on your birthday but then you were constantly with Roxanne and I figured it'd be better to let you know later down the road."

Her excuse is pathetic, but at least she gave me an apology, I'll give her that. "Thanks for telling me the truth," I play along, trying to be somewhat courteous to her. After all, if I can make peace with my mom, then I'm all for it.

"I've heard your grandmother has found a buyer for Roxanne's agency?" she asks, her eyes filled with curiosity.

"Yes, you know Oma doesn't exactly move slowly when it comes to business."

She laughs in her usual elegant and contained way, easing the tension between us. "I have to admit, I was quite shocked and angry when she told me what she was doing, but I know part of it was to make your dad potentially have a stroke." She grins and I return it. It's not like we have anything against my father, but the way he's been treating me since this whole situation began is well… typical. Almost expected. And now he can't do anything about me since I don't need to beg him for my allowance anymore. I can move on, and that is a massive relief.

"Well, I hope when the deal is signed you can meet with us to celebrate," I tell her. It's only proper that my mom could join us at the cocktail party. I know Dad wouldn't attend even if I asked him to, it'd be like rubbing salt in a wound, but maybe Mom would be more reasonable to put the past behind and move on.

"Listen, dear..." She leans forward, sitting at the edge of her seat, and I can tell she's having a hard time figuring out how to say something she knows I'm not going to like. "Are you a hundred percent sure about this? I mean, the fact Roxanne is selling her agency to be with you is a very noble gesture, but... are you sure she's not with you simply because of who you are?"

I frown at her question, failing to grasp what she means by that, so she adds, "You know, a young impressionable rich heir with a noble title?"

"Jeez! Mom!" I utter in outrage, shaking my head at her attitude. I can't believe she even thought something like that! Is this how she sees my girlfriend? Fuck! She reminds me so much of Elise during our last confrontation in the lecture hall.

"I just want you to be a hundred percent sure with your decision," she says, raising her hands in the air, like she's some kind of innocent lady.

Finally, everything is out on the table. Even after seeing how miserable I was after the breakup, Mom still has doubts about Roxanne and I. Frankly, it's time she knows the truth about me. After all, it's not like either parent has had a good handle on who I really am and how I've spent my life.

"Mom, Roxanne is the woman I love. You know love, that very feeling that made you marry Dad." That shot probably wasn't necessary, but it is definitely fun to see her eyes go wide. "I just hope that everyone can accept it. She's going to be part of our family and I'm going to be part of hers. I really hope that your choice is to support us rather than walk away. I've given this a lot of thought, I want you to know that."

She leans over and squeezes my hand gently. "I know, dear, and I trust you." Her voice is softer than before, letting me know she's trying for a more gentle tactic. "But some of the choices you've made over the past years have been... well, disappointing to both myself and your father, if I'm being honest." She's most likely referring to the year I went away and my constant refusal to go with my dad on hunting trips or to the office so that I could write poetry instead. "You're my son and I'll always support you, but I wouldn't be your mother if I didn't tell you how I feel." Fair point, and I appreciate her honesty.

"Why do you think I disappeared for a year?" I ask, confronting her. "I had to go and figure out who I was, not what somebody else wanted me to be," I admit, before rubbing a hand on my neck to ease the tension. "In fact..." I take a few deep breaths, still pondering whether or not I should tell her the truth, "...there's something I've got to tell you."

Mom's interest is immediately piqued, causing her to gasp. "Oh God, she isn't pregnant, is she?" Her horrified expression at even the thought of something as incredible as having a grandchild suddenly makes my blood run cold. It shows the true side of my family, one where status is everything and having a child with somebody they consider beneath them is a terrible fate. I shake my head in a frown.

"Um, no..." I actually feel a pang of disappointment for not being able to tell her the opposite just to piss her off. "What I wanted to tell you is that..." I swallow the lump past my throat, while Mom keeps staring at me, without even blinking once. "I never attended business school," I finally manage to force the words out. "Instead of staying in the path you and Dad had chosen for me, I transferred myself into the English program at the beginning of the school year."

Her lips purse together, and I can see that she's upset, but mostly disappointed. To me, though, that was something I really needed to get off my chest. "Well, I, um…" She clears her throat, her gaze returning to her lap as she ponders the best way to proceed. "That's not that bad." Her voice quivers at the end, and it's more than obvious that she's embarrassed with the idea that I won't graduate with a business degree. "After all, we should all pursue things we want in life."

"Like you did?" Again, it's probably not necessary and when she almost looks like I've slapped her, I feel bad for going too far. But now it's my turn to reach out and squeeze her hand. "I'm sorry, Mom. That was unnecessary and I apologize." But there's more that I need to tell her. "Dad told me to go and live my 'small pathetic life' when I went to see him in his office, so that's what I'm going to do. I appreciate everything that you and everyone else has done for me, but you need to know that I'm going to make my own way with or without your approval. If that means you can't support my decisions then so be it. There's a reason I've distanced myself and all I can hope is that you understand."

When I finish speaking, I realize Mom has been frowning the entire time. "Of course we do, Andries…it's just…."

"Just what?"

"Just… well, we only want what's best for you."

It's hard not to laugh out loud. Dad and her never really wanted what's best for me. They wanted what *they* thought was best for me.

"And my 'small pathetic life' is what's best for me. That's my decision, not anyone else's. After all, you always taught me to think for myself. Roxanne and this," I tap the portfolio, "is how I'm going to start."

There's almost something that looks like moisture in her eyes when I finish talking, and it's nice to see she has some emotion behind the stoic mask she always wears.

"Okay, then." Her gaze is fixed on the void, like she's trying to contain her tears from falling, and she takes a few deep breaths in and out, her chest raising and lowering as she does so. We keep quiet for a moment, letting the bombshells I just said sink in.

Not knowing what else to do or say, Mom stands up, smooths her dress, and when I think she's about to slap me or scold me, she just says, "We should go and see what your grandmother is doing to her flowers. After all, it's not like her gardener would want her anywhere near an actual plant."

My lips part at her well-put-together answer, and I blink twice in astonishment and in sorrow that she'd rather leave than dealing with her own son. My parents are never going to change. This is who they are. And I'm just better off without them, or just putting the mask of the perfect Van Den Bosch back on when they are around. Just for the sake of this afternoon, I decide to do the latter.

As we walk out of the house into the garden, the sun is shining and once I find Oma at the distance, it makes me realize that Mom suspected right—Grandma has managed to pull out something that she likely thought was a weed but has a bulb attached to it and one of the gardeners has already intercepted her. Oma is wonderful at many things, but gardening certainly isn't one of them.

CHAPTER 40

Amsterdam, April 8, 2022
Roxanne

When I walk into the meeting room, Margaret and three executives from Beate Uhse AG are sitting across the table and their lawyers have a mound of papers sitting on the maple wood surface. She nods at me and it's impossible not to smile at her. Even though I know it's strictly business, I feel like the fact she's the one leading the acquisition of my business is karma of the highest order since she's part of Andries' family. It's ironic that by pushing Andries away from the business that was part of my life, they've created a situation where now it's going to be directly involved with his own family.

Of course, Margaret has made it very clear that it's Beate Uhse AG and their managers who will be running the show, but it's still implying that one of the best escort agencies in the country is going to be part of Andries' family, even if indirectly. And that's enough to make me laugh as the lawyers start to go through the paperwork. Speaking of which, I'm glad we have agreed that the new managing director that'll take over will be a woman with experience in sex work and escorting and that will always put the safety of the girls first and make sure clients respect the agreements they sign. I'll give her some training for the first month, but I'm sure down the road things will go smoothly.

"Just to clarify, this payment…" one of their lawyers slides an envelope across the table, "…is for the corporation to transfer entirely to my client once everything is signed off. That means all properties, assets and also the client list, which we expect you to provide."

I've been informed of that ahead of time. Taking out the client list I know that Margaret's eyes will probably almost pop out of her head when she sees some of the names we deal with on a regular basis. After all, they are likely people she knows personally. Opening up the envelope with the check, seeing so much money on a piece of paper isn't something that would usually send a thrill through me, but this one in particular has a lot of zeroes on it.

After the papers have finally been taken care of and we begin to sign off on each mark, my hand almost aches by the time I'm done. Margaret stays relatively quiet through the whole process while the executives sign off on everything, but then once the lawyers are done and begin to tidy up, she asks me to stay behind for a moment.

Once we are alone, she leans toward me. "I want you to know I'm so very happy to be taking this off your hands. Not only because you're an incredible businesswoman and I'm sure you're going to use this money wisely, but also because it'll help my grandson. He truly loves you, I can see it in his eyes, and if this will help him, then it's worth every penny."

It's hard not to feel a rush of emotion at her revelation. As much as Andries' family and I have been at odds, finding out that there's at least someone among them who wants us to have a future together is so foreign to me. I reach out and squeeze her hand, feeling like it's appropriate. "Andries adores you and I'm glad there's at least someone in his family that supports him." She laughs slightly. "I hope you don't take it the wrong way, but I know what happened between him and his father…"

"What Sebastian sees as love for his children is an… interesting thing." She sighs. "My daughter chose a man who can be a bit… abrasive, to say the least. Especially when it comes to his first son." She pats my hand in return.

"Well, thank you for everything. It was very kind of you." She nods.

"Just take care of him. With your business mind, you'll be able to help him along the way."

"Are you, um, joining us for the celebration?" What a stupid question! I curse at my own stupidity. It's hosted by Beate Uhse AG itself! Of course Margaret is attending.

Her eyebrows raise, but she then smiles, nodding her head.

"Of course, I am. Shall we?" As she stands I offer her my arm and we walk out of the office together. Her movements aren't quick, but I can sense a strength in her body that I am enjoying getting to know. There is a lot more to the woman than meets the eye, I can tell right away. And while I don't know much about Lady Margaret, I'm sure I'll get to know her better over time. As we walk down the street toward our destination, she makes me laugh with all the stories she's telling me about Andries' family and some of the trials they have had over the years.

It makes me realize, just like with my family, every family has its own issues and sometimes things get difficult. The glue that holds the family together sometimes comes loose, and it takes effort to re-apply it and put it back together.

We walk into the restaurant that has been privatized for the corporate event hosted by Beate Uhse AG and while I scan through the crowd, my eyes are immediately drawn to Andries and his faithful friend standing beside him, Dan.

We make our way through the tables and once I reach him, he turns slightly in my direction as if feeling my presence approaching.

"Hey!" I greet amid the noise of the event.

As we greet each other with a tight hug, he leans to my ear and says, "I'm so proud of you." His words are enough to make my heart flutter in response. "Congratulations on getting that done."

Margaret gets a hug as well and his grandson tells her how happy he is to see her. I'm glad to see there's at least someone in his family who supports him no matter his choices.

Andries then waves a waiter over and the man grabs the bottle of champagne that lies on an ice bucket beside us. It's a formal affair, and with a sabre he lances off the cap, sending it flying across the room with a loud cheer from many of the patrons around us. As he puts the bottle down, another waiter appears with double the glasses we need.

"Um, Andries...do we really need all those glasses?" I ask him.

He replies with a smirk. "Turn around."

As I do so, I see my sister, her boyfriend, and what really makes my jaw drop—my own mother standing behind them and she's actually smiling. I don't think I've seen her smile in close to a decade and certainly not when it comes to greeting me as a celebration. I turn back to Andries, a flush appearing on my face. But it's not embarrassment, it's a flush of wonder that he managed to surprise me. And include my family, which he knows means a lot to me.

Mama walks forward and I pause, wondering if she will even allow me to hug her. There is a sudden silence as it seems the whole group stops to wonder what will happen. I'm elated when she opens her arms, and I can give her a proper hug for the first time in years. I can't even speak because of the thrill that washes through me. Shutting my eyes, I just let myself revel in this simple motherly gesture.

Turning toward Margaret, I manage to stammer out an introduction. "Margaret, I'm so happy you are able to meet my family. This is Yao, my mother, and my sister, Lili and her boyfriend, Robin." Margaret nods at all of them and especially my mother. Mama hugs Andries, whispering something to him out of gratitude, and even gives him a kiss on the cheek. Accepting the flute of champagne the waiter offers me, I raise it up as we all take hold of one, even my mother.

"Here's to the future!" It's simple and straightforward but entirely appropriate. As we all take a sip of our champagne, I feel the bubbles cascade down my throat. It's impossible not to feel a rush of affection toward my wonderful partner, and I kiss him hard as the others laugh. It is as if a massive weight has been lifted from my shoulder and now we can finally be free to move forward together.

The restaurant is stunning and after we sit at our table, the servers begin with plates of small tasting dishes while one of the executives at Beate Uhse AG stands up to do a speech.

My mother slides into the seat next to me, and, while everyone is quietly listening to the speech, she leans forward to my ear and says, "I must tell you...I'm sorry for the way things happened between us." I'm almost taken aback by the fact she's actually apologizing. It seems so out of her character that I'm left speechless. I can also see Lili watching us intently, and I know that she likely had something to do with it. "I'm very proud of you finally selling...that business of yours. And I do appreciate you giving the family the bookstore that we worked so hard to keep alive." I can't help but be utterly speechless at her empathetic and humble behavior. "I hope you can forgive me and be willing to give your old mother a second chance?"

I have to respond and turn to her with tears springing to my eyes. "Mama, I never gave up on us. I, um, I hope you know I never meant to bring dishonor to the family, I just wanted a better future for us." Her lips suddenly tighten but then she nods, her hand resting on mine, giving it a squeeze.

"I know, I know...." She shuts her eyes, trying to get a hold of her emotions. "Well, at least thanks to your former job you met one fine man I must say."

I have to giggle when Andries looks at the two of us, wondering why Mama is suddenly smiling at him, his lips spreading into a smile filled with pride. Taking her champagne, she sips it gently and swallows, still smiling at the flavors merging together.

Once the speech ends, everyone claps and I do the same, even though I have no idea what the executive was talking about. The food on the table progresses into smaller meals, and it is truly in the presence of a family coming together. I can see Andries wishes that more of his family was involved and wanting to celebrate with us. He takes my hand as a band starts to play and everyone at the table claps when we leave the table and start to sway on the dance floor. My head is spinning from the champagne and also the fact that it is actually over. No more business. Just the future. It's terrifying, but also so damn thrilling.

"I can't believe you got my mother here," I tell him, our bodies pressed against one another. "And that she actually spoke to me and apologized."

"When I told her you were selling the agency, she seemed quite happy about it," he says a bit shyly. "But if I'm honest, I think Lili had something to do with your mom's behavior."

"Thank you for everything," I say in a whisper. "Having my mother apologize and be willing to turn the page means the world to me."

"I understand." His eyes are twinkling and his lips curve into a small smile. "I wish mine could have been here too."

I can't help but feel slightly guilty, and I know that his mother would likely wanted to have come, but maybe there's more to that situation than I actually know. "Maybe your mom had other impediments?"

He blanches quickly. "I think now that she knows I haven't been going to business school her opinion of me might have changed a bit—and not for the better." My heart falls as I watch the disappointment in his gaze. "It doesn't matter. Everything is going to be great. For us, at least." He presses his lips against mine and the music comes to a close. But what he just said startles me. I didn't know he had revealed to his family that he hadn't gone to business school and instead was studying English.

"Wait a minute. Your family knows you aren't going to business school anymore?" I grasp his shoulder tightly, trying to give him the extra support he might need.

He nods, a prideful smile forming at the corner of his lips, pulling me closer to him, he then leans down to whisper, "There's something else you need to know…" I look him in the eye, trying to find some hint in his gaze. "I've booked a little getaway to Paris for us and your family, like I promised, for the Easter holidays."

I have to stop when he reveals his intention, but then I realize quickly that I really have nothing to hold me back from this trip. No clients. No trial. No family drama. With the Easter holidays ahead, it's the perfect opportunity to relax and spend a few days in a different city with the man I love. "That sounds wonderful. I, um, I can't believe you did that."

"Oh believe me it's pretty real, your mom and sister were over the moon when I told them."

Leading me back to the table, we clink our glasses with the group again. It's wonderful to be able to sit down next to my mother and not have it feel awkward or have tension between us. She's actually being warm and open to Margaret as well, and the two of them are sharing stories about their children. I even hear the word grandchildren mentioned from my mother more than once, and when I hear that, my jaw almost hits the table.

"So what do you think, Yao?" Andries addresses her, most likely in an attempt to change the subject of the conversion. "Do you have already a list of places you'd like to visit in Paris?"

"We definitely want to go to the *Shakespeare and Company* bookstore," Yao answers excitedly. "And of course, Librairie Delamain, which is the oldest bookstore in all of Paris."

My entire family with us in Paris? It feels a dream come true and I can't help but already picture the four of us strolling around the Champs Elysées, visiting the most beautiful antiquarian bookstores and doing all the touristy activities.

So much has changed in such a short time. My family seems to be repaired. The trial with Karl is nearly over. And instead of losing the man that I love, we are heading to Paris for a trip together and if I know Andries, it will be filled with only the best things. With my family along I'll be able to experience the city through their eyes for the first time, and that will truly be wonderful.

Reaching out, I take his hand and squeeze it. When we go home later tonight, I'll no longer be an agency owner, I'll be just Roxanne.

CHAPTER 41

Amsterdam, April 15, 2022
Andries

While Elise is back home to spend the Easter weekend with our family, I'm packing for the trip, and even though I'm familiar with what it takes to spend a few days in Paris, it's actually making me nervous. I guess it's different when you're planning on proposing to your girlfriend and the fact her family is going to be there with us. Everything is in place, though. I've made a reservation at the Ritz and all I need to do is talk to Yao about getting her blessing. I feel a certain amount of apprehension about telling her my intentions, especially after the grudge she held against her daughter for so many years, but the fact Yao agreed to come on the trip with us tells me that their relationship might be changing for the better. At least I hope so.

Meanwhile, Dan is draped across my armchair, glowering at me. I know he thinks this is all stupid and a bad idea, but he can shove it.

"Don't take that shirt," he comments as I lift up one of my summer collared pieces. "You're going to Paris, not St. Tropez." Shooting him a look, I place it off to the side. As much as he's boorish about it, he's always had better fashion taste than mine. "Have you picked out an outfit for the big day?" His last two last words sound a bit judgmental to me.

Instead of simply coming out and asking me if I'm sure, he's resorted to making fun of the idea. Like it's something stupid for me to do, which I know he thinks it is. He hates the fact he's losing a wingman, or a partner in crime, or whatever. I don't really care.

"Are you really, really sure about this, though?" Finally it comes out. "Marriage is like... forever, you know?" His longest relationship in the past few years had been about two months, so I understand his attitude about it, but he has no idea how I feel.

"I know, Dan. News flash for you she's the woman I want to spend my life with." I'm not even looking at him but I'm pretty sure he's rolling his eyes. A few more shirts go into the suitcase along with my selection of pants, and a couple pairs of shoes for every occasion. When I think about where the ring is I get a sudden flash of panic but heave a sigh in relief when I glance over to the dresser and see the carmine-box sitting there.

"Sometimes I think about spending life with a woman. Then I wake up," Dan teases as he stands up and walks in my direction. "And realize it was just a nightmare."

"Yeah, next to whatever flavor of the week you've managed to drag home from the club," I fire back. "And then they don't even get breakfast."

"That's how I'll know she's really special…" he begins without even a hint of irony. "If I actually want her to stay for breakfast." I chuckle, but reach for the carmine-box and open it to marvel myself once more at the emerald-cut diamond solitaire. Dan stands beside me, a gush of air rolling off his lips. "Are you *absolutely* sure about this? I can't talk you out of it?"

I shake my head again, this time laughing. "Dude, I have a jet waiting, I'm paying for a suite at the Ritz, and I have a ring. As if I'm really going to let this whole thing just go up in smoke now." He rolls his eyes and finally shuts up.

Once my suitcase is full, it's easy to wheel it to the door where my chauffeur is to take it to the car. Roxanne has already left with Lili and Yao to the airport, so I'm just the last one running behind.

"Well, I've got to go," I tell Dan, who looks at me with some pity in his eyes.

We exchange a last hug and a few pats on the back, and I hear Dan saying in a low voice, "Good luck, and don't forget to call me. I want to know how it goes."

* * *

When I arrive at the airport, my car drops me off through the private gate and I see that Roxanne and her family are already there. Yao almost looks confused when we walk out onto the tarmac and I point toward the freshly fueled up jet waiting to whisk us off to Paris. What would normally take hours of waiting is gone, and the plane has us deposited at Le Bourget in less than an hour. It's always been a fast flight.

Yao and Lili are quite quiet, both busy taking in all the sites as our private shuttle drives us from the airport into the downtown area. They try to snatch pictures from their seat each time they spot an interesting monument or a Haussmann building. Seeing them buzzing with excitement, I know it was the right decision to come here to ask the woman I love to be my wife.

Once the car stops in front of the Ritz located in the Place Vendôme, a gloved-hand valet opens the car door, welcoming us. I can't help but take a quick peek at Yao's reaction.

"Wow," Lili utters in admiration once she steps foot outside. The three women start taking in their surroundings, their eyes perusing the immensity of the square filled with nothing but high-end jewelry stores.

"Shall we?" I take Roxanne's hand in mine and we make our way toward the entrance, thanking the doorman as he welcome us in French, his head bowing slightly at us.

The palatial entrance takes their breath away, and I must say, despite having been here before with my parents, the immaculate beauty of the lobby and its Belle Époque decoration doesn't leave me indifferent either.

The porters take our bags and we are ushered toward the front desk. While I'm finalizing the check-in process, I watch Roxanne take a few pictures of Yao and Lili standing behind the marble staircase covered with a red carpet and tapestries spread on the paneling walls. They are smiling up to their ears and I find myself mimicking their smile. We're going to have such a good time here. I've booked a table at La Tour d'Argent—one of the most iconic establishments in Paris and already two centuries old—for the evening. Before we go, though, I need to find a moment to Yao before proposing to her daughter tomorrow.

Once the checkout has been made, I hand one key to Yao and another to Lili and let them know they are staying next to each other. I had asked Lili if she wanted to invite Robin along, but he already had plans to spend Easter with his family. Roxanne and I, on the other hand, are located on another floor.

When we reach the suite I've booked for us, my heart is pounding anxiously fast. I just hope she's going to like it.

Standing in front of the white double doors, I go and open them, inviting her in.

Roxanne paces slowly inside, taking in her surroundings, she scans through the high ceilings, the crystal chandelier centering the living room, the marble fireplace situated on her right, and the overall opulence of the place.

"Oh my gosh, Andries, this is..." she lets her words trail off as she paces around the ample living room. The décor highlights Asian lacquer pieces, gold-framed mirrors, and velvet furniture in beige and brown tones. "I..."

"Remember when you told me your perfume was Chanel Number Five, and that it was your favorite fragrance?" I ask, and her attention returns to me when she nods, visibly smitten. "I figured you might enjoy being in a suite that once belonged to its creator."

"You mean?" She blinks twice, her mouth gaping as she processes what I just told her. "This is Gabrielle Chanel's suite?"

"She lived here for thirty-four years," I say, causing her to gasp. "It was pretty hard to make a booking on such short notice, not going to lie, but I wanted us to stay here. I knew it'd be a special place for you." I conveniently leave the part where I had to contact the hotel manager who knows my father well. Being a Van Den Bosch had never been so helpful.

"You are totally crazy, this must have cost a fortune!" She walks in my direction, ready to rebuke. "Andries, you didn't have to—"

But I hold a finger to her lips, shushing her. "Hey. You deserve this and much more. This is just a one-time splurge to celebrate what you did for me."

She clasps her hands over my neck, her features softening. "I know but you don't need to spend so much, especially after what your parents have done."

"Don't worry," I tell her and seeing the frown forming on her face, I explain a bit further. "Oma found a few properties under my name that my mom had supposedly forgotten to tell me about."

She furrows her brow in confusion. "Wait. You own real estate that you knew nothing about?"

"I know it sounds silly, but yeah, Oma is a Van Dieren— another noble family that has been around for centuries and they own thousands of properties around the world. Most of them are being managed and rented out by their family office but I remember Mom telling me when I was younger that once I turned eighteen, a few of them would be transferred to me so I could have something that belongs entirely to me." I pause for a beat, observing her attentive gaze. "But since I left for a year and spent my eighteen birthday abroad, I guess she took it upon herself to never mention it again as some form of revenge."

"Wow," she utters in shock at the revelation. "What a petty thing to do. Your family is really something."

"That's why I don't really care if they disowned me." I shrug and before the mood gets too heavy due to such a serious subject, I take her hand and say, "Well, let's put this behind and check the rest of the suite."

We continue checking the suite like we are exploring some sort of museum. After all, this place has been decorated by Gabrielle Chanel herself. We find some of her personal objects such as portraits, drawings, and unpublished photographs, still unknown to the public. Then we walk into the bedroom and my first thought is to kiss her, to throw her down on the bed and make furious love to her because I've been craving her for days, but this will have to wait for now, as we have got ourselves a busy schedule ahead.

When she finds her luggage lying by the closet, she starts to unpack a couple of things including an elegant dress for the evening, which I'm thrilled to see is one of my favorites. It reveals just enough, but not enough to make her mother's eyebrows raise. When she catches my eye, I see her grin at me. "Don't get any ideas. I'm going to have a shower and get dressed. You promised Lili and Mama to take them to Shakespeare and Company upon our arrival."

It's refreshing that she can read my mind, after all.

The temptation to simply open the bathroom door is there, and I want to climb into the shower with her and soap her naked body down. But there will be time for that later. Instead, I take this opportunity to go and talk to Yao in private. Arriving at her room number, I knock a few times, and when she opens me the door, she seems visibly surprised to see me.

"Hey," I greet, slightly nervous at what I'm about to do. "Is the suite to your liking?"

"To my liking? My dear, this suite is even bigger than my apartment. Come in, come in," she ushers me inside and I giving her a polite smile, stepping in.

"See? It's huge!"

"I'm glad you are enjoying it, then," I find myself saying, and before I can place another word, Yao takes over.

"I've never been able to afford anything like this for my girls, so I hope you know how much I appreciate you taking us on this trip."

"You're welcome. I'm truly glad that you could all be here together, and I'm really excited for the future." Taking a deep breath, I know what I'm about to ask her will come out of nowhere.

"Speaking of which…Ms. Feng, I came here to ask you for your blessing, if I were to ask Roxanne to marry me." Her eyebrows raise immediately in confusion, and that doesn't help one tiny bit. "It's kind of a silly old tradition, I know, but you're the only parent she has. It'd mean a lot to me to know that you were okay with me proposing." The funny thing is, I don't really even care about my own family's blessing. I know my grandmother cares enough to be part of it, and that's all I need. If I need to build a life without the rest of my family, I'll figure it out.

"Oh!" she utters, like she just figured something out. "So this trip to Paris is because you're going to propose her?"

"Yes," I reply, swallowing the lump in my throat. "I intend to do so tomorrow afternoon, actually."

She gasps, but then her expression softens with a grin. "This is wonderful news! Oh my goodness! I must say, I never thought Roxanne would find a man like you. The fact that you know everything about her previous job and have decided to accept her and her past, that is very kind of you, indeed."

"I'm afraid it's not a matter of kindness, Ms. Feng, but of love." I pause for a beat, her eyes lingering on me. "I might despise the industry she worked in, but I also understand her circumstances weren't the most favorable. She wanted so much to help you and Lili."

"I know, Roxie would go through hell for us." Her gaze drops as she thinks something through. "I was mistaken about my daughter. And I regret the fact I wasted so many years holding a grudge against her for what she did." Her expression is taut with what looks like regret, and I can sense that she truly means it. "I hope that you and she can build a life together. I've never seen her so happy as she is with you." That's all I need to hear. A smile breaks out over my face I can't control. I have to hug her, knowing that she just gave me the blessing I was looking for, even if she didn't come out and say it.

"Thank you. You won't regret it."

* * *

When I reach back to the suite, Roxanne is still in the bathroom, so I busy myself choosing a new shirt and checking if my new pair of pants have a good crease. When she opens the bathroom door and sweeps out in her dress, her hair hanging down and still damp, my pants immediately twitch. God, she's gorgeous.

What her mother and sister don't know is that Roxanne and I have planned one stop before we head out for dinner. The restaurant is strategically located near *Shakespeare and Company*, one of the most iconic bookstores in the world. It's a place I know Yao and Lili will love, and the great thing is it also represents a large part of myself and Roxanne. Since we first kissed in a bookstore and bonded over our love for literature, it is something that will always hold a special place in our relationship.

Arriving at the store, Yao's eyes are wide and Lili squeals, walking in and perusing through the bookshelves. The store is so massive and full of incredible out-of-print copies that is hard to know where to even look. There're old editions of some incredible books behind glass that are available for purchase. For a while, we are all caught in enjoying the smells and sensations of everything around us. I knew that it would thrill all of them to see it, just as it always thrills me.

Walking through the stacks, I'm holding Roxanne's hand when her phone chimes with a notification. There're not many people that know she's here, so when she stops to look at it and I see her face fall, I know it can't be good news.

"What is it?"

She looks at me, her gaze filled with apprehension. "It's about Karl. The verdict came in." I can see her take a deep breath as she reads the news. "Guilty." There's a rush of breath that escapes me.

"So what are you upset about? That's great news, no?" Since Roxanne hesitates, I peer at her screen and start reading the article itself. "What?" I utter in disbelief as I read Karl's sentence. "Just three weeks in jail and a ten thousand euro fine?" The sentence is nothing. A token really, considering what he was accused of. Roxanne's testimony and how she went easy on him probably had something to do with that, but I brush those thoughts immediately aside as they'll only ruin our romantic getaway.

She squeezes my hand in reassurance. "I know. It's not fair. Honestly, it's a perfect example of what we want to get away from, right?"

I nod, trying to focus on the positive side; Karl was at least found guilty and that should be enough to ruin his reputation and also cause him all sorts of business trouble.

On that somber note, I know it's time we head to the restaurant to forget about what Roxanne just discovered. We quickly find Yao and Lili and I tell them we need to head out to make our reservation on time. Neither of them buy anything, but both of them vow to return later in the trip and I can see them pointing out things the bookstore that have given them ideas for their own store. They could turn it into the type of iconic place that this store has become.

The restaurant isn't far, and its refined atmosphere makes the place even more special. Since I speak fluent French, they realize we aren't the typical tourists and so we actually get good service. We decide to go for the tasting menu so we can taste several French specialities.

As usual, there are several plates on the table before we know it. The server pours the wine, and we all have a toast. "To our trip to Paris. And may it not be the last," I tell the table. I know Roxanne has probably been here dozens of times, but she was always on the clock or likely having to impress someone. Meaning she was not being herself. I want her to know somehow that she doesn't need to be anybody except the woman she is anymore.

The conversation flows since everybody is excited to be here and is in a good mood. We spend a lot of time talking about the bookstore of course. Lili really wants to expand, and I know that Roxanne is excited to see what they will do with the place.

With everything up in the air regarding my family, I don't know what I will find when I get back. Will they ever talk to me again when they find out I've asked Roxanne to marry me? What would our wedding look like? It sounds silly, but even just planning the event would be something that I could get excited about. Not a grand extravagant affair like so many of my family members have done, but something low-key, between close friends and family. A quiet party at my grandmother's estate would definitely fit the bill.

I'm getting ahead of myself of course. Refocusing on the present moment, I stand up, take a sheet from inside my inner pocket, and after clearing my throat, the three women stop talking, their attentions shifting to me, as they wonder why I'm standing in front of my seat, a paper in hand.

"I hope you're all enjoying the evening," I say, looking at Yao, Lili and Roxanne. "I've written a little something that I wish to share here in this joyous environment." Looking at my girlfriend in the eye, we exchange a complicit smile as if she knows what I'm about to do. "Roxanne," I begin.

"*The choices we make shapes our existence*
"*And you went above and beyond the distance*
"*To keep me close and in your heart*
"*I'm thankful we're now ready for a fresh start*
"*My gratefulness is overflowing*

"Wherever you are, I'll be going
"As my past, present and future is how I see you
"In your soul I found a love that's true."

"What a wonderful poem," Yao praises as she and everyone around us start clapping. Heck, even the waiters who were standing against the walls.

I bow my head slightly in gratitude and lowering myself back into my seat, Roxanne leans enough to give me a tender kiss on the lips. "Thank you," she says in a whisper. "It was so beautiful."

"Wonderful poem, sir," one of our waiters says in a thick French accent as he refills my glass of wine. "You're very talented. Are you a professional poet?"

"Hopefully one day," I tell him.

As my attention returns to the table, Roxanne and Lili are tasting another one of the dishes that have been set out and both are making faces that look slightly orgasmic in nature. Seeing my girlfriend with that type of expression only makes my pants stiffen, and when I sit down beside her and see the silky length of her bare leg, it's impossible not to let my hand slide under the table and move up her thigh. She smiles, not revealing anything to her sister and mother on the other side of the table.

I feel her hand grab mine and remove it from between her legs, but then her hand steals underneath the table and moves to my pants. When she expertly feels the hardness underneath my fly, I know she's got the same feelings I do because her hand gently circles around the tented tip that my erection has created and with a small, subtle movement she starts to rub, making my breath catch in my throat.

The sensation almost makes me groan out loud, and when we finally pay the bill and leave the restaurant to head back to the hotel, it's difficult not to run with my hand in hers. Everything we have been through together is making me want her more than I ever have before.

* * *

Once we are finally inside the room and alone together, I'm able to succumb to the feelings that have been simmering inside me all night. And I know that she has felt it too. With her family around, there wasn't a lot of chance to show our affection toward each other, but the city is like a drug and now we are both ready to take a long, hard hit of it. She shows me how much she wants me when she walks into the bathroom and then walks out wearing nothing except a small shift.

In the light from the window her body is flawless like always, her skin and smooth lines along with the curves of her gorgeous breasts and ass look like something out of a Renaissance painting. I'm sitting on the bed and she slowly paces in my direction, almost teasing me by not doing so quicker.

She stands in front of me and once her eyes meet mine, it's like an electric shock passes between us. "I'm not tired," she points out before I grab her and throw her down on the bed for a lingering kiss.

Her breasts are perfect curves in my palm, and the only thing between my raging erection and her naked body are two pieces of fabric.

"Me either," I breathe. "I've been dying all day long to be here right now, like this. With you." She can hopefully see the intensity in my eyes. It is the truth. And now we are going to finally be able to finish what she had started in the restaurant.

A hand reaches out, and she quickly undoes my belt and unbuttons my shirt, and I allow her hands to take care of it. We've made love so many times, but this time somehow it feels different.

"Like this?" she asks with a sultry tone as she wraps her hand around the head poking through my boxers and strokes it like she did in the restaurant.

I growl in response, the feeling being too good to speak.

Roxanne then turns over and her perfect ass is right in front of me. Touching it is a craving like I've rarely felt. It's curvy but firm and when she slides her panties down her pussy is slowly revealed with a hint of wetness between her puffy lips. She turns around and the sensuality of the moment takes my breath away.

I lean back and take hold of my underwear, sliding it down. Her eyes are fixed onto my groin and when my throbbing erection is revealed, it is sticking straight up. Whether it is subconscious or not, she bites her lip, and it is sexy as hell.

Without saying a word, she slides forward, and her hands find my shaft, making me gasp with how gentle she is. Squeezing it, she leans forward and moves herself into position to take me into her mouth. My body shivers at the sight of my sexy lover about to suck me.

"Hmmm," she purrs when she reaches the head of my dick. Kissing lower, her tongue dances across the shaft to my balls and gently sucks on one of them. I feel my cock shudder deep inside as she moves up and then takes me into her mouth. It's like the most incredible sensation. Warm, loving and still erotic like nothing I've ever seen.

"Goddamn...you are so beautiful," I tell her. There's a smile as she lets her mouth wrap around me again. Taking a deep breath, I lie back and enjoy her, nervous but eager to feel what she wants to give me.

Much to my chagrin, she slowly slides me out of her throat, the chill air of the room an uncomfortable welcome after the hot, wet heat of her throat. She uses her hands to caress my balls again, holding the weight of them in her palm as her nails tease the extra-sensitive skin.

"Am I going too fast for you?" she asks slyly.

"Not fast enough," I respond, thrusting against her grip.

She laughs, her voice low and sultry. Roxanne strokes my cock once, the wetness from her mouth easing the way. Precum is blooming on the tip, and she spreads it across the head of my member with her thumb before lowering her mouth and licking it all away.

The noise I make as her tongue touches me again is almost shameful in its helplessness. Only she can make me feel this way—and she's the only one I'd ever trust to be this vulnerable with.

I'm dying to feel her throat grip my dick again, but now she's decided to take it slowly, moving her wicked lips and tongue from my balls, to my shaft, and then the head again before starting back at the beginning. It's torture... delicious torture.

This close, I can smell her arousal and how much sucking my cock is turning her on, and in turn, it makes me even harder, if such a thing could be possible. Her licks and strokes get longer, more thorough, her saliva dripping down my shaft as she sucks me. Teasing turns into something more, and even though it seems like an eternity, Roxanne is finally swallowing me again fully, making ravenous noises as she does so.

Nothing can compare to the silken feeling of her pussy, but this is a close second. I won't come, not yet, but the temptation to shoot my seed into her pretty throat is almost all-consuming.

Using my hand to squeeze her hip, I pull her close so that I can dip a finger into her wetness, hearing and feeling her moan around me as I touch her. She's dripping and so ready for me. My other hand finds one of her tits and I tease her rock-hard nipple while she moans around my shaft, making me quake and moan in unison.

Grabbing her hips, I tug her closer and her mouth rolls off my erection. She gives out a light squeal but then spreads her legs, her glistening pussy staring at me. It's obvious what we both want more than anything, but I want to make it last. Moving down I take my first moaning slide of a tongue through her folds, and she gasps and grabs the back of my head, her hips and scent arching up into my mouth.

I suck her clit between my lips, making quick circles with my tongue before sucking again with force. Roxanne gasps, grinding herself against my face as I dip my tongue into the well of her pussy, tasting her deeply before moving back to that little bundle of nerves that is the center of her pleasure. I can feel her legs shuddering, and the way those shivers move all the way up her spine.

I alternate quick licks and sucks, exploring the outside of her folds before diving in again to make her scream. Roxie bucks as I eat her out, but I manage to hold her still enough that I am able to taste her fully. She's sweet and hot, and I am positive I'll never get enough of this.

Roxanne's fingernails scrape across my scalp, which tells me she's getting close. But I don't want her to come yet. When she does, I want to be inside her. I have to be.

I wasn't about to waste any time, especially when she beckoned me forward with one hand while cupping her breast with the other. "I want you," she breathes. "Get inside me."

Moving up over her body, I sigh when our eyes lock on each other. Like two pieces fitting together, my cock slides against her dripping slit and when I push inside, she gasps out loud, crying out with pleasure as my member sinks inside her. One easy thrust and it's like she grips me with her entire body.

Her hard nipples are rubbing against my chest, and she wraps her arms and legs around me, pulling me deeper into her. This is so perfect. Everything about this evening has been perfect. Fuck! I nibble her bottom lip, before moving back to her mouth while thrusting back and forth. We aren't just fucking. In my mind, I'm already making love to my wife somehow and the thought of it causes sensations I will never forget.

We are connected in every sense of the word. Mentally, physically, emotionally, and spiritually. Feeling her body flush against mine, her breath against my skin, and the beating of her heart, make this something more than sex. Something more even than making love. This is a bonding of souls... I guess all of our time together has been.

I raise up on my elbows, slowing the pistoning of my hips so I can look deeply into her eyes, skimming my hands down her beautiful body. I could come in seconds at this point, but I still want a little more time in this moment with her. I want to remember it for the rest of my life.

I tweak her nipples, making her writhe beneath me, before coaxing her to arch her body up so I can suck them between my lips and teeth. I nip at the hardened peaks gently, soothing the sharp sting with my tongue before moving to the other one. Over and over I tease her like this, watching the flush of pleasure make her neck and face rosy and feeling her pussy grip me tighter with every scrape of my teeth.

When she's nearly overwhelmed, she buries her hands in my hair again and tugs me down to press her lips against mine. We kiss deeply, so close that even breathing is something we share. Roxie takes one of my hands and pushes it to where we are joined, and I don't need any more instruction than that, rolling my thumb over her clit, drinking down her shuddering breaths with my lips on hers.

As I break the kiss, putting all my attention into the thrusts of my hips and the movements of my fingers between her legs, Roxie takes the opportunity to explore my body. She's getting close, I can feel it in the way her walls are fluttering around me, even as she runs her small hands over my chest, arching up to kiss my collarbone and neck. She can't get enough of me, just like I can't get enough of her.

When I erupt inside her, she gives out a gasp and pushed up into me, my love slipping into her like a fountain. I have been craving her for days, and my orgasm wracks my entire body to the point I nearly lose my rhythm. It starts from the base of my spine and explodes outwards, blinding in its intensity. It's the same for Roxie, I can tell by the way her body tenses as if electrified, her hands scrambling to grip the sheets as an anchor to keep her here on Earth.

"You're so incredible when you come for me," I manage to say between tremors. "The most beautiful thing in the world."

She whimpers, pulling me down against her and locking her arms and legs around me while the last aftershocks roll through our bodies. My love. My Roxie.

Panting, we both slow our movements, and I can feel her pulsing around me. Our lips find each other's and while I soften we kiss and touch and I can feel myself finally slip out.

"God, I love you," I tell her, and she kisses me again hard, sealing what I know is mutual love between us. Tomorrow will be perfect. The setting, the fact that I already have her mother's blessing. There will be no better time to ask the woman I love to spend her life with me. I'm excited for the next day, and that's something I haven't been able to feel for a long time.

CHAPTER 42

Paris, April 16, 2022
Andries

Waking up next to Roxanne after the night we had makes my body stir in ways that I can't possibly imagine. As soon as I feel her body next to mine, I'm terribly aroused again. Reaching out I touch her bare back and she pushes into me with a sigh, her ass humping against my erection causing a giggle from her.

"Well, good morning," I hear her saying with a tease.

I wrap my hand around her hip and start pinning soft kiss on the crest of her neck. Kissing her skin feels like the most delicious fruit I could possibly have in the morning, and I can't wait for the rest of the day when I know what's going on ahead.

Speaking of which, will my family come around and accept her once they know that I'm serious about our relationship? After all, Dad disowned me, Mom is supportive of him, and even my sister is on their side and accepts whatever they say in order to stay on their good side. Oma is supportive, and even Dan—as much as he grouses about the fact I'm planning on getting engaged—is there for me if I need him, I know that. I guess only time will tell….

"What time is it?" Roxanne rolls over and sighs, arching her back. Her breasts stick out perfectly and the temptation is there to take one of her nipples into my mouth and pick up where we left off last night. Still, the fact the proposal is on my mind makes me nervous enough to hold off. After all, the ring is still only about two feet away in the nightstand.

"Time to get up," I say as I sneak at the clock on the nightstand. "We are here to visit Paris, not to stay between the sheets." I lean over and kiss her shoulder and again she rolls into me, her perfect legs rubbing against mine.

"Fine," she purrs, sliding out of the bed. As she pads to the bathroom like she did last night after we made love, I still marvel at her sinuous beauty and how much she makes me crave her.

For the first time in my life, it feels like there's nothing preordained. Like there's a vast path opening up in front of me that could go in five different directions, and I have no idea which one I will end up taking. There is truly choice, something that my family had rarely offered me. The only thing I know for sure is that the woman happily humming at the mirror in the bathroom is who I want to spend it with.

Letting my morning wood subside, I climb out of bed and over to the window. The view is spectacular, and Paris even just after the sun has come up is already alive with by-passers walking to a market, biking to work, and some ladies still wearing evening dresses stumbling home from whatever apartment they slept in last night.

"Shall we go down and have breakfast?" Roxanne asks as she walks out toweling her hair. "I'm sure that my sister and Mama are already up."

I move up behind her and wrap my hands around her waist, kissing her neck. Again, she stirs feelings inside me I can't possibly describe. "Sure, I figured since Lili has never been here before, we could all go to the top of the Eiffel Tower together. What do you think?"

"Mmm...that sounds absolutely lovely." She turns and her lips find mine. Even just kissing her is enough to make my body erupt with passion. Just like we should always feel, especially in Paris. "Why don't you start getting ready and I'll round up my mother and Lili?" One more kiss and we manage to separate.

As I disappear into the bathroom, she goes to the bedroom to get herself dressed, and I can't help but wonder what her reaction would be if she found the ring box in the nightstand. It's right underneath the phone and would be easy to discover. After all, the Cartier box would be a dead giveaway. Would she be thrilled? Would she be upset or sad? I'd like to think she'd squeal and rush to me, throwing her arms around me and telling me yes right away, but there's still that feeling of apprehension. If she rejects me, especially with her mother and sister along with us, it would crush me completely.

Aside from my plan to propose later on, we have a touristy day ahead of us. Trying not to look too much like we aren't locals, I give Yao and Lili a lay of the land and make sure that they know where they are. After breakfast, we head out for the morning and the first stop is the Eiffel Tower, which I know is a good place to start with before it gets too crowded and the buses start to pile in. Once we reach the top, Yao and Lili become like teenagers and rush excitedly to take a glass of champagne at the bar before snapping a few pictures.

As I observe the three of them taking selfies with the view and their glasses of champagne, I can't help but think of the other men who have likely entertained Roxanne by taking her to places like this. I'm sure with her former life she was shown the best of everything, but it was as a completely different person playing a role and acting a part. Not somebody who is seeing it with fresh eyes and through the ones of her sister and mother for the first time. It gives me a warm feeling to know that I'm able to provide such an experience for her and her family, and also spend it with her when she is having so much fun.

The view is always breathtaking, and we are able to snap some perfect shots, creating memories that I hope will last a lifetime. Even Yao is able to let her hair down and smile and be a bit silly when posing for the camera. Once we are there for a little while the numbers start to swell, and I know it's time for our next stop.

We leave the Eiffel Tower and head to a cute, traditional brasserie with a wide terrace just around the corner which is perfect to make a quick stop for a croissant and coffee. I sit down with the three women at the terrace and immediately a waiter comes to take our order. As we take in our surroundings, we find people walking by on their way to work or we spot other tourists like us. It's almost funny to watch and actually guess what those by-passers are getting up to during their day. There's nothing better than simply sitting at a terrace and enjoying some French pastries in good company. Even Yao's demeanor seems to be great today.

Afterwards, we head to the Louvre, which is the next destination planned. But this is only an excuse to send Lili and Yao away. Once we reach the museum, I take Roxanne's arm and tell her that we should take a trip back to the bookstore we visited yesterday.

"I saw them looking at some first editions," I whisper to her. "It'd be a nice surprise to head back there and purchase those books for them."

She's got no idea what I have actually planned for us there and quickly agrees to head back to the bookstore as a surprise for her family. The ring box I've been carrying is literally burning a hole in my pocket, or at least it feels that way. As we walk through the Parisian streets hand in hand and talk about the city, I can't help but feel a swell of nervousness build inside me. When we reach the bookstore, it's almost difficult to step inside knowing what I'm about to do. This time though we are greeted by the store clerk, and after we exchange a few words, he leads us to the back end of the store. Roxanne thinks he's just going to show us the books her mother and sister saw yesterday, so she follows him without giving much of a second thought.

Then once we reach the back end, the clerk unlocks a wooden door and welcomes us inside a circular room. The walls are covered with ceiling-to-floor shelves filled only with antique hardcovers and collectibles. I thank him, and he closes the door behind him, leaving us alone.

"This is kind of a secret room that most people don't know about," I tell her, reveling in her excitement. "Some books here are even centuries old. It's a bit like your room for banned books."

It's the most appropriate spot for what I have planned. After all, our entire life together began inside an antiquarian bookstore, exploring banned literature, and this is a place that takes me back to the first time I kissed her between the stacks. Her gorgeous profile, not knowing anything about what I was about to get myself into or experience.

"This place is so incredible." She sighs as she paces the floor, perusing the shelves. "I could literally spend all day here." Her hand drifts over a couple of spines, her attention never leaving the shelves. "Oh! There's even a collection of poetry from Bei Dao." My hands are shaking, knowing what I'm about to do. While she's distracted, her back on me, I take out the ring box and squeeze it in my hand, my heart thundering a thousand miles an hour. It's time. There are no one around us and it's the perfect moment to do so.

"Do you know where the books are that we are looking for? I don't recall Mama coming here yesterday."

"I have something I need to tell you," I say, trying to make sure my voice doesn't shake.

She finally turns around, and when she does so, I kneel down in front of her, causing her to gasp in surprise, her hands going up to her mouth.

"Roxanne, I don't know how you managed to make me fall so hard for you. Dan believes you have put a spell on me," I start, and while tears are springing to her eyes, I see her smile and she lets out a brief giggle. "But the one thing I do know is that you were meant to turn my world upside down. And everything that we've been through since that first kiss in the bookstore has only showed me exactly how much I want you in my life." Her eyes meet mine and everything comes out as a rush.

"An antiquarian bookstore represents where we started. But I also want it to represent where we begin." I open the carmine box, revealing the ring she tried on at the shop with her sister. "Ms. Feng, will you marry me and make me the happiest man in the world?"

The pause feels like an eternity as she looks at the ring lying in the open box. A single tear runs down her cheek and she nods. "Of course. Of course, I will, Andries." When she says those words, a thrill runs through my body that's absolutely indescribable. I stand immediately up and, with a shaking hand, remove the ring and slide it onto her finger, knowing it would be a perfect fit. She gasps as the ring slides on and then I take her hand, looking into her eyes and pull her into me.

I kiss her hard, tasting a salty tear that has flowed down her cheek, and my heart keeps pounding hard inside my chest as I realize Roxanne is going to be my wife whether my family or anyone else tries to get in the way.

"I can't believe this," she breathes amid a few sniffles. "This is too good to be real." She wipes her eyes with her fingers, while I spray soft kisses on her head.

"It's very real, believe me," I say in a low voice.

We embrace each other, reveling in the magic of the moment in a comforting silence. But the truth is, I'm just as overjoyed and barely able to process this new reality—I'm officially engaged. Wow.

* * *

It's difficult to let her go, but we finally manage to make our way out of the store, my head reeling with the fact I'm now engaged. Roxanne is freely letting tears stream down her cheeks, showing as much emotion as I've ever seen her exhibit, especially in public. Some of the people walking by even almost stop us to see if something is wrong, but it's obvious that her tears are joyful, not sad. Her normally stoic nature has been eliminated by the romance of the moment as she continues raving about the ring I put on her finger. We have a bit of a walk before meeting up with her mother and sister, so I take a moment to talk to her about us being engaged.

"Whatever you want for a wedding, it's yours," I tell her. "I'm fine with something simple and intimate if that's what you'd prefer." She nods and agrees, the smile never leaving her face. Then there is a pause as she considers something.

"What about your family? Are you going to tell them?" she asks.

"Just my grandmother. I'm sure the rest of them will find out in due time." It's a tough decision to not contact the rest of my family, especially Elise who was simply caught up in the middle of everything. But this moment is for us, not anybody else and I don't want there to be any chance that it might be ruined by parents making stupid remarks about our future together. I send off a quick text to Dan with a picture of the ring on Roxanne's finger, knowing he will want to know everything.

Quickly my phone rings with a FaceTime request from the one and only Dan O'Brian. I'm rather happy he's the first one person I'll share the good news with. Even though he might have tried to convince me otherwise, I know he's got always my back and will support my decision. When I answer the call, his smile is wide.

"Hey, bud! Just thought I'd reach out directly and say congratulations to the newly engaged couple!" His voice sounds genuinely happy for us and Roxanne makes a big deal out of showing him the ring on her finger. He whistles. "Damn… that looks like a good, solid rock, Andries. Don't show any of my ladies that, otherwise their expectations will get too high!" Roxanne laughs, and so that I. She seems so happy she's almost glowing.

"Alright, well, I'll leave you to enjoy Paris!" he wiggles his eyebrows suggestively. "I'll start planning the bachelor party. I have some ideas in mind already." That part makes me laugh as well. I can only imagine what hedonistic situations I'm going to have to talk him out of before I get married. He can have his fun, of course.

The phone clicks off. I know that word will spread quickly now that Dan knows, and likely it means Elise will hear about it soon. It almost makes me wonder if my parents or my sister herself will even reach out at all once they hear about it. Part of me hopes that they do, and there's another part of me that hopes they just… don't.

Roxanne goes forward to search for her mother and sister as we stand close to the exit of the Louvre, and I take a chance to call Oma quickly. After all, she's the only supportive member of my family. When she answers the phone, it's almost funny to hear what she has to say. "Ah, Andries. I'm assuming you're calling me to let me know you're an engaged man?"

My eyes widen in surprise. How the hell did she know? "You must be psychic, Oma. I have no idea how you do it."

She laughs heartily in my ear. "Oh well, it's just putting the pieces together." She pauses for a beat, considering me. "Do you want me to tell your parents, or are you going to do that?"

It's a difficult question, to be honest. Since I'm over the moon with happiness, I want to share it with the world, but instead I say, "I'll do it myself... when I feel it's the right time."

"Alright, my dear, I promise I'll make sure I won't 'spill the beans,' as they say." I truly hope so.

I see Roxanne has spotted her mother and sister, so I tell her I need to go. Her congratulations is her signing off. And I know she means it, truly.

When Yao and Lili walk up to me, their hands filled with souvenir bags, they start gushing about the paintings they were able to see. I frown, exchanging a quick glance with Roxanne, but I notice her hand had been hidden behind her back all this time.

As they show us what they brought from the souvenir store, Roxanne says, "I actually also have a souvenir of my own." She reveals her left hand, the ring on her finger gleaming, and immediately her sister squeals loudly and throws her arms around her. Yao looks at me and smiles, then walks forward to hug me.

"My new son. And what a wonderful son you will be," she says it into my ear causing me to glow with pride. Being accepted by my future mother-in-law is something I never could have expected when I met her back in that hospital room so many months ago. Lili gives me a hard hug as well and then grabs her sister, the three of them walking in front of me as they start to chatter away about a possible wedding scenario.

What is the future is going to bring us? There's no way of knowing for sure, but as long as I'm with her, that is absolutely fine with me.

CHAPTER 43

Amsterdam, April 18, 2022
Dan

She's gonna kill me. I can already feel the anger pouring out of her skin as she storms into the tea room of the Astoria Hotel and races in my direction, her purse firmly pressed against her shoulder.

"So?" she asks without wasting any second, lowering herself into a chair in front of me. "Do you have any news?" Her big amber eyes blink a few times, staring right at me.

I cringe internally in anticipation to what is yet to come, but I try to hide it by rising my teacup until it meets my lips and I give a gulp. "I do."

"And?" she presses on, her tone filled with anticipation. Andries is my best friend and the fact he got engaged in Paris makes me want to cheer with his sister, but alas, I know all too well that Elise isn't gonna like the news one bit. I take another sip of my tea, heaving a long sigh as I ponder the best approach. "They are having a great time in Paris." I give her an awkward smile.

"Dan," she scolds just as fast, her body leaning forward and her forearms resting on the table. "Did he propose?" *Always so straight-froward...* "Yes or no?"

She might be younger than her brother, but Elise—unlike him—is not naive and is much less of a romantic.

I give her two nods of the head, my gaze dropping to my cup of tea.

"Fuck," she grits between clenched teeth as she leans back on the chair. "We have to stop this madness." A gush of air bursts from her lungs as she processes the news. "He's screwing himself over. Dad's gonna be furious."

I hum at her vaguely, before blurting a quiet, "Andries seems happy though."

"Happy?" Elise repeats with shock in her eyes as she leans forward again. "He's being eaten alive by a professional liar! I don't trust that woman *at all*." Her index finger even taps on the table as to mark her last words. "How can you side with him on this?"

The thing is, I'm not siding with anyone. I enjoy playing in both teams to keep a good relationship with both, and it helps to create a bridge between Andries and his family.

"What do you suggest we do?" I ask, intrigued, as I take the pot and fill her cup with some blooming tea. "Roxanne sold her agency, they are now living under the same roof, and they just got engaged." I pause for a beat, observing the frustration building in her accelerated breath. "Life goes on, Elise." I shrug.

"This is so fucked up," she snaps, head shaking in dismissal.

"Hey." I lay my hand on hers for a second, bringing her attention back to me. "Now that Andries is pursuing life on his own and without his family's support, your dad will have no choice but to rely on you to continue the legacy of the family business."

She huffs, rolling her eyes before she focuses again on me. "Who knows…." There's a trace of disappointment in her tone that squeezes my heart. "Maybe he wants to give another promotion to that Karl once he leaves prison."

"I don't think so," I tell her sincerely. "Karl is good at sales but he isn't family." Seeing the annoyance in her gaze, I add, "Let's be honest here, who's doing an internship at Van Den Bosch Industries?"

"Yeah, but I'm doing it only because my brother didn't want to." Her gaze drops to her cup of tea, which she holds between her fingers, then looking up at me again, she says before giving a sip, "Dad offered this internship to him, not me."

"And yet, you are the one doing it, right?" My tone comes off more enthusiastic than I thought, but I'm just trying to cheer her up. "Look, your dad just found out that his first son wasn't even attending business school and was lying to him since the beginning. It's a lot to digest." Elise remains quiet as she listens. "Give him some time, I'm sure he's gonna figure out you are the best choice out of the bunch."

She rubs a hand on the back of her neck, most likely soothing the building tension in that area, staring pensively at nowhere. "I don't think my brother realizes how much Dad would have given him, if only he wanted to follow the same path."

I scratch my stubble, ruminating for a moment at her statement, before saying, "I think your brother knows."

She squints her eyes immediately in confusion, so I explain further. "He met your dad at his office trying to get his allowance back, but Sebastian told him he'd have to do the internship and then work at his company." I hesitate for a moment whether or not to tell her the rest, but at the end of the day, she deserves to know the truth. "According to your brother, your dad even tried to pitch him to become the next CEO once he retires and told him that he could have whatever he wanted—even that he could keep seeing Roxanne if he accepted."

Her jaw drops at the revelation, but she closes the gap just as fast. She swallows the lump in her throat, her gaze dropping to her lap as disappointment emerges on her lovely features. I know she's always been the one aspiring to those things, which might be why Sebastian takes her loyalty for granted.

Silence fills the air between us while Elise leans back against the chair and seems to be considering everything I just told her. Suddenly, though, the ringtone of my iPhone buzzes nonstop, startling me in the process. As I take the phone to check who's calling, my brows rise immediately in surprise. "Oh, speaking of the devil."

I answer the call, putting the screen against my cheek.

"Hey!" Andries greets, his cheerful tone causing a sudden contrast with the sadness of his sister's. "How was Easter?"

"It was good, and yours?" I reply, unable to match his enthusiasm. "How is Paris?"

Elise's interest is suddenly perked, and she leans forward again to pay close attention to the discussion, even though she can't hear from her brother's side.

"It's wonderful, we are loving it." Andries seems to be on cloud nine, which is understandable when someone's just got engaged in Paris. "Actually, after I finish my degree, we are thinking of moving here for a few months to explore more of the city. There's so much to see and so little time." While Andries is speaking, I can't help but look at Elise as she frowns and tries to discern what her brother is saying.

"Well, I'm glad you are enjoying yourself." My answer is vague and Andries surely caught how uncomfortable I'm to be talking to him with his sister in front of me.

"Is she there?"

My lips twist into a smile—he knows me so well. "Yep," I reply with amusement, my eyes pinned on his sister.

"Can you put the phone on speaker, please?"

His request takes me off guard, and I can't help but try to figure out what his plan of action is. "Sure," I blurt out, before doing so and putting the phone on the table between us. "All set."

"Elise?" Andries asks, his tone always so bubbly. "Can you hear me?"

She heaves a long sigh in displeasure, before muttering a quick, "Yep, I can."

"Uh oh, you sound grumpy today." His humor makes me snort, but Elise shoots me a glare right away. "Is everything okay?"

She takes a few breaths, before saying with mild annoyance, "Well, I suppose I should congratulate you for the engagement, but I'm afraid I'm just lost for words."

"It's hard to accept, I know." His calm attitude radiates through the air between us.

"Is anyone else from our family aware yet?" Elise asks.

"Just Oma," he replies. Before his sister can jump in, he adds, "Elise, look, I know you don't approve of my engagement, but I'd truly appreciate if you could let me deliver the news to our parents."

"Well, if Oma knows already, then Mom and Pops do too."

"She promised me she wouldn't say a word."

"Yeah, right," she mumbles, her head shaking. "As if she's not gonna tell them while you are still in Paris."

Her iPhone pings with a new notification and Elise wastes no time to check it.

When I see the frown forming on her forehead, I can't help but ask, "What is it?"

Without saying anything, she turns the screen to me—it's an SMS from her dad: *Is it true that your brother is engaged? Call me now!*

"Looks like Pops already knows," she says to Andries as she stares again at her screen. "He wants me to call him."

"Shit." Bubbly Andries has now switched to worried Andries. "Well, yeah, call him, then…" He sounds vague, and a bit lost as if he's still assessing his next move. "Elise!"

"Yeah?"

"If we have an engagement party, would you talk to our parents and try to get them to attend?"

Our eyes widen in shock at the same time and we look at each other, both left totally speechless and flabbergasted. After a few seconds of silence, Elise speaks again, "Um, not going to lie, I don't know."

"Please, I'm pretty sure they are super mad at me right now."

While I'm always trying to be a supportive friend, I can't help but picture the reaction of Sebastian and Julia as they find out their nineteen-year-old son is engaged to a former prostitute. Jeez! I nod, agreeing with him.

"I'll see what I can do," Elise replies, her tone even. "Talk later."

After biding farewell, she hangs up and exhales louder than usual.

Before one of us can open our mouth though, her iPhone's ringtone is already blasting through the room. She freezes as she looks at the screen, so I lean just enough to peer over and it's nonetheless than Sebastian himself calling. Poor girl, she's gonna have to handle his anger like she's some sort of therapist. Elise heaves a long sigh, as if mentally preparing herself before answering.

"Hello?"

For a split second, I feel tempted to ask her to put the call on speaker but I'm pretty sure she'll tell me to fuck off if I do so.

"Yes, it's true, we just spoke to him," Elise answers. Her features deepen as she continues to listen quietly on her chair. "Now?" She sounds surprised and her gaze goes up to me. "Um, okay, I should be there in a few minutes." She rolls her eyes, most likely in return to what her dad's saying. "I get it. See you soon." A gush of air rolls off her lips as she hangs up, and looking up at me, she then says, "Dad wants to talk to me in his office, like right now."

How typical of Sebastian—when he's furious with something, everyone around him has got to stop what they are doing to go and meet him. I can't blame Andries not wanting anything to do with his dad's legacy.

"Do you want a ride?" I ask, given how stressed and anxious she already seems to be.

"Yeah, if you don't mind. I took an Uber here."

"Sure." I gesture the check to the waiter, and just a few minutes later, we are ready to go.

As we walk out of the tea room, I can't help but sneak a peek at the worry on her face. "Are you okay?"

"He didn't seem happy at all," she confesses, tucking a lock of hair behind her ear. "I'm just... I'm just wondering what kind of favor he's gonna ask me for this time."

Seeing the dread on her lovely features, an idea starts forming in my head causing me to ask, "What if I wait for you until you are done?" She slows down her pace, her interest piqued. "Then we can always go and get wasted somewhere so you can rant about your dad."

Her lips twist into a smile and her eyes glow in excitement. "Sounds like a great idea."

Despite knowing Andries for so many years, I had never been to the headquarters of his family's business before. The lobby area of the skyscraper is spacious and minimalist, and my eyes keep darting around as I take in its immensity. We head to the elevator, and once inside, Elise taps her keycard and then presses the button that grants us access to the executive floor.

Background music fills the space between us as we stand beside each other in silence, waiting to arrive. Her anxiety is clearly palpable even though she tries her best to conceal it by keeping her posture straight and her shoulders wide. The elevator finally reaches the top floor and once the doors open, I gesture her to go first. In the foyer, we are welcomed by a receptionist who immediately takes her desk phone to announce our arrival. She invites us to take a seat on the beige leather loveseat at the end of the room as we wait for Sebastian to come over.

Sitting beside Elise, I grab a *TIME* magazine which is lying on the low table in front of us and get myself busy flickering mindlessly through the pages. Meanwhile, I can't help but notice how Elise starts tapping her fingers nervously on her lap.

"Hey," I whisper. "It's gonna be alright. Relax, okay?" My tone is barely audible, but she replies with a quick smile in understanding.

"Oh, Dan, how are you doing?"

My gaze follows the joyous baritone voice from the other side of the foyer and it's none other than Sebastian himself, striding in our direction.

Both Elise and I stand immediately, and I waste no time in reaching out a hand to shake his.

"Doing great, Mr. Van Den Bosch," I reply politely as we shake hands and exchange a pleasant smile. "Just came here to drop Elise off."

"Oh, thank you, that's very kind of you." His attention goes to her and I take it as my cue to leave.

I lean slightly toward her, and in a low voice, I say, "Well, see you later."

Elise thanks me and then starts following her dad as they cross the foyer in silence. After calling the lift, I stand there, patiently waiting for it to arrive and peer over my shoulder one last time to watch Sebastian inviting Elise into his office.

***

For some reason, I didn't feel it was appropriate to wait for her at the executive floor. I could already picture Sebastian raising eyebrows at seeing me there after finishing the meeting with his daughter. It could create unnecessary questioning later on for Elise, and that's the last thing she needs.

So here I am, sitting in an armchair downstairs in the lobby area as I wait for her to finish. She's already been in that meeting for an hour, and my curiosity keeps growing at every passing minute.

Finally, I see her walking out of the elevator, her pace hastening in my direction and looking much happier now than when we got in. I leap off of my seat and go to meet her.

"So?" I ask once I reach her. "How did it go?"

Her gaze is more pensive than usual, and she looks at me with a growing smile on her lips. "It went well," she says, simply, before continue walking toward the exit. "Shall we?"

We cross the lobby area in silence, but I can't help noticing how her mood has changed. She seems happier—much happier.

Once we step outside, we go back to my car and I open her the door, always wondering about her sudden change of mood.

I get inside the car and after closing the door, I look her in the eye and ask, "Care to tell me why you have become so pensive and smiley all of a sudden?"

Elise just shakes her head with a chuckle. "I can't, sorry."

"No way," I reply just as fast. "I'm not gonna spend the whole evening wondering what's up with you. You've got to tell me."

"I can't," she repeats amid a quick snort. "You're my brother's best friend. You'd tell him as soon as you knew."

So the meeting involved Andries? I refrain myself from asking her that, instead I just say, "I'm also your friend." When Elise raises an eyebrow in suspicion, I add, "And I also know how to keep a secret."

"Do you?"

"Yep." Since she doesn't look convinced, I explain further. "For instance, I knew who Roxanne was since the day I saw her in Ghent but I kept my mouth shut."

Her eyes widen in shock and she blinks a few times processing what I just told her; I knew she wouldn't see this one coming. "Wait—you knew she was an escort, and you didn't tell my brother?"

I tilt my head to the side as I say, "Well, I knew she had an escort agency, but I didn't know she had been an escort too."

"Why didn't you tell him about it, then?" she presses on, turning her body toward me, her arms crossing over her chest.

Since I've managed to pique her interest enough to engage in a discussion, I turn on the engine and get on the road, heading to downtown. "Because it wasn't my place to do so."

"Bullshit," I hear her saying as I keep my attention on the road. "You are his best friend."

While I'm trying to keep my eyes pinned in front, I glance at her for a few seconds and say, "Yeah, but he was just too happy for me to interfere." I pause, refocusing on the road. "The point is, I won't tell him if you ask me not to."

"Dad made me an offer I can't refuse," she finally tells me. "That's all I'm gonna say."

I nod, impressed. "*That* good?"

"Yep," she replies, her tone filled with enthusiasm. "*That* good."

Elise is normally too proud to keep something like this as a secret and the fact she isn't telling me can only mean one thing, but I need to make sure of it, before talking to Andries. "What are you scheming, miss?" I ask bluntly.

"Oh Dan, stop being so damn curious," she insists, heaving a sigh in annoyance. "I won't be able to disclose anything more."

"Why not?"

"Because if you know, you'll tell my brother and I can't risk that."

Bingo! It's about Andries and his relationship with Roxanne! I knew it!

"Oh, I know what you and your dad are up to, then," I blurt out, a smirk spreading across my face. "You are gonna try to sabotage their relationship, aren't you?"

"Where are we gonna eat?"

Despite my tone being inviting and even joyful, Elise turns her face toward her window, trying to change the subject, but I'm already too mad at her to let it go.

"Fuck, Elise." I sigh, my irritation growing at the realization I was right. "I can't believe you're gonna do that to your brother."

"I said I'm not talking about it," she snaps.

"Elise, stop it." I put my hand on hers to mark the severity of the situation. Once her gaze meets mine again, I say, my tone more serious than usual. "No matter what your dad offered you to ruin them, it's not worth it."

She pushes my hand away from hers and disregard my comment just as fast. "Can we stop talking about it already?" Her tone is growing irritated, and she stares at me like she's about to shoot me daggers. "You know what?" I frown when she unfastens her seat belt. "Maybe it's better I go and eat alone."

"Fine," I reply before she forces me to stop the car and drop her off. "I won't talk about it anymore."

Her lips twist into a victorious smile. "Great." She then looks around and asks, "Any place in mind?"

At her question, it's obvious she's ready to switch the conversation to something else. And yet, I can't help feel angry inside at what she and her dad have in mind. What a bunch! "I'm thinking to go to Yamazato," I reply, unable to keep my annoyance at bay. "I'm in the mood for sushi. And you?"

"Fantastic choice, I love the food there."

While I promised Elise I won't talk anymore about what her and her dad are scheming against Andries and his fiancée, all I know is that I've got to warn him.

THEIR STORY CONTINUES WITH
BOOK 3, ELISE.

Don't have the sequel yet?

Enjoy 10% off on your next purchase using the code FLYER10 at melaniemartins.com (code has to be manually entered at checkout).